THE BOXED Angel

Robert DiGiacomo

To
Rachel

Thank you for
makes it more than
Just lunchtime

Library of Congress Control Number: 2013903423
CreateSpace Independent Publishing Platform
North Charleston, South Carolina

For Paula, Jennarose and Isabella
My Angels

PROLOGUE

Philadelphia, July 3, 1776

Dixon Hancock was about to commit a crime, and at sixteen, his first. The stone was the size of his skull. "This one's too heavy," Dixon said and dropped the block of granite he had pulled from the broken curb. He stumbled and nearly fell forward but leaned on his palms. The ale he had been drinking came up in the back of his throat. He belched and spit out vomit onto the back of his hands.

"Go' on. Heave the bloody thing, Dix," Dixon looked up at his new friend. Jeremy tilted his head back and took a long drink from a brown earthen jug of ale. He wiped his mouth with his left sleeve and let the jug drop to the ground. Dixon was seeing wavy images of Jeremy. He looked like a tall ghost, and his shirt was stained with mud and dirt. His dark hair puffed up above his forehead. Jeremy walked toward him, and his bare feet, long nails and grime and all, stopped short of the puke.

Dixon was on all fours. He closed his eyes and willed himself not to spew the rest of the contents of his stomach all over Jeremy's feet, although it would probably make them relatively cleaner, if anything.

"He's afraid to do et," another voice said. Dixon didn't have to open his eyes to know it was George. Loud and arrogant, George was bigger than Dixon. He stood only five ten, but he was a stocky brute, probably weighing twice as much as Jeremy, who was a full six inches taller. The wine jug George was carrying was sloshing around, and Dixon could tell George was close.

The three were in front of a large picture window; the pane was hemmed-in by a three-story red brick house. Dixon finally had the courage to open his eyes, and he looked up at the glass. A flicker from the oil-fired street lamp reflected in his eyes. He was suddenly cold; the morning chill at three a.m.held alight fog low to the ground. The full moon cast shadows behind his new friends, and he was aware of carriage wheels that cracked upon cobble-stone, echoing in the distance. He was suddenly worried someone would see them.

"Com'n, Dixon," Jeremy said. "We don't wish to stand here 'til the morrow. I don't think you're a coward like George said."

With the presence of George, Dixon renewed his valor, stood,butstumbled, and fell hard against a lamppost; he dirtied his once clean, white, linen shirt. Alice, his personal maid and nanny would be very upset.He thought of how he would dispose of the shirt without her knowing. Alice had raised Dixon from the cradle and knew everything there was to know, and had his clothes laid out each day. She knew how many shirts and trousers he had and sewed the tears in his undergarments. Now distraught, worrying about her wrath, Dixonlooked up at the burning oil, and slid down the post, his eyelids heavy. He desperately wanted to sleep, and began to fade out.

"Ouch," Dixon yelped as George kicked him in his thigh. "Wait, George. I'll do it." Dixon struggled to his feet, using the post as his crutch. "I said I would, and I will." The alcohol was playing tricks with his brain. He knew what he was about to do was wrong, but he felt compelled to do it anyway. Unlike George and Jeremy, who came from poverty, Dixon had been adopted into privilege by the Hancock family. His father, John Hancock, was wealthy and renowned. He had been elected to the First Continental Congress, and so the family had moved to Philadelphia from Massachusetts. Up north in Boston, making friends had not come easily for Dixon. Though quiet and shy, he had a deep desire to just let go of his manners and his well-to-do family. Moving to Philadelphia gave him the opportunity.

His new friend, Jeremy, seemed to like him regardless of his father's money and social standing. Soon after they met, he had introduced Dixon to George. George was a true guttersnipe who constantly badgered Dixonabout never doing anything on his own, always being at his father's coat tails.George would regularly slap Dixon in the chest and punch him hard in the arm.

"We got to toughen you up, mate. You're nothing but a right git."George said all too often.

Dixon had had enough of being the whipping boy, and tonight he was going to change all that. With his mind ale-clouded, he gazed up at the window.

Smash!

The sound of broken glass scratched his ears. He'd waited too long. George had pitched his wine jug through the window. Dixon Hancock's eyes widened as Jeremy and George darted in and began to pillage the dwelling. Curiosity and a few wobbly steps brought Dixon to the opening. He leaned on the windowsill, avoiding the jagged shards of glass sticking up from the wood frame, and peered inside.A single skylight two stories aboveallowed the moonlight in. He watched while the pair filled their pockets with anything remotely valuable.

Jeremy stuffed his shirt with candlesticks, and then he picked up an inkwell. "Bloody hell," he screeched as the ink spilled down his belly. "Dixon, grab something." Jeremy ordered. "I'm sure you don't have everything your bloody self wants," he laughed shamelessly.

Dixon climbed over the windowsill and made his way in. He crawled, more to remain hidden than worrying about the vomit climbing up his throat. He stood, pressed back into the shadows, and looked around the room. He was in the front parlor of a wealthy home. It wasn't much different from his own. There was a richly decorated sofa with soft puffy pillows on the backrest, and a mahogany desk across from where he stood. A large oil painting hung on the wall behind it. It was too dark to make out the image, but it looked like a landscape. There were brass and silver statues on various tables, and a large cabinet with glass doors and many valuables. He was tempted to steal, but he remained stock-still with his back pressed tight to a ceiling-high bookcase. Jeremy exited past Dixon, snickering at him as he jumped out the opening. Then George appeared in the moonlight, weighed down by an immense booty and stopped several feet in front of him.

"Do something for yourself, Dixon. Be one of us. Take something," George said.

Dixon remained stiff against the shelves.

"You're a weak little lad," George taunted him, "always chasing after your father's heels." Suddenly they both cocked their heads; a door slammed shut somewhere nearby. George rushed for the window, but tripped over a candle stand knocked over by the shattered window. George's momentum flung him forward, and unwilling to drop anything to stop himself, plunged at Dixonwho never had a chance. Dixon tried to raise his arms as a shield but George's shoulder plunged into his chest and left him gasping for air. George grunted, then made his way out as young Hancock slumped down the bookcase landing on his knees.

The heel of Dixon's foot struck a hidden mechanism, and, at the base of the cabinet, a disguised door popped open. Dixon stared at it in surprise. The opening was low, scarcely visible in the moonlight. Still hunched over in pain, he spied something inside. Curiosity overcame Dixon's earlier uneasiness, and he explored the compartment with his hand.

"Velvet," he gasped. Only the most precious of items would be kept within its cloth. His father kept gold coins in a velvet sack in his desk; his mother covered the silver spoons and knives with a velvet cloth. Young Hancock reached in with both hands. He felt a rectangular object within the cloth and tried to lift it out. "Feels like it's bloody nailed down," Dixon said to himself. He maneuvered his body squarely in front, and using his legs, hoisted the object from its hiding place. He placed it down on the desk and untied the gold braided cord. When he pulled back the cloth, he saw a brilliant, gleaming gold box. Elaborate engravings covered every square inch.

"My Heavenly Father!" he said aloud, as his thoughts were warped with desire and greed. The thought of independent wealth, without the support of his father, a life exclusively his own

shot into his head. Then Dixon again became aware of his surroundings. The home he was in was not his. This box, the entire
situation, was not right. But the ale was still swirling in his brain,
and the moonlight gleamed against the gold, the lustrous metal
shimmering in his bloodshot eyes. It penetrated deep into the back
of his mind. Overpowered by a sudden sense of greed, young
Hancock retied the sack and closed the secret door. The box made
of gold was now his.

"*Stop! Stop now, you lad!*"

Dixon heard a loud voice, followed by a whistle. He picked
up the sack, held with both hands, and hid in the corner by the
window. Again he heard the voice, and knew it was the night
watchman, Jones. An older gentleman, too old for the mili-
tia, he volunteered for the night shift. Dixon peered around
the broken glass. Rapid footsteps clacked toward the house.
George came running past, still clinging to his armful of stolen
valuables, but now shedding one with every step. The smell of
burning gunpowder was followed by the crack of a musket
shot.

Dixon witnessed what happened next, as if time had slowed.
Simultaneously, George's shoulders and elbows clinched backwards. His chest lurched forward and his feet stopped in their
tracks. The marble-size lead bullet blasted into the small of his
back. The ugly sound of shattering vertebra followed as the bullet exited his chest, spewing his organs through a hole the size of
a grapefruit. George's body fell limply, bouncing onto the cob-
blestones. The insignificant life he had left attempted to pull him
forward clawing at the granite street until he bled to (what Dixon
was sure was) a painful death. George's eyes remained open, as if
he were looking at Dixon, but it was the gaze of cold death, staring into darkness. Dixon looked at the horrible scene in shock
as the watchman, Jones, appeared out of the alley, dressed in a
dark blue overcoat and wearing a triangle hat pulled down to
thick eyebrows. He towered at six feet six inches tall; his face was
craggy, with a copper complexion unlike Dixon's pale white. As
Jones came closer, young Hancock backed himself further into
a corner.

The watchman slowed his pace, pointed his weapon at the unmoving carcass, then prodded it. "You'll thieve no more, lad." Jones said.

Jeremy was standing with his back to a brick house panting. He was overwhelmed with fear. Beads of sweat trickled down his face and his throat muscles began to tighten, as blood raced through swollen veins. After witnessing his friend's demise, he wondered if the same fate was in store for him. Terror blinded his reasoning, and Jeremy panicked. Abruptly, the thief darted out from his hiding place and ran foolishly; his stolen goods were left behind.

Dixon saw Jones turn, and watched Jeremy make off toward the river. Jones called out, but Jeremy kept running. The watchman had quickly reloaded and aimed his musket, and again he warned the runner to stop. His voice was followed by the gun's thunder. Dixon could just hear Jeremy muttering prayers, and a plea for mercy. The projectile hit him like a sledgehammer, blasting into his right shoulder, shattering the bones so thoroughly, that only muscle and skin were left clinging to the extremity. The boy screamed, but miraculously he kept his balance, traveling as fast as his legs would take him, the now-dead arm flailing behind. Jones again ordered him to stop. Dixon thought pain and horror must have forced him onward.

Crack! The musket shot entered behind his ear, exiting his face, relieving him of his forehead and eye sockets. The body crashed to the ground splattering internal fluids like a slaughtered lamb.

Dixon thought of giving himself in, but the shame he would bring to his father, John Hancock, would be immense. Escape was his only option. A small crowd of curious townspeople had gathered by the two corpses. He knew any minute the group would take notice of the broken window, and running would give himself away. Dixon was pale with fright. Either the ale swirling in his head, or the fear of getting caught gave him an inner confidence. He held the velvet sack in front of his body, away from the sight of the crowd, and made his way down to the end of the block. He turned the corner and walked to a small alcove in a six-foot-high brick wall. Dixon's body beaded with sweat, and his heart raced. He took several deep breaths, and his heart began to slow, thinking his escape was complete. Then, without sound or warning, watchman Jones appeared. His musket was drawn, a murderous look on his leathery face.

"Drop the sack, you rogue," Jones said.

Dixon hesitated, and then released his grip but held onto the velvet. The gold box smacked the brick walkway on edge, and then fell flat and displayed its beauty.

"Blimey," Jones gasped. "You'll not make another move lad, or I'll do you in like the others."

The gruesome deaths George and Jeremy had suffered flashed through Dixon's mind. He became nauseated, and could taste vomit once again in the back of his throat. If he threw up, would that distract Jones long enough to escape? Not with the musket only inches from his chest, so he swallowed hard. Jones stepped closer to the gold box. His musket was firmly aimed at Dixon's chest, yet his eyes stared at the box in fascination.

The impact must have caused the lock on the box to dislodge, because from within the box, a mysterious mist began to rise, and a cloud accumulated, just higher than Jones's head. The watchman took a step backwards while Dixon inched his body back against the brick, attempting to enter it. They both watched dumbfounded as the cloud gave birth to shape. A human torso formed, and arms protruded down the sides, extending to long-fingered hands. The stomach was rippled with muscle, and the waist tapered off, a trail of vapor connecting the ghost to the opening in the box. Its head, nearly eight feet above the ground, towered above the mortals. It acquired the appearance of a hooded skull. Eyes of black pearls blazed through a featureless face.

A menacing creature, Dixon thought, terrified as its gaze shocked his veins. Images of his life began flashing through his mind's eye. Scenes of when he and his father would fly kites in the park on holiday, and ride horses over the countryside at home in Massachusetts. Then his recent past fell on him, the scolding from his father for otherwise meaningless faults. Dixon knew his father was drained by affairs concerning independence. No longer was there time for day trips together. John Hancock had forgotten his family for the cause.

Dixon wept.

The towering creature turned its intent look toward the night watchman.

"Aye, you'll be a witch then, you rogue," Jones said. "Your sorcery will not ward off me."

The night watchman's bravery was renowned and unmatched in the city. He pointed the musket barrel at the smoky chest of the beast and fired at point-blank range. The bullet flew through the creature, taking a breath of mist with it. There was no time for him to reload. The ghost was moving closer.

Fast.

Jones reversed his hold on his weapon, the gun that protected the city streets, the instrument he had probably obtained from his father—who had received it from his father before him, just as Dixon would one day receive his father's weapon.

Now, the musket became an ugly club, its power reduced to a primitive level.

Jones swung the butt end high into the air, entering the ghost's midsection. The club's momentum slowed while it plowed through the mist, then exiting sharply. Again and again, he cast it into the approaching monster with no effect. His strength apparently drained, with one last futile swing, he lost his footing and stumbled back against the wall.

Jones stood panting, staring the beast down with fury and fear, when without sound, the beast dashed straight at Jones's sternum, vanishing into his chest. He lost hold of his weapon, his family heirloom, as he gripped his throat. The night watchman's eyes opened wide. Then his face turned pale and blank. His body fell forward, hitting the brick walkway. The bones of his face shattered, and blood splattered onto Dixons shoes.

Then the shrouded head of the ghost eerily appeared out of the center of the dead man's back. Slowly, it rose; black pearl eyes glowed, those abominable, deathly eyes piercing Dixon. The monster grew to form as the corpse withered. Young Hancock felt as if he were watching not just a man's body be consumed, but his soul as well. Jones's skull was the last to diminish, turning to powder and collapsing in a pile to be blown away by the breeze, while his clothes simply dropped flat to the ground.

Dixon remained motionless. He was petrified. Even if his mind were able to give the command to run, his legs would remain still. The ghost seemed even larger than before, moving at him. It abruptly vanished into his chest. Dixon let out a scream. His life was over. He was to be absorbed by the devil himself, on his way to hell for his one theft, his one mistake. How could this be? He knew he only had seconds, so he started to say the Lord's Prayer.

Then he felt a strong pressure on his back. He was still standing but unable to move. He wanted to fall foreword like Jones, but some other force kept him upright. The pressure on his back became a burning fire. He thought his skin was melting, when suddenly, a burst of smoke appeared from his back, leaving Dixon unharmed. The pain gone, he felt oddly energized by the act. The creature reappeared and hovered momentarily above him, and then slowly, the mist was drawn back inside the box, reversing its outward ascent. Descending, it paused, the black pearls stared at Dixon, and then the apparition disappeared into its cradle.

PROLOGUE NO. 2

Baltimore, MD, Six weeks ago

The oppressive heat of mid-July was unavoidable to anyone or anything in the open, so Dr. Abel Salinger sat comfortably inside his air-conditioned Jeep Grand Cherokee, and tapped his fingers on the steering wheel. He waited impatiently for the train, and looked out the front windshield.

The sun beat its heavy weight through the row of trees behind the railroad tracks. The rays splintered like flames onto the vast parking lot. If there were any moisture in the air, it would have been steam. Instead, waves of heat rose from the blacktop, blurring the scene. The parking lot had at least four hundred and seventy-six spaces, but only thirty-six cars and trucks parked, including Abel's. He has been counting them for the past hour, waiting for the train to arrive. Across the tracks was a forest of thick trees, many leaves light green, but some brown and gray. It hadn't rained in a couple of weeks, and the heat wave had taken its toll on the oaks and maples. On the parking lot side of the tracks was a hundred-foot-long loading platform with ramps in the middle and metal stairs on the right and left. The platform was five feet above the ground, supported by stout concrete pillars. There were three tractor-trailers side by side on the far right. Railroad workers shifted cargo pallets with forklifts and hand-operated pallet jacks into one of the trucks. The freight train was due any moment, and they rushed to clear the area.

Staring blankly, Salinger felt a sense of relief that this was to be his last pickup. Every two months for the past year, he had sat in this same parking spot, awaiting an identical freight train. Each time, he retrieved an experimental animal. Animals were the cargo of these trains—thousands of them, all destined for the testing labs at the Baroque Pharmaceutical plant.

The animal in question would be earmarked with a red tag, the only red tag. Usually it was a medium-size dog or large cat, although two months ago there had been that full-grown baboon. He was startled at first, but the animal was sedated,which made the transport much easier.

Dr. Salinger noticed several rail workers turning their heads at the same time, looking down the track. He looked as well, but the oak trees screened his view. He depressed the window button, and the pane slid down halfway. The heat hit him in the face,but he heard the slow-moving locomotive in the distance. Abel prepared himself for the flaming blast that his middle-aged body would not enjoy and turned off the ignition. He reached into the glove compartment and grabbed a key with a red tag, to match the animals. He got out of his car and braved the heat, then strolled nonchalantly in the direction of the off-loading area. He looked quite out of place wearing a white, short-sleeved, button-front shirt, paisley tie, and gray slacks. All were stained with sweat within minutes out in the open parking lot. He twirled the key around his finger and tapped his breast pocket to double check he had the quickly scribbled requisition he had made himself for the animal. He has never been given any instructions in writing to retrieve these animals, but six months ago he was approached by one of the dockworkers and he was barley able to talk his way past him. Since then he wrote up an order on Baroque Chemicals letter head. It wasn't an official requisition but it would satisfy the dockworkers.When he was about thirty feet from the tracks, the sluggish rail cars rumbled past, air brakes screeched and protested. It cast a partial shadow over him, better than the direct sun, but not much. After the train came to a halt, Salinger counted back eight cars. Thankfully, the workmen paid no attention to him stepping onto the car. Nor did they care. Abel knew the sooner they completed unloading, the quicker they could get to the bar—out of the intense heat.

Salinger examined the forty-eight-foot-long aisle. Shelves of cages were stacked floor-to-ceiling; all of the animals were dogs of many different species. They made a lot of noise, pleading for attention from the only person they had seen in days. In the past, Abel walked straight into a wall of stomach-churning odor. Now he knew better and put a handkerchief over his mouth and nose. All the animals were in frenzy, desperate for attention, barking, yelping, and jumping against the cages. Abel felt like the desperate animals knew of the barbaric testing that awaited them.

It was difficult to maintain focus walking inside the train. It felt hotter than the parking lot. The floor was covered with moist straw. It felt like he was walking in a barn, and no matter how tightly he pressed the handkerchief to his nose, the smell of piss and feces made his eyes water. He looked left and right, alternately scanning the cages when he saw the red tag flickering at the far end, about waist-high. Salinger quick stepped the thirty feet, opened the lock on the exterior cage, and grabbed the plastic and metal crate containing a full-grown dachshund. The dog lay on its side, unmoving and lifeless. With no time to feel pity, he knew he must leave before he melted or worse, passed out. Dr. Salinger attempted to leave from the back door only to find it locked, so he had to trek past the gauntlet of frenzied dogs once more, and a heart-wrenching journey it was. They were even more riled up, watching him leave with one of their own.

For a moment, he thought he heard a hum over the cries of the dogs. It sounded like a mass of footsteps thundering outside. As fast as he could, he went to the exit and looked out. He couldn't believe his eyes—a hundred or more men and women were charging the train.

"Oh shit."

Dr. Salinger stood at the opening and watched in amazement as the marauders entered the rail cars and exited, carrying the various crates filled with dogs, cats, monkeys, rabbits, mice, and any breathing animal. The assailants wore shirts from the Humane Society, Animal Rights Activism, and PETA. They were very organized. Some members carried bolt cutters, hammers, or screwdrivers to open the outer cages, while the balance of the group carried out the prisoners. They brought the animals to awaiting minivans and sport-utility vehicles whose drivers left the area immediately after being filled with cages.Dr. Salinger had to react. He placed the crate on the floor, opened its gate, and grabbed the dachshund. It was heavy and lay limply in his arms. Seconds before the invaders boarded his car, he jumped from the train, and attempted to blend in. He reasoned their attack would be swift, and they would not risk a lengthy withdrawal of the entire complement of animals. The confusion level would be high, and he could enter and leave in his vehicle unnoticed. He trampled across the parking lot, and for a split second became aware of the absence of the dockworkers. He hoped—no prayed—they did not alert the police right away, possibly giving him precious seconds more.

No such luck. Squad cars barreled onto the scene. The army of organized animal lovers signaled one another not to panic, and let the animals run free, shooing them into the wooded area behind the train. Then, the people remained to detain the animal-control police from following into the forest. Abel was seconds from reaching his Jeep. Even if he got that far, police cars were blocking all exits from the parking lot. He felt a tug on his back; a female police officer grabbed his shoulder.

"Stop right there!" she said with a deep scowl.

"Please, you must let me go!" Abel pleaded.

She was a brute of a woman, standing taller than the doctor—with the build of a middle linebacker. Her hair was pulled back in a ponytail, and she held Dr. Salinger by the arm. It felt like a vice clamping his bicep.

"I'm not with these people. My name is Dr. Abel Salinger. I work for Baroque Chemical,the company that owns this animal. I was…" Abel felt he was babbling on like a child who had just beencaught shoplifting a candy bar, insisting he was a diabetic who needed the sugar. "I was told to retrieve this particular animal. Please, please let me be."

The officer wasn't amused and escorted him to the sergeant's car.

"Sergeant?" she said.

"Yes, Officer Cummings?" The sergeant was an overweight senior policeman who needed heavy suspenders. His face was smooth and very doughy with perfectlycombed short hair, and a thick, pampered mustache. He continually dabbed a handkerchief at the sweat on his face and neck.

"Sergeant, this man claims to work for Baroque Chemical and says he was instructed to pick up this particular animal."

"He does, does he?" the sergeant said, a bemused look on his face.He studied Salinger closely. "Do you have identification, and a written order for the dog?"

"Yes, I have my work ID," Abel said, as he shifted the dog to his left arm, and showed his credentials. "And the written order is in my breast pocket." He second-guessed that last part but it was too late.

"Who gave you the order for this animal?" the officer said, studying the photo on the plastic card. He grabbed the paper from Salinger. Just then theradio on his shoulder clicked. "Sergeant Jones here," he said and held the intercom and tilted his head. "Yes sir, that's correct, sir. Right away."

"Officer Cummings, escort this gentleman and the dog to that black Chevy," Jones pointed toward the main road, where the car was parked under the canopy of a large beech tree.

Ushered by the powerful but less-than-feminine officer, Dr. Salinger noticed two men sitting in the front seat. Both wore sunglasses, despite the shade from the covering leaves.

"Place the dog in the trunk, will you, Officer?" the man sitting in the driver's seat said, and pressed the trunk release button. Cummings gave the man a quizzical look at the request but the man nodded. "Go on, and put the good doctor in the back seat." His voice was stern and held no sympathy for the dog while he flashed some sort of badge at her. Abel couldn't make out what or who it was, but he obviously had seniority over the police. After

Cummings assisted the doctor into the back seat, she turned and walked away.

Abel was edgy, looking at the back of their heads. Directly in front of him sat the driver. He couldn't see his face, only short brown hair and smoke that lingered from a filterless Camel cigarette. Black hair covered the passenger's head. From the side, he looked to be about forty years of age. There were squint lines on his temple, and he had the beginnings of wrinkles on his neck. They both sat unmoving, staring straight ahead; the tension was thickening with each passing moment. Salinger felt a barrage of questions coming, but there was only silence.

"Who are you two?" Abel finally blurted out, attempting to mask his cowardice.

No reply.

"I demand to know who you are, and what you want," Abel said.

Still, he got no reply.

Salinger kept talking, hoping for a reprieve, and hoping he wouldn't give away the truth about his assignment in his babbling. "I work for the Baroque Pharmaceutical Laboratories, I was instructed to come directly to the train and obtain this specific animal. The preliminary tests begun in Canada, and the deadline for the extraction of data will expire if it is not examined immediately. Awealth of information will be lost and possibly years of experiments will be defunct."

"Doctor, you and I both know that animal is dead, so cut the bullshit," the driver said between puffs. Then he started the engine. Salinger grasped for the handle butthe door had no visible interior handle or lock.

"Sit back, Doctor, and enjoy the ride," the man said from the shotgun seat.

Abel decided, or rather it was decided for him, that he was a prisoner, and any groping for an exit was useless.

Special Agent Joe Tyson smoked his ever-present Camel ciga-rette as he looked into the interrogation room through the two-way mirror. Rivulets of sweat rolled down the eight-hour growth of stubble on Dr. Abel Salinger's face. He sat alone on a metal fold-ing chair, elbows on a faded green linoleum table. Dangling from the ceiling was an old, rusted light fixture with three bright bulbs that heated the doctor's perspiring skull.

"He's been in there nearly five hours," Carl Fazolo said between sips of black coffee in a paper cup with Wawa printed on the side. "And, unlike inside the car, he's kept his mouth shut."

"Faz, I think it's time we grilled him." A slow smile crossed Tyson's face as he looked over at his partner.

"You got it, Joe. I'm all for a little TLC." Faz drank the last sip of his coffee, and cracked his knuckles. At six-feet-three-inches, and bearing broad shoulders, the FBI agent had proven an expert at getting information out of suspects. It was obvious Faz found interrogation one of his most pleasurable duties. He picked up a folding chair, and entered the interrogation room. Joe stood close to the mirror, cancer stick in hand, the intercom turned on.

A workaholic, Joe spent upwards of sixteen hours a day between the field and office in the federal building at Sixth and Arch streets in Philadelphia. This was his life. In his late fifties, he had no family and no connections outside the agency. Joe hoped to make some headway into the case that had been stalled for two months, while they waited for the doctor to make his move. Salinger had been on twenty-four-hour surveillance since Tyson received a tip from within Baroque Chemical that the pick-up was to be today.

Faz was his number one agent at the Philadelphia office and had been with Tyson for eleven years. In that time, Tyson had watched Faz through many interrogations. He'd seen the entire gambit. Faz had them crying, pleading for mercy one minute, then laughing and sharing family stories. He watched as they lied for hours and then broke down into a feeble child telling the story of how they stole for the first time in grade school. Faz was good, but every suspect was different, and Tyson wanted Salinger to spill everything he knew about the smuggling.

Tyson didn't know a lot about Faz's personal life, just that he was married with two preteen girls. On several occasions, Faz had invited Tyson over for dinner or to watch the Eagles game. Tyson turned him down every time. Tyson knew not to get close, because at anytime the shit could hit the fan, and a personal relationship would only get in the way.

Joe watched as Faz opened up his seat of power, and perched across the green table from Salinger. The doctor looked up, his hands down by his sides, clutching the bottom of his chair as though any moment, the floor might fall from beneath him. Agent Fazolo reached inside his breast pocket and took out a pack of Doublemint gum and offered Abel a piece. Salinger snatched the piece and shoved it in his mouth so fast it was as if he hungry enough to have eaten his own shoe. "Thank you," he said with uncertainty.

"Special Agent Carl Fazolo," Faz said, "you can call me Faz."

"Agent Fazolo?" Salinger's eyes went wide. "What type of agent?"

"I'm an FBI agent here in Philadelphia."

"FBI?" Abel pursed his lips, and then swallowed the gum. "I thought it was strange you took me all the way to Philadelphia. I thought you were police detectives or something. Why am I here, Agent Fazolo?"

Tyson could tell the doctor was keeping something back. Salinger was too nervous; he knew why he was here. Tyson was sure of it.

"Faz is fine. You can cut the agent part. Tell me, Doctor, why do you think you're here?"

"I haven't a clue," Salinger said. "I was instructed to pick up an animal at the train station, and now I'm here. That's all I know."

"Yeah, that's right, the dog." Faz leaned his forearms on his knees, and looked at the visibly frightened Abel. "What is your job at the chemical plant, Doctor?"

"I am the senior chemist on the third floor, in charge of all animal experimentation." Dr. Salinger had just a hint of superiority in his voice as he answered.

Agent Faz looked directly at the doctor. "Please bear with me, doctor, because I fail to understand why a man of your obvious position and stature," Faz waved a hand, almost like a salute, "would be sent on an errand that any insignificant lab tech could have done. That would seem odd to anyone, don't you think?"

Salinger was sweating profusely. "I don't question my orders. I just do as I'm told."

"And who told you to pick up the dog? This requisition order is signed by you. How can *you* sign a requisition when someone else told you to pick up the dog, and...why."

"Mr. Gull instructed me, and I told you the reason in the car." Salinger was visibly shaken, and he looked like a rabbit ready to bolt at the slightest opportunity.

"Mr. Gull. Would that be Jason Gull, president and CEO of Baroque Chemical?"

Salinger knew he had slipped up. He was never to mention Gull's name, but he had never been put in this position before. He didn't know what to do or say. If he told the truth, he could count on never seeing the outside world again. His only option was to go on lying.

"So, doctor," Faz continued, letting the doctor's slip of Gull's name pass, "remind me again. Why were you sent to pick up this particular animal? All of the animals were headed to Baroque anyway, well, except for the ones freed by the crazies from PETA, or whoever they were."

Faz knew Salinger had lied before and now with the man drained, mentally as well as physically, he would never remember what he had given as a reason. When people were put under such anxiety, lies were rarely duplicated. Salinger sat and stared at the green desk, silent, unable to look Faz in the face

"What were your instructions, Doctor?" Faz yelled and shot spittle onto the desk. Some got on Salinger's hands

Salinger knew Faz wouldn't just let him sit there. He had to say something, and he had to lie. "The dog was singled out for its specific breed and size, for certain testing in the lab and I..."

"Bullshit again, Doctor," Faz blurted. He stood, leaned on the table, and eyed him menacingly. "You said before this dog came from Canada, and the wealth of information would be lost, blah, blah, blah. For your sake, you should come clean, Doctor. Otherwise we'll put you in a cell with a man affectionately known as Stallion, and weld the door shut."

Salinger was trembling.

"Now's the time, Faz. Go in for the kill," Tyson whispered to himself.

Salinger's cheeks were puffing outward, and he was trying to swallow. It looked as though he would puke at any moment.

"Maybe you can answer this, Doctor," Faz said. "Enlighten me as to why a dog that size weighed more than triple its normal weight?"

"I don't know what you're talking about." Salinger's eyes were glassy and bloodshot, and he still couldn't look Faz in the face. Salinger covered his face with his hands and started to weep.

Faz pointed to the door behind him. A man wearing a white lab coat stained a deep crimson entered the room. He carried a stainless steel tray containing four glass tubes, each approximately one inch in diameter and six inches long. The glass completely encompassed a strange, silvery substance. There was no movement within the glass, and they couldn't tell whether it was a liquid or a solid.

"Perhaps you could tell me why we found these tubes in place of the dog's intestines, or would you suggest the animal was just constipated?" Agent Faz pulled at the doctor's hands and forced him to look up.

The man carrying the tray suddenly stumbled on his untied shoelace and nearly dropped the tray. Dr. Salinger leapt out of his chair, and darted to the furthest corner of the room.

"Be careful, you idiot. Do you want to get us all KILLED?" Abel barked.

"What are you talking about, Doctor? Tell me what they are. Now!" Faz approached him, grabbed the cowering chemist by the throat and cutting off his air supply. Then he raised his service nine-millimeter handgun and pressed it to the doctor's forehead.

Salinger gasped for air, eyes wide as silver dollars and attempted to respond.

Faz held tight for ten seconds before releasing his grip, but the gun remained, digging hard into his subject's skull.

Dr Salinger took a deep breath, and looked over atthe tray. "There is enough enriched plutonium-239 in those cylinders to reduce the entire eastern seaboard to cinders."

Abel said it so fast that Tyson was ready to ask Faz to tell him to repeat it. Then Tyson saw the lab tech trembling, his face ashen white, and his knees moments from buckling.

Tyson pressed the call button. "Faz, quickly, grab the tray!"

Faz turned toward the lab tech, and leapt like a squirrel, grabbing the tray milliseconds before the man fainted.

Joe Tyson reacted nearly as quickly. He picked up the phone, punched a four-digit code, and screeched into it. "Bomb Squad, room four-thirteen. Code red." Tyson hung up the phone, pressed the intercom button again, his voice calm. "Faz, as gently as possible, place the tray down, and get the doctor—and yourself—out of that room"

Like getting out of the room was going to help, considering the massive destruction potential just described, Tyson thought to himself as Faz put the plutonium on the table, and grabbed Salinger by the scruff of the neck. Faz twisted the doctor's right arm behind his back and then thrust him into the observation room.

Inside of ninety seconds, a crew of four men dressed in full body armor, flak jackets, Kevlar helmets, armor blanket pants, and safety shields, entered the observation room.

"What's the situation?" Ivan Collins asked. He was the senior man of the federal building bomb squad. He was a brute of a man with a barrel chest and a belly to match. His protective attire was specially fitted to his particular physique.

"The situation is we were all nearly killed, thanks to the doctor here," Faz spat and jammed the shaking, exhausted chemist against the two-way mirror.

Tyson quickly shot his subordinate a stare, knowing he would understand that this wasa time for composure. "At this moment…"

Tyson said, pointing into the room, "…we possibly have four test tubes filled with plutonium…"

"Enriched plutonium-239," Salinger whimpered, interrupting Tyson. "Very volatile."

"Enriched plutonium-239," Tyson continued, "lying on that tray in the interrogation room, and we're not sure of its stability."

Ivan looked at the material through the mirror. "I don't think there is any imminent danger," he said, "but I suggest we evacuate the rooms, and make a clear path to remove it from the premises."

Tyson gestured forFaz to release the doctor and follow Ivan's orders.

Faz roughly shoved the doctor. They entered a room down the end of the hall, another interrogation room. "Dr. Salinger," Tyson spoke, intent on not appearing too threatening, "we need to know everything possible about these tubes."

Abel adjusted his shirt, and asked to sit down, and whether he could have something to drink. Tyson nodded, gave the doctora chair, and continued. "Are they stable? Is there any danger?"

"The vials are high-density polycarbonate, so they pose no immediate danger, but they can break, and they can be deadly. And…" Abel paused, viewing the men around him, "with prolonged exposure, everyone within thirty meters would increase their chance of cancer by three hundred percent. If one vial broke open, the ionizing radiation released would wreak unmerciful havoc on the citizens of Philadelphia."

CHAPTER ONE

Philadelphia, Present Day

Asleep in his bed, Al Campo's eyes flickered. His internal alarm clock woke him seconds before the red digits of the clock radio changed to 4:15. Music erupted into the room; an orchestra played "The Barber of Seville." A large, thick hand reached for the volume, and mistakenly turned it louder—then quickly reduced it to nil. He groaned, and then rolled over to face the clock. The four was flickering on and off, the plastic face was cracked, and duct tape held the cord to the side. It was beat up, and that's how he felt. The light from the streetlamp shone through the thin shades and gave him enough light to see without wasting electricity. He kicked his clothes that were on the floor as he made it to the dark hallway and rode his hand against the wall until he felt the doorjamb of the bathroom. He flicked the light switch and kept his eyes closed, groping for the faucet and then splashing water on his face. His pupils barely focused, so he balled the heel of his hands into them, then pushed back his hair. Al Campo stood staring at his face in the mirror; his eyes were dark and sunken. He wondered if he needed to bother shaving his face, or his eyebrows for that matter. *When was the last time I trimmed them*, he thought. He hadn't arrived home from the local bar until midnight, after watching the Phillies lose in ten innings. He'd only drunk a few beers—because he knew he had to get up for work, but still he was dead tired. Al decided not to shave, but showered,

1

got dressed, and went downstairs—past an ornate twisted iron railing. At the base of the steps was a mahogany secretary desk with about twenty tiny drawers. He then turned to his left past a low coffee table made with an odd mix of oak wood with an inlaid design made from cherry. Near the wall, there was another, taller table of teak, on which rested a tall, bright brass lamp. He turned the switch and light flooded the dining room. The main table was long and too big for the room. It was also cherry, but the finish was flaking off, and black stains covered the top. Its cabriole legs were in bad shape. At the head of the table was his prize possession: a colonial Queen Anne chair, original and in near-perfect condition. He had never had it appraised, did not want to know how much it was worth. He just liked owning it.

Campo had a passion for refinishing, repairing, and just plain collecting antiques. Strewn throughout his home were forty or so pieces he had removed from other people's trash and which he had made look new with his own hands. Along with the furniture, he enjoyed collecting nineteenth and early twentieth-century books. He had hundreds of rare volumes in a special glass-enclosed case down in his basement. He lived alone in a modest townhouse on the outskirts of the city, and he spent most of his downtime restoring or collecting. He earned his living working for the local glass workers union, which meant he installed glass in office buildings and commercial spaces.

The coffee pot had about three inches of day-old coffee in it; he poured a cup and put it in the microwave. He leaned on the counter and sipped the hot bark-tasting liquid and thought about the day ahead. He and his partner, Stanley Barrett, were to meet at the warehouse, pick up the required tools, and travel in the glass truck to the Delaware State Psychiatric Hospital, where all of the patient rooms needed new glass. Hospitals, in general, were pleasant to work in, but Al was a little apprehensive about working in an occupied mental hospital. It was a concept he was going to have to get used to. They were scheduled to be there for three months.

With a second cup of hot tree bark clutched in his hand, he got into his half-ton Ford pickup truck, and headed into the city. Al normally left for work later, but it was Monday. He purposely drove out of his way because it was trash day in the Wynnefield district of the city. A couple of the refinished pieces in his home could be traced back to there, found on the curbside. City Avenue was empty of cars as he drove south, past twenty-story apartment buildings, the Lankenau Hospital and past St. Joseph's sprawling university. Campo then turned down Wynnefield Road, and encountered different scenery.

Like he had traveled back in time, there were large, majestic homes lining the street. No two were the same. Immense stone structures,built in the late eighteenth and early nineteenth century. Massive, fat, tall homes,manyhad stained glass windows stretching for twenty feet or more. Gargoyles stood on the upper corners,motionless with mouths wide open, awaiting a rain to spew water. One home had a circular stone tower rising fifty feet, capped with a slate shingle peak, and a horse and carriage weather vane topping it off. Al couldn't help imagining Rapunzel in that tower, dropping her locks to an awaiting prince. Slowly, he drove past the giant houses, their trash on the curb. Conveniently, streetlamps lit up the road well, and he could see the piles of trash from the truck. In front of the first ten houses, there was nothing of interest,but he still looked in amazement at the architecture he'd observed many times before. Though the houses were extensive and distinct, they were not completely well-maintained. Very few had homeowners living in them. Most had been converted to apartments and were rented to college students, or even religious groups using them as temples, churches, or rectories. The original owners long since gone, the heirs were forced to sell or rent due to the high maintenance costs.For many years, Campo has seen furniture that was original to the houses discarded. Too many beer stains, broken glass, or even just a chipped leg made the pieces undesirable to the tenants, but they were Campo's prizes.

Something in the distance caught Campo's attention, the rear brake lights of a small moving truck. The lights went dim, and the truck vanished down the hill into nearby Fairmount Park. As he closed in on the spot just vacated by the truck, he viewed a large object half on the curb, alongside a pile of rubbish."A couch," Al said aloud, with a twinge of excitement. He stopped his pickup just ahead of the piece of furniture. He stood in the dark and glanced up at the house. It resembled a medieval castle with an eerie appearance in the darkness, and not a single light on.

Campo inspected the sofa, andas far as he could tell in the dim light, it looked in fair condition, although others mightnot be so kind with the description. He knew it was very old, its needle-point designs long since faded on the backrest. The fabric seemed to have been covered over several times; many areas were torn, displaying upholstery from a former period. The carved wooden armrests and ball-and-claw feet showed excessive wear. Judging by the woodwork, Al guessed it to be maybe a hundred years old.

"I love it. I'll work on it this weekend," he said to no one. Campo grabbed the couch at one end, and lifted it toward the truck, careful not to damage it any further. It was heavier than he thought, and he had to put it down again to open up his tailgate. He lifted it again and got one end situated on the tailgate. Then he went to the other end and had a tough time getting it up. "Damn, this thing is heavy," he said.Then suddenly, he heard a vehicle come racing up behind him. It screeched to a stop just three feet from Campo's back. Al was startled, but not noticeably. He pushed the sofa completely into the bed of the truck and closed the tail-gate before turning around. There stood an old, rusted midsize Datsun pickup truck. Its headlights were off, but the engine was still running. Campo squinted at the silhouette in the driver's seat. Whoever it was, he was taking histime before exiting. Al didn't care one way or the other and decided to get into his truck and be on his way. As Campo walked towards the cab of his truck, the motor-ist suddenly erupted and approached, one arm extended, point-ing at him. Campo saw something in the guy's hand, but couldn't make out what it was in the shadows.

"Excuse me," the shrouded person said, his voice friendly.

"Yeah, what's up?" Campo replied.

"I believe that piece of furniture belongs to me," the character said. He stepped closer to Al until he was illuminated by the street lamp.

What Al observed was a man of medium build, with straight hair. He couldn't be sure, but it looked like he was wearing make-up, pale cheeks with a little red blush maybe, and his eyes had a smoky dark shadow around them. Odd-looking to say the least but what Campo noticed most was the intruder's outstretched right hand holding a Smith and Wesson .38 caliber gun, pointed directly at his chest. Now, Al had been in sticky situations in the past, and he knew the first rule when threatened was to not appear alarmed. (Or maybe that was with dogs? Whatever.)

"I'm sorry," Campo said. "I didn't see your name on it, but you can have the broken chair over there, dickhead." He pointed over to the trash pile, and attempted to draw the man's attention away from himself. The stranger's eyes never moved from his target, and Al now knew he couldn't catch this man off guard that easily.

"That's a very foolish remark, since I am holding a gun directed at your heart. Now, I would like my couch," the man said as he re-gripped the weapon, pulling back the hammer and squinting, taking deadly aim. They were only a few feet apart now as the gunman inched closer, allowing Campo little chance of escape.

Campo quickly assessed the area. The gun was too close to dive behind or under the truck. With the hammer pulled back, the trigger was like a sneeze that could go off unexpectedly. He could lunge for the gun, but again, his attacker was too close. He was going to have to make a move, and he realized he might have to take a bullet. *But why?* He thought. *It's only a couch, and a very old one for that matter. Is it worth getting shot over?* But Campo had never backed down from a fight in his life. He had been threatened and shot before, and he was still here to tell the tale. Plus, he liked the couch. He already imagined it sitting behind the oak and cherry coffee table, and this asshole wasn't going to stop that from happening.

"Take it easy,"Campo said and turned toward the tailgate. "I was just trying to add a little levity to the situation. I'll get it out for you,"

"No, I'll get..."That was all the intruder could say because with lightning quickness, Al began turning toward the tailgate, spinning a hundred and eightydegrees. He swung the back of his clinched hand, and clocked the gun as it fired; the bullet put a hole in the tailgate. Campo took the split second of surprise and leaned back.Then he kicked the man square in the chest, a blow that smashed the air from his diaphragm, and the man fell back against the hood of the Datsun, then dropped to his kneeslike a rag-doll. Campo wasted no time in bringing his fist upward to finish him off, but the man gasped for air and raised his head, so Campo's fist only grazed his cheek. The effect was still enough and the man fell to the ground.

"Now, I do believe this sofa is mine," Al said, then took the moment to walk to the truck's cab. He sped off down the street, ignored a red light, and entered the Fairmount Park neighborhood, heading toward Center City.

"What the hell just happened…over a fucking sofa?" Al mumbled and checked his heart rate, because all of a sudden his chest was beating through his shirt.

———◆———

The collapsed man slowly regained his breath. He stood, managed to pick up his gun, and got back intohis rusted truck. He rubbed his sternum hard,trying to release the pressure; he rubbed his cheek and looked in the mirror. The base makeup was smeared and a red bruise appeared under his eye. He picked up his phone and speed-dialed a number. "Yes?" a hard voice answered.

"This is Jason Gull. I missed…" Gull took a deep breath to regain his strength. "I missed the delivery; I want you to get everyone out to search for a gray Ford pickup truck. It has an old couch in the back. I think he's going to head into the city on the expressway. I'm on my way to catch up."

The person on the other end was silent, memorizing all his instructions.

"We can't allow him to get away. Our deadline is getting too close, and there is no time for another shipment, so get everyone—and I mean everyone—on this."

"Yes, Mr. Gull," the person on the other end said.

Jason Gull repeated the description of the truck and the driver, added the first three numbers of the Ford's license plate, and then threw his phone onto the passenger seat. Gull yanked the gearshift into drive and sped off in pursuit.

CHAPTER TWO

Ten minutes later Al pulled up to the building where he worked. The glass shop was a two-story, rectangular brick building with a large overhead door, and a single aluminum and glass entry door making up its façade. A wholesale coffee distributor and a lunch cafe were connected on either side. The building was out of place in this area, with its large steel door and delivery trucks coming and going. It was the only non-retail business on the street. There were brick row houses built in the thirties and a couple of newer apartment buildings. It was only a matter of time before the glass shop was bought and converted to apartments or office space. Al parked on the sidewalk in front of the overhead door. The interior lights were on, so Al knew Stanley was already there. He walked into the shop. It was larger than the facade suggested. The ceiling was twenty feet high, while the space from front to back was five times that. There were large tall wooden racks; dozens of pieces of glass were stacked on each. To the right was an industrial radial arm saw, a huge beast from the fifties, with a sixteen-inch blade, and long rolling tables extended from either side. To the left was a huge table covered with carpet. That was the main work area where the glass was cut to size for different purposes. Campo walked to the rear, passing shelving units loaded with hardware and miscellaneous tools. At the very back was a makeshift office enclosed by a demising wall with a glass door.

"Morning," Al said as he entered the office.

"Good morning," said a man sitting at a desk adjacent to the door.

"You would not believe what happened to me this morning," Campo said. He walked around the edge of an aluminum desk, a big, boxy computer monitor sitting in the center.

"Yeah, yeah, yeah..." Stanley Barrett said. "You can tell me about it on the way; we've got to get moving to beat all the traffic." Stanley, a tall,thin man in his forties, was, in essence, Al's boss, even though they were the only two workers at the company. Stanley swiveled to face Al and crushed a cigarette in the metal ashtray on the desk. He had short,sparse hair, gray spreading in the dark blond. His nose looked like it had been broken several times. He wore a dark T-shirt and jeans with dark brown work boots. Al and Stanley got along like brothers; they both had a sense of humor and basically no personal feelings that could be hurt while busting each other's stones.

"Hold on, let me get a fresh cup of coffee first, OK, sir?" Campo said. He went to the coffee station, basically a Mr. Coffee on a metal table.

Outside, Stanley stood and viewed the sofa in the truck, "What the hell piece of shit do you have today?"

Al stepped from the office, sipping his coffee. "That's no piece of shit. That baby is going to go in my living room when it's done."

"Yeah, in about ten years," Stanley replied.

"No way. I'm nearly through with the mahogany chest, and this is next. You've seen my work,what the pieces look like when I've finished them. Surely you could appreciate something like this." Al's voice held a lot of pride as he looked once more at the newest project he had collected.

"To be honest," Stanley said, examining the furniture, "no, I can't. Why don't you just go to Sears, buy a new one, and get a warranty."

"Never mind," Al said, rolling his eyes. "Anyhow, when I was loading this, ah...piece of shit onto my truck, this guy stopped and pulled a gun on me."

"Get the hell out of here! Where were you, North Philadelphia?" Stanley chided.

"No, I wasn't, but seriously—I was held at gunpoint." Al said. "Look, there is a bullet hole in my tailgate."

"I can't say it's not an improvement on the truck. You need a new one of these, too."

"How did we get on to me needing a new truck?" Al said and fit his pinky in the bullet hole.

"Forget the truck. What the hell did the guy want?" Stanley said and he examined the exit hole on the inside of the tailgate. "What caliber? Looks like a .38?"

"Yeah, a Smitty, but he said he wanted this couch," Al replied.

"No way," Stanley said. "So what did you do? Obviously you're not shot, and here's the couch."

"I did a roundhouse, knocked the gun out of his hand, and got the hell out of there." Al had a smug look, like what else would he have done.

"It seems too fucking strange someone would go to that much trouble for an old piece of shit, um, I mean furniture," Stanley snickered.

Al raised an eyebrow and smiled. "I agree, so there's got to be more to it than that, don't you think?"

"I guess so. Did you call the police?

"What, and be late for work...please," Al said

"Shit," Stanley said as he looked at his watch, "Let's get moving. The crazies down at the hospital might get impatient if we're late."

CHAPTER THREE

The thirty-mile ride to Delaware blew by quickly. The red sun was low onthe eastern horizon. The sky was clear and the dry heat was just becoming uncomfortable.The trees and shrubs along the highway were dry and light green, thirsty for a soaking rain that had been absent for more than a month. Warm air burst through the open windows, granting Al and Stanley no relief in a truck without air conditioning. Conversation between the two almost never ceased, and before they knew it they found themselves bearing down on the driveway of the hospital. Al turned the wheel of the truck and stopped at a ten-foot black iron gate connected at either end to two concrete pillars. Beyond the pillars the iron fence surrounded the entire facility. To the right was a simple sign with a white background and black letters. It read: DELAWARE STATE HOSPITAL, MAIN ENTRANCE

Al stuck his arm out thewindow, and pressed an intercom protruding from another concrete pillar.

"Hospital security, may I help you?" a crackling voice said.

"Yes, we're with City Glass," Stanley said across Al's chest, "the Facilities Department expects us."

"Yes, they told us to expect you. Do you know where to go?"

"Sure, I was here last month," Stanly said into the intercom. He leaned back. "Just go straight ahead, and the road will start to curve to the right," he told Al.

The gates rolled back, and they rode in on a broken blacktop driveway. Al made a slow, gradual turn. On his left was a small, square, one-room building with a hundred-and-fifty-foot silo attached. Etched into a concrete plaque over a garage door were the words: Boiler Room. On the right was what looked like several one-story buildings, but actually they were all interconnected. The buildings were made from beige bricks, flat and plain. There were brown aluminum-framed windows placed every ten feet or so. It looked monotonous, rows and rows of squat beige bricks and simple windows. *Boring*, Campo thought. Whoever the architect was, he must have been on Thorazine himself to create this. The road continued, looping around in a huge oval to the rear of the main building. Finally, they reached some sort of loading area.

"Back in over there," Stanley said, pointing to the trailer half of a semi parked parallel to the road.

Al threw the gearshift into park, and they both stepped out. He noticed directly to his right was a twelve-foot-high cyclone fence topped with razor wire. It stretched across the open end of a U-shape in the buildings. Behind the cage, because that's what it looked like to Campo, were two dozen patients, each of them puffing hard on a cigarette. Al assumed smoking inside the building was prohibited, and from the looks of the group, outdoor time must be limited. They all smoked excitedly, some probably consuming a pack in an hour. Al was perplexed looking at the group, not understanding any of their individual sicknesses. He simply wondered. A tall, gangly man wore a helmet resembling the kind required for bike-riding; the reason for it quickly became evident. All of a sudden the man screamed, and burst across the yard. Several feet before reaching the fence, he leapt up and crashed into the steel links—then tumbled to the ground. He sat briefly and caught his breath. He rose, and then proceeded to his starting position and repeated the process several times before he tired out. Another patient stood, staring blankly back at Al. She was short and stocky. Her button-front shirt was partially tucked into blue jeans, and she wore two different sneakers. Her black hair stuck out, wild and stringy. As she methodically toked on her cigarette, her dark eyes never blinked. Campo at first thought her gaze fell on him, but then he realized she was looking into nothingness. Feeling a hand touch his shoulder, he was startledout of his inspection.

"Al, let's go," Stanley said. "I just finished talking with Jim McPherson. He wants us to begin over here in Kpod."

"And Jim McPherson would be?" Al asked as he proceeded to follow Stanley into the back of the trailer.

"The superintendent of the facility," Stanley said. "While we get our tools and glass ready, Jim said a locksmith would be by shortly with a set of keys to get us in and out of the building."

They both loaded a hand truck and a glass dolly with the tools required, along with twelve pieces of replacement glass from inside the trailer. Stanley having been already here knew exactly what they needed. Moments later, a light blue Ford Ranger pulled up to them, and a tall, frumpy figure exited. His thick curly blond hair added to his tall body, and he had a flat, smooth face. Large blue eyes magnified by glasses stared at them. He carried a black satchel, like the bag doctors used on house calls in the fifties, and approached Stanley and Campo.

"Hi, what can I do fer y'all? I'm Jesse, the locksmith."

Now, Al knew there was a saying in Delaware: if you're south of Wilmington, it's like being south of the Mason-Dixon Line, and most folk have a southern drawl. Jesse, not being the exception, seemed to be proud of his southern accent, and drawled it out more than usual.

"Hi, I'm Stanley, and this is Al," Campo nodded as Stanley stretched out his hand. "Apparently, we need some keys to enter and exit the building."

"Yea'ah, that's ca-rect." Jesse said as he dug into his bag. "I give ya two sets so y'all can enter and go by the loadin' dock door over heah." Jesse pointed to a pair of doors with a concrete loading ramp leading to them. "Now where you gonna be workin'?"

"As I understand it," Barrett said, "we will be working in all of the perimeter patient rooms."

"Then y'all gonna need keys to the pod doors."

"And what about the rooms?" Al injected. "Do we need a master key or something?"

"No," Jesse said. "Them doors don't have any locks, just the administration and nurses' room at the center of each pod, but ya only said the perimeter rooms, ca-rect?"

"That's right," Barrett answered.

"Now I see, y'all are ready to get workin', so I'll let ya in the pod, then go an' make ya two sets akeys, and bring 'em back in twenty minutes. That work for y'all? " Jesse smiled as he headed the two men in the right direction.

"Sounds like a plan," Stanley said.

Jesse led the pair down several hallways, tools and glass in tow. Al thought the inside had the look of his old high school, smooth linoleum-tile floors, painted cinder-block walls and fluorescent lighting recessed into a drop ceiling. Everything was an antiseptic off-white, with the exception of the extra-wide birch doors, which had a natural finish and stainless steel handles; all without key-holes. Finally they turned down a hall, windows on one side and the first door with a lock above the handle.

"Do we replace these as well?" Campo asked, referring to the windows that lined the hallway. They looked in bad shape, and most of them were cloudy.

"No, just the patient rooms," Stanley said. "And I think that's plenty. There are about sixteen hundred of them, windows, that is."

"OK," Jesse began. "This is the door to KPod. I'll open it but if y'all have to git out fo' any reason, just ask one of the nurses or orderlies and they'll fetch a key to let you out. Back up, please," Jesse said to a face pressed up against the narrow piece of glass in the door.

Al recognized it as the same blank, expressionless face he had seen outside huffing cigarettes.

"Back up, I said," the locksmith repeated. Then the visage dis-appeared from view. "OK, y'all have fun. I'll be back in a jiff."

"Excuse me," Stanley said. "Jess, do you happen to know who's in charge of this pod?"

"Well, that'd be Mr. Wilson. Ya can't miss him. He's the huge black fella with a ponytail." The southerner nodded, then left the two men alone in a strange habitat to fend for themselves.

Instantly, several patients approached, gazing curiously, always in motion, sidling, pacing back and forth, rising up and down on their toes or waving arms at the twosome. Stanley and Al gradually, good-naturedly, made their way through.

"Hi!" one female blurted loudly. "What are you guys going to do?"

"We're here to replace the glass in the pat...bedrooms," Stanley answered, not knowing what word to use in place of patient. How stable or unstable they were had not been explained in the least, so Barrett would choose his words carefully.

"Hello, can I help you?" a woman said, her voice echoing through a speaker overhead. At the end of the hallway, a glass-enclosed office sat at the apex of two adjacent hallways. Inside, a woman stood leaning over a microphone.

"Excuse me," Stanley said, as he and Al all but pushed through the crowd of spectators with their tools and glass. "Yes, I hope you can. Mr. McPherson said we were to begin replacing the windows in this wing first."

"Replacing windows?" she responded and looked at the two men. Her eyes darted from the glass dolly to the bunch of tools and then to their faces again. Al took a long look at her while his partner spoke. She wasn't tall, maybe five feet. Her silver-blond hair fell straight below her jaw with trimmed bangs. She wore too much makeup in an attempt to hide her wrinkles, and it didn't much help. She must be close to sixty, yet she had an attractive figure pushed into snug jeans.

"Yes," Stanley continued. "The windows in all of the, ah, resident rooms are to receive new glass."

"Well, I don't know anything about that," she said and looked down at some papers on her desk. "So before you get started you'll have to speak with Mr. Wilson."

"Could you tell me..."Before Stanley was able to finish his thought, a high-pitched yell was heard down the hall.

From around the corner, a large black man came moseying toward them,his arms high overhead, grasping a young man, very thin, with his nose running. He was wearing one of those protective helmets, and he screamed obscenities at his captor. Mr. Wilson retained a simple appearance; a round and pudgy face matched his abundant stomach and torso. He had short, curly hair on top of his head and on his cheeks. Behind his neck was a tiny clump of hair.Al remembered Jesse saying Mr. Wilson had a ponytail; the tiny ball of curls on the back of his head was a weak attempt at best.

"That's Mr. Wilson," the nurse said."He's carrying Freddy to his room again"

With that said, the lumbering head of K pod, who looked more like a member of the Philadelphia Eagles, kicked open a steel door, and as gently as possible, tossed Freddyin like a flea."Now you cool off for a while. I'll come see you a little later," Wilson spoke in a smooth, yet rigid pitch, and then closed the cell door. The reverberating obscenities could be heard faintly throughout the pod.

"Excuse me, Mr. Wilson," Barrett said.

Black eyes darted aggressively toStanley,and the man took a hard step toward him,then shot a glance at Campo. Stanley looked a little scared at first, but the big man realized he wasn't a patient, and then settled back down. "Yes, gentlemen, how can I help you today?" He smoothed the top of his head with his meaty hand

Stanley explained their situation. Campo was getting anxious, wondering if they were ever going to get started.

"Where is Jim McPherson?" Mr. Wilson said.

"He apparently went back to his office,"Stanly replied.

"Wimp," Wilson spat, shaking his large crown. "Every time workers arrive, he's the first to skate away. Allright guys, I'll show you where to begin."

The pair pushed their carts slowly behind Mr. Wilson's wide body; his walk looked uncomfortable. Massive thighs collided, causing him to step outward, and his arms swung in a round motion, like spinning a discus.

"Now gentlemen," Wilson said, making his way down the leftmost corridors, Al noticed he was constantly turning his head, always looking at the different patients hanging about. No one ever met his gaze; they all turned away when he approached. "This is K pod," he continued."The new patient's pod. All of our residents here have arrived within the last twelve months, which means we don't know what to expect from them. Some may talk a lot or run up and down the hallways, or some may even react violently to otherwise normal situations. Like Freddie. You just witnessed me placing him into the restraining cell."

"Placing?" Al thought out loud, knowing Freddie had landed hard on the linoleum floor.

Wilson's bulk stopped in front of a door marked K-1-66, and he folded his massive arms. He made the buttons on his shirt work hard. "This is where you'll begin, room sixty-six, and work your way around each hallway to room K-one-three. Now the only rooms with windows are the resident rooms, and there are no locks on those doors."

"Yes, Jesse told us," Stanley said.

"So if a door is locked, it means no windows," Wilson added.

"Pardon me, Mr. Wilson." This came from Al. "We're going to be working with sharp metal, broken glass, and a torch. How can we keep the inmates, or rather residents, out of the rooms if there are no locks?"

"You'll have to keep an eye open for someone entering the room," Wilson said. "It shouldn't be too difficult. They mostly keep to themselves."

"Even Freddie?" Campo said sardonically.

"Freddie is an unusual case," the big man said, giving Al a sneer. "Plus he's coming to the end of his twelve months. He'll be moved to the violent males' pod soon."

"Violent males. I can't wait to work in those rooms," Al said, as Stanley motioned to him to keep his composure.

"All you need to do," Wilson continued, "is tell the station nurse," Wilson pointed back at the glass booth, "where you'll work the following day before you leave, so she can make sure the residents are out before you arrive. How many rooms do you think you'll complete each day?"

"Two to three rooms," Stanley answered.

"Fine, I'll empty these next three, but from today on, you're on your own." Mr. Wilson opened the rooms to find them unoccupied. "They're all yours, gentleman. Have a nice day." He turned, and strode out of view.

"All right," Barrett said, ready to finally get to work. "Listen Al, you start tearing out here, and I'll go to the next room. When you're done, continue to the last room, and I'll come behind you to finish the installation. Then, we'll clean up together and have an early quit."

"Sounds like a plan." Al saluted Stanley as he turned and walked away.

Al Campo set foot into the first room. Facing him were four single beds, two on either side, each neatly made with tan wool blankets and a white pillow sitting at the head. The bed frames were wooden and rested directly on the floor. Other than a piece of paper, nothing could be stored under them. Beside each bed, square wooden night tables squatted, each with a single drawer and shelf. Directly across from the entrance was a bay of six windows, with two closets on either side, constructed of the same natural pine asthe other furniture. Campo summed up the living space in one word…dreary. He put on his tool belt, and began removing the metal holding in the glass. Within an hour, five of the six pieces of glass lay in the trashcan.

Suddenly, Al became aware of a strange sound, a ticking sound. It wasn't a steady tick like that of a watch or a grandfather clock. It was faint and erratic, stopping briefly—then starting up again for short or long periods. Remaining silent and still, Campo definitely heard something. Slowly, he followed his ears, which drew him to the closets on the right. Turning the handle nearest him he found it unlocked. When it rotated on its hinge, the noise stopped.

"Shit!" he said nervously. Here he was snooping around in an unknown person's closet. It could get him fired. He saw the interior was filthy. To the left hung one dusty jacket. On the right were deep high shelves, practically devoid of clothes.

The noise started again. Louder this time, it unmistakably camefrom the next closet.

"I know that sound," he said, and gave a quick look at the door with no lock. He figured if no one had bothered him in the past hour, it would be safe to look. Then he opened the closet door to the right; the ticking was louder now. The contents were nearly identical, a minimal amount of garments. Either hospital rules limited the number of personal possessions, or the patients were destitute when they arrived here. One difference did catch Campo's eye. The shelves here were not as deep.

Tick, tick, tick…

The sound led him to the middle shelf. He sat down on the end table and moved several items out of the way: an eyeglass case, a can of deodorant, and a toothbrush. He felt around the back panel, and was able to slip a fingernail into a crease along the edge, discovering the rear panel wasn't milled to the sides. A piano hinge joined the rear to the shelf, and ran crosswise, painted a natural pine. It was barely visible. Having a knowledge of furniture making, he instinctively pressed against the back panel, andthat activated a spring magnet and released the hidden door. Slowly Campo lowered it until it met the shelf, which in turn, correlated to an internal fluorescent light.

His insight was correct. Illuminated inside was an old telegraph receiver, spurting out a message. It was similar to a model he had on a shelf in his basement.He had found it outside the old RCA compound several years ago, except this one had been modified a bit. Inside the glass dome the original brass violin-shape gears were intact, with the principal typing implements held together by a copper coil. Yet the base and receiver did not have a direct wire. Instead, a mini laptop computer,complete with power cord and keypad were in its place. Originally with these types of machines, messages could only be sent by wires strung directly from point-to-point and transmitter-to-receiver. But this was hooked up to the Internet.

Highly unusual? Not just that.Simply put, it was impossible, was Al's only notion. For a legitimate patient in a psychiatric hospital to have such a machine was ridiculous. His inquisitiveness grew stronger now. Even knowing full well that snooping around in a patient's closet wasn't morally correct and could get him fired; curiosity drove him to find out what the hell this person was up to. The machine stopped once again. Gently, he pulled the one-inch-wide paper message out, careful not to tear it. It was not typed in English. Another language. It looked like Arabic, but slightly different. *All those Middle-Eastern languages ran together in some way or another*, thought Al, but somehow he knew the writing. Possibly he had seen something like this back when he was in the service, but he couldn't put his finger on it right now.

Campo couldn't just rip off the paper to study it at home later. So he retrieved a receipt from within his billfold and tried tocopy the writing as best he could. Several minutes had passed since the last transmission. He replaced the items as best he could remember and closed the collapsible back.

All of a sudden he heard the knob on the main door turning. Fear of being caught shot through Campo's veins. He put the paper back in his pocket, and shut the closet just as the bedroom door opened. A man was standing in the entrance. He had thick shaggy hair, dark as coal, and a deep tan skin tone—not the kind obtained at the beach; he was born with that coloring. He stared at Al harshly—and remained soundless and still.

"Sorry, but you'll have to stay out of the room until I'm finished," Al said as he resumed working at the window.

The man held his evil stare.

Campo felt he was caught, and tried to ignore the possible consequences, so he turned his back to the entrance. He felt uncomfortable, so he looked around to see if the man had left. He hadn't. Instead, the man moved closer. Al had to act and call his bluff. He walked past the man, whose eyes followed him, and poked his head into the hall.

"Excuse me, excuse me,"Al hollered up the hall to the nurse's station. "There is a resident in this room. Could you please have him removed?"

The nurse down the hall nodded, and immediately called Mr. Wilson, who arrived in sixty seconds. "Come on, Alex," the big man said. "I told you. You have to stay in the TV room today." Wilson clasped his pudgy hand around the resident's arm, and escorted him out. Alex's gaze never left Campo.

"Sorry, Al, but he doesn't speak," Wilson explained. "He's also very slow in comprehending orders. But don't worry. He won't be back."

"No problem. He didn't do anything," Al said, raising his arms in indifference. Once they left, he moved the nearest bed, propping it against the unlockable door.He hoped he wouldn't have any more visitors. Just as he got back to work, he heard the handle turn once more. "Not again," he said, as the door was forcibly pushed inward to a four-inch opening.

"Yo, Al!" Stanley said. His long nose poked in through the crease.

"Sorry, hold on. I braced the bed frame against the door." Campo moved the bed and let his partner in.

"What the hell have you been doing?" Stanley said as he viewed the last window still intact.

"Well, I had an intruder, and he didn't leave until the big bouncer came to get him."Al looked at Stanley, hoping his excuse was believed.

"You too, huh?" Stanly smiled at Al.

"What's that?"Al asked.

"I had some guy come into my room. He looked like he hadn't bathed in a week, and he asked me if I wanted my feet massaged," Stanley said, shaking his head.

"Really?" Al said with a twisted smile. "So how was it?"

"How was what?" Stanley said.

"The massage," Al said as he pushed Stanley teasingly in the shoulder.

"I didn't get a…shut up, Al!" Stanley shoved Al back.

Campo laughed hard and said, "OK. Whaddya want?"

"I just got a phone call from the shop. We have to pack up and go do an emergency glass removal."

"No shit, where?" Campo asked. He was kind of glad to be getting out of the hospital after nearly getting caught with his hand in the cookie jar.

"The Baroque Chemical building. Apparently broken glass is hanging over an occupied area. Their maintenance crew attempted to remove it and one of them got hurt. They called the boss, and he told them we were right around the corner. So, temp in the new glass, clean up the mess, and meet me by the truck, I've already done that, so I'll tell what's-his-name—McPherson—what were doing." Stanley said the last sentence as he was heading out the door.

"You got it," Al said, hurrying back to finish. "See you in fifteen."

CHAPTER FOUR

L eaning his forearms on the rectangular cherry wood desk, the president of the United States signed his name: E. James Worthington. He wrote his veto onthe latest ridiculous congressional attempt at a budget plan for the next five years. While his bipartisan cabinet urged him not to veto, he stood firm on his policies."This budget is just as full ofjargon as the last," Worthington said, as he leaned back into the chocolate-brown leather captain's chair. "They try to sugarcoat it with miniscule boosts for education and healthcare. It's not nearly enough, and the funds to furnish them are to come from alower-middle-class tax hike," Worthingtonsaid to Sam Haggart, his chief of staff, who sat across the broad hardwood desk. He wore a blue suit jacket, open, displaying a soiled white shirt and dark tie. His legs were crossed, and a stack of manila folders lay on his lap. Sam had set up this private time with the president so that they would have a chance to discuss some issues without anyone else overhearing their conversation.

"Sir, the tax increase is across the board, as I've told you. All income brackets will be affected," Haggart said through thin lips under a sharp nose and close-set eyes.

"Bullshit, Sam. You know as well as I dothat the middle class would take the blunt end of the burden."

E. James sat forward—his face taunt and angry. The president's physique suited his role. He was in his fifties, and in excellent condition, with streaks of gray woven through his wavy brown hair, and wrinkles distinguishinghis noble face. "The national debt is not their fault; all they know is they work their butts off fifty or sixty hours a week and watch their take-home pay decrease every year.

"As I have said on the floor to those stubborn politicians, I want a budget plan to entice the upper class to invest their money in small businesses and the labor force. This does not mean if they raise the pay scale, they up the prices of the product or the rent or interest rates. I want the mega-rich bastards in the top onepercent to use what they can't spend in a lifetime on the needy people of America. I'm tired of seeing more billionaires taking businesses out of the country because profits dropped three-quarters of a point."

The president paused briefly, and then continued. "Have young Ben Alomar come to see me later. I would like to include a few chapters on that topic in my provision to Congress later this month." E. James moved the document to the side, and set down his pen. He leaned back in his chair. "Now onto new business. Those folders on your lap must contain something interesting."

"Well sir, the situation in the Middle East is rumbling even louder since the assassination of Amir Mohab, the president of Turkey. And our sources point to the self-proclaimed Caliph Karuza, but as of this morning neither he nor his followers have claimed responsibility for it," Sam said. He leaned his chin on his thumb and forefinger, his left hand draped across the folders while Worthington began rocking in his chair.

"Your sources, what do they say about this Karutzas…" the president asked.

"Karuza, sir," the chief of staff corrected him.

"…Karuza's," the president paused, raising an eyebrow at Sam, "motive for the killing?"

"They feel it's pure, one-hundred-percent revenge. Amir was very outspoken about his feelings toward Karuza. Every public and private gathering he attended, the president chastised him. Our sources tell us Karuza's chief advisor and cousin, Ammar, felt Amir Mohab had to be silenced. His followers would findhim weak for tolerating the president of Turkey's verbal abuse any longer."

"What do we know about this Caliph Karuza, Sam?" E. James said and began to fidget with the pen on his desk, rolling it back and forth.

"Our agents in Turkey feel he's up to something sinister. His speeches, which started out attracting onlya few followers, have grown into ten-thousand-member rallies. He's been linked through satellite and is now seen throughout the Middle East, North Africa, and Europe. Now, our own media have a piece on him at least once a week—with cable news leading the waytwenty-four-seven."

"The media," the president snarled. "They care littleas long as ratings go up."

"The media and his rise to power, sir, are not happening by accident," Haggart continued. "His cousin, Ammar, has carefully orchestrated the political and religious rise of his kin. He has associations from Turkey to Great Britain—the magnitude of his influence is unmeasurable, and sir…" The chief of staff adjusted himself in his seat, pausing a moment to possibly prepare Worthington for the seriousness of the topic they were dealing with. "Sir, we recently observed this man having a private meeting with Karuza and Ammar." Haggart laid a picture of a light-skinned man with a taunt face and tight crew cut onto the desk.

"And this man is?" the president asked, without taking his eyes from the photo.

"Valissi Pandanco, a former KGB agent in the old Soviet Union, and now director of the secret service for Premier Antoniv Andropov."

"Of the Republic of Georgia in Asia?" E. James said, looking up, staring straight at his chief of staff.

"Yes sir, I'm afraid so. We feel that Andropov's interests are the same as Karuza's, or possibly the caliph has something they want, or vice versa. We're still in the dark on that one. The photo was just faxed over this morning."

Worthington was visibly irritated at the lack of information. "You mean to say, in plain words, Andropov wants oil reserves to boost his floundering economy, and Karuza wants the nuclear weapons Georgia still holds in its arsenal."

"Yes, Mr. President. In plain words," Sam said.

"I've known Antoniv since my days working atthe United Nations. I don't believe he would be willing to give a self-proclaimed Arab Messiah any of his ICBMs, or the ability to use the threat of them. In the dispersal of the USSR, those missiles were to be disarmed. Even though we know differently, he wouldn't risk exposure. Besides, Turkey has only a small fraction of the Middle East oil wells." The president looked over to his chief of staff and waited.

"Our sources considered those facts, and that's why they feel something big is going to happen—and soon. Masses, numbered in the millions, have been accumulating in the region." Sam looked straight into the president's eyes.

"A massive invasion?" Worthington asked.

"That was the original thought, but they are congregating in Iran, Saudi Arabia," Sam was reading from his file, "Iraq, Afghanistan, Pakistan, Yemen, Jordan, and the whole of North Africa, even smaller groups in the West Bank. If an invasion was planned, who would be invaded?"

"That's all I needed to hear, Sam. Call the chairman of the joint chiefs, Admiral Alex Faustian."

"Sir, he's already ordered the Harry S. Truman carrier fleet to prepare to meet with the Enterprise carrier armada already in the Persian Gulf, adding an additional nine thousand troops to the region. This, incidentally, has been done without a media blast."

"And when did you plan on informing me, Sam?" E. James said, disapproving of the action without his knowledge. But after-the recent death of his wife, he'd been unable to maintain his mechanical pace of retaining all information.

"I just did, sir. This all happened in the last twelve hours. That's why I hurried this proposal of Congress into you. I didn't want a meeting of this length to be questioned. As of this moment, you, the admiral, Bruce Kellogg, the director of the CIA, and I are the only ones privy to this information."

"I think a meeting of the joint chiefs is in order, closed doors of course, first thing tomorrow. Also have Kellogg and Nate Breechart join us," President Worthington ordered.

"Nate Breechart, the FBI director?" Sam said puzzled

"Yes, I want to know if this Ammar character has any digs here in the US. If so, I want them squashed."

Sam jotted down a note to himself to call the meeting.

"And by nine a.m., I want a detailed dossier on this Karuza person, and that brother of his."

"Cousin, sir," Haggart corrected again. "Ammar Hassan."

"Yes, yes, cousin. Now I have an appointment, Sam. I'll see you tomorrow morning." President Worthington stood and ushered Sam from the room. The chief of staff exited. The president had given him a tremendous task to accomplish in the next eighteen hours.

E. James Worthington rose from behind his desk and pen. He referred to them as his personal prison bars. He entered the outer office where two Secret Service officers, one man, one woman, stood on either side of the Oval Office door. A middle-aged woman, with blond hair held up in a swirl above her head, sat at a desk and typed. She was very heavy in the hips, yet her arms and shoulders showed no signs of obesity.

"Betty," E. James said, putting on his raincoat and hat. "Did you call for the car?"

"Yes, sir." Betty Nilsson looked up, listened, and spoke with full attention toward the commander-in-chief. She'd been his private secretary since day one of his law practice. "It is waiting by the South Lawn."

"Thank you." Worthington left, the agents following. He was on his way to a Special Olympics event in the downtown Washington area. With the impending rain, it might be canceled, but he hadn't missed an event yet. The president was obsessive when it came to his engagements; rarely did he ever cancel an appointment or meeting of any kind. He felt that if they were important enough to be made, they should be kept.

CHAPTER FIVE

Istanbul, Turkey

CaliphKaruza stood in the center of the room, hands casually at his side. He wore a *thobe*, a robe commonly worn in the Middle East. A spotless *ghotra*, headdress of a sheikh, sat on his head.

To his left, nearly half a foot taller than the caliph, was his cousin and chief advisor, Ammar, who wore similar raiment except forthe headdress, and that absence exposed his thin silver hair. Opposite Ammar on Karuza's right was an evil-looking man who stood commandingly, his body rigid. He was known as General Sabu, the Butcher, the caliph's strong arm. He was recognized everywhere in the Middle East as a ruthless, cold-blooded murderer of women and children from the Iraqi invasion of Kuwait. He wore desert tan military garb, black high-laced boots, and a tan beret on his thicket of black hair.On his hips were two holstered German-made Lugar pistols, antiques from World War II that were in perfect condition. He had been recruited by Ammar to stealthily build an army of followers, to make ready the way for the return of the Prophet.

They stood silently in front of tremendous bronze doors. Even through the thick metal, Karuza could hear the crowd murmuring in prayer. Slowly, the doors opened and silence was complete as the three figures walked into the daylight. The trio saw a massive gathering of people spread throughout the gardens of Hagia Sophia.

Tens of thousands of followers gathered to see the self-proclaimed caliph, His Holiness, Karuza. With its tall pinnacles surrounding a towering central dome, Hagia Sophia was ahome for the caliph and his religious zealots who would follow him to his glory.

Originally, Hagia Sophia had been built as a church by Constantine the Great and remolded at the hands of Emperors Justinian and Theodosius. It became a mosque when the Turks conquered Constantinople, the most important time in history for Karuza. In the twentieth century, it became a museum. Recently, Karuza gained support from religious sympathizers, convincing them it was where the new empire would begin. And he made the temple his place to begin the new realm of glory.

Karuza stoodin the shade caused by the massive multi-colored marble walls. The shade was growing smaller as the Earth's lone star rose in the eastern horizon to his back. The populace sprawled over every available expanse. They crushed foliage, climbed trees, inching themselves closer, eager to see the holy one who had been heard on the radio, seen on television, and had his message delivered in leaflets to hundreds of thousands of believers, preaching the words of the Prophet. They massed here for weeks, day and night, to seek the glory promised by the Prophet.The three stood at a white marble podium. The stone had blazing streaks of red in its grain. Perched on top were a dozen microphones. Karuza was told the center three were reserved for the loudspeakers, while the balance supplied audio to the various radio and television stations. The crowd suddenly erupted into applause, cheering and chanting Karuza's name. The caliph gazed out at the throng-absorbing reverence, allowing the ovation to continue several minutes. He gradually elevated his hands, palms facing the congregation, and they silenced.

"Believers, my followers, my most gracious supporters," Karuza's voice echoed over them, reaching the ears of even the most distant. "I have been blessed with the vision of His Most Revered Holiness, Allah. While I slept, he appeared to me and privileged me with his tasks. I am to prepare the way for the return of his son, the Prophet." The mass exploded into a semi-violent roar of approval. "He has…" the caliph paused, and lifted his hands. When calm resumed, he continued. "He has ordered me to bring all believers together, joining as one nation, creating a loyal world, ready to receive His Son. When we are united without war between us, no more distinction, whether Iranian, Libyan, Turk, Omani, we are all One, and when we, all of us, are one, Allah will send the Prophet back to us, so he may begin his reign of justice throughout the world."

Again the mass cheered, only to be quieted by the caliph. "All believers," Karuza said. He laid his arms on the podium, speaking commandingly at the microphones. "Come, join together in masses like the one before me. Combine in prayer. Send Allah your relentless faith. He will hear you. He has told me so. Once the power of millions…billions join asone nation, we will rise up." His Holiness reached up, clenching his fist, and slammingit on the marble. "Rise like a mountain and tower above all others: Christians, Jews, Buddhists, and Hindus. Believers in the Middle East, Europe, and Asia, come and join me here in Istanbul. In the West, travel to your capital. Send the message that there is only one nation, and the Prophet will be its ruler. Now join me in praying for blessings on Allah's son. May his arrival be swift and safe."

Karuza and Ammar bowed their heads, as did the gathered thousands, but Sabu kept his eyes wide to see his military guards watching the crowd. Once the sermon was completed, the Butcher's men would begin recruiting volunteers for the army.

The caliph raised his head and hands. "Blessings of Allah are upon the loyal believers and to their prayer of the swift return of the Prophet."The crowd cheered and applauded, then chanted Karuza's name. "Ka…ru…za! Ka…ru…za!"

The three men led by Caliph Karuza turned and walked back through the massive bronze doors. They entered a gigantic room with tall narrow columns surrounding a central dome made of white brick that appeared to float over the vast floor. Colored marble, matching the exterior, covered the walls along with a brilliant mosaic sunburst spanning the floor.

"That was a tremendous audience, my caliph," Ammar said, as they crossed through the sunbeams.

"The loyal believers are our strength and power," Karuza spoke in a soft tone, unlike the power he projected in front of the microphones. "Once the path is laid, they will secure our future."

"Yes, a very moving speech, your Holiness," Sabu added

"A very emotional speech indeed," a voice said from the shadows. "And just the way I like them, short and sweet." The voice was louder now, with a distinct Slavic accent. A silhouetted figure emerged from behind a white and green marble column. He was dressed in a black suit that contrasted with his pale complexion. He had short, blond hair and green eyes with a long, slender nose. "You even had me believing in the return of the Prophet for a moment, your sacredness," he said sarcastically.

Karuza shrugged off the remark.

But Sabu felt his caliph was dishonored, and he reached for his weapon. "You insolent bastard, I'll kill you for speaking to His Holiness in that manner."

The caliph reached out his hand, preventing the Butcher from drawing his weapon.

The blond man strolled up to the three, standing face to face with Sabu's ominous stare. He returned the threatening glance, and then he smiled in a demeaning way, infuriating the general.

"What is it you want, Valissi?" Ammar asked.

"In particular?" Valissi began as he reached into his breast pocket, pulling out a Turkish cigarette, and lighting it. "Why is the president of Turkey now lying in a Roman morgue, and the assassin known as Akmid Mohan laid outnext to him?"

"I ordered his death," Karuza said. "The president's mouth ran on too long. His insults were to be tolerated no more. Don't worry, Valissi. He won't be missed. His life would have been over in six days anyway."

"This does not please Premier Andropov," Valissi said.

"The caliph's name was disgraced whenever the president spoke publicly," Ammar barked. "To allow him to travel throughout Europe would be seen as a sign of weakness. He had to be terminated once he left Turkey, and Rome was suitable."

"The premier considers this a foolish act of retribution, and he does not condone the fact he was not informed. You know how sensitive he is," Valissi said as smoke seeped from his mouth.

"Taking the chance of relating our plans to Andropov could leave an avenue of implication for your premier," Ammar's timbre changed. "We thought it best to remain silent."

"I do not deem it necessary to explain my every move to you, Valissi," Karuza said as he walked across the domed room with his cousin and the Butcher in tow. "We agreed I would be left alone until the next moon."

"Remember, my divine Karuza," the Slavic accent of Valissi echoed, chasing the three as they walked away. "Premier Andropov does not like failure—and he will not tolerate any more individual acts of vengeance. Remember who elevated you to this level," Valissi was yelling now. "And who can bring you down!"

His Holiness paused before an arched entrance while Sabu opened the huge mahogany door. The caliph turned, waved limply, and said, "Goodbye, Valissi."

The three entered a library, extensive walls of texts rose thirty feet high. There were balconies on three of the four walls. The fourth was a gigantic stained-glass window Karuza had ordered installed. Its images displayed the Turks conquering Constantinople, a great battle scene of horses and men fighting in macabre silence. The ceiling was domed in glass, allowing the sunlight to illuminate the entire room naturally. They sat on low couches with no apparent framework that seemed to move with the user. In front of them was a mahogany table upon which a pot of Turkish tea sat. Ammar stood and poured a cup for each.

"Has Yavuz in America checked in as scheduled?" Karuza said, and then sipped the hot tea.

"No," Ammar said. "And if he had, we would have been notified immediately after the speech."

"His response was due an hour ago," Sabu snapped

"That is true," Ammar continued, "and the reason for the delay is unknown. We had sent our regular transmission, only this time we instructed him to commence Operation Slaughter, and reiterated that this would be our last exchange. The weapon will be delivered with further instructions. Then we specifically ordered that a reply was necessary."

Sabu thrust out a fist on the table in frustration at the incompetence of his subordinates. Yet the Butcher held in his almost uncontrollable rage. "Holy One," the Butcher said, and looked at the caliph as he drank the steaming liquid. "We've been sending the same transmissions in a random pattern every week for the past five months. *Remain. Await further orders.* Never has Yavuz been even a minute late in responding. The first time we send a new message, no response. We must assume his position has been compromised, and he must be replaced."

"I disagree," the caliph's cousin said, shaking his head. "If we send in another unit, and Yavuz is still intact, we jeopardize the whole operation."

"If we send in no one, and Yavuz is dead, we have no operation!" Sabu spat angrily.

"Enough!" the caliph said, raising his right hand. "We will wait for Yavuz to respond. He is a resourceful agent, and he will contact us when it is safe to do so. Until then, we remain on schedule. Up to this moment, all of our plans have fallen into place, as I have foreseen." Karuza stood and sauntered over toward the stained glass window, continuing his thoughts out loud. "Believers across the Middle East, Europe, and North Africa have been rallied by the millions; they speak of the return of the Prophet. With their devotion toward me, their caliph, their savior on Earth, they will follow us to the new regime."

Karuza pointed up at the images on the window. "I will continue what they created. I will take back the world that was stolen from us, with an army of a hundred million believers united as one. From here in Istanbul, to Jerusalem, onto Europe, and with the firepower Andropov holds in his arsenals, the Americans will fall. Then, all countries will bow to the new world order. Only six days until Operation Slaughter, and our wait will be over. The destiny of our prayers nears, and the Prophet will return. I will stand beside him, displaying what we have created for him, and then we shall live where our ancestors roamed and migrate to new lands."

At that moment, sunlight illuminated the stained glass. Brilliant rays burst through in colors that seemed to have texture and dimension. Their brilliance shone down on Karuza like a multicolored spotlight.

Sabu and Ammar's mouths gaped at the marvelous display.

The caliph stared at the window, grabbing the colorswith his hands, absorbing the heat of the sun; his *thobe* glowed like a nebula.

"This is a sign from Allah," Karuza embellished, while his cousin and Sabu dropped to their knees and watched their Holy One caress the splendor. They prayed out loud, blessing the light.

"I, Caliph Karuza, with the Prophet by my side, shall rule the civilized world."

CHAPTER SIX

After a fruitless attempt at catching up to the gray Ford and the couch, Jason Gull traveled south to the Pennsylvania/Delaware border. Once he crossed the state line, he turned onto an unmarked road. The pathway began as blacktop. Then, a mile into a forest, it changed to hard-packed dirt. Through a series of twists and turns, Gull drove at a speed that might have looked unsafe to a driver unfamiliar withthe surroundings. But Jason had traveled this road to work every day for the past twenty-five years. Basically, he created the avenue, traversing low brush in his early days before the creation of the Baroque Chemical and Pharmaceutical Corporation.

While joyriding in a four-wheel-drive jeep in his mid-twenties, he recklessly collided with an old outhouse, demolishing it. He ended up in a ditch with a blown tire, and no spare. Stepping from his jeep, he walked uphill and approached a thicket of vines devouring a structure. It was the nineteenth-century home of the DuPont family, long forgotten by the heirs. It was designed in the extravagant style of artistic expression prevalent in seventeenth-century France, when Louis XIV was king, hence the title Baroque, which Gull created from the ground up. He was able to buy the property from the state of Delaware. It consisted of thirty acres, the mansion, and a run-down chauffeur house, which he had torn down, making room for parking.

Finally,his rusted old truck swerved around the last landmark, and halted in front of an eight-foot-tall cyclone fence, strewn with razor wire. A sign dangled loosely from the links. DANGER! ELECTRIFIED FENCE! KEEP AWAY! NO TRESSPASSING!

Jason beeped his horn three times, waited fifteen seconds, and beeped three more times. With a sudden shudder in the ground, a circular portion of the earth surrounding the vehicle gave way. Slowly, the ground descended, and Jason sat patiently as he sunk thirty feet. When the platform came to rest, sensors automatically switched on fluorescent lighting. Now inside a private parking area, the floor spun ninety degrees, and he backed his auto into a vacant spot. Then the earthen elevator rose and concealed the entry.

In the round parking area were a collection of Gull's favorite automobiles: a BMW Z4, a convertible Ferrari, his four-wheel-drive Jeep Cherokee, and his everyday vehicle, a Volvo 980. He grabbed his briefcase, walked around a raw concrete column, and entered a wardrobe room with a complete bathroom. Thirty minutes later, the chairman of the Baroque Chemical Corporation exited. Dressed in his usual Armani business suit with his hair slicked back, his middle-aged intellectual face showed confidence, and a sense of power over all he owned. Waiting for him was a chauffeur-driven electric golf cart.

"Good morning, Mr. Gull," a man in a navy blue security uniform said.

Jason gave his standard response. "Good morning." He never talked to his employees other than his officers or secretarial staff. Small talk would give the impression they were on equal ground, and Gull wished to remain unreachable. A new driver accompanied the chairman each day, creating the separation he desired. They drove silently underground to a private elevator reserved only for Gull and a few select others. Inserting his security key card, the stainless steel panels slid open. He entered, pressed the top of three unmarked buttons, and faced the rear of the car. When it stopped, the back doors opened, and he walked into his private office on the second floor of the Baroque Company.

Gull sat on his throne, and controlled all facets of the operation, from research and development to sales and marketing. Compared to the chemical giants of DuPont and Merck, Baroque was a fly on their backs. But with $300 million in sales last year, and revenues expected to double this year, Gull's company would soon be on the map.

Most of his dealings were with foreign governments, selling drugs thathad not yet been approved by the United States Food and Drug Administration. He sold AIDS pills to countries in Africa, andcancer medications toAsia. Wherever the need, Gull would supply the remedy at an inflated cost. He sat down behind an inch-thick glass-top desk and pressed the intercom on his phone.

"Mrs. Anderson, I've arrived," he said. He pressed another button on his desk, and it released the magnetic lock onhis door, and it opened.

Gull watched Mrs. Anderson, his personal secretary, get up from her station in the outer office, pour a cup of coffee, and sweeten it with cream and sugar. She was in her mid-fifties, about as attractive as a walnut. She was one of the few employees who had been with him from the very beginning. And she was the best at what she did, never asked questions, never interrupted, and never, ever came unprepared. She approached the chairman's open door, and rapped softly. She walked onto his deep iron gray carpet, and bent around the two sturdy metal chairs in front of his desktoset down the cup and saucer. Then she quietly left without a word spoken. The magnetic lock engaged as the door closed.

Gull was about to take a sip when a red light began to blink on the intercom. He knew immediately what it meant, so he pivoted his chair to facetwo large wooden panels. He depressed a switch on the arm of his chair, and watched the panels separate. A huge video screen came to life as an image faded into focus. Seen from the waist up, a rotund man stood, arms folded behind him, sport coat opened, a sagging belly spilling out. His droopy cheeks, under eyes showing no signs of pleasure, were streaked with red veins,as was his bulbous nose.

"Gull, is everything in order? Are we on schedule?" the man asked.

"Well, Mr. Vincent, good morning to you too, but we've encountered a slight hindrance in our schedule." The question was asked of him regularly, and he always responded with a simple

"Yes." Although Gull's reply was casual, he attempted to mask the seriousness of the problem.

Vincent's eyes tightened. "How much of a hindrance, Gull?"

"One, maybe two days at the most," Gull replied.

"I do not have to remind you they must be completed and shipped no later than Friday." Vincent was rocking on his heels and seemed very agitated. "Maybes and uncertainties are not permitted in my timeline. I don't wish to risk contacting them unnecessarily. But if I must tell them there may be a delay, I need to know as soon as possible. Will they be ready for shipment on Friday?"

"They will be ready, Mr. Vincent. You have my word," Gull said through clenched teeth.

"Good. Now, after completion, all data relating to this project, and all personnel directly involved with final assembly and testing will need to be eliminated." Vincent said.

"Testing?" Jason feigned mild surprise. When and how he was going to be able to do the tests was his problem. A live subject must be used for a positive result. Well, Mr. Vincent did say all personnel must be eliminated. "Of course, Mr. Vincent. Everything will be destroyed, as we have discussed in the past."

Vincent used his pudgy thumb to press a button on a remote control in his hand, and his image vanished without another word. Mr. Vincent checked in on Gull's progress nearly every day. It was always brief, and Jason loathed the inquiries. After two years on the project, the end was near, and Gull was ready to rid himself of the only superior the chairman of Baroque Chemical had ever had in his life since his father was alive. Spinning around again, he hit the intercom. "Mrs. Anderson, tell Bracken Guttone to come to my office at once."

"Yes, Mr. Gull."

Within five minutes Gull released the magnetic seal, and Bracken walked in, ducking under the door header. He was a huge man, standing six-feet-eight-inches tall. He had a broad, protruding chest supporting steel-beam shoulders. His thick arms stretched the fabric of his suit jacket taunt. His waist was nearly half the dimension of his upper body, giving him a perfect V shape. His tanned jaw was square, like a rough-cut brick, and his forehead was the equivalent of a sledgehammer. Thin blond hair was pulled back and tied in a shining ponytail, and his eyes glowed ice-blue. He approached his boss, and stopped several feet in front of the glass desk. He stood with his vice-like hands folded at his waist.

"Any information on the Ford truck?" Jason asked, looking up at his chief of security.

"The search, so far, has turned up nothing, and with only the first few digits of a license plate number to go on, it may take longer than two hours, sir," Bracken couldn't help using the excuse, since he was being questioned the moment the head honcho arrived.

"I understand—but he must be found. Our research—and possibly our very lives—depends on the recovery of that couch. Not a minute goes by without a search!" Jason laid his briefcase on the desk and retrieved a file. "Doctor Salinger has been located."

"That's very fortunate," Bracken said with a smile.

"Yes. Very fortunate for us, not so fortunate for the doctor," Jason said, handing over the information. "You are to take care of him tonight. He's in the Pennsylvania State Penitentiary. Everything you need to know is in the file."

Guttone grabbed the folder, and placed it under his arm. "Will that be all, sir?"

Jason looked up at Guttone. "One other thing—when you find the man and the Ford, make sure there are no survivors or traceable evidence."

"Of course, sir," Bracken grinned. "Perhaps a bonfire of sorts."

CHAPTER SEVEN

Upon arriving at the glass truck, Stanley saw Al sitting in the driver's seat.

"Yo, Al, move over. I'll drive," Stanley said.

"Why's that?" Al asked.

"Because the plant is in the middle of nowhere, and for me to give you directions would be like reading the Bible to you," Stanley said, as he started the truck, and headed out through the fence. "I worked there several times before, and it will be easier if I just drive us there."

"No problem," Campo said, slouching comfortably. "I'll take in the scenery."

Stanley wasn't kidding. He made so many turns Al didn't know which way was up. They ended up on a long stretch of road with no signs or markings of any kind; both sides of the street had thick forests. A damp mist stuck to the windows as they drove through a dense fog. Campo enjoyed the cooling breeze gusting in the window. The visibility was reduced to maybe a hundred feet.

"This is strange," Al said. "I don't remember fog in the forecast, just dry heat for the next five days. Is there a large body of water in the area? Maybe it's evaporating, and causing the moisture?"

"I don't think so," Stanley said. "Call me crazy, but if I remember correctly, the last time I drove here the fog was here as well."

Campo took a long look at the surroundings. He noticed the bushes, plants, and trees were a lush, vibrant green, unlike the plants near his house and anywhere in the tri-state area for that matter. This heat wave had dried up almost everything.

As they breached a hill, a break in the woods opened up, and Stanley made for it. Campo lost his train of thought as the Baroque Chemical building burst out from the mist. Fronting the main building were deep, fluted stone columns flattened against the walls, with bronze sculptures capping each one. Polished brass doors shone brightly across the entrance, as windows with the same glimmer traveled down the façade. The decorations seemed to go on forever, as the various stages of buildings lasted as far as the eye could see. They approached a security shack, and a retractable gate barred their entry. On the driver's side, a man poked his head out of a window that Campo recognized as being made of bulletproof glass. He had a blue uniform and a blue baseball cap that had BCP, for Baroque Chemical and Pharmaceutical, on it.

"Can I help you gentlemen?" the man said while holding a clipboard and pen.

"Yes, were here from City Glass. Apparently there is an emergency?" Barrett said.

"Yes, I was informed you were coming. Head on up to the main entrance, and they will sign you in there," he said and closed the thick glass window.

The gate slid open, and Barrett pulled in and parked in a visitor's spot across from what appeared to be the main entrance.

"When was the last time you were here?" Al asked.

"About six months ago. I replaced the glass in that brass window, but I've never been past the main lobby on the inside. You ready?" Stanley asked, and got out.

The duo headed up the steps and were met by a security guard wearing a drab blue uniform and a silver badge with the Baroque Chemical name and insignia on it. He was of medium build and a look of boredom stretched over his pie-eyed face.

"May I help you gentlemen?" he said, not letting the two enter.

"Yes sir, my name is Stanley Barrett, and this is Al Campo. We're here to remove some broken glass. We received an emergency phone call from..." He stopped and looked at a piece of torn paper, where he had jotted down a name. "...Phil Cooper," he finally said.

"Yes, I was told to expect you. I'll call Mr. Cooper," the security guard said. "In the meantime, would you sign in? I'll check you into our computer, and print up a couple of one-day badges."

Al and Stanley were led into the lobby area. It looked drastically different from the outer building; the walls were covered with gaudy, almost offensive, artwork. There were paintings of semi-nude men and women with their bodies covered in tattoos. The frames were bright gold, hanging on walls painted a flat, dark blue. Al was caught up staring at them when Stanley called him.

"Al, do you want me to sign in your name?" Stanley looked at Al as he started to sign the book. Signing into work was as common as eating lunch, and the two of them frequently wrote each other's name. They considered it a formality that didn't hold much credence. Before Campo could answer, the security guard spoke up.

"That's not allowed," the guard said as he looked up from his keyboard and computer screen. "You will have to sign in, individually."

"Oh, no problem," Barrett said, handing over the pen

"Gentlemen, I will need to see some form of identification, like a driver's license," the guard said, looking up again.

"Why do you need that?" Al said

"Just to verify your identity, sir," the guard said.

Stanley passed his identification over first as Campo looked for his in his billfold.

"Shit!" Campo said.

"What's the matter?" Stanley asked.

"I can't find my license," Al said nervously, looking in all of his pockets. He traced his memory to when he last had it. He didn't use it at the bar last night. Hell, if he were carded at his age, he would kiss the person. No. He remembered seeing it last when using his credit card. He had to move it first. That was last night at the gas station. After the bar, he got home late, and threw his billfold on the dresser. Nothing fell out. Fell out! Dread rose in his mind, thinking the only place he could have lost it was when he removed his billfold in the hospital this morning.

In the closet at the hospital! What if the person who had the hidden transmitter found it? What if they suspected he was snooping around where he didn't belong? What if…Al's mind was whirling in thought.

"Sir, I need some form of ID, or you're not permitted inside the facility," the guard said, snapping him back to present.

Al looked once more, and then offered the guard his union ID. It was the only other picture card he had.

"This will be fine," the guard said. A few moments passed as he typed in the proper information, and two temporary badges were printed up.

Al wondered further about his license, and about the patient who interrupted him in his investigation of the transmitter. He couldn't help but think about the language used. Arabic, maybe not, but definitely similar. It could be a form of Middle Eastern dialect he hadn't seen before. But somehow, he had to find out what that patient was up to before he was implicated.

"Here you are." The guard passed them their respective IDs and badges. "Pin them on your shirt, and don't remove them for any reason. They must be visible at all times. When you leave, they must be returned here so you can be properly signed out."

From behind the guard's console, Phil Cooper came down the steps, practically jogging toward them. He had short, red hair that glowed with an orange tint; freckles spotted his face, arms, and hands. When he met the two workers, his eyes were wide.

"Hello, I'm Phil Cooper," he said, extending his hand. "Thanks for coming out so quickly. It is a bit of an emergency."

"No problem, I'm Stanley Barrett, and this is Al Campo. Where to?"

"I see you already have your badges and tools. Good. Follow me, please." Cooper started walking with Al and Stanley at his heels.

They left the main lobby, and Cooper led them down a hall made of cinderblock walls painted a glossy white. Photos showing aerial views of the Baroque Chemical building and surrounding area hung neatly. Phil and Stanley engaged in small talk while Campo studied the photos. He was amazed to see how much ground the plant covered. He could also see the maze of road-ways they had traveled to reach the facility. Occasionally, as they walked they passed doors with slim wire glass windows, and Al would sneak quick peeks. They turned several times left and right. Campo wondered how Cooper kept his bearings. The corridors all looked identical. Finally, they turned down a hall that appeared to have an ending. Campo approached one last pair of doors. As he neared it, he heard a strange, yet familiar noise growing louder as he got closer. Al looked through the pane of criss-crossed wire glass as Stanley and Cooper walked on uninterrupted. Campo saw walls and walls of jailed animals, all yelping and crying for help. The immutable pitch twisted his stomach. From monkeys to rats, dogs, cats, guinea pigs and rabbits, all seemed frantic to escape the cruelty of the testing facility.

In the far corner of the room, a lab tech was handling a monkey that was screeching and clawing at his light blue smock, fighting his imprisonment, yearning for a call from the governor. Pulling and pushing the little arms away, attempting to do his job and nothing more, man against monkey, the tech fought the crying ani-mal in frustration. Then, as if drawn into a moment of reserved passion, stored away like a childhood memory, the worker allowed the animal to take hold of his neck and hug its ancestral counter-part. The man gently stroked the hairy back, leaned towards the little monkey, and appeared to whisper a soothing message. Slowly, lovingly, the tech lowered the now-calm animal into its jail cell without struggle. When the technician locked the cage, Al thought he might have seen him wipe his eyes. He could tell, although on occasion some animals are treated with affection, it would never replace his desire to end the cruelty.

"Yo, Al!" Stanley woke him from his trance.

It was difficult, but he was able to shake off the images and jog to the end of the hall and meet his partner, and the maintenance head. They stood at a dead end with no doors or windows, and no continuation of the hallway. "What's up? What are we doing here?" Al said.

"One moment," Phil said, as he lifted his Nextel combination phone/radio and spoke into it. "This is Philip Cooper from building maintenance. I have with me two men from the glass company." He released the button on the radio and directed his attention to them. "Now gentlemen, before you enter…"

"Enter where?" Al said, puzzled.

"This is a highly classified and secure area," Phil said, staring down Campo. "I have to instruct you not to touch anything not pertaining to your work. Do not leave the work area without an escort, and do exactly what you are instructed to do and nothing more. If a problem arises, stop and have them made aware of it—and they will find a solution. Also do not talk loudly—and no cursing."

"Excuse me?" Stanley interrupted. "When you say *they*, who are you talking about?"

"Anyone in there besides yourselves,"Cooper replied.

"Where the hell are we going?" Al asked in frustration. "I'm not sure if you know it or not, Phil, but we're standing at a dead end!"

The sound at first was like that of a dump truck switching gears; then it sounded more like ball bearings pinging through steel tubes. Stanley and Al took an apprehensive step backwards, keeping an eye on the rear wall. Somehow the whole barrier began to move, rising vertically out of the floor, creeping effortlessly upwards until it cleared the tile. When it had cleared the floor, a new set of pings and bangs quietly accompanied the mass outward. It must be hinged at the ceiling, thought Campo, as the bottom pushed away from the trio. Soon two huge hydraulic plungers were visible on both sides, elevating the panel, holding it parallel to the floor.

Al examined the unusual door and guessed it to be six inches of solid steel.

"Gentlemen," Phil said to the curious onlookers, "when you're finished, they will direct you back here, where I'll meet you. Remember my instructions, and work safely."

"You're not coming in with us?" Stanley asked.

"Nope, I'm just your escort to here; I don't have clearance for that department. We hired you two because one of our men got seriously cut trying to remove the broken glass. You two are the experts. See you when you're finished." Phil said, leaving them.

Al and Stanley stepped onto a black and gray granite floor. Campo gave his partner a light shove so he would move away from the strange door beginning its descent. Directly across from them, nearly thirty feet away was a most intimidating sight. A lone desk sat, empty of its worker, and hanging precariously above it was a gigantic piece of rough-cut granite. Its shape was irregular, but was mostly upwards of four inches thick, extending the length of a car. Four stainless steel chains suspended it from the ceiling and they appeared inadequate to support such a weight.

"I guess the owner of this place wanted his own piece of the rock," Al said as Barrett smirked. From an adjacent door a woman emerged. She was radiant, wearing a skirt and fitted blouse that tightly displayed an hourglass figure. Her long, dark, wavy hair bounced with every step her bare legs took. Al sensed controlled sexuality, his gaze fixed on her movements. She knew she was beautiful. The looks she received from admiring men told her so, and the looks from envious women told her so much more. Comfortable with her beauty, it came without trying. Al felt she remained modest, yet she never let her guard down because of it. He looked briefly at his arms as goose bumps arose.

"Hello gentleman," she said, her sensual ruby lips curving into a brief smile. "You must be Mr. Barrett and Mr. Campo."

"Yes, we are," Al said with a smile as they approached the desk. Immediately he noticed the lack of a wedding band or engagement ring on her left hand. "I'm Al, and he would be Stanley. May I ask you something?" he said while Stanley watched his Casanova partner, and rolled his eyes waiting for a line from the latest movie Al had seen. But it didn't come.

"Yes, you may," she said politely

"Aren't you nervous sitting under this piece of granite?" he asked, pointing upward without taking his eyes from hers. Their odd color gave her an even more exquisite look; they were golden, and they glistened inher face.

The receptionist glanced up. "It's been so long since I've even realized it was there, I don't even think about it any more. Now if you'll follow me, I'll show you to the trouble area."

They followed her back around the desk to a long narrow hallway. Al couldn't take his eyes from the shapely figure, and how she walked. She made several turns, eventually leading them to a large cafeteria. The ceiling was two stories high, and composed entirely of glass. The second floor was also encased by rows of panes, extending floor to ceiling. At the far end, a yellow caution ribbon surrounded an area below a broken pane. Ragged and splintered glass protruded from all sides of the opening.

"You may access the second floor by the stairs to the right." She lifted her arm and gestured with an open hand. Then she turned and walked back the way she had come, saying, "I'll be back when you're finished."

"How can we contact you when we're done?" Stanley said.

"I'll know," the young beauty replied.

"Excuse me," Al said, fearing he might not see her again. "May I know your name?"

The beauty stopped in her tracks, turned, looked straight at Al with her glowing eyes, and said with the sweetest smile, "My name is Domeni, and I am happy to meet you, Mr. Campo."

"The pleasure is mine, and you can call me Mr. Right," Al said as he gave a wink.

Domeni's smile grew wider as her face flushed. Then she returned to her desk.

Campo closed his eyes; warmth flowed through his veins, and he felt a desire he had long been without—not lust or passion, for they could be found at a nightclub or corner bar. He was dizzy with inner feelings of romance, imagining the soft touch of a loving hand or the gentleness of a loving cheek pressed to his chest, squeezing for security. It was the exchange of comfort between two people in love. For some strange reason, these reflections shadowed the image of Domeni.

"Now that's what I would call a gorgeous woman in every sense of the word," Al said to Stanley.

"All right, Romeo, she's gone. Now let's get to work." Stanley shook his head as he began to get his tools ready for the job.

As they arrived at the broken glass, there was a large Rubbermaid trash can on wheels. The area in front and around the glass was encircled by yellow caution tape, and there was a padded drop cloth, like the ones used by moving companies, covering the carpeted floor. The pair donned their work gloves and began the delicate task of removing the shattered remains.

"Easy with that," Campo said as Stanley handed him a shard of glass with a piece of duct tape dangling from it.

"What's your problem?" Stanley said. "Just grab it, and put it in the trash can."

Al hesitated. "It's not the glass, it's that frigging duct tape. I'm allergic, remember."

"You're a sis," Stanley said. He never did believe in Al's condition.

"You know, if you never see it for yourself, you don't believe it," Al said. Then he took the piece of tape off. He licked a spot on his arm to wet it, and then rubbed the sticky part of the tape on the moist spot.

"What the hell are you doing?" Stanley asked.

"I'm going to prove a point," Al said. Within seconds, miniscule pink blisters started to form on his arm. They slowly grew larger to the size of small jellybeans. He poked them with his fingernail, and they burst, spewing liquid. "Do you see what I mean now?" Al said as he took out a tissue and dabbed the area. "I am allergic to the adhesive on almost all tape, especially duct tape, and glue too. Did you see how fast that shit affects me? It sucks—trust me. This spot will itch and then burn for about fifteen minutes before it calms down."

"You've got problems," Stanley said as he resumed work.

Both men continued without instruction. Having worked-together for several years, each knew the other's moves in close contact. After Stanley removed a piece of glass by cutting away the silicone with his utility knife, he handed the shards to Campo. He was able to work and view the upstairs at the same time. The decorations were similar to those in the lobby: deep-colored walls, brass-framed artwork, and mirrors. Gaudy, shining molding surrounded the doors, and they stood on what was possibly the thickest carpet either had ever felt in a commercial building. Campo kept panning his eyes down below, eagerly seeking the beautiful Domeni. Unfortunately, she did not appear. He then checked outthe area around them. Only one office door was visible down the hall away from the steps. The balance of the floor appeared to be a maze of similar corridors.

"Al, hold this," Stanley said, needing an extra pair of hands to remove a larger piece of glass. Campo obliged, then heard a sound from the office door. It was the noise of a magnetic lock, and he was familiar with the sound, having installed many in his years with the union. Too busy to turn completely around, he pivoted his head slightly and saw with his peripheral vision the image of a sizeable man rumbling toward them. After Campo removed the glass, he turned around and faced the man head on. He felt like his eyes needed to open wider than their lids would permit to fully see the mammoth before him.

"Gentlemen, I'm Mr. Guttone, head of security," he said, his icy-blue gaze studying the men.

"How are ya?" Barrett said from a kneeling position in front of the opening. "I'm Stanley and this is…"

"How long do you estimate this will take?" The man said, cutting him off and ignoring their outstretched hands.

"In an hour, we should be wrapped up, ready to leave," Stanley said as he glanced over at Campo, who nodded in agreement.

"That's very good. There will be an escort ready for you when you're finished." Pleased with the time frame, Guttone made his way downstairs.

"A rather polite gentleman, don't you think?" Al said

"Yeah, at one point I thought he was going to give you a hug." Stanly laughed at his joke and turned to get back to work.

Forty-five minutes later, Stanley installed a piece of ready-cut plywood into the opening and Campo cleaned up the surrounding area. Within moments, two men appeared downstairs. They removed the caution tape and organized the cafeteria.

"I'll tell you what," Campo said. "I'll bet there are a hundred surveillance cameras in this place, and everyone is watching them.

I mean with gorgeous telling us she'll know when we're done, and Arnold Schwarzenegger saying there will be an escort ready when we're done, and then these guys showing up the second the plywood is in place. It must be a bitch working here. Probably can't take a crap without wondering who's watching you on the commode."

Just then Al heard the release of the magnetic lock again, and another man stepped out.

"Al, you ready?" Stanley asked.

"Yeah, let's go. Where's our escort?" A millisecond passed, and two security guards wearing deep-blue uniforms approached.

"Gentlemen, Ms. Conti instructed us to lead you out," one said.

"Who's Ms. Conti?" Al asked.

"The young lady who escorted you here, sir. Will you follow us, please?"

"Damn, I was hoping she would be back to lead us," Al said.

"Don't worry, Romeo. We have to pass her desk to exit this vault," Stanley chided.

CHAPTER EIGHT

Jason Gull exited his office, and felt a bit of optimism after handing Bracken his assignment. Finding the couch and its abductor was a difficult mission, but there wasn't a doubt in his mind it would be done. Guttone was the ultimate warrior in Jason's battles. His chief of security had been raised in the rugged mountain terrain of western Canada. His mother named him after the bracken fern that grew heavily in the region. He was born weighing an astounding thirteen pounds, and had grown resilient to the cold, harsh environment of the Yukon, just like the large, coarse fern that was his namesake. Ten years together, and not one failure or submission to imperfection. Without Bracken, Gull admitted internally, he could not have achieved his extreme success.

Gull walked down the hall and saw two men conversing with his security officials. He slowed his pace, and studied the strangers. One he didn't know at all, but the other looked very familiar. As he got closer, memories of the morning escapade flashed in his mind. That face, he never forgot a face—especially not the face of the man who could put an end to years of work, and not to mention costing him a billion dollars. Gull's initial instinct was to command his men to apprehend the sofa thief; however, a mock explanation eluded him.

Think, think…He felt sure this man wouldn't recognize him after his quick change this morning. First, he had to call Guttone. He stopped in the middle of the hall, and never let his eyes veer away from his subject. He grabbed his phone from his jacket pocket.

"Bracken here."

"He's here!" Gull said in an excited voice.

"Who's here, sir?" Bracken asked.

"Your assignment, that's who. Did you see the two workers in the hall as you left? The taller one with dark hair. He's the man who stole the couch. Now get back here! I'll stall him until you arrive." Gull had to think of something quickly.

"On my way," Bracken said.

Jason followed them down the stairs to Domeni's desk. "Excuse me, gentlemen. Could I have a word?"

The two men looked over at the oncoming man, then back at Domeni sitting at her desk.

"That's Mr. Gull. He owns the Baroque Chemical Corporation," Gull heard her whisper.

"Yeah, what's up?" Stanley said in a polite, yet intimidating manner.

"You are glass men correct?" Gull asked the two men.

"That's us, but don't spread it around. People always want favors." Al said.

Gull ignored the sarcasm, determined to keep them there long enough for Bracken to return. "I was wondering if you could measure a desk of mine to be fitted with a glass top." It was Jason's first thought.

Al glanced over at the clock on Domeni's workstation. "It's getting late, and we still have to make it back to the shop and unload," he said, looking at his partner.

"I know, but it's only a table top. It'll take two minutes," Stanley said

"Fine, you go ahead, Stanley. I think I will stay here and get acquainted," Al said as he looked down at Domeni.

"Thank you," Gull said, relieved his ploy worked, also that the man didn't recognize him. "I'm Jason Gull," he said brazenly, and reached out a hand.

"I'm Stanley," he said and shook his hand. Then Barrett motioned to his partner. "And this is Al Campo," Al gave him a firm shake, and stared him right in the eyes, seeing something familiar.

Jason noticed the queer look, and quickly turned to lead Barrett to his office. "Ms. Conti, see that Mr. Campo is comfortable while we're gone. We'll return shortly," he said over his shoulder.

"Gladly," she said

"A better idea I have not yet heard," Al said as the two of them locked glances. Al Campo studied Domeni's face. Her skin was tanned and smooth; there was not an imperfection on it. Almond-shaped eyes looked back at him. He wondered how this adorable woman ended up in his path. Al knew his life had been less than noble—and even catching a glimpse of such a lady was a reward not worthy of his past. It seemed the man above was trying to tell him something.

CHAPTER NINE

S lowly, he paced the hall, from the TV room to the nurses' station. Yavuz Cusafa stared at the tile floor. His movements showed no signs of the burning impatience he felt, waiting for the workmen to leave his room. As he reached the end of the hallway to the television room, he observed the other residents talking to themselves, looking blankly at the walls, or peering dumbly at the TV screen. Yavuz stole a glance at the clock; he was overdue in receiving his transmission, and late in responding. He had been a resident atthe Delaware State Hospital now for six months, going by the name Alex. He had wandered into the facility intentionally, masquerading as a disoriented indigent seeking help. He had never spoken to any of the staff or to the other residents. He maintained a speechless profile that allowed for no explanation of a past or education. Since new John or Jane Does arrived every so often, the name Alex was given to him by the admitting nurse. Even though Yavuz did show he understood the hospital staff, with head nods and hand and eye motions, the doctors incorrectly diagnosed him as a paranoid schizophrenic who had suffered an emotional trauma and lost his power of speech.

Cusafa's mission was simple, at face value. He had to infiltrate and assume a residency at the state hospital, set up a hidden transmitter/receiver, and await orders. Every week a transmission would be sent, giving instructions for his assignment, and an immediate response was required. So far all messages had been the same: "Remain. Await further orders." Yavuz's reply was a pattern which reversed itself, and increased, and decreased with the weather, the first response was a standard "Message received * 68/343#11315." His response always began with *, followed by the posted day's lowest temperature, followed by a number that had been chosen before he left, and then his operation number, which identified which agent he was. The second number would increase if the date were an odd number, and would decrease if it were even. Home base would only accept his reply if all sets of numbers were correct. Without this code, base would assume he had been compromised.

Staring at the other residents for six long months rankled on his conscious mind. Although he was a professional operative, having years of undercover time in his past, this situation and the duration made him stale. He feared he was losing the quick reflexes possibly required for this mission. He ached for action, and felt he couldn't have been sent all the way to the United States to be given an assignment of little value. Six months was an eternity in anticipation. They must soon send him his mission objectives. Today's transmission might be the one, and a stupid worker was in his room.

Yavuz traveled up the hall, more deliberate pacing. He paused by his room, hearing the faint sounds of the worker, then continued to the nurse's station. Unexpectedly,the door to his room opened. The workmen had gone. It was another resident who had been making all the noise in there. The workmen must have left when he wasn't looking. It might not be too late. Quelling his haste, he shuffled into the room at his customary lethargic pace and closed the door behind him. He opened the closet, activated the hidden door, and the transmitter rolled out. He saw the message and without reading it, he quickly typed in his reply and sent it off. Relief came over him as his reply was accepted. Now the message. It was written in Arabic, his native tongue. He tore off the paper and read it. Yavuz's mouth fell open, and he read it again.

"Allah be praised," he whispered aloud. "The time for the Prophet's return has come." Cusafa knelt and used his fingers to pull a thin rug from under the bed. It wasn't a beautiful carpet, nor was it decorated like the prayer mats he was used to. He had gotten it when he first arrived from one of the laundry orderlies, and with hand signals asked if it had just been cleaned. It was to be his prayer rug for the duration of his stay, and it was suitable enough. He spread the rug between the bed and open closet and bowed in silent prayer. He lifted his head and looked to the heavens, palms up then back to the floor over and over again and murmured his song to Allah.

"What's this?" he said between bows. On the floor of the closet was a plastic card. Yavuz picked it up. It was aPennsylvania driver's license. There was a picture on it, and the name under the picture was *Al Luciano Campo*. "A spy! Here in the hospital," Yavuz said through gritted teeth. "Impossible! No one knows I'm here. I must warn home base of this."

"What are you doing?"A man said in a whining, nasally voice.

Yavuz turned in shock, and looked straight at a fellow resident. It was the one who wished to massage everyone's feet. The man stood there looking at Cusafa. His hair was molded to the side of his head, and his glasses were askew on his face. His blue jeans were torn at the crotch and at the knees, and his white shirt had blueberry stains. He squinted at Cusafa. Then he looked up at the open closet, and the transmitter inside.

"And what's that thing?" he said, "no one else has a closet with that in it. What are you doing with it?"

Yavuz reaction was slow from the lack of physical and mental exercise, yet quick enough to catch the intruder off guard. He lunged from the floor and rammed his forehead against the would-be massage therapist's breastbone, knocking him backwards onto the bed. The man gasped just as Cusafa cupped his hand over his mouth. Cusafa was ready to choke his victim, but bruises around the throat would cause suspicion. He held his palm over the man's mouth, and sat on top of his chest, his knees pinning down the man's arms. The man's legs kicked up and outward. Yavuz grabbed the pillow, and pushed it into the face. Holding both hands over it, he pressed on the pillow with his full body weight. The victim's struggle continued, thrusting his chest and legs in a futile attempt to survive. Yavuz held firm until three minutes had passed, even after all movement had ceased. He lifted the pillow and saw the familiar distorted face of death.

Yavuz went to the door and peered out to make sure he wasn't heard. He came back and positioned the corpse in the fetal position, covering it with blankets up to the neck and closed the dead man's eyes. Cusafa quickly replaced the machine. He then closed the closet doors and exited the room, spied both ends of the hallway, then proceeded at his lethargic pace up the corridor without anyone taking any notice of him at all.

CHAPTER TEN

"**S**o would it be forward of me to ask you out on a date?" Al said to Domeni, and leaned his hands on her desk. "Given the fact we only just met."

She smiled. "Yes, a little I guess." She could feel her face flush. *What is it?* she wondered. He wasn't the first man to ask her out. Hell, hundreds of men had vied for her affection, and not one had ever made the hair on the back of her neck stand on end by simply asking a question.

"OK then," Al continued, and stood straight again. "Why don't you ask me out on a date? I won't think it forward of you."

It was his delivery, no…the way he looked at her, no…it was the way he carried himself as he spoke, or just how damn handsome he was. Domeni felt shy and giggled at his candor. "Mr. Campo," she said, looking down at the desk, almost afraid to look into his dark eyes, unable to speak.

"Please, my name is Al." Al smiled his most engaging smile as he stared at this stunning woman. He sat back onto his heels, laid his forearms on the desk,and met her at eye level. He was close to her now, their faces only a foot apart.

She could smell his masculine aroma, feel his body warmth, and finally she met his gaze. It was a good thing she was sitting down, because her knees would have buckled under her, and the embarrassment…unthinkable. His face was full of tenderness and warmth. How could any woman resist?

"Al...would you like to go out on a date with me?" She felt like a freshman in high school, probably because that was the last time she might have uttered those words.

"Funny you should ask. I would love to," he replied, and moved his hand close to hers on the desk. Theirs fingers nearly touched. "Say where and when, and I will be there—with bells on."

Domeni's hands were trembling, but she tried her best to not let him see her anxious fingers, as she wrote her phone number and address down on a Post-it, and handed it over. "Friday evening sound good?" Domeni asked without even checking her calendar. It wouldn't matter anyway. She would cancel a date with John Travolta at this point.

"Friday...ah, I'm busy, but I'll cancel my plans," Al said.

"No...no, uh, how about Saturday? I don't want you to cancel anything important," Domeni stuttered.

"It's fine. I had planned to clean my fish tank, but it'll wait," Al laughed.

Domeni's pleasant smile was as wide as her face would allow. Maybe it was his sense of humor, no...it was everything about him she found addicting.

Domeni saw Stanley and Jason conversing as they came down the stairs towards them. She knew it was time for Al to leave. She looked back at the handsome man she had just made a date with and smiled.

Al reached over the desk and took her hand. "I look forward to Friday evening," he said, and then kissed her palm.

There went the hair on the back of her neck again.

"All set?" Al said, turning toward the men.

"Yeah, it's only one tabletop, and it's square to boot." Barrett replied.

"Thank you, gentlemen. The guards will escort you out," Gull said as they exchanged handshakes, and he made a quick exit.

Campo and Domeni exchanged one last look, and he left.

—◆—

By the time the glass workers reentered their truck, Bracken Guttone was parked out of sight in his jet-black XKS Jaguar. It had clouded windows, and appeared empty to passers-by. He sat inside talking to Jason Gull on the phone. "Yes, Mr. Gull, I have a visual, the taller dark-haired man. I'll follow them to his truck, and when he is alone, I'll take him." Guttone pressed the end button and drove off, following the orange truck.

She looked at her hands at two and ten o'clock on the steering wheel, wrinkled, bony, and dotted with brown blotches. They were the hands of an old person, a grandmother, or in her case as of two weeks ago, a great-grandmother. Beverly Foltz was heading home from her latest visit to her sister's house on James Street in Newtown, Delaware. She had seen her sister on this same day, every year for the past twelve years. Beverly, or Bev as friends and family called her, lived in Gladwyne, Pennsylvania, about ten miles west of Philadelphia. She wiggled in her seat a bit and slowed down as a large tractor trailer came racing past her on I-95

"Slow down! What's the hurry?" she yelled.

Bev hated to drive these days. Her car was a big, nineteen-eighty Mercedes Benz sedan. It was in prime condition. Her husband Benjamin would wash and wax it every day, and he had the engine running like a Rolex. He was very meticulous about the things they owned. Bev remembered all the time he spent painting the exterior of their house. If he saw as little as one shred of flaking paint, he would scrape and prime and paint every square inch of the siding. He was her steady rock, her soul mate, her one true love. He had also died twelve years ago today. That was her reason for traveling to her sister's house. That first summer after her husband's death was the loneliest in her life. He sister's shoulder was the one she cried on the most. Of course, there were her children, Fred and Craig, and their wives and children. But they all had their own grieving to do, and Bev did not want to burden them with her sorrow. It was Leann, her sister, who had introduced her to Benjamin. She was the one who knew her the best, and the one who could make her sorrow manageable. The two used to share the trip. Bev would travel to Leann's one year, and Leann to Bev's the next, but Leann had lost her husband three years ago and now in her ninetieth year, she had lost her ability to drive. So for three years in a row, Bev made the journey alone. Her sons would protest each time and offer to drive her, but in her selflessness, she would not allow them to be away from their families or work just to be a taxi driver. Bev was strong. Bev was determined, and Bev could do it all by herself.

The road ahead was blistering with traffic. Cars sped past like rockets, some waving their hands in frustration at her, others yelling curses as they passed. She drove along, fixed at fifty-five miles an hour, and would not change her speed, no matter how much other drivers complained. She was a good driver and she would go at the speed limit. Bev heard her cell phone ring on the passenger seat next to her, but she wouldn't take her hands off the wheel. She stole a glance at the screen and saw it was her son, Craig. He and his wife, Jean, had just become grandparents, and he was probably just calling to see how her lunch with Leann went, and to make sure she was OK.

"But of course I'm OK. I am a grown woman, and I can do it all by myself," she said aloud.

But Bev was suddenly struck with a sense of loneliness. She was headed home after a nice lunch with Leann. They had drunk mint tea, eaten tunafish sandwiches, and watched the birds flutter around the many birdhouses Leann had in her back yard. But she was going home, alone. Benjamin was not there, but his memory was. It lingered in the now chipped paint on the siding. His smell was pungent on his favorite chair. His shoes were still nestled beside it. His clothes were still in the closet and his pictures, their pictures, were everywhere. Bev started to weep. She looked in the rearview mirror and saw tears run down her face, carving paths in her makeup. Bev didn't wipe them. She just let them fall. Her phone made another noise, signaling she had a message. Craig must have left one. That's it. She would go to Craig's house. Their daughter Julie would be there with the newborn, the house would be full of people, and Craig would come home after work. Maybe they would let her spend the night, and tomorrow she would feel better. Tomorrow the anniversary of Benjamin's death would be over, and she could spend time with her children, grandchildren, and her new great-grandchild. Bev gripped the wheel with renewed confidence. She was still crying, but they were now tears of joy about what was ahead.

Bev normally held the wheel tightly, but her grip felt too tight, even to her.Something was wrong. Her left hand was really tight. She couldn't move her fingers, and then a shocking pain ran from her fingers through her arm and into her chest. Suddenly she couldn't breathe. She gasped for air, and then a thundering pain hit her in the chest. Her eyes rolled backwards, and she slumped over the wheel. Then, she fell against the side window and banged her head.

Bracken had followed Campo and Stanley through the winding roads of the Baroque plant, eventually heading onto Interstate 95. He had just swerved into traffic, three cars behind the glass truck when a tractor trailer cut him off and he lost sight of his target. He slammed his hands on the steering wheel and accelerated around the truck. He went to fast and Bracken had no time to react. A Mercedes swerved out of control from in front of the truck and plowed into the side of his Jaguar. Guttone lost the power to steer as the heavier car forced him into the next lane and smashed into a Honda. The Jaguar's front tires blew out, the steel rims screeched until they hit the grassy median. Bracken's car lifted off the ground, rolling three times before landing tires down on the hard dirt gully. Smoke and dirt seemed to be everywhere. Guttone was shaken up a bit, and he did a cursory inspection of himself. He was amazed to find that he was unhurt, except for a bruise on his hand.

He unlocked his seat belt, and tugged on the door handle, but the door panel was crushed and wouldn't budge, so he exited throughthe shattered window. Several cars had stopped, and offered assistance. Guttone waved off their kindness as though they were meddling panhandlers. He staggered back to the road on foot, and looked north to find that the orange truck and his assignment were now out of sight.

CHAPTER ELEVEN

He sat at a white table made of chipped Formica and metal banding. He attacked a low-quality meal of mashed potatoes, peas, and Salisbury steak on a Styrofoam plate. Dr. Abel Salinger filled the empty void that ached in his belly. He washed it down with a glass of orange juice that was not nearly enough to quench his thirst. He raised the glass above his head, requesting more juice. Behind him stood a thin, short man dressed in dark slacks, and a gray suit coat hanging open, giving Abel a visual of the FBI-standard 9mm Glock handgun holstered inside.

The agent grabbed the cup, refilled it, and handed it over to Salinger, who smiledat his high-paid servant. He was told he was under guarded arrest, which meant he could wander anywhere in the facility with an escort in tow. Even when going to the bathroom, someone followed him. He was under constant supervision.

Abel was not going to attempt an escape—or even consider the effort it would take to relieve himself of the pestering glance of his bosom buddy. No, Salinger was comfortable knowing the FBI needed him for future testimony. It felt like a year had passed since his arrest, since he had spilled his guts with all the information about the plutonium and his involvement in the illegal dealings of Baroque Chemical.

Special Agent Joe Tyson told him he did not supply enough information for the government to legally close down the plant. Since Salinger's order to retrieve the animal had been written in his own hand, they couldn't tie anything back to Baroque Chemical. Plus the details he had given of Jason Gull's blankets of security meant even the use of an effective search warrant would be useless in producing enough evidence to make an arrest. With the fleet of lawyers Gull would throw at the FBI, he would skate off with a slap on the wrist. Dr. Salinger had explained his involvement was preliminary, only a single vial of plutonium obtained at a time. He would take it to the plant, where his team would transfer the material into the special reactor core, and it would be enriched. Salinger would draw from it the ionizing radiation in gaseous form. That was a stable product. He then sent it to the downstairs lab, never to see it again.

"Doctor, I'm not a chemist," Tyson said in his interrogation. "But how is it possible to turn a dense metal like plutonium into a gas? From what I've read, its melting point is about five thousand degrees."

"Actually," Salinger said, "it melts at a temperature of 1,186 degrees and its boiling point is 5,850 degrees. You've got it backwards."

"Whatever the temperature, how is it done in the Baroque Chemical plant?" Tyson asked.

Abel could tell he didn't want to start a debate. The doctor felt more in control now, because they were talking on his level. Salinger sat with his hands clasped in front of him as he spoke. "Jason Gull has invented…no that's not fair. He paid a brilliant German scientist to invent a reactor which reduces the normal specific gravity of plutonium from 19.84 down to almost nil." Abel looked Tyson in the eyes while he avoided eye contact with Faz. "Instead of creating combustion, the fission process is interrupted, and a gaseous element is formed. We extract the gas and send it off."

"In its new form, what possible uses could Gull have for it?" Tyson asked as he puffed hard on his cigarette.

"Jason Gull has created a new form of power from Plutonium. The possibilities are whatever can be dreamed up by the user." Salinger said.

"Where in the plant does the material go, Doctor?" Faz asked, and when he did Abel looked down at his hands. "We need to know to conduct a search."

"I don't know. To some ultra-maximum-security area. That's the label we print on it. It wouldn't matter if you found it anyway. It's no longer plutonium, and I don't know of any laws that restrict possession of an unknown element," Salinger said this from his memory. Jason Gull uttered the same words when the doctor had expressed concern in being arrested for his involvement.

Abel finished his second glass of orange juice. Then he was taken back to Joe Tyson's office, and seated across from the SAC, which Abel had learned was short for Special Agent in Charge. He was always nervous that, at some point, the rug was about to be pulled from under him. Especially with Faz sitting in the room— ever since Faz nearly choked him to death, he'd been leery of the agent.

"Doctor, we're sending you to a maximum security facility, where you'll be safe." Tyson said, leaning back in his chair. Faz sat next to Salinger with his hands folded on his lap.

"I don't understand. You said there would be no prison term," Salinger said. "I don't have any thing to say if I go to jail." He sat back like a schoolboy and folded his arms.

"Well, Doctor, you can't stay here any longer," Tyson said, shifting papers on his desk. "There are too many people who know your whereabouts, and this facility is not equipped to house witnesses for long periods of time. An indictment of Jason Gull might not come for months, and a safe house is unavailable. The best chance we have of keeping you out of harm's way will be in the Pennsylvania prison system."

Salinger was about to protest, but was interrupted by Faz. "Don't worry, Abel. You can rest easy. You will be separated from the other inmates and be under constant supervision. The warden has my strict instructions that you are not to be treated like the other prisoners, and an entire wing of the prison will be yours."

Every time Faz mentioned the word "prison," Salinger cringed, but he received an affirmative glance from Tyson and his face softened. He knew he would need every possible protection from the wrath of his former employer.

———◆———

The cell was considered posh under the circumstances. A lone light bulb with a pull chain hung from the center of the ceiling. There was a toilet with a seat, and running hot and cold water and working electricity. The walls and concrete floor were freshly painted a drab gray. A single metal-frame bed was pushed into the corner, and a desk from the library had been brought in, with a shelf full of novels and reference books to the doctor's liking. A laptop computer (without Internet access, of course) sat on the desk, and a stack of CD-ROMS filled the drawers. He was also permitted casual clothing instead of the state-issued blue scrubs.

Abel thought about his amenities. Once he got used to them, he might like it here. Solitude had always suited him in the past. He was told that he was permitted to leave his cell at any time, bodyguard in tow. The guard was present constantly until Abel's cell was locked-down for the evening. Last night, he arrived late and went directly to bed. But today, he had taken a late shower at nine p.m., the only time he could have one in private. The warden gave him the opportunity to shower earlier, right after the general population, but Salinger decided to wait. He stepped out of the bathroom, wearing a white terry-cloth robe and slippers; his protection greeted him.

"Hello, Dr. Salinger, I am to escort you to your lock-down this evening."

"Where is Paul?" Abel said. "I thought he was to be here until lock-down."

"Sorry sir, Paul's shift ended at nine-thirty. He would have been here, but you showered late, and he left ten minutes ago. My name is John," he said.

Abel became a little nervous. John looked like he was about seventy years old, and couldn't out run a slug. How was he to protect him?

"Don't worry, Doctor," John said and reached out his hand. "I've got fifteen years experience in the protection of witnesses. They all testified." Abel shook his hand, and felt slightly relieved by his strong grip. They proceeded to the wing where his cell was located.

"So do you like sports, Doctor?" John said.

"Yes, I do, men's tennis most of all." Abel was glad for the chatter.

"How about baseball? Those Phillies may have a shot at the pennant this year, huh?" John continued talking as they walked. They came to the end of the hall and approached a door made of gray steel bars. John displayed his identification to the camera and the gate unlocked automatically.

"Only if their pitching keeps pace after the all-star break," Salinger said, and then they went down a series of halls, and stopped at another steel gate. This was the doctor's wing.

"You go ahead to your cell. The door is open," John instructed the doctor, as he showed his ID to the camera once more. "I'm going to fetch a cup of coffee. Would you like one?"

"No, thank you. I want to get some rest, and the caffeine will keep me awake all night."

"Decaf?" John asked.

"Thanks, just the same, but no." Abel smiled.

The steel closed between them, and John was off. Abel strode down the hall, whistling a tune he couldn't quite remember the name of that was stuck in his head. He walked past empty cells and glanced inside—only darkness. His was the eleventh cell; the first ten were not equipped with luxuries such as running water and electricity, so he ended up in the middle of the block. He drew near, the sliding gate was open as the guard had said, but strangely the room was dark. Salinger was sure when he arrived last night the light had been on, but couldn't be certain.

"You could have left the light on for me," he yelled to no one in particular, and assumed his guard was out of earshot for the moment. "I'm new here, you know."

He entered his lightless room, and the gate automatically shut and locked itself behind him. Abel turned, but saw nothing. He turned again toward the blackness and groped his hand awkwardly in front of him, searching for the pull chain to the lone fixture. Finally, he made contact and yanked it downward. One-hundred-fifty watts illuminated the nine-by-eleven chamber and blurred his vision for a moment

He rubbed clear the haze and then gasped at what he saw. There, directly in front of him, half-sitting on his bunk, one foot on the floor and the other resting on the bed was the titanic Bracken Guttone. He was dressed in neat prison garb, his immense muscles visible through the snug material.

"Mr...Mr. Guttone, what are you doing here?" Immediately he thought of lying, but with his past success at the game, he wondered internally why he tried. "Are you going to help me to escape, because there isn't much time. My bodyguard will be back in a few minutes."

"You've been very perfidious, Doctor. Mr. Gull has confided in you for many years and is terribly upset about you cooperating with the FBI."

"I don't know what you're talking about. I haven't told them anything. Just help me escape, and I'll explain it to Jason, personally," the doctor pleaded, and he began to perspire.

"I'm sure you have a very entertaining story to tell him, Doctor." Bracken put both feet flat on the floor, and stood, raising himself with his hands on his knees. He took two large steps towards Salinger, whose legs trembled, the fabric of his bathrobe shaking. Guttone towered over his prey, just inches away, like a grizzly bear looming over an unsuspecting camper.

"You don't understand. I'm on your side," Salinger pleaded. He cowered and began to cry. "I haven't told them anything. Please, I'm on your side."

"I'm sure you are, Doctor." Guttone said.

Abel looked up into the eyes of his grim reaper, seeking mercy and found a face devoid of remorse. He tried to scream, but no sound was heard as Guttone's antler-size hand gripped his throat. Bracken pressed on his jugular, and Abel clawed at the larger man's fingers with little effect.

In a display of tremendous strength, the giant Bracken stretched out his arm and lifted the doctor by his neck. Salinger's jerry-built legs flailed wildly. Guttone watched with a total lack of remorse, and studied his face as it contorted into an ugly mask. The doctor's eyes bulged, and his tongue thrust out seeking air. His skin turned red, then blue, then ashen white. With one final desperate struggle, Abel swung his fist down and hammered Guttone's forearm. Bracken quickly jerked his arm, breaking the doctor's neck. Salinger's legs stopped moving, and his hand fell off the monstrous wrist as a puddle of urine formed on the concrete. The giant carried the corpse to the bed and covered it with blankets, then closed the eyelids. Guttone went to the mirror, adjusting his clothing and golden-blond ponytail. Once he was satisfied that he looked unruffled, he pulled the light cord, then left the prison.

CHAPTER TWELVE

The president's chief of staff, Sam Haggart, sat on the president's left. President Worthington sat at the head of a long, narrow conference table. The table was inside a huge conference room on Level Nine, under the White House. The walls were paneled with oak, and the doors were adorned with hinges and doorknobs of polished brass. Picture frames were displayed around the room, their exposed metal frames glimmering under the four chandeliers that hung from the white plaster ceiling. This was the room where the president held his top-secret meetings with his cabinet. Around the perimeter of the table were nearly fifty chairs, but at today's meeting, only one end was occupied. The oak doors opened, and Sam nodded as a group of men entered. In walked FBI Director Nate Breechart, then Bruce Kellogg, the CIA director, who sat next to Sam. Then two members of the joint chiefs, Admiral Alex Faustian and General Morris Bartow, filled in the space next to the president. Before their arrival, Sam Haggart placed manila folders in front of each chair.

"Shall we begin?" The chief of staff said.

"By all means," General Bartow said in his southern drawl.

The group opened their folders, and Sam began. "Now for those of you who haven't been watching FOX news lately, the man in the photo is a self-proclaimed caliph, Karuza, a religious zealot. He has been preaching in Istanbul, Turkey, for the past year. At first his sermons had only a few listeners, but he carried on preaching, proclaiming that he was speaking on behalf of all true believers in the world, claiming that he was Allah's chosen instrument to lead the way for the return of the Prophet. Since then, people have flocked by the thousands to hear him speak, calling themselves New Believers. Now if you'll turn the page." There was another picture of a man dressed in Arab clothing with thinning gray hair.

"Excuse me, Mr. Haggart," Morris Bartow broke in. His thick hands were clasped on the desk, his southern drawl more pronounced. Sam leaned back, and then rubbed his hand over his brown hair. "Are we going to look at pictures this morning, or are we going to get to the reason we've deployed another carrier fleet and sent several thousand of our boys over to the Middle East?"

Sam was well familiar with the general and his coarse nature. He had to sit through many meetings listening about the general's tough upbringing and his constant interruptions. He would bide his time and hope the president would chime in. "Yes, General," Sam Haggart answered. "But I'd like to give you all a brief outline of the past year before I turn it over to Mr. Kellogg. So if you'll permit me…"

The president gave Morris a patented "Worthington" stare.

"Why certainly, Mr. Haggart," the general conceded. He leaned back in his chair and folded his hands on his stomach.

"This is Ammar Hassan," Sam continued and held up the photo. "By blood, he is Karuza's cousin, but they were brought up like brothers, as neither had any siblings. Their parents moved around frequently together, so their original origin is unknown."

"Then they are not Turkish?" FBI Director Nate Breechart said. He sipped from a bottle of spring water he brought with him.

"That's correct," Sam continued and glanced around the room looking at each member of the meeting. "We do know they hail from somewhere in North Africa, possibly Libya or Egypt. Ammar has been masterminding Karuza's scheme to eventually rule Turkey. Not as president, or prime minister, but as caliph— and then, it seems, his intention is to become of the leader of what they're calling the New World."

"Why Turkey?" Bartow said. "You said he's not from there. Why not set up shop in an oil-rich country like Saudi or Kuwait?"

Sam stood and gathered everyone's attention. "I'll now turn over the meeting to Mr. Kellogg, who will be able to answer your question better than I." He poured himself a glass of ice water.

"Thank you, Sam," Bruce began. He was wearing a light green business suit and no necktie. "First off, General, Turkey is geographically in a key point of the Eastern Hemisphere, joining the European and Asian continents. In Karuza's mind, that puts himat the center of the world, and at the center of millions of believers. Where else would Mohammed choose to return?"

"Mohammed?" the president said, "I though he's been preaching the return of the Prophet?"

"Well sir, he has never mentioned who the returning prophet is, and we can assume he's not talking about the return of Jesus or Buddha. In the Muslim culture, prophet means Mohamed"

"Well...I don't want us assuming anything at the moment," Worthington said. "For now let's keep it to what we KNOW."

"OK sir," Bruce continued, "Well, the movement at least for the past two decades has been strongest in Turkey, where the rich and poor are separated by a huge divide. Ammar has been writing his cousin's speeches, carefully teasing the poor; they sense the promise of reform and equality. They will follow Karuza by the millions."

"When you say millions, Bruce, are you being precise? Where and how many are we talking about?" the president asked. He sat relaxed for the moment, resting one hand on the table while with the other he squeezed a soft exercise ball.

Bruce cleared his throat and continued. "Sir, across the Middle East there are approximately a half a billion Musli...I mean followers. Most are aching for a new nation not separated by boundary lines, or hiding under the veil of the PLO."

"So his influence is not limited to Turkey," Morris said.

"Yes, General. Since his speech yesterday when he boasted of the return of the Prophet, whom they assume is Mohammed, groups have been massing in every capital across the Middle East, Northern Africa, and Europe. Even the New Believers here in the US have been accumulating in Washington." Bruce started to return to his seat.

"I noticed the crowds on the mall," Admiral Faustian said. "I thought it was some sort of convention."

Bruce turned toward the admiral. "It seems they will continue to grow, and at a staggering pace."

"My agents across the country," said Nate Breechart, finally deciding to enter the conversation, "have been watching all the leaders of the New Believers here since this character began his vocal pilgrimage last year. And they have reported that mosques have been sponsoring bus trips cross-country to bring their members to the capital, as Karuza instructed. We've also discovered funding being funneling in from foreign governments, subsidizing individual paychecks while on the migration."

"What governments, Nate?" the president.

"I was hoping Mr. Kellogg could enlighten us, because the FBI has been unable to determine their origin. We do know the funds enter along the Eastern seaboard, most likely New York, where the movement is strong." Nate Breechart leaned back in his chair, having said all he knew.

"Well, the origin could possibly be in the Middle East," the CIA Director said.

"Could be!" Bartow said. "I'll wager the ranch its origins are in Turkey, from this Karuza character."

"He wants to start a worldwide revolution," Worthington said, "Sam, yesterday you mentioned a meeting between an ex-KGB agent and Karuza."

Haggart cleared his throat and returned to his seat before speaking. "Yes sir, I did. If everyone will turn over the photo of Ammar, you'll see Valissi Pandanco standing to the right, facing Karuza and Ammar."

There was a fourth figure in the picture Sam didn't mention. It was Sabu the Butcher. Morris Bartow immediately recognized him; shock and dismay flushed his face. He remained quiet while the chief of staff continued.

"As the president stated, he is a former member of the KGB, and is now working for Premier Andropov of the Republic of Georgia."

"So far," Kellogg started in, "we've been unable to determine the nature of the meeting, but we do know Pandanco and Karuza were arguing."

"About what?" E. James asked. He was now leaning forward and tossing the ball from one hand to the other.

"Our agent had difficulty with his sound equipment," the CIA director said. He was as upset as the president about the lack of information. "And by the time the problem was corrected, the conversation had ended. As for the monies funneling into the US from Turkey, as you've suggested, General, we can't find any evidence that Karuza or Ammar have the enormous sums required. They're not oil-rich sheikhs."

"Then there's your answer." Morris said.

"To what question?" Kellogg said.

"This Pandanco friend of Karuza's is supplying the big dollars to support their cause," Bartow said to the group. The men looked over at Bartow, curious about what the general knew and they did not.

"Whose cause, Karuza's? Or the Republic of Georgia's?" the president asked.

"I'd say both." Morris leaned his forearms on the table, clasping the photographs together. "Listen gentleman, in my experience in the Middle East, since the fall of the USSR, each of the newly-formed Central Asian republics tried to enlist various Arab nations to assist in their recovery—secretly, of course. They offered to hand over the Soviet weapons left behind, weapons that would be obsolete in a contemporary war, but which are nonetheless dangerous. To a nation such as France or the United Kingdom such weapons would be useless. But to a country like Libya or Iraq or Iran, these weapons were miles ahead of anything they could possibly muster themselves, and they exchanged them for oil, or huge sums of money. Where do you think Iraq obtained those Scud missiles they used in the Gulf War? Now the scenario is reversed, Georgia's economy is struggling, but that is by design, I assume by Andropov."

"What are you talking about, Morris?" the CIA director asked. "We have reports the Georgian government has been floundering at a consistent pace since Russia cut them loose. If they have money stashed, it would be an unbelievable feat of secrecy."

"Pardon the frankness, Mr. Kellogg, but your reports are based on the news media, and what you see on CNN. To be honest, your office doesn't have the manpower or the funding to provide proper data," Morris said, as his eyes moved to the president and back to the irritated Kellogg. "You see, gentlemen, within the Republic of Georgia lies one of the only diamond mines in western Asia—and it's a big one. Once the Soviet Union fell, all mining operations were turned over to Andropov, and he has kept the wealth of the mine a secret, while stockpiling diamonds."

"He's also taken over operation of over fifty ICBMs," Admiral Faustian added.

"Maybe more," General Bartow continued. "Andropov obviously can see value in Turkey, but what his purpose there is, we still don'tknow. So we need to find out what Karuza and Ammar are up to before Andropov moves in to exploit it."

"I couldn't agree more, General." Worthington said. "I had presumed the reason for this meeting was to inform me of their propose."

"As of this moment, sir, Karuza has done nothing wrong in the eyes of the United Nations," the CIA director said.

"What about the murder of the prime minister of Turkey? Are there any leads implicating Karuza or his followers?" the President asked.

"Other than hearsay," Kellogg paused, "nothing. The assassin was killed by the Roman police."

"So much for a confession," Morris added.

"He was traced to a terrorist group in the Sudan, but they said he was a rogue killer, available to the highest bidder. Our sources confirmed the Sudanese response," Kellogg said.

"Listen gentlemen," Worthington spoke, standing, leaning on the wooden table, his eyes moving from one man to the next. He clenched the soft ball under his palm. "I am troubled by the fact Andropov is directly involved with the growing movement. I want answers—not more questions. Find out what Karuza's next move is, and put a twenty-four hour eye on Valissi Pandanco. I expect results. Immediate results!" The president stood erect, briefly nodded at Sam Haggart, and left the room.

CHAPTER THIRTEEN

A l drove north on Interstate 95, oblivious to his surroundings. His thoughts were consumed with images of
Domeni, and anticipation of their date later in the week.
He was taken aback by the thought he even had a shot at meeting a
woman like her, and even more surprised she accepted his offer. Al
was confident in himself, but his opportunities with women had-
been few and far between. Never had a woman consumed him so.
He was filled with high expectations they would hit it off. They
only had one brief meeting, and Al felt he had known her all his
life.

What will they do? Where will they go? It didn't matter. The
sensation he had when he was in her presence was enough. Al
had never been married, and he truly felt love only once before.
It was years ago, and it ended harshly—and then in tragedy. He
would always regret his past love experience, never being able to
mend what had happened. Maybe that's why his opportunities
had yielded so little. He was always afraid of making the same
mistakes. It took a woman—not just any woman, either, but a
statuesque beauty like Domeni—to draw out desires long-hidden
behind his fears of love. There in the truck, Al swore to himself
that he would allow himself to forget the past, and take hold of the
future—and that future would include Domeni.

Sitting in the passenger seat, Stanley also seemed unaware
of his environment. He had fallen asleep not ten minutes after
leaving the Baroque Chemical plant. They arrived at the shop

only to find it empty. The owner had stepped out for a reason unknown to them, so they entered their respective vehicles, and went on their way. Stanley headed north, back to the interstate, and Campo traveled west, to his part of the city. The route he took home was quicker than the drive in the morning, and he arrived at the back alley of his townhouse fifteen minutes later. The rear of the red brick townhouses raised three stories. All the homes were identical, with the exception of trim color, and some homes had wooden decks. Every one had four windows, a garage door, and next to that, a back door led into the basement. Al built a small shed facing the concrete driveway, hiding his central air unit beside it. Farther toward the alleyway, he kept his trash cans, which never moved until the men picked them up, emptied them of their contents, and returned them to their original position.

Al backed into the driveway, and immediately jumped into the bed of his truck to unload the couch. He knew if he went inside to a cool, air-conditioned interior it would be hard to force himself back out into the July heat. Al took a good look at the worn fabric and decided it had to be removed. So first he tossed the cushions over the side into the stationary trash cans, and then he dug out his Leatherman pocket tool, expanded the cutting blade, and tore into the backrest cloth like Anthony Perkins. Indiscriminately, he yanked strips of cloth from the tacks holding it in place, and threw them carelessly towards the trash cans. Soon the wire and burlap backing was exposed. Their condition was questionable, so he left the backing in place, and jabbed the knife into the seat cloth. Al heard and felt the point of his knife glance off something metal. Just the wire braces, he thought. He stabbed into the seat again, and this time he felt something solid. He tore back the deteriorated cloth to reveal a box approximately a foot square. The top had an emblem painted on it, and Campo knew immediately what it was. It was the symbol for radiation: three trapezoids surrounding a small black circle.

"What the hell is this?" he said. "Son of a bitch! This is why that guy wanted this couch so bad this morning!" He lifted the item; it was about half as thick as it was wide, with the same symbols printed on its sides. Campo figured its weight to be about forty pounds, it could be uranium or plutonium or any other heavy metal. Al was familiar with the characteristics of those elements from what he remembered of a high school field trip to the Salem nuclear power plant in New Jersey. That trip had made a great impression on him. It made him realize what awesome, destructive power could be harnessed by man, and used for a positive gain. He was taught to respect nuclear power plants for all they could be used for, especially after the Chernobyl accident.

Once again his curiosity was triggered, and he wanted to open the latch on the side, but the material inside most likely needed the shielding of the lid and, in all likelihood, he would be exposing himself to contamination if he opened it. In an instant Campo felt a bit apprehensive. Whoever that man was this morning, and where he came from, smuggling a radioactive substance meant at least ten to twenty in the federal pen. This guy wasn't going to let an altercation stop him obtaining his property. Al had an uneasy feeling, a sixth sense he'd acquired years ago having been in harm's way many times. Quickly he searched up and down the back alley, peeping over the toolboxes on the side of the truck.

Usually, this emotion was followed by something bad happening, but Campo forced himself to relax, knowing it was another time, and another place, far in his past. His next move, he thought, would be to take the box to the nearest police station, and be rid of it, but first he would thoroughly check the other side of the couch, in case anything else was hidden. He jabbed atother side and heard a clank, but this time it wasn't as loud. He ripped back the cloth and expected to see the symbol for radiation, but instead newspapers lined the area. They were brownish, and crumbling. Al pulled them out, and studied the writing. It wasn't a typical news font; the print was a strange form of italics. Not bothering to read any of it, he searched for a title page, and turned over the frail publication. The name smacked him across the face. At the top of the sheet in bold black was the word, "GAZETTE." Above the word, in smaller letters partially legible due to the decay he was sure it read "T EPENSYLNIA."

"Holy shit," Al said. He knew the Pennsylvania Gazette hadn't been published in nearly two hundred years. Campo flushed with excitement. Goose bumps grew on his arms and the hair on his neck stood on end. He found the date under the title, "3 July 1776." He remembered the metal sound, and he set the paper aside. Al dug through some straw padding, and uncovered a purple velvet bag, its soft texture seemed untouched by the years. It looked as though the bag contained another box, the same size as the othercase. Campo, eagerly but carefully, lifted the object from its tomb. It was heavy, but it felt very different than the other box had, and he knew with overwhelming excitement that it was not another radiation case.

Campo set it on the tailgate, and he leapt to the concrete. After he untied the velvet he opened it, reached his hand inside and let his mind wander into possibilities. Definitely metal—he felt grooves and ridges.Then he slid his hand under it, lifting the weight, drawing away the cloth. His hands tingled, and he felt a strange electrical vibration enter his palm. He brushed off the queer feelings, blaming them on his excitement and static electricity. Suddenly Al's face was litby the reflection of sunlight bouncing off solid gold. The metal was untarnished. The box had the appearance of being newly forged from fresh gold. He knew this must be an ancient artifact by its design, and unmatched sculpting. He gulped down the lump in his throat, and ran his fingers over the priceless object, grinning from ear to ear, forgetting all about the case with the radiation symbol. That strange tingling sensation ran through his fingertips again and a chill ran down his spine. Campo relished the thought of wealth and easy living. His ship had finally come in—or so he thought. He looked to see how the box opened, and he found a keyhole in what appeared to be the front, yet there were no seams visible to define a lid.

"The sack," he said, "the key must be there." He lifted the velvet up by pinching the back and shaking it. A folded piece of paper fell out, but no key. Al unfolded the parchment; it also strangely looked new. The writing was in ink, and written in an old script similar to the newspaper, only writtenby hand.

Al Campo turned, and sat on the tailgate of his truck, and began to read:

"To the poor misfortunate fellow who unearths this box of dread. I dare say, do not be deceived by its beauty, for within its dreamlike luster lies a demon of horrid measure. Only death and despair at the hand of Beelzebub himself can be found within. As to why I live to tell this tale of woe, that escapes my ability to comprehend or reason. I must relate unto you my story. I myself bear witness. My name is Dixon Hancock.

I am stepson to the most noble statesman, American patriot, and member of the Continental Congress, John Hancock. I have shamed him so terribly that I fear my only recourse is to champion his name in the fight for freedom from the horrible tyranny of England and her King. I am to leave this evening under the cover of darkness, traveling north to the city of New York where our troops have massed to fight against the King's Redcoats. But enough of my own pitiful self!

The evening before last I found myself in the company of two rabble-rousers. Jeremy, whom I had known before that evening, seemed a kindly soul, and I, without friends in the city of Philadelphia, took to him. The other lad, George, came with Jeremy. He was full of ale and wine sacks. Their influence deepened my craving for adventure, my desire to escape the toil of constant schooling and discipline. After drinking much ale, my thinking had turned and twisted, and I began feeling rebellious. Jeremy and especially George were prompting me to commit thievery as they themselves would on any other day. My mind was clouded with ale, and before I was able to stop them, George had cast his bottle, rending a glass pane.

They ransacked and pillaged the house, and although I knew the wrong they were committing, I too entered through the window. As I said, ale was driving my defiance, and by way of a stumbling George. Then I uncovered this box of gold, and as you are now dreaming of riches, I was guilty of the same. I took the box from its hiding place and made it mine. When suddenly the night watchman Jones surprised us three, Jeremy and George fled swiftly, but Jones's musket ball was all the quicker, and took their lives, as I witnessed. This assault brought back my senses; it was then that I realized the house I was robbing was the home of my stepfather's dear friend, Benjamin Franklin. With no time to waste on remorse or regret, I also sped away, but my emotions would not allow me to leave the box behind, so I stole it with me.

Traveling as fast as my legs would carry the weighty object, I hid in the alcove of the square, I was breathing a heavy draw, weighing my next move when out from the shadows the watchman, Jones, appeared. His musket drawn on me, fear took hold of my hands and the box fell with a mighty sound. By some way the piece opened and what happened next, I assure you is no tale of nonsense but of truth and absolute assurance, such as my eyes have witnessed.

A mist appeared and began to rise. It moved—not like morning fog in Boston, but as something having a mind of itself. It formed into the monstrous shape of Beelzebub! Jones fought bravely to his end, and the devil entered his body, and upon leaving took the watchman's soul as I saw him devouring the flesh and bone. Hovering above me, the creature stared me down, and I closed my eyes fearing I was to suffer the same fate. But mysteriously, it had no effect on me, and slowly seeped back into its chamber. It did not leave me unaffected, as I am forced to live with this horrible memory.

Returning to my stepfather's home unnoticed, I examined the gold box, looking for the seam through which the monster had appeared, but somehow it had mended itself, leaving no crease, only a keyhole for which no key was found. It must be within the walls of Benjamin Franklin's home. I am too ashamed to return the stolen property, so I am hiding it with this letter until I return in glory as a hero of the Revolution. I beg of whoever uncovers this box, leave it where it came, and forget all you have seen and read of it.

You may writhe in anguish as watchman Jones did.

With direst warnings,

Dixon Hancock

Campo sat, perplexed, staring blankly at the letter. At first, he was mesmerized by its context; then skepticism took hold.

"This is a boy, a frightened thief, and he's attempting to keep others from his prize. So he made up this story when he had to leave home, so no one would want to take it for himself," he mumbled out loud.

Al's next thought was of its value. First there was the letter, handwritten the day before the Colonies declared independence, and in perfect condition. The author had said he was the stepson of John Hancock, and it would make it easy to verify its authenticity. It would also be a great starting point in locating the origin of the box, which was probably older than Colonial times. Al thought of something else—the fact Dixon didn't mention its contents convinced him the real valve was to be uncovered upon finding the key. He searched the velvet once more, then scoured the couch in vain. Campo needed more information.

This was when he was at his best, facing a task requiring fieldwork, and he could feel the adrenaline rushing through his extremities, into his brain. He had forgotten the first box entirely. Looking through the back window he read the digital clock on his dashboard. There was still time to go downtown to see his friend who worked at the University of Pennsylvania.

The streets in the University City section of Philadelphia were still crowded with summer students and teachers. Drexel University and Penn were tangled together in a combined four-hundred-acre campus. Campo figured most of Penn's student body had off during the summer months, but he knew Drexel's four-semester program was in full swing. Al drove down Spruce Street into the heart of Penn's campus and attempted to find a parking spot. It was futile. He checked his clock, and knew he had to park soon, before his friend left for the day. The buildings lining the street were either carved out of the eighteen-hundreds or the twentieth century. There were several new buildings, currently being constructed, along with several older buildings receiving upgrades. The street had orange cones and temporary metal cyclone fencing lining the entire east side,which left little in the way of parking. He decided to use a spot he called the "pray you" spot, because each time you pull up there you "pray you don't get a ticket." Out front of the University Museum, he drove around the circular driveway of the Museum's giant rotunda that housed the main hall exhibits. Campo loved its architecture, and never tired of looking at the five-story dark-brown veneer, and circular, pointed, slate roof; thousands of brown bricks stacked tightly together created a smooth façade. Shooting from left and right the museum's wings spanned the entire city block.

Campo reached into his glove compartment and grabbed his university ID badge; his friend had given it to him some five years ago to makeit easier for Campo to visit.He placed an expired Construction Vehicle Parking Permit in his side window, and exited the truck, hoping for the best. He had returned the gold box to its velvet bag, and then put it into a brown paper shopping bag. Now he held it tightly to his side like a schoolbook. He walked several blocks, through a myriad of brick walkways, and concrete paths. The weight of the object became cumbersome, and he had to switch carrying positions constantly. Eventually, Al advanced toward a lofty, gothic structure. He looked up at a towering, central fortress-shaped centerpiece. Its color was a strange terra-cotta red, with dragon-head sculptures poised on the stone walls. The lower section was elliptical and was capped off by a stone and glass dome. Large red stone columns supported a flattened portico with stone steps that led into the main entrance of the Fisher Library at Penn. Al entered the principal hall, and instead of setting foot in the book section, went downstairs past a security guard. The guard glanced over, and Campo flashed his U of P pass clipped to his pocket. The guard nodded, and Al continued. The box was getting heavy now, and he labored down the stairs relieved his friend's office was at the bottom.

"PRIVATE: Department Of Architecture, Archives," was printed on the door. Al rapped his knuckles against the yellow-stained wooded door, pine from the look of it. But probably as old as the building because each time he knocked some of the old varnish fell to the floor. Almost a minute passed without an answer, and the box felt like it had tripled in weight since he had left his truck. Ready to place it on the floor, and knock again, he heard the deadbolt slide and saw the handle turn. The door creaked open, and revealed a man who looked like he belonged on the racks with the Egyptian sarcophagus. Herman Seller looked up at Al Campo, and flashed a kind smile. Every time Al saw his friend, it seemed he never aged. He had the same face: so wrinkled he could be mistaken for a piece of flesh-colored cellophane. Herman's leathery, textured skin looked pliable, but filled with history.

"Hello, hello, Mr. Campo," Herman said in a raspy voice. He pushed up his bifocals, which seemed to always be hanging on the tip of his nose. "How are you this afternoon?"

"Very well, Herman, but I've told you a thousand times my name is Al. Mr. Campo was my father!" he said, and placed his free hand tenderly on Seller's shoulder. Al was always intrigued byHerman's sparse white hair; it shot straight up from his head. The man's back was crooked, so he stood slightly hunched over, peering at Campo with squinted eyes.

Al walked in, closing the door with a flick of his foot, and noticed his friend walked slowly, as if every movement ached. "Herman, how have you been?" Al asked. "It's been a while since I've seen you."

"Oh fine, fine, yes, it has been a while. Well, Mr. Campo," Herman looked up at Al as he spoke, side-stepping the question about his physical condition.

Al rolled his eyes, knowing Herman would never call him by his first name.

"What rare artifact…no…furniture, you always bring furniture, and an occasional book, yes, books, that's what you deal with, books. You've brought in some fine examples. I always remember the copy of *Hamlet* you returned to the library after it was stolen, very generous of you, very generous indeed! Then there was the copy of the Samuel Clemens book we found to be a forgery, oh yes, I remember…"

"Herman," Al interrupted the old archivist before he described every book he had brought in over the past ten years, "I need some information on Benjamin Franklin."

"Franklin, yes of course, very diverse and complicated man, a genius but very vague at times. Have you looked into a book by Carl Van Doren? He did a biography on him several years ago. It was very comprehensive." Herman started looking through some books.

Al took hold of Herman's arm kindly and turned him to face his direction. "Professor, I own that book, remember? I got a copy of it when I was researching an old Franklin stove—you recommended that bio then. But the information I'm looking for delves a little deeper."

The two men walked over to a table in the center of a cluttered room. Campo loved coming here. All around them were tall shelves, perhaps twice as tall as he was and loaded with everything from neatly stacked volumes of books to loose piles of papers. The walls held endless books, manuscripts, folders, letters, and any other possible literature the archives department had gotten their hands on in the two-hundred-plus years since the university's inception. Campo had to wait a few moments, because the desks and tables were also covered and Herman had to move a pile of magazines to the floor. The table they picked served as Seller's desk; even though it was a mess, it was the best possible place to rest the package. Campo was used to the stacks of books, and did not mind the disorder, mainly because the one thing missing among the piles was dust and dirt. The ventilation system was state of the art, and it was kept up to date with timely maintenance. Al knew Herman insisted on the upgrades because the condition of the archives depended on it.

Al removed the paper bag.

"What a beautiful velvet cloth, yes, very fine indeed," Herman said.

"If you think the sack is nice, what's inside is really going to blow your skirt up."

Seller looked down at his trousers. "I'm not wearing a skirt, Mr. Campo."

"It's a figure of speech, Herman," Al said, then he untied the cord, and pulled away the sheath.

"Oh my heavens…" Herman said. He caressed the metal engraving with wrinkled fingers and palms.

Al saw the look in his eyes and was wondering if Seller felt the strange electrical sensations he had felt earlier, but he didn't mention it.

The professor tried to move the box but its weight was too much for his weak hands, so he bent down with his glasses tight on his head. He opened a drawer in the desk, pulling out a magnifying glass and then studied the engravings. "It's exquisite, yes,

yes, exquisite indeed.Where did you find such an extraordinary piece?" Herman said and squinted. His face and magnifying glass were nearly touching the box.

Al explained how he found it in the couch, leaving out the first package he had found, and then handed Herman the letter. Seller sat down on his chair, on top of some papers, and patiently read through it twice. All the while he rubbed his chin and nodded to himself. "Well that's…that's the most extraordinary story I've ever read. Amazing, amazing indeed," Herman said, and continued to study the letter.

Al could hardly contain his excitement. "Yes, I agree. So what do you make of it?"

Herman stared at the letter, then at the box, then back at the letter.

"Well, Herman, what is it?"

"I am not sure, young man." Seller finally set the letter down, and studied the carvings of the box. He took out several loose-leaf papers, grabbed a sharpened pencil, and made rubbings of the images and symbols.

"Do any of the markings look familiar?" Campo said, aching for information.

The professor looked closely at the box. "I can't say, but they appear to be some form of hieroglyphics."

"So it's Egyptian?" Al rubbed the engravings and felt the tingling again.

"No, Mr. Campo, the word 'hieroglyphics' only refers to a form of symbol writing. The ancients in this country who painted their rituals in caves also used hieroglyphics. These particular symbols are not familiar to me, but it is a starting point. Also, these two young men Dixon mentions." The old archivist pointed to the paragraph. "He does not tell their last name."

Al looked at the letter. "Maybe he didn't know them very well. He does say he had only met the second boy that evening."

"Yes, true…true, but…" Seller turned the page. "Here it is.'… the watchman, Jones.' That's a last name. At least I believe it to be his last name, we must assume it could not be his first."

"And he was on guard duty," Al interjected. "You can trace back to the date, and find records."

The professor shook his head and looked at Al. "Not so easy to do, Mr. Campo. Records two hundredyears ago were not as today, no, not at all like today."

"But it's a good place to start; there could possibly be an account of the theft in a police report of some kind," Al said as he watched Herman meticulously rub every square inch of the box onto paper, labeling each. "Also, he says he got it in Benjamin Franklin's home. We can search every possible written record of him, and maybe something will turn up."

"As you know, Mr. Campo, I am fluent with the details of Franklin's life, and I do not recollect any mention of a gold box such as this."

Al looked closely at the box and then at the professor. "I know, old friend, but with something so significant, another look may be worth it." Al laid his hand on Herman's bony shoulder once again and gave a soft squeeze. "Herman, listen, how about I leave the box and the letter in your trusting hands. I want you to take as much time as you need. I would like to know a few specific things, though."

"Yes, of course, Mr. Campo, of course," Herman said and finished up with the rubbings, and ventured over to a stack of binders precariously piled in the corner. Despite the maelstrom of information, Al was dumbfounded that Seller knew exactly what and where every volume was. He could find a sidebar written in the margin of a letter dating 1875 by Henry Cabot Lodge.

"First," Al said, "I'd like the box dated—and if Franklin didn't have it made, then who did? Did he actually own it, or is that a fabrication of Dixon Hancock? Also I'd like to find the key so we can open it and find out what's inside."

Herman's expression changed like a tempest, and his hunched frame almost stood erect. "Mr.Campo, I...I don't think opening the box would be very wise."

"You believe the story to be true?" Al said. "Herman, if it were true, how could such a find be kept secret all these years? And with Benjamin Franklin himself owning it? Even he would have exploited it for all he could. Why, in his own autobiography he pats himself on the back so many times I lost count. He would have loved to show off such a find."

"Yes, yes, that's true, he does speak highly of himself…very well of himself indeed." Herman said.

"So, Professor, let's just start out authenticating it first. Then we'll worry about a monster appearing later. Here's my cell phone number. Call me if you find out anything. In the meantime, I'm going downtown to Benjamin Franklin's home on Arch Street tomorrow to see if I can turn over any stones."

Campo shook the old man's hand, and went off toward the exit.

Herman read the letter composed by Dixon once more, and began his research.

CHAPTER FOURTEEN

The second day at the state hospital began uneventfully. All the equipment and material were already in place, so there was no need for them to meet at the glass shop. Al and Stanley parked next to each other, adjacent to the forty-foot trailer containing the glass and metal. The pair again worked in separate rooms, Al ahead of his partner, and they continued where they left off. Like Mr. Wilson had said, the rooms were empty, but Campo had learned his lesson, and propped the bed frame against the door.

Al's mind was completely engrossed with the gold box. He wanted desperately to find the key and what fortune it held. Last night after his meeting with Herman, he went home and searched every book he owned—and the Internet—for information on Benjamin Franklin. He couldn't find a reference to the box, and he fell asleep while reading. All day he checked his cell phone, looking for the message indicator to blink. Maybe Herman would call, and it wouldn't ring because his reception was fading in and out, but the service would accept the message.

Come on, ring.

Campo completed his third room and walked out into the hall. He was stopped abruptly by one of the residents standing in his way. It was the dark-haired man from the previous day. By the look in his eyes, Al could tell he was looking for something. He recalled his missing driver's license. He felt the sinister gaze of the resident, as if the man were aware of Campo's meddling. Something more was apparent: his face showed intelligence under a studied attempt at masking it. This man was involved in a mischievous game, possibly a dangerous game, and Al had stumbled onto it. Al put on his best look of indifference, but he feared the resident saw his guilt.

"Excuse me," Campo said, returning the stare. Their eyes never left each other as he rolled his tool cart around the patient, and made his way to the enclosed nurse's station. "Pardon me, Miss. Did someone turn in a lost driver's license?"

The middle-aged woman looked around the desk, and in the drawer. "I don't see anything, but I can leave a message for the evening nurse to look for it."

"Thank you." Al said. "Oh, should I leave my name so you know whose it is?"

"That would be fine."The woman took down Al's name and number and promised to call if his ID should show up.

Al was sure a patient had it, and he didn't know quite what to do about it. The resident would probably deny having it. Besides, what proof did Al have that that's where he lost it? The one thing he did have in his favor was the message he had copied down. Maybe it contained an incriminating message, and Al could exploit it to have the resident turn over his property. Right now, he didn't even know what language it was in, and the time to do research was not there. An idea hit him suddenly. A neighbor living up the street from him was a professor, and was fluent in many languages. He'll drop off the note, and perhaps find some clues.

———◆———

Yavuz entered his room, and closed the door, leaning his back againstit. "American devil, he knows."

Yavuz snatched a chair, and wedged it under the doorknob. Then he opened his closet, retrieved his transmitter, and typed a coded message to his superiors:

"This is Cell One. My cover may have been compromised by an unknown. I am requesting instructions." Yavuz sat and awaited a response He looked over his shoulder at the barricaded entrance, not wanting another intrusion like yesterday.

Moments later the machine sprang into action. He read the message.

"Cell One, remain; await further orders to complete your mission. All is well; the return of the Prophet is at hand. Send all known information to Base, and Allah will show the way for elimination."

Yavuz bowed his head as he saw the reference to the return of the Prophet, and he prayed for his safe return. Then he typed in every piece of information written on the driver's license, and pushed the send button.

"It is in Allah's hands now,"

Stanley and Al were able to finish their quota of installations, plus a few more, by one o'clock, and they decided to leave early instead of starting work in rooms thatwould have to be emptied. Upon reaching their trucks, Stanley seemed to be in a bit of a hurry, so he simply said, "I'll see you in the morning, Al, same bat time," and he exited the hospital grounds.

Campo wasn't as rushed, so he took time to check his oil dipstick. Since he'd been burning oil lately, he thought it was a good idea. He pulled out the long steel wand, wiped it off, returned it, and pulled it out again. He held it to the side and angled it to avoid the sun glare, looking at its reading. As he did, his eyes focused across the parking lot. He saw a black Chevy sedan facing him, with two men sitting in the front seat. Al deduced they must have the car running, because he saw billows of smoke rising from the exhaust pipe. Campo returned the dipstick and grabbed a spare quart of oil he kept behind the seat of the cab. He took his time pouring, and held the Chevy, and its passengers in his peripheral vision. That done, he jumped into his driver's seat and proceeded to the gates. The sedan didn't move as Al left, and he blew off the situation as paranoia. Within five minutes, he was cruising north up Interstate 495 out of Wilmington, heading to the Pennsylvania state line. He put on his left turn signal to change lanes into the merging traffic where I-495 and I-95 integrated into one highway.

He checked his side-view mirror; there was a tractor-trailer to his immediate left, so he hit the accelerator and swerved in front of the semi.

There it was! The black Chevy—Al only caught a glimpse in the mirror. It was to the left of the truck, but for some reason, he couldn't see it any longer. He put on his turn signal once again, and moved into the far left lane. Nothing was in the mirror; it had to be his paranoia. Why would someone be following him? He sped up to the maximum of sixty-five, passing several cars onto an open highway. The trailer was far back now, and no other traffic was around him. Suddenly, there it was again. The Chevy was in the right lane, keeping a steady pace with Campo.

What the hell?

Al slowed his speed to fifty until the sedan was a car-length away. He could see the faces of two men. In the passenger seat was a dark-haired man, his eyes determined, fixed on Al's face in the mirror. The driver seemed relaxed, casually resting his right wrist on the steering wheel, a cigarette dangling from his lips. Campo didn't recognize them. For the past ten years he had kept his nose clean, and been a diligent taxpayer. What could they want?

"Shit." Campo reached under the passenger seat, and felt the case with the radiation markings on it. "I forgot about that stupid box." Al traced his memory, but he couldn't understand how he came to be followed. From yesterday morning until now, it had been routine. Go to work. Go home. Talk to Seller. Go to work. He hadn't mentioned the box since he found it. *Then again, he's been nearly shot, found a box possibly containing a volatile substance, another box with a hidden secret monster and oh yea, a secret computer in a mental patients room. Other than that... same old same old.*

"Shit," he said again. "It's that asshole with the gun, all right. Let's see if these bozos are really following me."

Campo's exit was coming up quickly, so he slid over to the exit ramp, and so did his pursuer. He waited as long as he dared, then spun his wheel to the left, fishtailing erratically, slamming onto the gravel shoulder, and bouncing back into interstate traffic. The other driver's reaction was quick, but he miscalculated, and turned the wheel too far. The rear quarter-panel smashed into the sand barrelsthat divided the off-ramp and shoulder. They erupted like a dirt gusher, spewing their contents in every direction. The trunk popped open, then slammed shut, lodging in the twisted metal as the car skidded back onto the highway. Somehow the driver managed to veer into traffic without colliding with another vehicle. He must have stabbed his foot solidly on the gas pedal. The black car raced downthe road, making up the lost distance.

Campo gazed at the reflection, and he decelerated without noticing. Quickly he realized the tenacity of his hunter, and he sped up. His pickup was no match in a race against the bigger, more powerful engine. His broad truck and heavy tool boxes held him back. Al weaved in and out of the thickening traffic headed toward the Philadelphia International Airport. He aimed his vehicle at the airport exit and cut off a tour bus with an advertisement for malt liquor. The unsuspecting driver hit his brakes to avoid the collision and the sedan was forced to slow down, and pass behind the bus on the right losing ground. Campo contemplated which road to take into the airport, Arrivals or Departures. He decided on the latter because in the six lanes available, cars would be double, triple, or even sometimes quadruple parked and because of security reasons they were only allowed three minutes to unload and pull away. This would increase his chance of losing his tail. He headed in, and immediately had to dodge vehicles and pedestrians at a dangerous speed. The terminals were crowded with all sorts of cars, taxis, small busses, and people unloading luggage. He saw the faces of people walking high above on the glass pedestrian bridge that connected the parking garage to the terminals. Their mouths were agape watching this gray Ford truck barrel through the area. Campo had to slow down a bit to avoid killing a pedestrian or cab driver, and that gave the car chasing him time to get back on his tail. Campo's knowledge of the airport was not the best, but he did remember that there were about four main terminals and about a thousand feet of road between each. After the first terminal he hit the gas hard and then had to decelerate again as more people were unloading. The driver of the pursuit car had no remorse; he nipped several autos, tearing off side-view mirrors while sideswiping others, then continuing onward as though nothing had happened. He and his passenger were waving violently in an attempt to make Al pull over. Al's eyes stared forward carefully, watching as he avoided collisions every second, bowling through the continual moving parallel of cars. The next time he looked back was inthe clearing between C and B Terminals. The sedan was right on his tail. The black car's chrome bumper whacked Al's truck, jolting Campo forward.

"Mother…"

Al looked back again to see his chasers screaming and motioning at him to pull over. He ignored the gestures like a lawyer walking past a vagabond on a city street, then hammered down hard on the gas. The Ford's motor tapped into energy it had never before harnessed, downshifted, and leaped ahead into B Terminal. It was packed; there must be a trip to freaking Disneyworld judging by all the kids who scampered around with their tiny suitcases on rollers, decorated with Sponge Bob and Minnie Mouse. Cars here were parked four deep with their trunks open and people all around. He was going too fast, dangerously too fast but he saw his chance. In the far left lane was a slow moving vehicle. Well, all vehicles were supposed to be slow moving here. Campo was the exception. His timing would have to be perfect. He slowed just enough to force the Chevy to brake slightly.Then he raced forward like a greyhound out of the starting gate, spurting between the parked cars and the sluggish one a split-second before the driver of the parked car opened his door. The driver never knew what happened as his door was blasted off its hinges. It rocketed upward, smashed into the glass walkway, high in the air. The driver of the now door-less automobile got out immediately, screaming obscenities, but he quickly and wisely retreated into safety as a deadly shower of glass rained down.

Campo witnessed the accident, and saw the black car sped onward, its front end crushed, the right headlight smashed, and the windshield cracked, the fracture spider webbing out in all directions. He drove his pickup at top speed and merged back onto Interstate 95. Traffic was thinner on this stretch of highway, which had six lanes to spread out. The black car quickly bore down on him, when suddenly his truck began sputtering, and losing acceleration.

"No, no, no, come on, you son of a bitch!" Al swore, and looked at the fuel gauge. Its needle pinned on "E." Heavy with tools and bodyweight, the Ford pickup decelerated rapidly. He steered it onto the gravel shoulder, and his pursuer did the same. Then Al slammed on the brakes, causing them to stop inches away. His options were not all gone, not gone at all. He needed a plan and quickly. The two men sat, apparently waiting for Al to make the first move. He reached over to the glove box, located a box of stick matches, and a giant, emperor-size Dominican cigar. He bit the end and spit it out the window, lit a match and rolled the cigar in his mouth puffing the tip into life. The entire time he watched through the puffs of smoke in his mirror at his soon to be prey. He pondered his options, and thought for the first time he had no reason to run from these men. Hell, if they wanted him badly enough they could have just shot out his tires, or exited the car, and drawn weapons on him, but they didn't do any of that. It was a crucial mistake on their part, underestimating Campo's potential. Al figured it was time to take the offensive, but he waited patiently.

Then it happened. Both men opened their doors at the same time. Campo darted out, hunched low, going full-tilt, and he was on them in seconds. He caught the driver by surprise while the man was still half in the car. He crushed the door into the man's throat, pinning his neck and left arm between the door and the top of the vehicle. The man reached his right hand into his jacket; he was going for the gun Al could see in a shoulder holster. It was a .38 caliber revolver, a cumbersome weapon, and powerful. Campo jammed the hot tip of his cigar against the back of the hand going for the gun, and the driver let out a gurgle. Al reached in through the open window and grabbed the weapon with his left hand and held his body weight against the door so the driver couldn't move. Then the other guy rounded the trunk, and yelled something like *stop* or *freeze*, some stupid shit he ignored, and Campo hurled the heavy steel weapon with his left hand, striking the attacker between the eyes. The man dropped like a stone to the road.

Campo wedged the door hard, holding the pressure with his full weight. The man was gasping for air. The top of the door pushed tightly against his throat, and his right hand was wedged between the door and the car in an attempt to keep from choking to death. His left hand Campo had bent over the outside of the door. He was pretty securely trapped.

Campo took a puff of his cigar, rolling it in his fingers. He blew out a couple smoke rings and admired the flavor of the tobacco. His captive stopped struggling, and Al waited until the color changed in his face, from pink to blue. Then Al released a little pressure to let him breathe in a gasp.

"Who and why?" Al said and drew another puff from his cigar.

His captive mouthed some indistinguishable words, so he relieved the pressure again.

"Joe Tyson, FBI," the man said in a choked gurgle. Then Al put the pressure back on, hard.

"FBI, that's bullshit," Al said. FBI was the last thing he expected to hear, but the man looked the part: gray business suit, white shirt, and paisley tie. It was though his mother had dressed him for a job interview. Campo quickly traced his memory again, positive he hadn't mentioned the box to anyone.

"I am!" Tyson said through gasping breaths. "Check my ID."

Al reached inside the inner jacket pocket and pulled out identification for Joseph A. Tyson, FBI, Philadelphia office. He masked his surprise and released the man.

"All right, what do you want?" Al said and straightened out Joe Tyson's tie and shirt as the agent rubbed his neck and swatted off Al's hands.

"What the hell is wrong with you?" Tyson said, leaning back on the hood of the car. He grabbed his ID, then looked at his partner lying on his back unconscious. "Didn't you see us waving you over? You could have killed someone."

"I'd say you were more likely to have injured someone the way you were driving. Speaking of injury, I wonder if the other guy is all right," Al said with a nod of his head.

Tyson walked over to his partner. "Help me get him off the roadway, and into the car." Tyson said and inspected his partner's face. There was a bloodied gash on the bridge of his nose. "Other than a massive headache, and a welt the size of a grapefruit, he'll be fine." Joe tapped Faz on the cheek and tried to revive him, but he was out cold. He and Campo brought him to the passenger seat, and Tyson slung the seat belt over his chest and waist, then closed the door.He looked at Campo, tightened his jacket, and adjusted his tie. "Get in the back seat," he said and shoved him on the shoulder.

"No need to get physical," Al said.

"Get physical?" the FBI man said, poking a finger at Al. "I should arrest you for battery of a federal agent, and a dozen other misdemeanors and moving violations. Now get in the goddamn car." Tyson reached down to pick up his gun and got in the driver's seat. He let the weapon lie on his lap, with his hand firmly on the handle and trigger. The safety was on but Tyson had his thumb resting on it. He half-turned in his seat and watched Campo get in.

"Good, you can give me a ride to the gas station. There's one a couple miles up the road," Al said. Campo immediately smelled the fresh scent of cigarettes and figured he'd puff on his cigar again.

"You really do like to agitate, don't you, Mr. Campo?" Tyson said and took out another Camel. "I'm dead serious, and angry enough to put you in jail for interfering with an official investigation."

"Whatever, let's get this over with so I can be on my way." Al sat in the black leather bench seat, leaning his back against the corner of the door and backrest. He put his left leg on the seat and got comfortable. "All right, what investigation?"Al looked around the back seat. He couldn't see the door locks. The seats were worn and had a couple of marks on them.

"What do you know about Jason Gull?" Tyson said. While he waited for Al to answer, he checked Faz's pulse on his neck, and held his hand in front of his partner's mouth to make sure he was breathing OK.

"Jason Gull...um...Jason Gull, Jason Gull. I know that name." Al rubbed his chin and raised an eyebrow, looking at Tyson's reflection in the rearview mirror. "I know...he's the tooth fairy."

"Mr. Campo, I am trying to keep my composure, and you mocking me is not helping." Tyson squeezed his hand around his gun, then thought better of it and slipped the weapon back into its holster. "This is an important matter, and I would appreciate it if you would cooperate." The agent turned and stared down at Campo.

Al was getting visibly pissed as he looked the agent up and down. "You know, you people crack me up. Why don't you cut the bullshit? How the *hell* am I supposed to know what the shit it is you want. As far as I remember, Jason Gull is the owner or president or CEO or some crap like that of the chemical company I worked at yesterday. And that's the extent of my knowledge of him. You'd do better to tell me what you know, and what exactly it is you want from me."

Tyson was getting just as angry as Al, but he was doing his best to keep his cool. "Yesterday, Mr. Barrett and you were called to an emergency at the Baroque Chemical Corporation. Several hours later you emerged, and left in an orange truck."

Campo was rolling and bobbing his head."Yeah, and…"

"As you left, a black Jaguar followed you out; the driver of the vehicle was Bracken Guttone, an employee of Gull's."Tyson stopped to take another draw of his Camel.

"Yeah, I remember him. He was the dickhead Sasquatch guy we met while we were working, but I didn't notice anyone following us," Al said, as he recalled the time in his mind. "Jesus, will you open up the back windows in this car? I can barely see you through the smoke."

Tyson turned the key and depressed the window buttons. "Well, he was, until an accident on the interstate caused him to lose control."Tyson had a slight smile on his face ashe finished his sentence.

Al leaned forward. "How do you know he was following me? He could have been going anywhere, and coincidentally left at the same time."

"Originally, we didn't know he was tailing you, but our sources said Bracken was very interested in you, and gave orders to find out everything about you." The agent paused for a few seconds to judge Campo's reaction.

Al decided to play dumb. He wasn't sure this guy was for real, and held back his cards. "Why would anyone I only met once, and in passing at that, be interested in me?"

Tyson wasn't buying Al's act one bit, so he continued. "He was specifically interested in where you lived. That's when we made the connection. We were hoping you could tell us why," Tyson said, and for the first time his demeanor was pleasant.

"I haven't a clue," Al shot back, not falling for the nice guy routine. "Listen, Mr. Tyson, I went to the plant, I worked in the plant, and I left the plant, that's about it. It was a routine job; I've done about a hundred such emergencies in the past ten years. If this Bracken wants to know my home address, I'll give it to him myself. I've got nothing to hide."

Tyson started the car, then swerved onto the highway. He kept both hands on the bottom of the steering wheel and rested his forearms on his lap. "Mr. Campo?"

"Will you stop calling me, Mr. Campo? Al will be fine."

"To do that, Mr. Campo, this conversation would take on a personal tone, and I'm still considering arresting you." Tyson stared straight ahead and purposely passed the next exit. "We believe Jason Gull is involved in a smuggling operation originating somewhere in the Philadelphia area. Up to the present we have no hard evidence to convict him, and anything you may know that could shed some light in the gray areas might help us possibly make a connection."

"I haven't any connection. That's just it. Why anyone would be interested in me, Mr. Joe-Average-American, is bizarre to say the least." Al held back, still unsure of the situation. He didn't know it, but Tyson knew he was. "Do you think he has the wrong guy?"

"We have agents heading to question your partner, Mr. Barrett, but Bracken wasn't very interested in him. He was only making inquires about you. Can you tell us why?" Tyson turned and stared Al straight in the face.

"I'm tired of this. For every answer I give, you come up with more accusations. Just drop me off here, and I'll walk back to my truck." Al went to open the door before the vehicle had come to a complete stop, but there was no handle

The agent took the next exit and pulled into a gas station.

"Mr. Campo," Tyson unlocked the door. Al kicked it open and tried to get out but Tyson grabbed his shoulder. "Wait a second."

He pulled a business card out and gave it to Campo. "If there is any information you may remember that may be of interest, please give me a call. And remember, I *do* know where you live, and I can still arrest you for battery."

"So do it then." Campo snatched up the card, slammed the door, and Tyson drove off. Campo went to the attendant and bought a two-gallon gas can. As he stood at the pump, a black sports Audi pulled up next to him. A woman exited the car. She was tall and had black straight hair. She wore a skirt, no stockings, and high heels. She gave Al a sideways glance. Campo smiled and she smiled back. Ten minutes later, she had dropped him off at his truck. He had written her phone number on the back of Tyson's card.

"Well," he murmured to himself, thinking of Domeni. "You never know."

CHAPTER FIFTEEN

Campo decided to take a scenic route into Old City, and he got off at the Market Street exit. He fingered the card that Tyson had given him and read it once more. "FBI," he said to himself. He was ready to toss it out the window but flipped it over and saw the phone number of the woman that had given him a ride. "You never know" he said again, and stuck it in his pocket. He turned down Sixth Street, and then onto Chestnut Street, where Independence Hall sat in the middle of a plethora of historic buildings and artifacts. He drove past the glass and steel building that housed the Liberty Bell, and Independence Hall where this country was born. Then made another left onto Fifth Street, past the tall brown stone building called the Bourse Building. It was only two-thirty and the city streets were still buzzing with late-afternoon lunches, tourists snapping photos, horse-drawn carriages clopping on aged cobblestone. Families were taking in the many historic wonders Philadelphia had to offer.

Al's route guided him to the edge of Old City along Arch Street. Once there, he parked at a meter, and filled it to the maximum of two hours. He walked down past an interesting mix of old and new structures, a multicolored modern clothing store was next to the red brick building of the first US Post Office. Across the street, a generation beyond Colonial days, there stood a used record store with stereo equipment lining the sidewalk. It blared music so loudly, the ground vibrated. Down further, Al noticed a tourist sign directing passersby toward Christ First Church, the

Liberty Bell, Thomas Jefferson's house *and* Benjamin Franklin's home. He headed up a slight incline on Arch Street and saw the rebuilt home of BenFranklin. Campo was a bit disappointed to read on a sign posted out front of the red brick building that the dwelling was a fake, reconstructed just thirty years ago, but after his research last night came up with nothing, he hoped the inside might still hold some clues.

He followed signs that led him to the back of the building, down a brick path with an iron fence on his right that opened up to a grassy park. The back door was wood and glass. Once inside he was surprised to see he was led down an enclosed corridor that led into a museum in the basement. The red brick re-creation was merely an exterior façade. He traveled along a carpeted hall that went in a circle; the halls were bare except for directional signs pointing to the museum. As the routetook him towards the basement, Al felt his weight pulling him on, and his momentum eventually flattened out in a small, dim foyer. In it, a National Park Ranger sat behind a desk. He wore a blue-green uniform with a Park Service badge, and a wide-brimmed hat. His face was round, and had a pleasant and welcoming look. Campo also noticed that he carried a sidearm clipped to his belt. These guys were serious.

"Welcome to the Benjamin Franklin exhibit," the ranger said and handed Al a flyer that had information printed on both sides. "You may walk along and view at your leisure, and if you have any questions, don't hesitate to ask."

Yes, I do have a few questions. How about a strange gold box that was stolen from Franklin's home two hundredyears ago? Campo was dying to ask, but he knew better. He was just going to have a look around on his own. He turned the corner, and the first thing he saw was a huge portrait of the man himself. It was a famous one from Al's recollection: Franklin was in his later years, painted from the chest up. Balding, with stringy gray hair falling over a fur collar, a puffy shirt matted down by a gold watch-chain that disappeared into the bottom of the frame. His lips were taunt, and slightly curled in a way similar to the smile on the face of Da Vinci's Mona Lisa. It was a look of confidence, an air of nobility.

Al knew from his reading he was a worldly figure, known for his experiments in electricity, and for his philosophy on life. He stood alone as the first genius of the newly formed United States, a country he helped shape in nearly every way. Al stood staring at the image, trying to pry information out of the confident eyes, the stern yet smug face. He looked like a man who thought highly of himself, who knew he was smarter than anyone else. He boasted of it often in his autobiography—yet he knew he wasn't perfect. Upon further inspection, Al saw a number at the bottom of the painting.

"Excuse me," Al said, and got the ranger's attention. "What's this number here?"

"That would be the print number," the ranger replied. "This portrait is a copy of the original,which is hanging in Washington DC."

"Oh, I see,"Al said.

"Yes, actually," the ranger continued, "of all the artifacts in the exhibit, only two are original—the rocking chair, and his secretary desk there in the corner." He pointed his finger to Al's left.

"Thank you." Disappointment covered Campo's face as he paced past the fake items lining the walls. There was an old-looking printing press, an iron stove, several bookcases with fake books in them.Then he approached the rocking chair. Wooden and worn, there was nothing special about its design, curved spindle back-rest, flat seat. He wondered how it was possible that the chair had survived two hundred years.The secretary was next to it. That was more of a piece of furniture, possibly chestnut with cherry inlay decorating the front face and drawers. Its top was chestnut, and it had many marks and scratches in it. The top back had several let-ter holders with worn edges on the thin wood. Four drawers, two on either side, were mounted next to the legs, and there was one long narrow drawer in the center. A queer thought occurred to Al. Maybe the key would be stored in one of them. Probably not, but something else was on his mind. Refinishing furniture was Campo passion, and in the past ten years he had brought similar desks back to life by sanding off old varnish and stain, although none had the historical significance of this. What he did remember was that many of them had hidden drawers, known only to the furniture builder, and to the owner—unless of course someone like Al Campo came snooping around. Al looked back. The Ranger was out of his line of sight, and no other visitors were around. There were probably cameras, but at this point he didn't care. He leaned over the guardrail, and checked the most common areas first, along the legs where they met the body, and had no luck. Then at the back, and again there was nothing. For several minutes he tried every area he could imagine. Then he stopped, leaned back again, and checked on the Park Ranger, who was now engrossed in a novel. He gazed at the furniture, and wondered where a man of brilliance such as Franklin…That was it. Al vaguely remembered reading how Benjamin in his later years became forgetful. Then it hit Campo that someone who was forgetful would put things where he could easily find them, which meant hidden, but in plain sight. It was a slim chance. He slid open the large drawer in the center. The inside was bare, except for a worn, green velvet lining along the bottom. Velvet, he recalled, was the material holding the box. He ran his fingers along the edges and slid a fingernail into the seam where the velvet met the sides, and glided it around each corner. The fabric was attached to a thin cardboard, no, not cardboard. They didn't have cardboard in the eighteenth century. It was a very thin piece of wood, and he was able to lift the fabric out in a stiff, flat piece. At first he could see nothing in the dim light of the display, but he felt the bottom of the drawer, and sensed something different. The base was loose from the flattened bottom! Again he worked his nail around, and this time a thin sheet of aged paper feathered up. It was the exact dimensions of the bottom of the drawer, and colored with tung oil to match the wood, easily missed by someone not wanting to damage the relic. Al held it to the limited light, and knew it was written in Colonial times. The words were in French, and it began with Benjamin Franklin's name.

"Wow!" Al was so excited, he forgot where he was.

"Do you need help, sir?"

Al looked up. "No, thank you, I'm fine. I'll be leaving now," Campo said as he replaced the velvet, closed the drawer, and gently bent the paper. It wasn't brittle, the tung oil had kept it pliable, and he was able to fold the letter up, put it under his shirt,and made a quick exit.

He found the streets were still full of people, and decided to walk along Arch Street. He dared not look at the letter in the open, but before he headed for his truck he decided to check out Benjamin Franklin's grave. He'd seen it before, many times in fact. He had passed it on foot a few times, and at least a hundred times in the car while stopped at the light. A steel fence barred him from entering the area, but the engraving on the flat marble stone covering his grave, covered with pennies, was visible from the sidewalk. He studied the marble slab.When he heard a siren in the distance, he panicked, and then thought it best to get back to his truck.

Once back in his truck, he opened the letter carefully and examined the writing in the afternoon sun, and oh how he wished he could read French. When a sudden guilt crept up on him, he wondered how he came to be in this position. He had actually just stolen a relic, possibly undiscovered, for his own gain, and it might contain nothing pertaining to his endeavor. He promised himself once the letter was translated, he would return it to the Park Service, and with a bit of sorrow he decided to turn the gold box over to the University Museum in Seller's care for proper display. Of course, he'd do that after he found out its origin and what it held. It was only fair that since he discovered it, he should be the one to unwrap the mystery behind its existence.

Campo's next move would be back to Herman Seller's dungeon.

Thirty minutes later, the archivist was examining the document, wearing his bifocals. His eyes narrowed in an attempt to unlock its secrets.

"Herman, do you read French?" Al asked.

"No…no, sadly not, Mr. Campo," Herman said, looking back at Al.

Al looked at the professor, "Then shouldn't we find someone who does?"

"In a moment, yes, just one moment. I may have found something interesting, yes very interesting," Herman said, holding Al in suspense.

Finally after several minutes, Campo blurted out, "Well, what is it?"

"You see here?" Herman pointed at the bottom. "It is signed 'Francois Quesnay.'He was a close friend of Franklin's while he was visitingVersailles in 1767. This man was the physician to the king, yes, yes, the king of France. We have other letters here in the library written to our subject and signed by the doctor. Yet all of those were kept neat and tidy in Benjamin's memoirs. Indeed, he was compulsive in his care of his personal letters."

"So the question is: why hide this one?"

"Mr. Campo, we are now in a bit of a quandary." Herman paused and set the letter on his desk of papers. "First, you bring a gold box with a compelling letter attached, which I might add I am no closer to finding any clues for, and today this. Indeed, Mr. Campo, we are entering a world of discovery, and we may even rewrite a few history books in the process, extraordinary... yes, simply extraordinary."

Al was excited to see Herman's enthusiasm, but hearing that the old man had made no progress on the mystery of the gold box was a little disappointing. But what could he ask for in a day, miracles? It was just that in the past ten years he had brought Herman dozens of items, and usually the old man had information either immediately, or within a day. Yet, Al mused, this was all together different from an antique book.

"Herman,"Al said, laying his hand on Herman's shoulder. "I want you to know no matter what we discover, or what develops, I'm going to leave it all to you to break the news to the world, and keep these items in the university for public display."

"I always knew you would, Mr. Campo, yes, yes, you always have the best intentions, the very best intentions, indeed," Herman said, as his wrinkled face tightened into a wide smile of approval.

"I will make a copy of this, and send it over to my friend in the French department."

"Herman, as always, I trust you beyond all things, and I'll wait for your call to let me know the letter is translated," Al said. Then he left Herman in a trance, staring at the letter.

CHAPTER SIXTEEN

L ow on the horizon, the sun continued its descent. The heat of the day tapered off, and a cooling breeze sent drifts past the face of Umitz. It was a welcome wind. The beads of sweat running down his forehead and neck accepted the change of temperature like a cooling drink after a desert hike. Umitz had been perched on the black tar rooftop, hiding behind a brick chimney across the alley from Al Campo's townhouse. He had been there nearly six hours in anticipation of his target's return from work. He wasn't alone. His team consisted of three: one man sat in a silver Mercedes on a parallel street north of the alley. Umitz reasoned if Campo were to sense a trap, he had to travel north because at the end of the street it turned to the right, and it would be the logical turn to maintain momentum. The third member was posing as a worker, tilling soil in a community garden on the front block of the target's street. In the event he careened south, his man would blast him with a compact M6 submachine gun he had hidden in a plastic bag under the earth.

Umitz became impatient. He was not used to the humid heat, and he was unable to stop sweating. His body was weighted down with crossing straps over his shoulders that tethered a body harness in place. He had stripped down as much as possible; he wore only a T-shirt and blue jeans. They were purchased this morning, directly after he received his orders. Attached to the harness was a rappelling clasp hooked to a rope strapped to the chimney. If he needed, he could rappel down to the ground rapidly, and finish off his prey. During the long wait, Umitz had loosened the harness, and it draped over bony shoulders. His thin frame was crouched down with his knees bent, and his toes supporting his body. He backed his body up against the heated chimney. Every half hour or so, he would rise and stretch his legs, quietly walking to the center of the roof, making sure curious home owners didn't see him. He looked at his watch; another thirty minutes had passed. His knees cracked as he rose, and his back ached from the harness digging into it. Umitz strode to the center of the roof, leaving his silenced automatic rifle lying on the black tar roof where it had been for the last hour. The sweat on his hands made the grip slippery, and he didn't want his aim to be affected. He leaned forward, stretched his back, flexing the joints, shaking his hands and arms to loosen stiff muscles.

Then he heard the sound of tires bearing down the alley. Swiftly snapping the harness together, Umitz hunched down by the chimney, and saw a Nissan Maxima cruise past the driveway of his prey. Frustration flooded his brain; a hundred times in the past few hours he had repeated those same movements. He did not know what type of vehicle his target would be driving; he only received an address, and a description of the subject. Maybe the man would not arrive until after nightfall, or not at all that evening. His orders were to eliminate the target by any and all means at his disposal. The Prophet's return required it. Failure would not be accepted. Umitz would wait as long as it took—no matter what the harshness of his environment. At this instant he was tired and dehydrated, but fueling him on was the pure stamina he earned through his years of terrorist training, Allah would not be disappointed. The assassin would give his life to secure the future of His Holiness, Caliph Karuza. Once again he heard echoing sounds from the passageway below.

"Praise and good graces to you, Allah. May this be my victim approaching," he said, bowing his head, and then he peered around the bricks and mortar. He saw a gray pickup truck drive down slowly, then turn into a driveway at the top of the block. Holding in his screams of rage, Umitz slammed his fist into his palm.

Al Campo had too many thoughts whirling around in his head. The gold box, the object marked with the radiation warning symbols, FBI agents questioning him, message from a hidden transmitter inside a suspicious patient's room. Mostly though, it was the image of Domeni's glistening eyes and their imminent date on Friday evening. And Al thought his life was boring.

As he drove, the past thirty-six hours flashed by. He wanted to focus on one event at a time. First and foremost, come hell or high water, he would be at Domeni's home on time—but that was three days away. Next, he figured Herman Seller had his end under control, and he was going to keep Special Agent Joe Tyson on hold for now, at least until he had time to re-think his situation. Then there was the message from the hospital. That mystery had yet to be solved. Al's neighbors, who lived at the top of the street, he remembered were foreigners. He knew this from the way the women wore veils and covered their bodies with the *burka*. He knew they were Muslim, and the head of the household was a professor of theology at Temple University and spoke many languages, one of which was Arabic, and Campo thought he could decipher the message. Determined to translate it, he headed toward that house. Al pulled into the back driveway at the top of his back street. He rapped on the door, knowing someone was almost always home, and probably in the basement livingroom. A few moments had passed, so he knocked again. The curtain in the window was pushed aside. He recognized the babysitter's face, and smiled. The dead bolt turned, and she swung the door open.

"Hi, Mr. Campo." Her bright, face shone.

"Hello, Mary." Mary was a teenager who lived on Al's street. She often babysat for the family's children, along with several other families on the block, so Al knew her well. "Is Reza or Turgut home?" He pronounced their names slowly.

"No, I'm sorry. It's just me, and their little baby girl, Hunan," she said.

"Oh," Al said. "When do you expect them back?"

"They said around nine o'clock tonight," she said.

He looked at his watch. "OK, could you give Turgut this, and ask him to give me a call when he gets home?" Al handed over a copy he had made of the message, with a note asking Turgut to translate it, and his cell phone number. "It's not important, so he doesn't have to call me this evening if he arrives late."

"No problem," Mary said, then closed the door.

Campo hopped back in the truck, and pulled into his driveway.

———

On the rooftop, Umitz radioed his men. "Target has arrived; I will eliminate, and rappel down. Swiftly and quietly prepare yourselves." The assassin kept his eyes on the target through the back window of his truck, and reached for his automatic weapon. He clasped the handle, but it did not move. Turning to look, his saw that his gun had partially melted into the tar coating of the roof. As the sun went down, the black muck had cooled and hardened, and now the gun was embedded in the surface. Umitz made several futile attempts to free the weapon, using both hands and pulled with all his strength, (where was a fossil digger when you needed one). The sludge held firm. In frustration he kicked at it, and cursed the roof and the unbearable humidity. Then he reached for his sidearm, a nine-millimeter automatic he had purchased here in the States. At close range, it was a vicious and brutal killer, but at this distance it would be pure luck to strike a subject in a vital area in one shot. Umitz reached over the red brick chimney, holding the weapon with both hands. *Something's wrong*, he thought. His target had left the vehicle, and was nowhere to be seen. How fast could he have gotten out and into his house? He'd only taken his eyes off him for a minute. Umitz's eyes burned red, and his skull was pounding. After waiting in the unbearable heat on this expanse of Black Tar from Hell, his plans were dashed in the literal blink of an eye. Now he had to make an attack inside the dwelling. Umitz looked upward, and noted that complete darkness was approaching. The assassin would wait until then to make his entry. His mind calmed down as he began contemplating his new strategy. He was about to radio his men when Allah graced him. His target exited the back door, and walked toward the driver's side of the truck. Umitz waited until he was seated at the wheel. He would have a clean shot through the back windshield at the skull. Carefully he aimed his nine-millimeter, holding the handle, with his right hand, while his left steadied his arm. He exhaled and held his breath

＊＊＊

Al opened the pickup door. He had just used the bathroom, relieving himself after the long day. Too tired to make himself dinner, and with nothing in the refrigerator that tickled his taste buds, he decided that a hour or two at the Greeks Tavern with the wide-screen TV, the Phillies and Sarah, the bartender with her beautiful blue eyes and tight clothes would make for a good night. He jumped into his seat, turned the ignition, and heard the rear window shatter, and saw his dashboard splash red. His reaction was so fast he didn't feel the burn of the bullet piercing his shoulder; he rammed the truck into reverse, and swerved out of his driveway. His attacker fired as fast as his fingers would allow, blasting the passenger side glass and door panel. One bullet caught Al in his thigh while the rest peppered his seat and dashboard.

Umitz ceased firing as the pickup raced down the street. He alerted his men, and leaped over the front of the house, rappelling to the grass. In mid-stride, he unbuckled his harness, and climbed into the open door of the Benz.

Campo knew he was hit, but how severely he was wounded, he left to the remote corners of his mind. The wounds were painless and unimportant; the instinct to react and escape took over. Adrenaline sheered through corpuscles, expanding their diameter, bringing power to his brain. Al raced down the street, and was met by the crackling sound of an M6 submachine gun, its bullets drilling through his windshield. He ducked his body on the seat behind the protection of the motor, and thrust his foot on the gas pedal. He heard a thud as the gunfire stopped, and Al looked up through the shattered glass to see the body of his attacker thump over the hood; his head thudded on the roof, splattering red and cream-colored ooze on the pane. The cadaver flipped into the air, making a belly landing on the concrete street. Campo sat up straight, squinting out at the distorted view. He spun the steering wheel, and headed up Seventy-Seventh Street. He reasoned the last shooter wasn't the first, and figured another onslaught was coming his way. Without warning it came. A barrage riddled the side panel of the Ford, and luckily missed rubber. He lost control briefly, and sideswiped several cars, tearing off side-view mirrors like twigs off winter branches. He looked back and saw a silver Mercedes careen around the corner. Two faces were visible. The driver's was stern and rigid, clinging to the wheelwith both hands, while the passenger was screaming and firing erratically out the side window with an automatic weapon. The bullets sprayed the air around Campo's truck as he violently wrenched the steering wheel in a sweeping motion. Al knew he didn't stand a chance at outrunning the faster foreign car. His knowledge of the city roads, and meandering side alleys were at best a slim gamble to help him escape, and live another day. He turned right, then right again into the crisscrossing streets in the outskirts of Philadelphia. Darkness was drawing nearer and he hoped to lose his attackersin a confusing sequence of twists and turns.

Campo heard the now familiar clatter of gunfire; once again he swerved back and forth, and then turned sharply left. It was then he noticed his pant leg and seat were drenched with blood, and suddenly a sharp pain throbbed in his shoulder. He reached his left arm over to the exit wound above the collarbone feeling ripped flesh through the shirt. His entire front was stained a dark crimson. Slight panic crept up on him—if he didn't stop the blood from seeping out, soon he was going to pass out and die while driving. Knowing now time was short, he decided to make a move to a long stretch of roadway called Lansdowne Avenue. Lined with rail tracks, the street had a continual flow of trolley cars. These were the same cars he would curse in the mornings on the way to work. Inevitably, whenever he was running late, he would find himself stuck behind one stopping on every corner, but now they might very well save his life.Al sped down the narrow street, and blew past red lights with his hand depressing the horn, barely escaping collisions at every intersection. His pursuer for the moment ceased firing, but continued on his tail, quickly gaining on the straightaway. Then he came up on Forty-SecondStreet, and sure enough—two trolley cars were traveling in opposite directions. Al lurched the pickup into oncoming traffic speeding to the Forty-Second Street trolley stop and squeezed between the two massive transit cars, one heading east, and one heading west. As Al burst through, the driver of the Benz attempted breezing through the same seam, but a split-second too late. The luxury car was designed to absorb an impact, sparing the passengers the hard thrust of a collision, but the moving trolleys, weighing in at roughly forty thousand pounds each caught the Benz at an angle, and crunched it at its mid-section. The trolleys continued moving, causing a horrid sound of twisting metal, exploding tires—and for a moment, the cries of the two men being crushed in a tomb of German machinery.

Campo continued for another mile, leaving the macabre scene behind for the police to sort out. Daylight turned to dusk as he pulled over into an abandoned gas station in West Philly. The darkness and the fact that he could see no one else chasing after him, allowed him to feel safe enough to tend to the new holes in his body. He unbuckled his belt, and tightened it around his upper thigh. He winced as the seeping fluid slowed for amoment. The wound in his shoulder seemed to subside and clot a bit; his shirt was stuck to his torn skin. He searched around the cab of his truck, looking for a rag or something. He reached under his seat and felt the hard metal case he had found in the couch. He cursed himself, knowing his new condition was due to that stupid box with the radiation markings. Then he bent over onto the bench seat to look under the passenger side, and he felt his shoulder wound tear from his shirt. Blood seeped onto the seat and he fought back the pain when his hand felt a clump of old napkins. He pushed himself up, jammed the napkins under his shirt, and pressed hard. He needed medical assistance, and soon. A hospital was out of the question. He reasoned his would-be assassins would have to report back after his demise, and when they failed to do so, they would most assuredly check every emergency room in the area. Where could he go? He took for granted they knew every relation, every co-worker of his, and to compromise their safety for his own life was unacceptable.

Al scanned his memory for old safe houses, but he hadn't needed such hiding places in more than ten years, and in fact, who had he even been in contact with from the old days anyway? No one. He didn't know where he could go. He drove without direction, and leaned his weight on the steering wheel. The only feeling he had in his leg was pain from the tightening of the leather strap. He was forced to use his left foot to control the pedals and his right arm dropped to his side. He nearly gave up. He was so weary and tired, his mind grew lethargic.

"Snap out of it," he commanded himself. "Think hard—if you want to live."

Suddenly, it struck him, a place from his distant past, a past long forgotten by his inner self. No one, not even his closest friends, would know where to find him. He pressed on the pedal with renewed confidence and headed east toward Camden, New Jersey. Now if he could just manage to stay alive until he got there.

CHAPTER SEVENTEEN

Deep puddles of blood welled together, running this way and that as the movement of the vehicle swayed the pools of blood on the vinyl-coated floor. Al's pant leg and seat were saturated, as well as his T-shirt. Unable to stop the bleeding, he was only barely able to keep it from gushing out. The truck swerved at times, and he continued to blink his eyes in an attempt to warn off the inevitable faint that was creeping closer.

After he lost his attackers, he made his way through West Philadelphia into Center City, crossing over the Benjamin Franklin Bridge into Camden, New Jersey. The darkness was complete, and the bridge was lit up by bright spotlights, their light shining on the blue-painted support towers. Al concentrated on the lights. Their glow helped him to realize his life was hanging in the balance, and the light at the end of the tunnel could either be safety, or the grim reaper coming to collect.

He exited onto Route 676 and looked for the Kaighn's Boulevard off-ramp. He was headed for an old friend's house—old was the key here, both because his friend was probably in his late seventies by now, and because Al hadn't seen him in twenty years.

His name was Gerald Thomson, the Reverend Gerald Thomson. The reverend had, in many ways, saved Campo's life. At age seventeen, Al had been involved in a terrible auto accident. He had been driving, and his close friend had died. Campo fell into a deep despair while in recovery at Cooper Hospital in Camden. The doctors knew depression was halting the healing process, and the reverend happened to be in an adjacent room, consoling a member of his church. Al's doctors asked if he would go to him and see if he could help.

Gerald walked into the pale white room, and saw the boy lying with his back propped against the backrest of the bed. His face wore a look of gloom, and he stared blankly at a television screen mounted on the wall. The boy's eyes were red, his face bruised not from injury but disheartenment. There were no intravenous tubes entering his arms, only a cast preventing movement. A tray of food sat untouched, a straw poking from a carton of orange juice.

"Hello, young man, I'm Reverend Thomson." Thomson was a stocky black man with stick legs. He weighed 180, but he looked heavier. He wore black trousers and a shirt with a clerical collar. His face was round and smooth. His kindness shone through tender dark eyes. He sat down on the lone chair in front of the fallen soul. "The doctors asked me to come in and sit for a while, is that OK?" In response, he saw anguish and sorrow in the downcast countenance of the teenager. "Well, I guess I'll just sit a while," the reverend said. "I've been on my feet all day, preaching sermons, walking to homes of the elderly folks who are too weak to make it to the church. Then there's those of them in the hospital." Gerald looked at Al, then looked out the window at a clear blue sky and continued. "Most have lost hope—but when they see me come in, it brings a smile to their faces. We sit and pray for forgiveness of our sins, talk of better times, and of Jesus. Although they have lost their ability to attend my church, faith holds a special place in their hearts."

"You said you've been on your feet all day?"

Gerald looked back at the boy, whose lips were barely moving. "What's that, son?" Gerald said, as he leaned in to hear the boy.

"You just said you were on your feet all day," the boy repeated.

"That's correct," the preacher said.

"Then you said you sat and prayed with the people in this hospital," the boy said and he glanced over for a moment.

"I did, didn't I? Well, I guess what I meant is I wanted an excuse to sit and talk with you," Reverend Thomson said. He leaned back in his chair and rested his hands on his knees.

"Why?" the boy asked. He tilted his head forward and looked Gerald in the eye.

"If you could see your face in a mirror, you would know why," the priest said, resting his elbows on his knees.

The boy frowned, as tears welled up and his lip quivered. He struggled to hold back his emotions.

"What's wrong, son?"

Using his free hand, the young boy rubbed the tears running down his black and blue cheeks, "I'm still alive," he said. No longer having the strength to hold them back, he let the tears fall. "I don't deserve to be." Crying heavily, at the weight of death on his inexperienced shoulders. He could only feel bitterness at having been the one to have survived.

The reverend rose up and moved to the bedside, resting his wide palm on the boy's head as tenderly as a mother would hold a child to her bosom. He sat on the edge of the mattress, slung a comforting arm around him, and let him cry out the pain. The boy sobbed into his shirt.

"It's not your fault, son," Gerald said, looking out the window to the blue sky, and he hugged him gently. "You're alive not by crime or fault, but for a reason. In life, we travel many paths. Some are chosen by us, or by the ones around us. Then there are times when the road we take is chosen for us, without our own influence. It is in those times when we must trust in the Lord—for he watches and guides us through spirit, and in him we find the strength to overcome the choices, and many roads we take on the way to sit with the Almighty. You see, son, all lives must come to Him, for he granted us life, and has explained the way from birth to gain His favor, and when He is in need of angels, He grants passage to the souls most in need of His good graces. Your friend is being comforted by the hand of the Lord, as my hands console you at this time of need. Be strong, son, and have faith in the Lord, that He will guide you through your life on the way to His arms."

The young Al Campo's prayers for reformation were initiated within the reverend's consoling hug. His new mentor taught him to forgive himself as he would others, to spend time healing—not hurting, to believe in his friend's ascension into paradise, and to trust that he was not hurting. Words of wisdom had never before sunk into his soul as they did in that hospital bed. After that visit he became mentally healthier, and was released from the hospital.

From that day on, Campo returned each week, and sat at the front of the church listening to his friend. After mass he would go to the reverend's home, and they created a lasting friendship. It had been nearly thirty years since they first met in that hospital, and Campo's life had taken many roads and paths on his own. Now once again by the path chosen for him, he needed the reverend's consoling arm on his wounded shoulder. Years had passed when Campo did not write his friend, and even since he had been back in the area, he hadn't called or contacted him. There were many reasons, though Al felt his old friend would understand without any hesitation.

Campo was becoming weaker. The blood loss was taking its toll on his muscles, and his brain was shadowy with memories. He needed to find the reverend and fast. Where was the home of his old friend? The times had changed the city of Camden. Kaighn's Boulevard was a nasty place during the daytime, and darkness brought out the vilest; drug dealers, prostitutes, and gang members roamed the street. Burned out buildings and crack houses lined the pavement. He knew he couldn't knock on the wrong door, or it could be fatal. He passed the Zion Baptist Church, Gerald's house of worship, and the only landmark Campo was sure of. Vaguely, he remembered where to turn from the walks they had taken after service, but so many years had passed. Too weak to hold his right arm up any more, it hung past his knee as he hunched over the steering wheel. Pain was no longer a factor in his right leg, and his left leg was shooting pins and needles. He was barely controlling both pedals.

Al's eyes blurred at times, and he looked for a familiar street sign to jog his memory. Most of the signs were torn down by vandals, so he prayed for a miracle. Something familiar caught his vision; it was a dented, blue mailbox on the corner, and the streetlight above illuminated it enough for Al to see that one leg was bent.

"That's the street," Al said, renewing his effort.

Turning down the road, Al saw row homes lining either side; they were unkempt, and run down. Abandoned cars lined the two-way street. Campo remembered it never quite looked like this. Reverend Thomson and he always entered the home from the back alley. Campo was uncertain which front door it was, so he drove around back. Scarcely conscious as he slowly crept his shot-up Ford truck past the houses, he desperately hung on, hoping to see a familiar sign. Ahead was a concrete deck with a steel railing surrounding it. That's the house, he thought. It has to be. Campo had more desperation than confidence, but if he didn't receive medical assistance soon, he would die. He pushed on the brake as hard as his numb foot would allow. It wasn't enough, and the truck rolled and bounced to a stop against one of the steel supports of the deck, causing a bell to sound. He was already leaning his full weight on the steering wheel, so he wasn't jolted into another injury. He opened the door, and gravity took hold and he crashed to the pavement. Unable to bend his wounded leg, he dragged himself to the back door. With his last bit of energy, he pulled his body up to use the knob. He propelled his arm like a sling and rapped on the glass. Too tired to do it again, he let his hand fall to his side. What seemed like an hour to Al was only a minute before he heard the door unlock. Through desolate eyes, Campo saw a black man standing before him, a round face with a red Phillies cap on. The man was too young to be his friend, and he gave one last conscious breath.

"Is…is this…the rev…erend's house?" he asked and fell to the ground, then faded out.

CHAPTER EIGHTEEN

Republic of Georgia

Premier Andropov stood in the center of a teardrop-shaped clearing surrounded by a zigzag pattern of boxwood trees. He looked back at the capitol building's rounded frontage. Behind it, rising high above the capital city of Tbilisi, the Caucasus Mountains glowed in the bright sun. Their snowcaps melted, and water flowed, sparkling down into the nearby Kura River. His city teetered on the verge of breaking out into the world, looming with power hidden inside the missile silos left by the collapse of communism. Although his citizens sought no such rise to power, they were still reeling from the after-effects of the collapse of the USSR, more than twenty-five years beyond its passing. His bulky stomach acted as a cantilever as he arched his back, compensating for the girth. He wore a yellow-collared shirt and blue trousers, and stood with his arms at his side. He pulled a handkerchief from his back pocket, and wiped the moisture from his brow. Then another guest entered the area from within the boxwood bushes, and walked directly to Andropov. They had other plans in store for their country's future.

"Hello, Valissi. It is good to see you again," Andropov said.

"Good day to you, Premier Andropov," Valissi said, saluting his superior and clicking his heels and bowing slightly. He wore his standard tailored business suit. Only today he regretted his choice because the sun seemed to cook him where he stood.

"Valissi, we are friends—a salute is not necessary," Andropov said, extending his hand.

Valissi smiled, and shook the firm grip of the large premier. Valissi felt miniscule compared to the premier like a Beagle standing next to a Mastif. He always remembered, when he was a little boy in Moscow, watching the 1960 Olympic Games, when Andropov was a member of the Soviet wrestling team. How he had dreamed of one day becoming an Olympic hero like Andropov. Ever since Andropov's rise to power, Valissi strived to be his companion. Andropov promised a healthy political career, and took Valissi along for the ride. Before the demise of communism in Russia, Andropov was granted a position as premier of the Georgian Soviet Socialist Republic. After its fall, he retained his title, and his power over the new republic. Soon after the fall of the USSR, a group of men, including Andropov, discovered a hearty diamond mine. They kept it a secret, obtained massive personal wealth, and funneled only a small portion to the country. They had larger plans for Georgia, and in four days those plans would be set in motion.

"Walk with me, my friend, through the garden," Andropov said. "I fear my cabinet suspects I am mistreating our country, and their ears are pinned to the walls of the Capitol building."

Valissi nodded, and the two walked side-by-side through the tall boxwood maze. Valissi kept his arms folded behind his back, and his superior continually wiped his perspiration.

"Sir," Valissi said. "As I've told you in our communications, after the assassination of the president of Turkey, a link between the assassin and Karuza was made. I spoke with Karuza, and he contemptuously mocked your disapproval of the killing."

"I expected as much from the Arab," Andropov said, nodding his large head. "He must retain the illusion of power among his followers. He will begin his reign on my terms; he knows where he stands. The ordering of the execution gave him a taste of power, and your words will sink deep into his mind."

"Yes, but I do not trust him. He allowed a foolish mistake so near the deadline to Operation Slaughter. The attention he is creating may cause a delay."

"Nonsense," Andropov snapped. "Slaughter will continue as planned. Karuza is very shrewd; this recent happening will focus on him, leaving his operatives well concealed. The world will be watching Turkey, waiting for Karuza to make a coupattempt. Meanwhile, the leaders of the Middle East will still make their public appearances as scheduled. After Slaughter has commenced, the caliph will have been watched so closely there will be no way to implicate him. Then, gaining support from all of the Arab nations, Karuza will sympathize with their needs, and he will become ruler of the Nation of Believers, whatever that means. I don't care." Andropov paused and gazed upward, looking at the brilliant mountains shadowing his country. "You see these mountains, Valissi? Our ancestors thought of them as protection, yet throughout history invaders like the Arabs, Mongols, Persians, and Turks traversed the rocks, and sacked our city. Now when our Georgian army seizes control of the OPEC oil supply, these mountains will be our pedestals. Through Karuza's new power, we will hold the most powerful nations in our hands. When the United States joins us, the world will come to know Georgia as the only superpower in the world. First we choke the oil supply, causing massive price increases, and then we hold the world for ransom."

"What are you saying, sir? The United States will never agree to such aggressive tactics, and why would they join us against the world?" Valissi became nervous, and slowed his pace, looking at the premier.

"When the new president is sworn in, he will stand behind all our decisions, wanting world peace, not World War three. I have that guarantee," Andropov said with a convincing smile. He walked a little faster now, passing by a hibiscus bush that was trimmed with yellow flowers.

"Sir, with respect, President Worthington has three more years left inhis term," Valissi said, with a tinge of doubt toward his superior. He was almost walking sideways, keeping his eyes trained on the premier.

The pair turned down another path. The boxwood bushes were higher here, and the ground was made of fine red gravel. "Valissi, my friend, there are plans outside of your knowledge. Worthington will be assassinated at the start of Operation Slaughter, and the vice-president will be sworn in that same day."

Valissi stopped his movements, and peered up at the sweating leader. "Sir!" he said, and stared at the face of the former wrestler; serious, flat eyes communicated a foreboding confidence, reassuring Valissi that he was in the presence of a genius at work. "So Vice-President Carel Vincent will take over?"

"Yes. Mr. Vincent is my pawn," Andropov said. He pulled out a pack of cigarettes and offered them to Valissi, who took one.

"But how,when?" Valissi said, and produced a lighter and litthe premier's first, then his own.

"He is an American capitalist," Andropov said between puffs. "It is easy when you use money—along with the promise of the most powerful seat in the world. Of course, his power will be guided through the premier of Georgia, or he will be removed."

"What of the people in the USA?" The former KGB agent stated, wondering how much more he hadn't been told. "How will they be controlled? You cannot believe they will sit still and watch their government follow a foreign rule. They are a Christian country, and they will notice the change—and change is not good in their eyes,"

"Valissi, we have many operatives working in the US, swaying influences, and gaining power," the big premier said. He adjusted his pants around his round belly, then unfolded his handkerchief, re-folded it with a fresh side facing out, and rubbed his forehead with it. "The Believers gather in Washington, and millions more are on the move. They leave their jobs and await the coming of the Prophet. While we supply funds to them, they cannot deny our rule. Once Vincent is in control, he will use their power of numbers to influence Congress to grant the president authority to confront Karuza head on, and make a deal securing the United States' future oil supply. Only it shall not be based on money. Karuza will demand the president and the US remain neutral as we swallow the Middle East and Europe, along with dismissing all foreign aid to Russia, its former republics, and all the countries in the east."

"Then you have no intention of using Georgia's nuclear weapons as a bargaining chip." Valissi said and crushed his cigarette out in the gravel.

"I did not say that, Valissi," Andropov said and tossed his smoke into the bushes. "When Europe is in our grasp, Russia's economy will disintegrate, leaving them an easy mark. We will control all of the weapons in the Eastern hemisphere—then we shall threaten the Americans with destruction, unless they surrender to Georgian rule."

CHAPTER NINETEEN

Cold and dead was how most people would describe the contents of the black coffee mug on the desk, all but hidden amid the piles of papers and files. Herman Seller lifted the cup to his lips, completely absorbed in examining the translated letter found by his friend, Al Campo. He took a long sip; his eyes behind the rims of his bifocals did not waver from the page, as the sludge ran down his throat as easily as if it were a fresh cup. Seller jotted down various notes to himself on scraps of paper torn from useless documents. What he found in the letter fascinated him, and he thought he should call his friend to inform him of his findings. He dialed the number Campo had left. Waiting patiently, he listened to the fourth ring. Then Al's voice instructed him to leave a message.

"Yes, yes, Mr. Campo, this is Herman Seller from the university but of course, of course you already know that. So I was reading the translation of the letter you discovered, it is very interesting, very interesting indeed. You see it is a handwritten letter from France, in which the king's physician asks Benjamin Franklin specifically to investigate the strange happenings regarding a certain gold box. The box was described in detail. I'm assuming the letter came before the gold box, so Benjamin would know what to investigate. It seems to refer directly to our gold box. You see, the doctor was called to tend to the king's young son, the Dauphin; the boy was in shock and continually babbled on about seeing a ghost. He was found in the king's bedroom, where supposedly he and another young boy, the son of visiting royalty from Africa, were at play.

"The young prince was hiding behind the curtains, crouching on his knees, mumbling about the great ghost that had attacked them. The first members of the royal family to arrive on the scene asked what had happened to the young prince from Africa, but little Louie just continued his ramblings. Apparently the visitor was never found, except for his beaded necklace and his loincloth. The last paragraph stated how, after some recovery time, the Dauphin admitted they were playing with the gold box, and that was where the ghost had appeared from."

Herman paused, looking at the letter. Something new caught his eye, each time Seller read the paper, another fact jumped out at him, but this time it was a revelation.

"Mr. Campo, I feel I've discovered something interesting, yes, yes—very interesting. I will call you back with new developments."

Herman hung up the phone, and gathered his notes, along with the translationof the French letter. Then he grabbed the letter written by Dixon Hancock, and placing all the documents carefully into a folder, he exited his archival domain, heading toward the University of Pennsylvania's main library.Stepping through the aluminum doors of the modern brick and stone building, Herman glanced about the room, always amazed at the luxuries he had to do without. There was a state-of-the-art computer system containing every file, book, magazine, or index card that had ever passed through the nation's Library of Congress, along with countless publications of the university's private collections. Despite Herman's environment in the basement of the old library, and the lack of a modern computer system at his disposal—or even a washroom on the same floor as his work area, Seller was content with his position at the school. Forty-some years ago, Herman had beena *somebody* here at Penn. He was one of the top professors in History and Archaeology, having been involved in some expeditions with the world-renowned University Museum of Archaeology's team of experts. His research contributed to the deciphering of more than a thousand different symbols and alphabets from inscriptions around the globe. Articles of his work could be found in three issues of the National Geographic Magazine. The last article involving Seller also showed a photograph of him standing beside a newly uncovered sarcophagus found in Thebes. Many days and nights Herman spent in his library pondering those days inthe past, out in the field where the action was. These days, his mind drifted more often—due to alack of work sent his way. All of it was due to his limited computer experience, poor vision, and his knack for repeating himself to the point of losing his thoughts. Therefore his days of traipsing in and out of underground tombs were over. The only stimulation challenging his wits now were the rare projects and artifacts brought in by his friend Al Campo, and of course, his memories of past glory.

Herman walked past several computer desks lining the wall on his right. To the left were large desks where students gathered in silent study. Behind them were volumes of the most commonly used reference books, arranged on shelves stacked floor to ceiling. He looked above at the second and third floor balconies circling the room. They also had their share of texts neatly stacked in order of author. Seller marveled at how the world traveled so fast, passing him by like a tornado, sucking away everything he knew as real, and replacing it with science, moving at the speed of light. Einstein was correct in his theory that when someone travels at the speed of light, he transcends time, arriving in the future un-aged. Only in Herman's case, the motion occurred in his mind, causing him to age in what seemed like seconds, while arriving in the future. He stepped up to a rounded console in the middle of the room closed off on either side, only permitting library staff beyond. A middle-aged woman, not completely unattractive, sat peering at a computer screen. She had long, straight black hair; her body was thin, yet not well shaped, not like a statue, but straight and narrow. She glanced at the hunched-over Seller, and, showing her kind smile, she approached the counter.

"Hello, Mr. Seller, how are you today?" she asked, leaning on the desktop, folding her arms, her voice bright and bubbly.

"Hello, hello, Margaret, I'm fine, thank you," Herman said, knowing Margaret had a tendency to jabber on unrelated topics, causing Seller to forget his original intentions. Many times he found himself leaving the library without what he'd come in search of.

"That's good to hear, Herman. What can I do for you today? More text containing non-translated Egyptian script for you to work on?"

"No, no, not today," Herman said setting down his folders. "What I need is all the microfilm you have from the eighteenth century of the Pennsylvania Gazette, specifically the latter part of the era."

"Oh, I see! You're getting more up-to-date with your research," she said, not attempting to access the information on the computer.

"Yes, yes, that's right…" Seller said, but he was cut off.

"I'm very glad to hear that," Margaret said. "Because I was beginning to grow tired searching through countless computer screens, staring at mummies and statues in search of those writings…"

"Yes, yes, that's very good to hear," Herman interrupted. "But you see, I'm in a bit of a hurry, so please may we continue this conversation tomorrow."

"Why of course, Professor, right away," Margaret was slightly annoyed as she began punching the keypad, and Seller could see it in her face. The archivist made a mental note to himself to send her some flowers later, and apologize.

The computer's hard drive responded, and a dozen access numbers appeared, glowing in the librarian's face. "Which one do you want professor? I'm only permitted to acquire one roll at a time. Month and year separate them. For instance, I have a roll dating from 3 March 1772 to 30 December 1772."

"Oh, I see," Herman replied, puzzled. "Let me check." He opened the manila folder on the desk, and located the letter written by Dixon Hancock; at the top was the date: 3July 1776. "I would like the month of July in the year 1776, please."

Margaret fed the date in, and within seconds the printer under the counter sprang into action, producing a copy of a receipt. "One moment, Professor, I'll be right back." She disappeared into the back room, and returned flipping the disc in the air. "This is dated

3 January to 31 August 1776. The file has it labeled incomplete, but I hope it has what you need."

"Yes, yes, let's hope so. Thank you very much, Margaret."

"Could you sign here, Professor?"

After scribbling his name, Herman sat at the first screen by the door. He began scanning the contents page by page. Time passed slowly. Hour after grueling hour he agonized over the small print. His vision was poor to begin with, and the script writing of the age was blurry, and it seemed to run together. Five hours and nine months of newspaper headlines later, he leaned back in the hard wooden chair and rubbed his eyes beneath his glasses. Margaret must have taken notice of the professor's anguish, and in her effortless kindness brought him a fresh can of soda from the vending machine. Seller thanked her, and gulped down the bubbles to relieve his parched throat.

Herman needed to view the entire film from start to finish because the paper clippings were not in any order. His body ached. His fingers cracked with stress, and his eyes were about to give up on him when his blinking eyes lit on a familiar word. Squinting hard, blinking several times, and rubbing out the dryness, he resumed his scan.

"Yes…yes, there it is," he said. "Jones. Harold Jones!" He read it again. The name appeared in segments of two pieces of torn paper pasted together; they referred to an article on another page. Speedily he referenced the page and there it was—a small column with the caption, "Watchman Harold Jones awarded medal for bravery."

Herman read the entire clipping, not very lengthy, but what he needed was there. It stated how Harold Jones had been born in England, and his mother was Beatrice Agnes Jones. His father had been royalty, not British royalty but of African blood. Beatrice was briefly engaged in an affair with the emissary for the Egyptian emperor while he was on a tour of the European nations. Beatrice never let anyone know of her shame, having a child out of wedlock, and his father remained a secret until her death, when Harold divulged his true father to the people of the New World. To his surprise, the officials gladly allowed him to remain a watchman, due to his mother's devotion to the cause of independence. He became a loyal colonist, and the medal was his third in two years.

"Egyptian," Herman said. "There it is, yes, yes, there it is." He learned back in his chair, emotions bordering on horror and ecstasy. To any rational person this would sound crazy at best. After jotting down the microfilm catalogue number, and the exact area of the article, he printed out a copy, and returned the film to Margaret. "Thank you, my dear," he said, handing back the film.

"Any time, Professor. Did you find what you were looking for?"

"Yes, yes, I did. Thank you for asking." *Flowers, don't forget the flowers*, Herman reminded himself.

The professor returned to his basement domain. He was excited but nervous. His explanation couldn't be verified without more research, but he wanted to look up one other thing. He set down the files and rummaged in the corner of the room. He found a decrepit text of the Old Testament. It was a large volume, and he needed both hands to lift it. The book's hard cover was a dreary brown color, the edges were frayed, and the binding was separating. He flopped it open and leafed through the dry pages. He came to the book of Exodus, and found 12:12. He read aloud, "I will come down this night, and I will smite all the first born of Egypt. I will execute judgment. I am the Lord."

CHAPTER TWENTY

A middle-aged man entered through arched doors, carrying a silver tray in front of him. He stared down at the pot of Turkish tea and cups on the tray. He hung his head, apparently to protect his eyes from the glare, but his real intention was to avoid being photographed by the cameras dangling from the ceiling. Yoseph was here for a reason other than to serve tea. Without looking up, he knew every inch of the room. He strode around a table made of teak, shaped in an oval the size of an automobile, resting in the center of the room. He passed ancient marble columns circling the room, as arched windows separated the stone supporting the concave ceiling above the pale, white floor. The sun was low, and its rays splayed, brightening the snow-white room with gold beams. He looked down at the red seats of eighteen high-back padded chairs surrounding the table. He set an empty cup in front of each. On the far side, a lone chair stood out, facing away from the sun, embroidered with gold ribbon, and with bronze armrests. He knew this to be Karuza's seat. Yoseph placed Karuza's cup last, and then he turned to face the window, rising high to the ceiling. Across the street, a modern office building was several stories higher than the temple. He placed himself directly between the chair and rooftop. He looked from the backrest to roof, again and again, repeating the motion, studying the distance, and deducing an angle of fire. Footsteps rang through the hall. He heard them approaching, and quickly poured tea into each cup. He finished his duty, and passed the entering group without attracting attention.

Fifteen men entered single-file, all wearing desert-tan fatigues, black military boots, and tan berets on their heads. Sitting down, they all sat stiffly, hands folded on their laps. Nearly identical in appearance, they all had the same dark hair and thick eyebrows. Some men had full mustaches, the rest were beginning to grow them, and they were all between the ages of twenty-five and thirty-five.

Moments later Karuza walked in, flanked by the ever-present Sabu on his left and Ammar to his right, who was carrying a silver briefcase. The three rounded the table silently. Sabu slid Karuza's chair back as his leader sat, then seated himself—glancing proudly at the troop of men he had assembled. Ammar placed the case on the table, spun the dial to the combination, opened it, and produced manila folders. He handed them over to Sabu. Coolly the butcher walked around the table, placing a folder in front of each man. The folders had no markings on them, and they were sealed with edge banding, guaranteeing their security.His Holiness sat, relaxed, in his chair, watching the eyes of each man looking down at his respective packet. All the men were handpicked by Sabu. Not all were Turkish; several were Iranians, along with Iraqis, a Syrian, and a Saudi. Karuza felt confident of the loyalty of the men before him; he could see his destiny in their eyes. Each man considered it a privilege to sit at his table, and would gladly die for His Holiness. He secretly envied their valor, for Karuza feared death—the possibility he might not see his vision become reality was too much to bear. Never had the caliph knowingly put himself in harm's way. Since his rise to caliph began, Sabu had been his personal bodyguard, as well as hiring hundreds of others to protect him. After the last folder was laid down, Sabu sat, his posture perfect, hands clasped. He looked to Karuza, who sipped the tea, then placed the cup down, and addressed the ensemble.

"Gentlemen, you have all been granted a great gift by the grace of Allah. In my waking hours of the day, Allah appeared to me in my meditation, and gave me sight of you fifteen loyal Believers. Your faith and devotion to the return of the Prophet, Allah, and myself has been unmatched by all else in the world." As Karuza spoke, he looked upward, palms facing out, praising Allah. Then he gazed at each one and continued. "You are all to become my sword; you will begin the preparations for the Prophet's return. The events I have described to the masses, you shall bring into reality."

The fifteen sat tall in their chairs, drawing energy from Karuza's ebullience. He knew they were all prepared to die for their caliph, although they would prefer to live to experience the reign of justice he promised. None would utter words describing their pleasure—no one.

"Each of you," the caliph continued, "has in your possession your individual obligations to our cause. Do not open them yet— they are for your eyes only, and while Sabu, Ammar, and I know the contents of the files you hold, we will not know which man has which operation. Your task, gentlemen, will be to eliminate from power the leaders of the insolent countries preventing the return of the Prophet: Morocco, Iraq, Algeria, Tunisia, Libya, Egypt, Sudan, Israel, Turkey, Lebanon, Saudi Arabia, Kuwait, Yemen, Iran, Afghanistan, and Pakistan."

There were rumblings around the table. Sabu slapped his hand down on the hard wood, quieting the men as Karuza went on. "Simultaneously," Karuza voice was stern as he continued. "They will fall due to unexplained illness. It is Allah's wish, and you fifteen devoted followers will be the hands that deliver their fate."

The group of men now sat quiet, but all were questioning themselves about how to accomplish such a massive assassination plot. Leaders of nations do not leave themselves open to random killers, or even premeditated assassins. In their faces, Karuza saw the question, and yet he did not answer them. The Butcher slowly rose from his seat, leaning his hands on the table; his glare met the eyes of each one of his team of assassins. Satisfaction emanated from his expression; he was pleased with his selections and was confident they would carry out their missions. He stood straight, then started circling the table, his hands folded behind his back.

"In each of your files," the Butcher said, "there is a ticket for transportation to your respective countries. Some of you will travel by plane, some by rail—or even taxi cab. And from this point on, you do not know each other. You may see one another on the bus, or pass in the street—do not communicate—do not speak. Alone, you will accomplish your task. When you arrive at your destination you will take residence in your rooms, which have been prepared for you near your target area. Money for your stay has also been supplied in the folders. You will remain secluded until the time of your mission." Sabu paused and continued striding mechanically around the table while Karuza sat silent, his eyes shut in prayer, and Ammar remained alert, watching every facial expressionof the trained professionals. Then Sabu spoke again. "Your targets will be in or around a predetermined area for the massive operation. Your caliph will make a moving speech, accusing the leaders of these countries of wrongdoings and treason against the Believers' mission. This will draw them out in the open if they are not already within range for the assault." He then stopped directly across from Karuza, standing with his legs spread at shoulder width, and hands behind his back. "Questions?" he barked out. Directly to his left a man raised his hand. "Yes? Armand, you may speak."

The man pushed his chair back, rose, and stood at attention. He saluted Sabu, bowed graciously to Karuza and Ammar. "Blessings and peace of Allah be upon you, your Holiness, and to you, the Divine Ammar." Then he turned to Sabu. "And to you, General Sabu, it is my greatest privilege to be assigned to your command once again, and granted the gift of such a noble mission. I am Major Armand Satchan, from Iraq."

"Your question, Major Satchan?" Sabu said.

"Sir," Armand said. He stared straight ahead, standing at attention. "His Divine Holiness mentioned these men were to die of an illness, and we were to be the hands to deliver the sickness. How may we properly plan in such a short time to poison our targets, and in the public eye? As you say, His Holiness will draw them out. I am willing, as are the rest of the men, to give our lives for Allah, but if we are discovered attempting to poison these men, eventually the governments will trace us back to here."

"You may stand at ease, Major Satchan," the Butcher said. "I remember you from Iraq. As I recall, you were given several medals for your dedication to accomplishing our ultimate objective."

Armand allowed a crooked smile under his bushy mustache. Sabu knew he was pleased to know he was remembered for his valor. The major stood relaxed as Sabu continued.

"There will be no need to poison your targets, or be within arm's reach of them. On the contrary, I expect you all to seek the protection of rooftops or the branches of trees, or the cover of a city bus. Concealment will be of the utmost importance. You are correct in thinking the government officials will become wise to our actions, so you must not be discovered!"

Again rumblings were heard, as the group of assassins turned their heads back and forth, looking in silent questioning at one another. Then their attention was grabbed by Sabu's growl.

"Gentleman! His Holiness is not demanding your lives, only that nothing may be linked to the caliph. Your mission is top secret from beginning to end. If you are discovered, you will take your cyanide pill, but we trust in your expertise. There should be no need for suicide. Allah has showed his light to our caliph, and success is promised. A new and revolutionary weapon will be sent to each of you on the day of the massive operation. It will allow you to inflict the proper death to each victim from a safe distance. Questions about this weapon are not permitted at this time. Upon delivery, instructions will be supplied—in code of course—along with your folders. Every situation has been anticipated and accounted for, giving you the perfect opportunity to kill the dogs who prevent the caliph from sitting as ruler."

Just then Sabu saw a reflection out the window above Karuza's head; his instincts thrust him forward, leaping onto the table, using the men's shoulders as rungs to climb. He charged at the caliph, screaming for him to move from the seat. Karuza was deep in prayer, and opened his eyes just as Ammar shoved him sideways. Then the barrage came; the window disintegrated as a hail of bullets crashed into Karuza's chair.

Sabu stood on the teak table facing the onslaught of blistering glass, drawing his twin German Luger handguns from his hips.

He fired, screaming like a madman. Sections of the hardwood exploded into splinters as the gunfire spread across the room, missing Sabu by inches. The fifteen assassins lurched in every direction, seeking cover as a new stream of bullets rained through an adjacent arched window, smashing through furniture everywhere. Men were scattering aimlessly while Sabu stood his ground, emptying his weapons. Armand alertly dove into the hall, and grabbed an AK-47 Russian machine gun from the guard outside the door; he tossed it to the general. The Butcher wielded the weapon like he was cradling a child, and fired at the rooftop of the building across the street until the attack ceased. Sabu was panting and grinning evilly, eyes wide in fury while sweat streamed down his face. His gaze showed an expression of mingled thrill and vengeance.

"Attack!" he screamed, "I want the heads of the perpetrators in my hands! Now! Head for the rooftop—and bring them back alive!" Amazingly, Sabu was unharmed, yet the table all around him looked like it was ready for the furnace. Of the fifteen men in the room, only minor flesh wounds were taken, and they all ran for the rooftop. The Butcher looked about the room. There was no sign of his caliph or Ammar. He leapt from the splintered remains, and found Karuza's fragmented chair. It was lying on its side. The posh backing was peppered with bullet holes, and white padding showed through. Sabu thrust it aside, and saw his caliph leaning against the marble pillar. Ammar was lying across his lap. Karuza's cousin and advisor was unconscious. A wound in hischest was gushing deep red blood. The caliph pressed his hands to the wound in an attempt to stop the flow. Veins were filled near to bursting in Karuza's eyes, and his forehead crinkled with anger. Sabu saw tears drip from his eyes.

"Your Holiness, are you harmed?" Sabu said, then turned to the men clustering behind him. "Get a doctor, you fools, now!" He took off his beret, and held it to the damaged torso. A crew of doctors rushed into the room immediately, tending to the unconscious body, pricking him with needles, and attacking the wound, temporarily stopping the blood. They rushed him out on a stretcher as the crowd all watched. Hatred and revenge filled their faces. No one knew then if Ammar would live or die.

CHAPTER TWENTY-ONE

General Morris Bartow strolled down the hallway on the southeast side of the Pentagon carrying a heavy packet. It was thick, and showed signs of wear. He gave his standard nods toward the staff as he passed them in the hall, one by one the men and women turned sideways to avoid a collision with the general's massive, lumbering body. General Morris Bartow was a large man, huge in fact. His height and mass were clearly remarkable. He wasn't obese, just plain large. He walked into his outer office where Alma, his Jamaican secretary, immediately handed him a clump of messages.

"Coffee, if you would, please, Alma," Bartow said as he entered his main office. He tossed the file onto his desk, and leafed through his messages. Three were from his wife, reminding him their son was due in from duty in Europe, and how important it was to be home early. The rest were various unimportant requests from lobbyists asking for his support for various military funding. He took the stack of papers, and dropped them in the wastebasket. He removed his medal-burdened jacket, and loosened his khaki-colored tie, unbuttoned his collar, and sat at his desk. Alma entered with the steaming cup of java, sat it on his desk, received a "Thank you," and left. Morris reached into his bottom drawer, and grabbed a half-empty bottle of Southern Comfort. He splashed some into the coffee, and took a quick swig from the bottle before returning it to its place. He leaned his heavy forearms on the edge of the desk, untied the string around the three-inch thick file, and opened it. The first page was a summary of the contents, which read in part: Classified military activity in the Middle East and Eastern Europe, 1980–1998. Special projects director, Colonel Morris Bartow USMC.

Bartow began reading through the file page by page; most of it was basic intelligence reports from various field agents during the time period. The general knew what he was looking for: the Butcher. When Sabu's name appeared, he knew then he would be in the right place. An hour rolled by and half the stack of papers was turned over before he glanced up at the wall clock in disbelief. He downed the rest of his coffee, and replaced it with straight Southern; he took another drink, and set the cup in its saucer. Upon turning the page, the name jumped out at him like a jack-in-the-box, from a decoded telegram sent in 1995.

MAJOR ALFONSE CANDALINI CRITICALLY WOUNDED STOP FOUND IN BAGHDAD STREET HANDS AND FEET BOUND STOP BEATEN AND TORTURED TO THE POINT OF DEATH DOCTORS SAY HE WONT LAST TWENTYFOUR HOURS STOPREQUEST WITHOUT DELAY RETALIATION AGAINST THE GUERRILLA FORCES LED BY SABU THE BUTCHER AND HAND THAT INFLICTED BEATING STOP

Morris recalled the telegram, and the difficult decision to refuse the request. Shortly after the incident, Bartow was promoted to general and sent back to the States, and the operation he was commanding given to his next in command. He was looking for more information though. He wanted more information from the period after he left, because he knew that after Saddam Hussein no longer had the resources to pay for his military might, Sabu the Butcher had been recruited by Ammar and Karuza. Bartow leaned back in his chair, his hand resting around the cup of whisky on his desk. He rolled his head, closing his eyes, searching his memory. His mind recalled reports of inhuman savagery and mayhem that Sabu unleashed on the helpless people of Kuwait. He was a ruthless murderer, and he used his power to recruit forces for Saddam's military might, but Saddam became impatient and, against Sabu's counsel, had forced an attack on Kuwait. Morris cringed at the thought that if Sabu had had more time to prepare—even a year more—the Gulf War might have had a different outcome. It had been more than twenty years since Sabu had been seen in public, and who knew how long he had been preparing for Karuza. The general sat there, dreading the worst, and knew it was time to take action. He knew that Karuza, with Sabu at his side, could only have death and dominance on his agenda. The general would have to drum up all possible resources, and take his findings to the advisory committee with the president.

Morris pressed his intercom. "Alma, I'm going to need you for some dictation."

"Yes, General," Alma replied, "but if you don't mind me saying so, your son arrived today, and your wife did call three times."

"Shit!" Morris mumbled. "You're right as always, Alma! We'll do it first thing in the morning. Come in early, so I can have it ready for my meeting with the committee."

"Yes, sir." Alma said. "Should I call your wife, and tell her you are on your way home?"

"That would be fine," Bartow closed the Top Secret file, and locked it in his top drawer. He finished his Southern Comfort, and headed home.

Black and white surveillance monitors gave the room a moonlit appearance; shadows mixed with flickers of light bounced across the ceiling and walls as they were set in motion. One man sat with his hands manipulating the various dials, joystick, and keypad changing the images on screens running six across and two high. John Dunn's face was thin and freckled; his eyes were set close together, floating over a flat nose. Blond hair projected outward in scraggy dreadlocks, and his face had a two-day growth of beard. Over the past twenty-four hours, with the exception of a few trips to the vending machines, this room and these screens had been his home.

Under the orders of Bracken Guttone, he scoured the tapes and collected every second of video from the hundred or so cameras that recorded every move of Al Campo, and his partner Stanley Barrett, while working in the Baroque plant. Normally Bracken was a fiend for neatness, and would never allow any employee to look as unkempt as Dunn did at this moment. But because he was so efficient, and the best computer wizard Bracken had ever met, he made an exception for him, and him alone. Finally Dunn was able to painstakingly install three hours of footage on one monitor, all in sequence from Campo's entry to the parking lot to his exit. He tapped the intercom, heard the dial tone, and punched four digits.

"Yes, Dunn?" Bracken said.

"Mr. Guttone, I have what you've asked for, ready to roll."

"On my way."

Moments later, the mighty head of security squeezed into the small monitoring chamber. John could smell the faint scent of his cologne. He realized that he must smell like a day-old cheesesteak, especially with the remnants of one from yesterday in the trash can next to his desk.

"Where would you like to start?" John asked with his hands poised over the controls.

"When they first arrived," Guttone said and closed the door.

It was what John had assumed, and he simply pushed the enter button. He saw the queer look on Guttone's face and knew it was the odor. He opened his desk drawer and rummaged for a stick of gum or mint, or even a scented glue stick, but came up empty. His boss would have to suffer for the moment.

Guttone stood squarely behind the video tech, his massive arms folded across his front and his ice-blue eyes concentrating on every move his quarry made. His body dwarfed the small surveillance room, or closet rather. There was barely enough space to stand behind Dunn's chair. With no windows, the lone door was closed on Guttone's right and ventilation was brought in through a vent above it. John, who normally did not mind his tight accommodations, felt claustrophobic, with the mass of muscle and bones towering above his shoulders.

"How long have you been in here?" Bracken said, not taking his eyes from the screen.

"I'd say about a day and a half," Dunn said. "I haven't left since you gave the order."

"Well, after this, leave, and take a bath. You stink," Bracken said, and he pulled out a box of breath mints. He tossed three in his mouth and studied the screen. Minute by minute the video played, and Bracken gazed intently as the screen jumped from one space to another, catching every motion of Campo and Barrett from the back, the side, front, and even overhead. The head of Jason Gull's security had every ounce of energy concentrated on picking out flaws in his opposite number. He knew he would find Al Campo one way or another, but time was passing, and a sense of urgency drove him forward.

In ten years of service to Jason Gull, he had never failed. Their partnership ran deep. Bracken's income reflected his ability to maintain security in and around the plant, along with personal security when Gull went abroad. Even though Guttone was not responsible for the lost plutonium, once Jason gave the assignment to him, he attacked the task as though his arm had been taken from his body, and he had to recover it. He was as reliable as the sunrise, and having his perfect record tarnished, by a blue-collar worker no less, was like an eclipse taking its time skirting the inevitable pass. He cringed at the thought of having his paycheck reflect this incident. The hours passed, and Dunn began squirming in his chair. The video was boring to him, having seen every frame a hundred times or more, and the shadow of his superior made him even more buggy. Guttone was quiet, and fixed his gaze on the screen. Then suddenly, he spoke.

"Stop right there," he ordered. Dunn nearly had a heart attack, lurching forward, smacking the pause button. Bracken took a good look. The screen displayed Campo talking with Domeni at her desk. Since the video had no audio hook-up, he had to guess what the two were saying. "Play that back slowly," Bracken ordered.

John moved his joystick for several seconds, and clicked a button on top of the instrument, frame by frame the images moved in slow motion; the angle was from above, and to the right of the two. Domeni was speaking, and then Al's lips also moved, Domeni wrote something on a small piece of paper, and handed it to Al.

"That's it. Stop." Bracken ordered. "Can you zoom in on the piece of paper she's handing to Campo?"

"Without even trying." The tech used his mouse to manipulate the zoom and focus, and gradually the note occupied the full screen. It looked like a million ants scattering around a dead cricket. "I can do better," Dunn said, anticipating Bracken's response. He tapped keys in an alternating sequence. With every depression the form's cloudy appearance mushroomed into focus.

Bracken felt like he was changing glasses at the optometrist until his vision was crystal clear. At last the wording was legible: 405 Inglewood Road, Ardmore, Fri. 7:30 610-555-1212

"Check our files. That must be Ms. Conti's home address. Apparently, Mr. Campo has a date with her Friday evening," Bracken said, pleased with the positive outcome of his search.

"Sir, pardon me for saying so, but if I recall, Mr. Campo went into hiding two days ago. Do you really think he'll come out into the open, and risk being caught?"

"Dunn, you know as well as I do every healthy man in the company has tried to get a date with Domeni, yourself included. All have come up with the same response, a pleasant, but stern no."

Dunn looked at the trailing video, watching Domeni, contemplating Bracken's words. "I guess you're right. I would risk a deal with the devil to go out with her just once."

"As would our prey, Mr. Campo." Guttone said and rubbed his chin. A broad smile spread across his face. "He has a date with a goddess, and we'll make it a first date to remember. Let's see, Friday is a day away. We still have time to catch up with his friend, Stanley Barrett."

CHAPTER TWENTY-TWO

Stanley Barrett pulled into the empty driveway, and pressed the garage door opener on the visor of his white Chevy pickup truck. He rolled into the vacant spot in the four-car garage next to a covered fifteen-foot Boston Whaler fishing boat. He stepped from the vehicle and glanced at the house. There was no sign of his four teenaged kids or his wife. Typical for this time in the afternoon. Most likely his wife was still at work, and the kids were out and about with friends. Stanley came home early after Al Campo was a no-show for the second straight day at the state hospital. He called his partner, leaving messages on both his house phone and his cell after yesterday's absence. Then he repeated the process this morning, asking him to call as soon as he got the message. Stanley never bothered to call their boss at the shop the day before, deciding to cover for Al, in case he wandered in late with a hangover. It wouldn't be the first time one of them had done it. This morning, Barrett became a bit worried about not hearing from his friend overnight, but never called the shop. He knew he would be able to accomplish more than half the quota for two men, which he did, then left early. Barrett's worries were valid, but without knowing what Al was up to, he didn't know how to find his friend. He had every confidence Al was OK. Maybe he had decided on a little R and R, confident Barrett would cover for him. Even if he didn't, Campo was the sort to tackle the heat from the boss just the same.

On the way home, Stanley had made the decision to take the boat out and do some fishing on the nearby Delaware River. An avid sportsman, Barrett fished in the spring, and all summer long, while in the winter he hunted the various wild game Pennsylvania had to offer. Even in the punishing heat, the sky was clear, and the breeze light; the river almost ached for him. He stepped to the boat, and rolled back the protective liner, displaying a pearl-white beauty of a boat. It had a center console, rear bench seating with a seventy-horsepower Mercury outboard motor mounted to the back. Barrett, unlike most boaters, meticulously cleaned, and scrubbed the entire outer surface after every outing. The boat looked like a showroom piece. Stanley often was reminded of an old joke about people who owned boats. "The two happiest days of their lives were the day they bought the boat, and the day they sold it." That wasn't the case with Stanley. He loved getting out on the water where he could enjoy life simplified. He grabbed one of his many freshwater fishing rods from a homemade bracket, snatched a tackle box, checking its contents, and placed them both in the Boston Whaler. He jumped into the truck, pulled out, and positioned it, doing his best to line up the trailer latch and tow pin. While getting out to connect the two, something made him look at his house. Through the living room's large picture window, he thought he saw some kind of movement. He jerked his head, looking once again, and half-expected one of his kids to come through the back door. Nothing happened, so he shrugged it off, deciding he must have seen the drapes being blown by the air-conditioner kicking on. He stood at the meeting point of the two vehicles, and saw the hitches lined up poorly. He removed the chocks keeping the boat trailer from rolling, and muscled the hitch over the ball, and secured the two vehicles together. The truck sank slightly as the full weight rested; busily he attached the electrical wires to connect the brake lights and turn signals on the rear of the trailer. He then washed his hands in the garage sink, and noticed the time, so he went over his mental checklist. Silently satisfied at his results, he started toward the house. Again the curtains moved, or was that what he thought it was. Faintly he heard the air-condensing unit running on the far side of the house.

Why am I so paranoid? he wondered. It was just another day, and the fish were waiting.

He walked toward the house to change out of his work clothes and into shorts and other regalia for the inevitably wet conditions. Stanley's house was a split-level. The back door opened to the basement floor, which was partially underground. Barrett had converted the large space into the main family room. Also on the same floor were the powder room and laundry, opposite the picture window. He entered, and casually looked about, seeing the curtains still, and no one home. He charged up the six steps three at a time into the main floor, where the kitchen, dining room, and formal living room were positioned in an L shape. Up six more steps were the bedrooms and a full bath. Then four additional steps led to his master bedroom. He returned in five minutes, dressed in blue bathing trunks, a white sleeveless T-shirt with a Boston Whaler boat pictured on it, and fitted, waterproof, non-slip rubber shoes. He stopped in the kitchen, grabbed a piece of leftover fried chicken, crunched it in his mouth, snatched a six-pack of Budweiser, and hit the last set of steps.

He didn't see it coming. As he reached the bottom he was met by a shock. Someone thrust the butt end of a shotgun into his stomach, blowing the chicken into the distance, and the beer flying upwards. His body plunged backwards, and he fell, hitting his head on the corner of the top step, knocking him out cold.

Dizzily he woke, to find himself being slapped into consciousness. Bleary-eyed, and with his head pounding, he was restrained by two men holding his arms outward, pressing down on his shoulders, forcing him to his knees. In front of him stood an immense figure, his heavy paw slapping his jaw until he finally worked up enough energy to speak.

"What the fuck is going on?" Stanley said, and the man stopped the abuse.

"Mr. Barrett, so good of you to join us," Bracken Guttone said calmly, as though he was at a high school reunion.

"Who are you, and what the hell are you doing in my house?" Barrett said and spit blood.

Bracken smiled. "It pains me that you don't remember me from our first meeting, or I should say the pain is yours." Guttone nodded to the two men restraining him, and they wrenched Barrett's arms, twisting them to a dreadful position. Stanley let out a horrible cry, and they relieved the pressure. Barrett's face took on a bewildered look as he recognized the giant.

"You're the asshole from the Baroque plant," he spat out.

"There we are, you do remember me!" Bracken settled himself into a soft recliner directly in front of his captive; he crossed his legs, and brushed his suit pants smooth. "Mr. Barrett, I care little for you and your family. I only want to know one thing, and if you provide me with the correct answer, this will all be over shortly."

"Fuck you, jerkoff. Ahhhhh!" Stanley screeched as the two goons wrenched his arms again, nearly tearing them off, or at least, that's what it felt like.

"That was not the answer I was hoping for," Guttone said as he folded his hands on his knees, making himself comfortable. "Although my friends here do seem to be enjoying your attitude. Please allow me to ask first, and then you may have an opportunity to respond. Where is Mr. Campo?"

Stanley gave a sideways glance at the two men holding him. They were both the size of linebackers, with broad shoulders and large hands. He knew fighting them would be impossible. And he couldn't let them think he knew anything. "Who the hell is Mr. Campo?" Stanley said and prepared himself for agony, and held in the grunt of torture. His head was whirling in pain, as his torturers crushed his bones together. He had to stall, and think of a way out. Memory became acute during times of stress. Barrett thought; all of his guns were locked in the gun cabinet on the third floor, and even if he were to escape from the hold the two men had on him, he would never make it that far. All his weapons, save one, were there. He had stashed a .22 caliber handgun, loaded with silent rounds, in the drop ceiling above the back door. His house was lucky enough to backup to thick forest, but he thought it was unlucky to have hundreds of squirrels and rabbits and possums and freaking raccoons rummaging in his trash, the grill, and any vegetables he tried to grow. Many mornings the animals would be causing havoc in his backyard, and he would race upstairs to the gun cabinet, but by the time he returned it was too late. So he took the liberty of hiding a weapon closer to the door, without his wife or kids knowing about it. His wife, if she knew, would scream at him for the idiocy of it all, and if the kids knew about it, they would more than likely take the gun out and shoot it at the wood pile or each other. He ended up with about twenty squirrels and a couple raccoons in the trashcan before they got wise enough to only come when he wasn't home. The .22 would be his only chance, but he couldn't remember how many bullets were left. It had been awhile since he used it.It was a better plan than any other he had managed to think of, but now he had to wrestle the goons off, and make it to the ceiling, just ten feet away…easy, right?

"Mr. Barrett" Bracken said, uncrossing his legs and leaning forward. "I'm not sure you realize the severity of my situation.You see, Mr. Campo has something of mine—and I need it back."

"Let me guess, you want the stinking couch he picked out of the trash," Stanley was only playing the game, never realizing how close to the mark he had just come. It was a mistake he couldn't have seen coming.

Brackens blue eyes flew open; it was the first promising event in the past forty-eight hours.

"So he told you of the couch?" the giant said smiling. "That's good news. Then you know where he is hiding it; tell me now, and this will all be over quickly."

Barrett figured that no matter what he said, they were going to kill him—and he wasn't about to go down without throwing a punch. The two goons were increasing the tension on his shoulders the longer he remained silent. The pain sliced into his back and neck as though he was being operated on without anesthesia. The men bent his arms backward until they were nearly touching at the elbows. Barrett held on, knowing they hadn't gotten any information from him yet, and hoping Guttone wouldn't let him pass out again. Stanley's flesh on his chest was stretched to tearing point, and he was about to give in and scream.

"Enough!" Bracken ordered. "Mr. Barrett, this is pointless, and I am in a bit of a hurry. I may have to leave Cal and Jim here to greet your family when they arrive home, if you're not more cooperative. Now, you wouldn't want that, would you?"

The pressure on Barrett's back was lessened, and he looked up at the man sitting in *his* chair, and gave him an evil stare. "Mr. Whoever the Fuck You Are, if you call off the goons, I'll sit down and tell you everything you want to know." Stanley knew any attempt at exchanging vile threats in protecting his family would be pointless, and the only way to save his wife and kids was to act upon his plan.

Bracken couldn't see any harm in letting the man sit comfortably. He had him three-to-one, and after a search of the home, he was sure there weren't any surprises his captive could pull. "I don't see why we can't sit and talk like gentlemen, Mr. Barrett. Remember, don't try going forthe gun cabinet, or I will execute you where you sit. Cal, Jim, release him."

Barrett fell to the floor, then raised himself tohis knees, rolling his shoulders briskly to ensure they still worked. "May I sit down?" he asked, motioning to a sectional sofa. Then he looked at the goons, noting that they were relaxed, and didn't have their guns in the ready position. Both men had short-barreled shotguns slung around their shoulders. All he needed was one quick motion in the process of rising.

"I'd prefer you remain where you are," Guttone said and eyed his prisoner with a furrowed brow.

"My legs are near dead asleep," Barrett said and checked the goons again. They were relaxed, thinking him a non-threat.

Guttone thought for a moment, knowing he was talking to a dead man. "Very well.You may rise and stretch your legs, then back to the floor."

It was all Barrett was hoping for. Making as though he was having difficulty standing up, when one of the goons reached to help, Barrett grabbed him by the wrist, and flung him crashing into the seated Guttone, who went end over end. He spun and blitzed his shoulder into the other man's body, bouncing him to the floor. Then he went for the ceiling. He leapt like a cat lunging for an out-of-reach bird and knocked the ceiling tile, jarring the weapon loose. It fell, as did Barrett. Twisting his body, landing with his back to the carpet, the .22 landed on his lap. He seized the weapon, pointed it and fired at the nearest goon, hitting him in the waist. He pulled the trigger again, and struck the second man in the back. The third shot never came because when he pulled the trigger again, he was out of ammo. Stanley remained on his back with the .22 leveled at Bracken. He could see the broad shoulders protruding beyond the chair—oh, how he wished he had a full clip. Barrett cautiously got to his feet, keeping his gun aimed at Bracken. Then he backed up to the wall, getting a better look at his foe.

The massive body of Bracken lay in wait for the third shot. He pressed himself into the corner behind the recliner that he knew was no protection against the bullets. No shot came, but he wasn't foolish enough to come into the open. Bracken also didn't carry a firearm of his own. With his size and strength—and the attendants surrounding him—he had never needed one, until now. Cal and Jim were lying on the floor. He heard Cal moan, but Jim was unmoving. Both their weapons were slung around their necks and out of Guttone's reach.

"Mr. Barrett," Guttone said. "I do believe we have a situation in which I am prepared to make concessions." He was lying, assuming his opponent had the upper hand. But why didn't the third shot come? Barrett fired on the others without thought, and Bracken knew he heard the hammer cock for a third shot during the melee.

"Get up slowly, and keep your hands out where I can see them," Stanley commanded.

Bracken did so, and stood, straightening his suit jacket and adjusting his tie. He stared at the weapon. Stanley's hand was steady, and his face focused, but his eyes betrayed him. Bracken knew the gun was empty.

"Why don't you just fire that pop gun, and finish the job you started?" Bracken said lowering his hands, and stepping forward.

"You son of a bitch," Stanley said in anger, knowing the bluff was over before it started. He hurled the pistol, and ran straight into Guttone's concrete body with the desperate hope of knocking him back. The giant simply ducked the projectile, and received the blow like a soccer ball. Stanley backed up to give it another shot, this time fist first, going for the jaw, but the giant's powerful bare knuckles met his, and he heard the dreadful sound of shattering bones in his wrist.

Stanley wasn't done. Although reeling in pain, he threw a left hook. Bracken caught the throw with his huge palm, this time in mid-swing, and twisted it until the elbow snapped. The bones in Barrett's arm crumbled. Writhing in agony, he began kicking violently, but was flung backwards as Guttone thrust his steel-like forearm into Barrett's chest. Guttone took time to straighten his jacket and trousers before picking his victim up by the throat. Stanley's useless hands clawed at the mammoth arm holding him captive. Stanley hungby the neck, helpless to escape. The familiar sight of his victim's eyes bulging, Bracken shook the last breath from the man's lungs, and he lost consciousness. Guttone dropped him like a wet rag, and yelled in anger.

"Goddamn it," he said, noticing blood had splattered onto his jacket sleeve. He furiously entered the bathroom, removed the expensive jacket,and rinsed it with cold water. He grabbed the terry-cloth hand towel and rubbed briskly. He repeated this several times, then held it close under the light. Satisfied the drycleaners would be able to remove the rest of the stain, he slung it over his shoulder, and looked back at his henchmen lying semi-conscious, and moaning.

"What a mess," he said, shaking his head. "There is only one way to straighten this one out." He grabbed a pack of matches and a cigarette from Cal, who was writhing on the blood-soaked carpet, and walked up to the kitchen. The stove was gas-fired, so he turned on all four burners at once, blowing out the flames, allowing the fumes to escape. He stepped away, and lit the cigarette, then folded it into the match pack, keeping the hot end extending outward. He saw a microwave cabinet across the room, and placed the homemade detonator on it. In approximately five minutes the pack of matches would ignite, and by then the gas fumes would have filled the air, causing an explosion.

He knew it would take forensics weeks to unscramble the pieces. Striding to the back door, he exited without so much as a backwards glance. He walked through the woods to his new Jaguar parked on an off road, and drove through the brush, making it to the main highway. His car reverberated on the blacktop as the concussion from the explosion was felt for miles. He drove discontentedly, feeling Barrett might have been holding back information, and cursing himself for being so lenient and foolish.

"It'll never happen again," Guttone said aloud and heard the siren of the fire station bellow.

CHAPTER TWENTY-THREE

Darkness woke him, the absence of light for so long a period of time triggered an alert in his brain. Al felt a cold tingling running through his bloodstream. His eyelids were crusty and difficult to open. With effort, the hairs on the upper and lower lids tore apart as clouded light pierced his retina. He didn't know why, but he did not use his hands to wipe the caking particles free, as he managed to blink several times. Al Campo looked straight up at the graying ceiling. Shards of flaking paint hung precariously, and needed only an open window's breeze to shake loose. He looked left without moving his head, and saw dingy, decaying wallpaper rising up to cobwebs hanging across the upper corners. The smell of alcohol whiffed past his nose. Baffled abouthis whereabouts, Campo closed his eyes again. *I must still be sleeping*, he thought. Then he opened his eyes again with nearly the same difficulty as before. The view was the same; to the right there was a half-open, old wooden door with its white paint chipped and flaking. Light beamed in from the other room, full of dust mites, showing the balance of the room contained a beat-up, inexpensive dresser, a large-framed mirror leaning against the crumbling paper, and the single bed he lay on.

"Where the hell am I?" Al whispered in a dry, raspy voice. Then he remembered. "Wait …the attack at my home…then the chase….and the reverend's house." He remembered someone answering the door, then blackness. The man who answered must have been a good soul to put up a stranger. Campo attempted to raise his body, but pain shot through his shoulder, forcing him down. Now he remembered being shot. He reached his hand to the wound, and felt a neat dressing. Then he felt his thigh, and found the same. His hand had a bandage as well, but it was holding an IV in place. No matter where he was, it was a good place.

Again, he pushed himself up, and agonizingly braced himself on his elbows. He viewed a single window at the foot of the bed, with the drapes drawn completely. His body was stiff, and he ached even where no wounds were present. He was familiar with these aches; they were from being unconscious too long. Al struggled upward, and swunghis legs over the side, keeping his bandaged leg straight while flexing the other. His knee creaked loose. He sat upright slowly and methodically stretched every muscle possible. Finally, he exercised his wounds, bringing much-needed circulation back. He felt stronger, in through the nose out through the mouth, rhythmically bringing oxygen into his lungs and brain. He felt seventy-five percent, so he decided to exit the room and find out who had been granting him such hospitality. The door creaked open as he limped onto worn hardwood in the hallway, towing the IV stand behind him. He followed the dim light, walking as quietly as possible, but knowing he was as loud as a freight train. He moaned as the dry scabs over his wounds broke loose, tearing his body hair, stretching with his movements. He made his way to the end of the hall, using the wall as a crutch, dragging his leg. He smelled fresh coffee and something sweet in the air. A man appeared in front of him, and Campo could only guess it was the same man who had answered the door.

"Hey Uncle! Look who's up and about," the man said over his shoulder, looking at Al in mock surprise. "How about a little help?" he said, inserting himself under Al's shoulder.

Campo welcomed the lift, and they both hobbled towards the light. At that moment, Campo realized his only attire was his boxer-briefs, and he felt slightly embarrassed, thinking about how these people had to undress him to tend to his wounds. All self-consciousness left as he saw a black man sitting at a table in an otherwise empty kitchen. His face was round and gentle, indicating strength and pleasant kindness. His brown eyes were glistening.

Reverend Thomson's face was weathered, and Campo felt deep dismay seeing how his old friend had been worn down by years of hard work. Sympathizing with his congregation, and years of futile attempts to save the unsavable had taken their toll. The years since Al last saw his friend were difficult ones, and Campo saw an old man sitting at the table, but in the fearless eyes he spied a glimpse of his old friend, and was comforted deeply when a tear fell from his eyes. Without a word spoken Reverend Thomson stood, and gave him a bear hug. He still maintained his strength, and strong hands pressed into Al's back. The reverend was careful not to press too hard, being careful with Al's fresh wounds. Campo returned the embrace, and had to partially support his weight on the reverend because his breath was stolen. Gerald released him, and sat his old friend down on a chair next to his. He placed a cup of coffee and orange juice and a slice of lemon pie on the table, then sat back in his chair.

"I guess I found the right house?" Campo said, then swallowed the glass of juice completely. Then he sipped the hot coffee.

"Thank the Lord you did my boy," the reverend said. "When my nephew Jonathan saw you outside, you looked like the ragged end of nowhere."

"I still do," Al said, bringing a smile to Gerald's face.

"Son." The reverend had always called him son. "Son, the last time I heard from you must be going on twenty years. Your last letter came from over seas. I still have it…I mean, them."

"How many of them?" Al asked, pleased to hear his letters had been read and appreciated.

"All of them," Gerald said and waved a hand at his nephew. "Jonathan, go and get me the shoebox on top of my dresser, would you please?" Jonathan, standing at the door to the kitchen, nodded and went to his uncle's room.

"You know, Reverend," Al said, grabbing his friend's hand and squeezing it. "It has been a long time. How are things at your church?"

"Son, it's been difficult," Gerald said, his tone solemn. "The followers grow fewer with each passing year. Drug pushers are taking over the streets, as corruption and violence become the staple of this neighborhood. My Zion Baptist church stands untouched by graffiti, which gives me a certain sense of pride and accomplishment, knowing they still have respect for the church. The few parishioners who attend my masses I cherish and give myself fully to each sermon, and it shows."

Al sipped his coffee, and looked at his friend. So many memories flashed into his mind, how close they were, how many times he had confided his secrets, not to a reverend, but to a friend and father figure. Where had he been while the reverend deteriorated? So many times his shoulder was Campo's comfort, and he had just left him wondering. He knew Gerald wanted to know all about the past twenty years, but what could he say? He felt guilty as hell about dropping off the face of the planet, and then reappearing out of nowhere with two bullet wounds, and a truck that looked like it fell off a cliff. He couldn't tell him the reason for his disappearance—it would be too difficult to explain—and he knew his friend would never ask him if it weren't in his heart. There was a heavy quiet between the two. The reverend waited patiently to hear all about the trouble he was in, and how he could help. Al knew the reverend was not going to ask. Campo had to speak of his own free will. He took another sip, then massaged his shoulder.

"How long have I been here?" Campo asked, afraid of the answer.

"Well..." The reverend paused. "Jonathan carried you inside two days ago."

Al cringed at the thought two days of his life gone with out a trace, but relieved that whoever was after him had been unable to locate him for forty-eight hours. It was a small comfort, knowing he wasn't out of the woods yet.

"I guess I picked the right place to hide out," Al nearly bit his lip at the last statement as the reverend's door of opportunity was opened.

"Hide from whom, son?" Gerald said as his nephew re-entered the room and set a brown shoebox on the table.

"To be honest, I'm not really sure. You see there was this couch at the side of the road..." Campo explained everything he could remember that was pertinent, including the gold box, the box with the markings for radiation, and even his run-in with the FBI. The Reverend's face took on a somber shadow, concern for his friend's safety resting heavy on his shoulders, even after all this time apart.

"Where are the boxes now, son?"

"I left the one with the professor, and the other is in my truck," Al said, then thought of his vehicle sitting in back of the row house in plain view. "Damn, my truck is out back still, I have to move…"

"Don't worry about it," Jonathan spoke from the doorway. "I pulled it into the garage. It barely fit under the door, but I managed to squeeze it in."

"Son," Gerald spoke, "do you feel the man who approached you when you found the sofa is involved?"

"I didn't think so at first," Al paused and scratched his chin and felt the two-day growth of hair, "but after I put all the pieces together it seemed to fit. I think the FBI was serious about this guy at the chemical plant, Jason Gull. He must have sent a lackey after the couch, and when I interrupted him, they came hell-bent after me."

"Did the feds have ID?" Jonathan said.

"Yeah, it was legitimate," Al said and drank his coffee. He felt his muscles getting warmer, so he started rolling his good shoulder around and bending his leg.

"I think they know more than they told you about this Jason Gull," Jonathan continued. "For three men to attack you in broad daylight, heavily armed and risking exposure, there has to be more to the story. I don't remember seeing it on the news, or on the Internet. I could have missed it though. Have you opened the radiation box?"

"No way. I don't know if there is any shielding in it—it's too risky."

"Son, I want you to listen to me." The reverend reached out and laid his hand on Campo's, holding it in his. "Call that FBI agent, and turn over that thing in your truck, and be done with it. Someone wants it bad enough to risk their lives for it, and you need to get as far away as possible."

"I don't know about that, Uncle; if he contacts the FBI, they might be in on it, and just have him killed when they pick it up. On the other hand, if he calls, and the call is traced, he might expose himself, and get killed anyway.

"I don't believe so," Gerald said, staring down his nephew. Then he turned to Al. "It is your only course of action, son. Please do as I ask."

"You may be right, but Jonathan has a point. I don't know all that much about the FBI agents, and they could be the ones who sent the hit squad. Right now I need to keep calm and reason out my options."

The reverend wanted to change the subject. "Here we go, son," he said as he withdrew an envelope from the shoebox, and read Al's letter. "'Dear Reverend, I finally received my orders, I'm not allowed to say where I'll be going, but I'm definitely looking forward to a new assignment far away from this place. As soon as I arrive I'll write again. For now, you can send your letters to the same address as before. I miss you, and always have you in my heart, your dear friend, Al. April 21, 1992.' That date seems like an eternity ago."

"Date!" Al said, as the word sparked in his foggy memory.

"Yes, April twenty-first, nineteen…" Gerald repeated.

"No, no, I'm sorry," Al said. He could feel the blood pulsing in his veins as he remembered the image of Domeni. "I just remembered I have a date with a beautiful woman Friday night. What day is it?"

"Son, I think going out on a date would be a little unusual under the circumstances," the reverend said puzzled.

"Yeah, but you haven't seen this woman," Al said, seeing her gold eyes flash in his mind. "She's something special—and I have a feeling deep in my stomach. Right now I am getting energized just thinking about her!"

"It's Thursday evening, about eight o'clock," Jonathan said as his uncle gave him a piercing glance.

"How long have you two been dating?" Gerald asked.

"Tomorrow night will be our first date." Al smiled and looked down at his bare legs and chest. "My clothes. Are they wearable? I can't go like this, and I think a trip to my house for new ones would be a little dangerous."

Robert DiGiacomo

"A little!" the reverend said, "Son, you are underestimating these people. They want to kill you, and you'll only be putting this girl in harm's way."

"Not true," Al said. He rubbed his hair back and took a quick sniff of his underarm. "No one knows we have the date, and besides, they would probably think I would be insane to go, but they don't know who they are playing with. I know my past is a mystery to you, but trust me when I say, they don't intimidate me in the least."

"Your clothes are nasty," Jonathan said. "And basically trash. My clothes won't fit you, but I went out and bought you some new ones, sizing them from the old."

The reverend's stare was threatening. "You're not helping the situation, Nephew."

"Uncle, how can he pass up on a date he feels so strongly about? If he's willing to risk his life for her, she really must be unbelievable. I think he is doing the right thing. After his date, he can drop the box off at the federal building, and make a run for it."

"Son, don't bother with all that," the reverend said and slapped the air toward his nephew. "Call the FBI. Then call this girl and make new plans. If she's that special, she will understand."

"Reverend, you know I love you," Campo said and gripped Gerald's hand, "and I feel ashamed about leaving you in the dark for so long, but I think I can handle these characters, and I don't wish to wait another second to see her again, much less a day. Trust me, I'll be all right."

Gerald knew it was useless to argue, and just shook his head, saddened. He made one last attempt to keep him there. "You're in no condition to drive. Stay here tonight and get some rest. We'll talk about it again tomorrow."

"Old friend," Al said, "you're probably right, but I'm feeling pretty good right now. By the way, who fixed me up? Did you take me to Cooper Hospital?"

"No son, with bullet wounds there is always a police report, so Jonathan took care of you right here. He's an ER intern at the hospital."

"Doctor…well, thank you. So what's my prognosis? Am I able to travel? " Campo asked as he put on the pants and socks Jonathan retrieved for him.

"Sure thing," Jonathan said. "The bullet passed through the flesh on your shoulder, causing a gash and a tear in the muscle, superficial. I put nine stitches in, and rubbed on some ointment. It's already beginning to heal. Your thigh was pierced, entering on your right side, and exiting cleanly. The damage to your muscle was minimal, and I closed up both wounds with three stitches each. I have been giving you IV antibiotics for two days now, so there should be no risk of infection. Aside from the discomfort and pain, you're fine. Just be careful not to rip open the stitches and keep them dry until at least Saturday. If you want you can come back next week, and I can remove them and check the wounds. All in all, you are lucky and I think the new scars will do justice to all the others on your back, chest and legs."

"What about this?" Campo asked, referring to the IV in the back of his hand, brushing aside the remarks about his battered body. The last thing he wanted to do was explain all of his previous wounds.

"Let's see," Jonathan said as he took the IV out of Campo's hand and pressed a cotton ball to the small puncture. Then he began to put a piece of adhesive tape over it.

"Forget the tape, Doc. I'll keep pressure on it until it clots," Al said as Jonathan helped him get dressed. He looked over at his friend's somber face. The reverend tried his best to smile. Al knew his friend was genuinely concerned, but he also felt it was only a matter of time before they found him here. He had to leave to protect them. "So Doc, what's the bill, including the clothes?"

"It's on the house. Anyone my uncle calls son—and there aren't any—is like my brother, so forget about it."

"Sorry, but I won't forget about it. How about a couple of pain pills, and I'll be on my way?" Campo pulled a tan polo shirt over his head, easing it gently past his wounded shoulder, and then laced up his new sneakers.

"The first thing you have to do is get something to eat, and plenty of fluids in you before you leave. As for the pain, I can hook you up with something. I'll be right back." The doctor left the room for an instant, and returned with a brown paper bag, dumping it in front of Al. Then he passed him a bottle of Tylenol.

In front of him lay Campo's wristwatch, his billfold secured with a rubber band, some pocket change, and his cell phone. Gerald went to the cupboard, and brought out rolls and deli meat for sandwiches, along with a half-gallon of orange juice.

"You and I have the same phone," Jonathan said. "So I gave it a full charge. Also I programmed my uncle's home number, and my cell number, in case you need anything, or you want to come back and stay a while longer."

"Thank you, Jonathan. You've been more than gracious. I am indebted to you and your uncle." Campo ate like a starving child, as the three sat and talked for another hour or so, avoiding any conversation about the current situation. They kept to the past, telling Jonathan how they met and so on. Finally Al rose from his chair, feeling full of food, and ready to leave, Gerald hugged him, and held on tightly. Then, with a tear in his eye, he let go, and went upstairs. Al had to wipe the moisture from his own eyes as he thanked the reverend's nephew again. Shaking hands, Al felt Jonathan pass him something. It was car keys.

"Don't worry about him. He's tired. It's way past his bedtime," Jonathan said. "Your truck is pretty banged up, so why don't you take my Durango. I just picked it up a week ago. I think that girl should ride in something a little nicer than a Ford pickup with fifty bullet holes in it."

"Doc, I couldn't."

"Don't say no. Besides, it will give you a reason to come back and visit us when this all blows over."

Before Al could speak again, Jonathan turned him around and gave him a shove toward a jet-black Dodge Sport Durango. Without another word, Al jumped in, and took off down the street. His thoughts were consumed with his old friend. The reverend was getting older, and Al was leaving again. The thought he might never see the old man again crossed his mind, and suddenly Al felt guilty and lost. He gripped the black leather steering wheel and reminded himself to return, to take care of his friend. Al's eyes welled up, and the muscles atthe back of his throat tightened. He stopped the car at the corner, and looked in the rear view mirror, seeing the doorway where he had collapsed, and the metal post supporting the deck. "I will be back," he said aloud. Then reached his hand under the seat and felt the metal box Jonathan had put there from his truck. Then he drove away.

CHAPTER TWENTY-FOUR

Al Campo raced over the Ben Franklin Bridge back into Philadelphia. He acclimated himself to the new Durango and its functions. The air-conditioning system for starters was Greek to him. He's only ever owned standard package pickup trucks with simple levers and buttons. This was a whole new system; everything was electronic and operated at the touch of a button. Simple enough, he thought, and twenty minutes into his drive, he finally managed to get cool air to come out of the exhaust ports, blowing that new car smell in his face. With that task accomplished, he focused on where and how he was going to spend the next twenty-four hours. The summer sun faded in the distance, and he felt he could move fairly freely without being noticed by his enemies. He knew his home was out of the question, and all of his close friends would probably be under watchful eyes. The only place he would feel safe and at minimal risk would be with Herman Seller at the archives department. No one knew about the relationship between him and Herman, mainly because he never discussed the old man with any of his friends. Herman had little or no interest in involving himself with anyone outside the university, and he most likely did not talk about Campo. Every time Al had brought something to Seller, he had asked if it could be kept between them. He decided to head for the university. It was late, so he thought he should call and make sure his friend was still there. He held the cell phone in his right hand, resting on his lap. His right shoulder was still sore, so he drove with his left. He turned on his cell phone, and waited until the green light indicated that he had a signal. The phone beeped, and the digital display read off the date and time, then there was another beep, and the envelope icon lit up. He had messages. He wanted to call Herman first, so he put on the speaker, dialed, and Herman answered. With as few words as possible, he explained his situation and hung up. Herman was all too happy to have Al for a guest. Besides, he had a lot to tell. Next came the messages. The female voice of the voice mail said he had five messages. Pressing the pound key, they began playing

"Hello Mr. Campo, this is Herman Seller…" Campo saved that one, knowing he would be in the man'scompany soon enough.

"Next message."

"Yo, Al! Where the hell are you?" It was Stanley Barrett. "If you get this message before noon, call my cell. If not, I'll see you tomorrow."

"Shit!" Al said. "I forgot about work."

"Next message."

"Al, I hope you get this message." It was Stanley again. "I'm getting a little worried, and I want you to call me, I'm covering for you at work, so don't call the shop. But when you get this message, call me."

"Next message"

"Al, give me a call as soon as you get this message." This was Neil, the owner of the glass shop. "I need to know what's going on. Jim McPherson from the hospital called me, and said only one of you had showed up these past two days, and I can't seem to get hold of Stanley. His phone has been disconnected or something. I'm not angry, but I need to know what's going on."

"Next message"

"Hello, Al." This was a female voice, and she was crying. Al thought he recognized the voice through the tears, and to his horror he was correct. "This is Karen Barrett…there has been a terrible accident…Stanley was in our…" She could barely contain herself. As she went on, the sobbing mounted. "Our house exploded…" More weeping. "There was a gas leak, and my husband was inside when it exploded. Oh Al, he is in intensive care, and they don't think he is going...going to make it. Dear God, please. He has been in and out of consciousness, and he keeps calling your name, saying something about how they are coming after you next. Oh Al, please call, he says you're in danger. What does he mean?" Her sobbing became uncontrollable, and she was barely able to speak through her gasps. "I...I can't talk anymore..." she said, and then hung up the phone.

Al pressed the off key, and clenched his fists on the steering wheel. Memories of the past attacked his senses: the auto accident twenty years before, and his ultimate reason for leaving. He had always felt the death of his friend was on his shoulders. Now his best friend was involved in an explosion—apparently at the hands of his new enemy. Campo pushed his pain back into the recesses of his mind where he could control it. At first, he thought he should call Stanley's wife, but they would surely be watching the hospital, and probably listening to every phone call in and out of the switchboard. She did say Stanley was alive—and that was positive. It would have to suffice for now. His next move would have to remain the same, to get to Herman Seller, hopefully, out of reach. Because in due time, vengeance would be his.

Campo entered the dimly lit archive room. The sharp tang of horseradish hit his nose and he had to blink from the powerful smell. Seller was leaning over his desk, eating a roast beef sandwich, the gold box set before him; he was jotting down notes on a yellow pad between bites.

"Herman, my friend, do you always eat a full meal at this hour, and with so much horseradish. Jeez, did you put the whole jar on it?" Al asked, and walked into Seller's domain.

"You know, Mr. Campo, I had forgotten to eat, yes, forgotten to eat this evening, and my stomach was growling," Herman said between bites. "I hadn't noticed it until you called. I had some roast beef in the icebox, and decided to make a sandwich, and you can't eat cold roast beef without some spice. I love horseradish, love it indeed.Would you like some? It is very good, very good indeed."

Al ventured forward and saw the professor's sandwich lying on a paper napkin on top of two thick books, the white juice from the horseradish leaking through the napkin. "Maybe later Herman, thank you, I got your message, but didn't listen to it because I knew I would be seeing you. What did it say?" Al asked, pulling a chair next to the professor and moving some books and papers aside. Al sat down carefully, minding his wounds, leaning his elbows on the desk.

Herman finished chewing, wrapped the paper around the soggy sandwich, slid it to the side, and referred to his notes. "Mr. Campo, we have discovered some very exciting things."

"Herman, you make it sound like you have someone else working with you," Campo said curiously, fearing Seller might have involved a colleague.

"No, no, Mr. Campo, forgive me. I'm just reverting to old habits. When I was working with the team of scientists from Penn, credit would never be taken by any individual, so we never referred to ourselves in the first person."

"No problem, Herman. Please continue," Al said.

"Yes, yes, of course." Herman thrust his tongue in the side of his cheek and around his front teeth and smacked his lips. "Without giving you all the details, I will just tell you the letter you discovered contains clues about an incident involving a child. This child disappeared without a trace; no, I'm sorry. Only his waist garment was found. This information struck a chord in my memory—and as I'm sure you know, my memory is not what it used to be. The years of stagnant researching in these walls have made me a trifle disadvantaged in the…"

"Yes, Herman, I understand." Al hated like hell to cut him off in mid-sentence, but he had a feeling if he didn't, the professor would soon lose his train of thought.

"Of course, of course," Herman said and lifted a manila folder from under the gold box. "As I was saying, after reading the letter, I re-read the pages arriving with the gold box. Again, I saw a connection between the two."

"Does the letter mention the gold box?" Al said.

"Yes, directly."

"Freaking awesome," Al blurted out, startling the old archivist, "Herman, can we date it? Does it mention a key? Where does it come from," Al rambled on with questions. He stood and walked around in a circle. Herman looked at him with a smile on his face and let him continue. "Does it mention how old it is? Does it say what's inside, or why Franklin never mentioned it in his writing?"

"Finally, a question I can answer," Herman interrupted him. "Yes, it does, but please, Mr. Campo, let me finish telling you what I've discovered."

Al looked at Herman. He was leaning all his weight on his left leg and felt his wound throb from the sudden movement. He sat down gingerly and said, "Sorry, Herman. Please tell me what you discovered."

"Indeed, Mr. Campo, the box was sent to Franklin by his friend in France, the king's physician. The story is grand in detail but let me go on with how the contents of the letter left me questioning the origin of the item. As I said, a young boy disappeared, and his disappearance was connected with the gold box here." Herman set his hand on the lid and brushed across it. He rubbed his fingers together and looked down at them.

"What is it, Herman?" Al said, "You feel it too, don't you? A tiny electrical tingling, right?"

"Strange, very strange indeed," Herman said and then looked again at Al. His eyes were red and tired. "Where was I in the story, Mr. Campo?"

Al thought he would wait to pester him about the strange feelings later, figuring he'd better get as much info from Seller while he was still half-awake. "The boy's disappearance and the gold box..."

"Ah...yes, the disappearance, indeed," Herman said. "So...I went to the library, to confirm my assumption. You see, Mr. Campo, Watchman Jones and the young child who disappeared were both Egyptian."

"And that is supposed to mean something to me?" Al said, shrugging his shoulders.

"Yes, yes, don't you see? The ghost contained in this box is the Angel of Death."

Campo's eyes opened wide, and he shook his head in doubt. "The ghost that Dixon talked about, the one he called Beelzebub, the devil, Lucifer?"

"Mr. Campo, in ancient Egypt, Moses set forth to free the people of Israel, and he accomplished this at long last by sending the Angel of Death to kill the entire first born of Egypt. Then the Angel swept through the city, and he passed over the Hebrews."

"I'm familiar with Passover, Herman," Al said and stood again. He walked around and messaged his thigh and then rolled his shoulders. He could feel the stitches creak and stretch under his shirt. He stopped and leaned on the back of his chair. "Let's put this in perspective, shall we? The angel of death came from God, from heaven or hell wherever. And you expect me to believe it was captured and stored in this box for...five thousand years and somehow ended up in Ben's abode? I don't think so, Herman. It's fiction, fantasy, science fiction, if you want, or even religious fiction. You've been stuck in this hole for too many years, my friend,"Al said.

"Only God knows the how or why, but I did some more research. I am only beginning to decipher the inscriptions on the surface, but one held a clue to how it came to be in France. There on the side is a cross on a shield; it is the insignia of the Crusades. I found the old manuscript of Raymond of Aguilers; he was a monk who chronicled the first Crusade. He was there when the Holy Lance was discovered by Peter Bartholomew."

"Do you mean the Spear of Destiny?" Al asked, having some knowledge of the artifact. "That was never proven to be the actual spearhead though, but what does it have to do with our box?"

"I am getting there, Mr. Campo. Be patient, patient indeed," Herman said and rubbed his eyes under his glasses. "The Holy Lance was immediately taken from the site and given to the two brothers, Godfrey of Bouillon and Baldwin of Boulogne, both descendants of Charlemagne. Afterword, Raymond of Aguilers dug deeper in the earth and discovered a "magnificent gold box." He described the box in little detail but mentioned that a strange tingling entered his fingers and through his arms the longer he held it. He eventually passed it to Raymond of Toulouse of France, his master, and the one for whom he was recording the events, well for him, and Pope Urban. Raymond did not know what significance the box held, nor did any of the religious scholars of the time, so it was brought back to France and never noted again until the young prince from Africa spotted it while he was visiting Versailles, and was consumed by it." Herman looked at the box solemnly, and leaned back in his chair. "This box, Mr. Campo, is not for man to play with and use at will. It is dangerous and powerful, and those two attributes combined can only mean death and destruction."

"Herman, I don't mean to sound doubtful, but it is a little far-fetched. I think if we open it, we'll know exactly where it came from. Anything in your search mention a key?"

Herman's face drooped. He was sure his findings were valid, but he could not prove his idea. "Mr. Campo, I don't think that would be very wise, not wise indeed. A key should never be found, and if one is, then it should be destroyed."

"Hold on, Professor, lets not jump before we tie off," Al said and reached for the manila folder. "Are the letters in here?"

"Jump? Tie off?"

"Old friend, I'm not saying we should open it without knowing everything possible about the origins and contents beforehand. I just thought if a key were found, more answers would come with it. You said you just started translating the carvings; maybe they contain helpful information. So let's just take it slow. If we find a key, we hold off until we are certain it's safe. In the meantime you can finish translating it."

Herman was a bit relieved by Al's tone and his apparent caution. One thing was certain in his mind. Even if a key were found, as long as Herman was alive, this box would never be opened. "Yes, yes, Mr. Campo. We shall proceed with prudence."

"Great. Now where is that roast beef? All this talk has gotten me hungry!" Al said, and got up looking for the icebox. "You know, Herman, we may be sitting on a very important discovery. This could get you right back to the top of the archeological world again." Campo found a small mini-fridge by the door. He took out the package of roast beef and two slices of cold rye bread. Herman resumed eating his sandwich, and listened intently to Campo's reminders of better days. "You may even be featured in National Geographic again. That would make me very happy, to see you renowned again, and to watch the staff here at the museum gloat at your discovery."

Herman smiled at the thought of his superiors reading all about a discovery made right under their noses. His vanity began to shine through, but he would still remain firm on his decision not to open the gold box.

"Herman, do you have any more horseradish to go with this roast beef?"

CHAPTER TWENTY-FIVE

Jason Gull pushed a button on the ceiling of his Volvo 980, and the gates to his private residence rolled open. He drove along an oval driveway, coming to a stop at the front door. The home was constructed in the Spanish style, with tan stucco and red terra-cotta roofing shingles. Large, thick mahogany doors had deep, hand-rubbed grooves in them. On either side was crackled glass windows, and the front porch floor was dark brown stone. To his right was an alarm pad with a keyboard face. He waved a personal key card in front of the sensor, heard the click of the door, and he stepped into a grand foyer. The ceiling was tall—thirty-three feet to a giant stone and crystal chandelier. He hit a button on his smartphone and it illuminated the entire room. His hand ran down the top of a crackled glass handrail lining diagonal steps zigzagging around the foyer to the upper and lower floors. As he went down the stone steps, he tapped additional buttons on his phone, and lit up his art work lining the walls. His décor of bright pastel colors painted in stripes and diamonds, glistening gold frames hung squarely on the walls, seemed to give him pleasure, and a degree of comfort being in his solitary domain, where he felt safe. The paintings were by obscure and unknown artists. Gull commissioned each painting and described in detail what he expected from them. He especially liked the super-modern eccentric furniture he helped design, and arranged in a fashion to promote standing. In one corner stood a stuffed white bear, its leg bent—appearing to have room to sit down. None of his few houseguests ever even attempted doing so. Next to it, a chair deco-rated with the skin of a tiger using the animal's head at the top as the backrest, and the paws for armrests.

Jason tossed his key card and wallet into a tray positioned on the seat of a yellow 1950 softail Harley-Davidson roadster that sat at the base of the stairway. He walked to his right where there was a black granite bar top. Behind it were dozens of bottles of liquor. A bottle of XO brandy sat on the bar with a glass next to it. After pouring himself a glass and taking the bottle with him,he stripped off his tie, unbuttoned his collar, kicked off his Italian loafers, and sunk into a plush suede recliner. It was the only piece of furniture inviting enough to sit in. He stared at the ceiling and breathed in the cool moisture and temperature-controlled air vented through-out his house. The aroma was subtle today. His air-conditioning system had a state-of-the-art filtering system that would produce different fragrances each day, and today's was lilac. He rolled his glass around and watched the legs of the brandy cling to the sides before sliding back down. He felt like he was clinging now. He was on the brink of becoming one of the mega-rich and power-ful, one of the world's elite one percent. Or he teetered on the edge of failure, and most assuredly, his death. He sipped his XO, and pondered. Who was this Al Campo who had nearly destroyed plans that had been set in motion nearly two years ago? How could he be so elusive—just a lowly blue-collar worker, an insignificant piece of scum. Gull had trampled and steamrolled over hundreds of similar men on his way up. The file—compiled for him by Bracken—lay open on a cracked-glass table with a stone base.

Gull had been studying it the night before, trying to find some hint about where Al Campo could be hiding. The strange part of the file was that it seemed incomplete. When Bracken compiled a dossier on a subject, he always included the birthplace and date. Information on his relatives and his childhood friends appeared along with every bank account and legal transaction ever made by the subject. It helped Jason deduce his habits, and spot flaws in his personality. This file contained nothing of that sort. The file actually started with his first day of work at the glass company ten years ago. It contained nothing to help him get into the mind of Al Campo, nothing that would allow him to cause harm to the ones he loved and considered his closest family. The whereabouts of his mother and father were unknown, and there was no mention of him having any siblings. Campo's exact age could not be determined; no birth certificate was produced with his name, at least, not in this country. He was a diligent citizen, paid his taxes, went to work everyday. He had no traffic violations, had never been arrested, not even a parking ticket. He sent money to various charities, mainly children's charities, and gave small donations to the Fraternal Order of Police, and Wounded Warriors. He'd never been married, had no steady girlfriend, and no children. He spent time at a local bar called the Greeks, in the nearby town of Narberth. He had a few acquaintances there, none of whom could be called close friends.

The further he read, the more frustrated Gull became. His time was already running thin, and he was now a day late. He knew he could stretch the delay only one, or at most two more days. Bracken would have to find Campo—and fast. He sipped his brandy again, and then set it next to the open file. A black lacquer humidor lay next to it, and he grabbed a Cuban cigar from inside. His fingers rolled it back and forth as the blue flame of a mini-torch ignited the leaf. He drew in the smoke, took a deep breath, and melted back into the soft cushion.

From within the smoked glass windows, the man watched as a dozen armed men dressed in black lurked outside Gull's gated property. Hoods covered their heads, and they wore automatic weapons slung over their shoulders. They climbed the stucco and iron fencing, and spread out over the landscape. One man made his way to the security gate, and installed a key card connected to a small transmitter, deciphering the code, and the gate began to open. In rolled the dark Cadillac limousine. It stopped next to Gull's Volvo. Three men worked at the front door keypad, using the same descrambler, and unlocked the big wood doors.

A stocky brute wearing a gray suit exited the limo. He was bald, with a thick beard and eyebrows with caramel skin. His deep-set eyes darted back and forth to his men who secured the area. One of them motioned from the entrance, signaling it was safe to enter. With a calm demeanor, he entered the home. He was aware of the aroma of fine cigar smoke. He took the steps slowly and looked at the strange artwork on the walls as he followed one of his henchmen. The room was dimly lit, but he could see the figure of Jason Gull restrained in his chair by two men holding guns to his head. Gull was silent, due to the duct tape on his mouth; he noticed an empty glass, a bottle of brandy, and an open file on the table in front of Gull.

"Hello, Mr. Gull. My name is Quaffa," he said in English with a heavy Middle-Eastern accent.

Gull appeared to nod, and looked straight ahead.

"I am His Holiness Caliph Karuza's personal messenger," Quaffa said, and paced in short distances just in front of the table. He didn't look at Gull but kept his eyes down, giving him the sinister look of an animal in a cage. Gull's eyes followed him as he continued. "He is very displeased with your deliberate attempt to avoid his requests. Our weapons have not yet been delivered, and they were due this morning. His Holiness sent word of his concern, yet you only stated a promise of delivery. That is not acceptable, and I am here to instruct you as to when they are to be delivered!" Quaffa stopped and looked directly at Gull for the first time, his hands behind his back, bending slightly towards him.

Gull felt a trickle of sweat roll down his cheeks and his armpits were drenched. He was aware that his hands were trembling, so he made tight fists and then relaxed them. He didn't want Quaffa to think he was defiant.

"His Holiness is not unreasonable; he understands how delays happen, so he is giving you two days to deliver the weapons. Two days!" Quaffa held up two thick, dark fingers in front of his prisoner.

"Now," Quaffa said, and he resumed his short pacing. "I am sure you would like to know the consequences if you fail us again. First," he held up his forefinger. "I personally will castrate you while my men hold you down. Then," he put up his middle finger, "each of your toes will be cut off one by one. Then" he held up his pinky, "your fingers, and then," Quaffa made a fist and pointed it at Gull who couldn't keep from trembling, "we will remove a new body part every three minutes. In my experience, a man of your physical health might even last until one of your legs is removed..." Quaffa studied Gull, looking him dead in the eyes. "That has happened only once before, but we can only hope you will be strong enough to survive that long. Do I make myself clear?"

Gull raised his head then lowered it until his chin hit his chest.

Quaffa leaned down and picked up the Cuban cigar lying at Gull's feet. He puffed hard a couple of times, and drew smoke through the hand-rolled gem. "A fine cigar," he said. Then he poured a glass of brandy,told his men to release Gull, and to tear off the tape.

Jason sat forward, and rubbed his mouth.

"I..." he started to say, but stopped in mid-sentence as Quaffa held up his hand with the cigar to his lips. "No words, Mr. Gull. Just the weapons—in two days." The brute turned and walked to the door. The balance of his men flanked him, every other one walking backwards until they shut the door behind them.

Jason crawled on his knees to the window, and watched the invaders leave his property. Then he turned, picked up the bottle of XO, and took a long drink. The burning fluid gave him some bravery after his complete cowardice moments before.Then he called Bracken.

"Yes, Mr. Gull," Bracken said.

"What is the status of our search?" Jason said. Then he did something he hadn't done in nearly ten months: he lit a cigarette.

"Sir, I will have him soon,"

Gull closed his eyes, steaming with fury. He held it in check, and answered."Do you have any leads about where the product is?"

"None, sir, but we will have him, as I promised." Bracken seemed annoyed at the question, but Gull could care less. He needed this problem solved fast.

"Bracken," Gull said, anger in his voice, "the urgency in finding the product has increased to a deadly level. You must intensify your search."

"Yes sir," Bracken said.

Gull knew it was a response just to pacify him. The search could not be more intense than it was, but no other answer would suffice.

"Sir, should I concern myself with taking him alive?" Guttone said. He sounded like he already knew the answer.

"If at all possible, yes, but just get the product and bring it to Wolfie." Gull puffed hard on his cigarette and blew out the smoke slowly.

"Understood," his security chief said and hung up abruptly.

Gull slammed down the receiver, his mind racing for a solution. Should he run, and take with him what he could? He had considerable resources abroad, and the ability to disappear. But that option could always remain on the back burner. He still had two days. If he could somehow obtain more plutonium…impossible! Another solution was needed. He picked up the phone, and speed-dialed once again.

It was answered on the first ring."Yes?"

"Mr. Vincent, I was just paid a visit by Karuza's men," Gull said and sucked on the smoke like he was drawing in life force.

"What's that? I wasn't aware of any meeting," Vincent said.

"Well sir, it wasn't a planned visit. They just left several minutes ago. The delay in our delivery has caused some concern on their end. They have given us an additional two days for shipment."

"This isn't all part of that problem you spoke of earlier, is it, Gull? Because you assured me that was not going to be a problem," Vincent said.

" No sir, but we are having trouble refining the product. Is there any way you could stall them, and keep them at bay while I complete the process?" Gull said, his tone joyless.

"Negative, Gull. Their deadline is approaching, and it cannot be moved back. The course of history hinges on their success, and their success is hinged on you completing the weapons on time."

"I understand, sir. I will have the weapons as promised," Gull said confidently, even though he didn't know how. He hung up, and once again dialed.

Answering the phone this time was an older man, his voice heavily accented. "Yes, hello? This is Wolfgang speaking. Who is calling, please?"

"Wolfie, this is Jason Gull. We have a problem. I need the weapons in two days."

"Ah, have you secured the balance of the plutonium?" Wolfie said.

"No, that's the problem. We haven't. I need the weapons just the same. Would it be possible to use the amount of product we have already, and disperse it evenly into the fifteen?"

"Yes, that is possible, but the weapons were designed for a distance of three hundred meters, and with a reduced level of Jasonium, they will not be as effective. They may even fail to operate."

"Would it be possible to extract enough plutonium from the reactor core to use in the weapons, and when more is secured, replace what we took?" Gull was grasping at straws now; he almost knew the answer before Wolfie said it.

"Yes, it would be possible."

"Wonderful. Have your people get right on it," Gull said

"Ah, but you didn't let me finish. There are two problems with that solution. The first is it would take nearly a week to extract the core material safely, and the second is that once we did, we wouldn't have enough heat to melt the plutonium into gas and thus creating Jasonium. We need the core to create the new element."

Jason squeezed the receiver so hard it cracked in his hand, and he bit through his cigarette. "Wolfie, I need those weapons in two days. How can it be done?"

"Mr. Gull," Wolfie said. Now he seemed to be getting annoyed. "The only way is to obtain more plutonium, and for the weapons to be ready in two days, I'll need it in twenty-four hours so I'll have time to prepare the Jasonium. The weapon casings are all ready, so I just need the product."

"OK, Wolfie. Just be ready when I bring in the plutonium." Gull hung up the phone. That was more bad news he didn't need. Now all he could do was wait, and have faith that Bracken would come through, and then the rest would be on Wolfie. He poured the rest of the brandy down his throat. It warmed him through, and he sunk once again into the recliner. Then he smelled something burning. "Now what?" he said and saw the burning ember of his cigarette burning a hole in his carpet. "Shit," he said and crushed it with his foot. His fate rested with Wolfie, for he knew Guttone had never failed him. Gull closed his eyes and thought about the German-born physicist, now in his early nineties. It always amazed him how his appearance was that of a much younger man. His hair was thick and coarse, not completely gray, with dark streaks throughout. His face had few wrinkles, and he wore heavy-framed glasses. He stood half a foot shorter than Gull, with a thick-boned structure.

Gull remembered the stories Wolfie would tell over and over of his first days in the United States in 1937. After he left his home-land of Germany, fleeing the new fascist regime, he hoped to enter Princeton. He was denied entry, but luckily ended up in Chicago, where he received his doctorate. The German told Gull how he had his idea of refining radioactive material into gas several years after he was present at Enrico Fermi's famous self-sustain-ing nuclear chain reaction at the University of Chicago in 1942. Thereafter, Fermi was transferred to the atomic bomb laboratory in Los Alamos. The young Wolfgang was left with the aftermath of recovering continuous data from the nuclear reactor. While the scientists at Los Alamos were inventing the A-bomb, he worked on his theory of transmitting the power of the atom into light, specifi-cally a laser beam of light. His research had been suddenly halted when the school's financial backing from the government stopped. From there, he finally attained a professorship at his dream univer-sity, Princeton. His research had long been forgotten until a bril-liant young graduate student entered his advanced physics class. That student's name was Jason Gull.

Jason was a dream student for Wolfgang, continually pestering the professor with questions about the unknown effects of quan-tum physics, and his thoughts on nuclear power beyond weapons of mass destruction, and supplying illumination for millions of electrical customers. So interested was Gull that Wolfie brought out his old data sheets from the fifties. Gull's interest was imme-diately piqued, and the two men started on a mission to create a laser beam generated by nuclear power. Once Jason graduated, he was on his way to the world of bioengineering, and he did not see Wolfgang for ten years. Then, armed with a personal fortune and the Baroque Chemical plant in his grasp, Jason asked the aging professor if he would work only on his research and theories for him. It would all be funded by Jason and Baroque Chemical. Jason would also totally support the physicist.

He saw the scientist was eager to get back into his past research, but it meant leaving Princeton and his teaching. Gull sweetened the deal giving him unlimited resources, and told him he could leave at anytime, and return to New Jersey.

He lied.

In the vast facility, Wolfgang made tremendous progress, quickly turning out a prototype, and within ten years, he had developed an upgraded model. The weapon had a laser scope for pinpoint accuracy—and the laser beam could not be seen with the naked eye. It could project a dose of radiation so powerful that if it were fired into a human's heart, that person would die instantly, and the death would be attributed to a heart attack, or related coronary death. The deadly ray could be fired from up to three hundred meters away, and deliver death at a slower pace, depending on the target of the laser. During those years, Wolfgang knew nothing of the outside world. Jason dominated Wolfgang's life, and kept him away from the public eye. He wanted him all for himself. The possibilities of such power consumed Gull, and wouldn't let go of the German. When Wolfie had finally asked to return to Princeton, Gull's response was harsh and threatening.

From that day onward, the German never asked again. Gull made sure Wolfgang knew nothing else besides the walls of the research facility, and his private residence inside the plant for years—and Gull had no intention of ever letting him leave alone, or alive.

Gull was so close to attaining his dream, and one man stood in his way—Al Campo. He was deep into the effects of the brandy when the phone on his lap rang.

"Hello, this is Gull."

"We have him," Bracken Guttone said.

CHAPTER TWENTY-SIX

Coal-colored clouds, bursting with sparks of lightning, pushed northeastward, and extreme winds sent dark shadows climbing the treetops, bringing on the evening a bit early. Facing west in the eastbound lane, a lone car was parked, its driver viewing the fast-approaching tempest on Inglewood Road.Sitting behind the wheel of the black Chevy sedan, Special Agent Carl Fazolo caressed the bulbous bruise above the bridge of his nose. He rubbed back his thick, black hair and scratched his scalp, staring blankly up the street. They were parked down the block from Domeni Conti's home, waiting for the man who had caused the bump to his forehead. The street had trees lining both sides, tall oaks, their fat trunks planted in the middle of each home's yard. The houses were all two-story brick colonials, set close together and having shared driveways. He watched as cars sped past, traveling fifty or sixty miles per hour, far beyond the speed limit. They abused the law since the rural road had recently been transformed into a four-lane road with double yellow lines striping the middle. Now it looked like a highway with houses on either side.

"What time do we expect our mark to arrive?" a man said from the passenger seat. "Mr. Tyson didn't have time to brief me before I left."

"Seven-thirty."

"Another half hour," the passenger said as he looked at his watch.

Faz glanced at the agent next to him. He didn't know much about the man until this morning when Tyson brought him in, with information on Campo's whereabouts. Faz only knew him from the office floor and his chirpy "Good morning, Agent Fazolo," that he would say every time they crossed paths. His name was Craig Stortz, and this was his maiden field assignment. Short and stocky, he was muscular due to his obsession with exercising, both at home and at the gym. He would even have push-up competitions with the other agents at the office. He almost never lost, except once. There was a pretty female agent transferred to the department. She was a tiny girl, only five three and about ninety-nine pounds soaking wet. She witnessed Stortz's boasts and his competitive manner and challenged him. To Stortz's and everyone else's surprise she banged out a hundred push-ups in two minutes, while Stortz was only at seventy-five. She stopped, looked at him, and said, "You really want to do this?" Stortz looked unfazed so she banged out another hundred as Stortz collapsed on the floor after number 125. Faz smiled as he took a sip of coffee remembering the incident.

His hair was cut in the military style. He sat tall in his seat, and his wide torso was a bit out of proportion. It gave him the appearance being tall when he was sitting, yet he stood only five-foot-eight. Craig had been in the agency for two years doing filing and research, most of the grunt work for the other twenty senior agents of the Philadelphia office. For six months, he had been begging Joe Tyson to have a chance in the field. Today was the day Tyson finally gave in. Stortz was twenty-eight years old, married with two sons, who were six and four years old.

After graduating from the Law Enforcement program in Arizona where he was born, Stortz entered the FBI school, and quickly shot to the top of his class. He received the highest honors out of Hogan's Alley, the FBI's physical training program. Joe Tyson had picked up his file fresh off the pile of graduates and handpicked him for the Philadelphia office. Joe disliked having to put him through the piles of paperwork and research, but knew he would ace his way through the grunt work, and now he was ready to cut his teeth on a field assignment.

"What type of vehicle do we expect him to arrive in?" Craig said impatiently. Sitting around was what he had been doing behind a desk, and he was eager to get some action.

"Last he was seen in a gray Ford pickup truck," Faz replied. "But he could be driving anything. The attack at this home could very well mean his truck was shot up, and he doesn't seem to be stupid enough to drive a car with bullet holes in it. It might attract attention." Faz drank his coffee as he looked up the street at Domeni's house.

Stortz wanted to ask more about the attack at the home, having only heard preliminary reports, and they were not very clear. But he could tell from Faz's tone he was in no mood to answer questions. He recalled Joe Tyson's instructions very clearly: "Do whatever Faz tells you to do. Do not question his orders—and keep your enthusiasm in check. This should be a routine pickup." Keeping his eagerness to a minimum would be difficult, because after Tyson said he should go, he could feel his mind and muscles working overtime. He even knocked out fifty push-ups on the floor of Tyson's office after thanking him. He looked at Faz's stony features and sensed he didn't like having to babysit the new guy, so while keeping his eyes wide, he made small talk. "I hope those clouds mean it's going to rain soon; my lawn needs a drink," Stortz said and adjusted in his seat. His pants were beginning to get moist from the vinyl seats.

"I don't think it's in the forecast. Those clouds are here to tease us. It won't rain." Faz said and gave a half-glance at Stortz.

"Well, one thing's for sure. If it doesn't rain soon, my entire lawn will be dead in a matter of days. Did you see that, sir?" Stortz blurted out. "That car slowed down a bit."

"Yes, I did see that. It was subtle, but he did slow down."

Stortz jerked his head around, his eyes following a dark, green-colored Jaguar that had passed Domeni's home. It held up its speed, and then continued, passing the Chevy very fast.

"Did you get a good look at him, sir?" Stortz asked Faz who was staring into the rearview mirror.

"Not really, but I don't think that was Al Campo. I can't be sure, but it may have been one of Jason Gull's men. He went by too fast, and I couldn't get a good look."

"Should we call in to Mr. Tyson?" Stortz asked, not from fear, but because he remembered his superior instructing Faz to call in if anything unusual happened. If Gull's men were wise to them, it seemed a good reason to call in.

"We'll wait a few minutes. He might circle the block and drive past again." Faz said and looked from the rearview to the side mirrors. "Besides, I can't be sure it was one of them anyway," Faz said dryly.

"I think maybe we should call it in anyway, just to be safe." Stortz said with raised eyebrows.

Faz looked over at him with a who-the-fuck-are-you-talking-to stare, and without a word told Craig to keep his mouth shut. Faz was in charge, and all that was on his mind was to meet up with Campo so he could repay him for the bruise he had taken to the head at their last encounter. Ten minutes went by and they waited patiently and alert. The agents expected the Jaguar might come around the corner at any moment. Then they heard something, a pinging sound, and it was coming closer. They looked through the side view mirrors, and saw a young man, maybe twenty years old, bouncing a basketball. He wore long, green mesh shorts, and an old and worn 76ers tank top, with a baseball cap pulled down to his eyebrows. His shirt was wet and sweat ran down his face. Faz dismissed the kid; he remembered seeing a community park with courts and a ballfield around the corner, so he turned his attention back toward Domeni's home.

The kid dribbled closer, and with the speed of a track and field star raced to the open window of the sedan, he reached behind his back, and withdrew a high-powered dart pistol from his shorts. A tranquilizer dart struck Faz in the neck just below the ear, and then one was sticking out of Craig Stortz's bulky chest. Craig fought the effects of the drug, tugging his gun from his holster, but another dart stabbed his thigh. The two agents slumped over unconscious within seconds of each other. The young man threw the weapon into the back seat, opened the driver's door, pushed Faz out of the way, and then started the car. He jammed it into drive, pushing hard on the pedal. The tires burned as the kid spun the car into a 180-degree turn, and raced down Inglewood Road.

Silently and slowly, a gray Ford cargovan, its tinted windows concealing four heavily armed men, rolled to a stop in the exact place vacated by the Chevy.

CHAPTER TWENTY-SEVEN

The front was built of gray stone and bright white mortar that had recently been upgraded, while the balance of the house consisted of faded red brick. The painted trim around the vinyl windows was kept up to par, and was meticulously clean. The front door was a rich, English brown, its polished sheen glimmering. The place where Domeni made her home was particularly well-organized. That was not to say the other homes were untidy, but Domeni's parents' home stood out from the rest. The front lawn, though small, was thick and green. It was trimmed tight to the ground, like a golfing green. The shrubs were clipped in perfect circles, and summer annuals flourished in the sun. Inside, Domeni sat poised in front of her mirror, putting the finishing touches on her makeup: lipstick, and a touch of mascara to highlight her auric eyes. She was "excited to say the least," as she had told her girlfriend an hour ago on the phone, and as before, the hair on the back of her neck stood on end whenever she thought about him. On the surface, Al Campo appeared to be everything she desired in a man. He was tall and dark, with wavy hair and a kind face, not boyish—but strong and weathered from working in the field, a masculine sexuality she was drawn to. He had large, powerful hands she knew could caress her skin as gently as a fur, but also hold her tight, filling her with security. There went the hair on her neck. She rubbed her shoulders and tried to relax. She didn't want to appear like a giddy schoolgirl, but that was exactly how she felt.

She completed her ensemble by putting on a short denim skirt, and a tight white pullover that accentuated her breasts. She pulled out her hair from the back of the shirt, adjusted her boobs with the palms of her hands, and then put her bare feet into high heels. A quick turn in front of the mirror, side, front, and rear, and she decided she was pleased with what she saw and was sure Al would be as well. She went to the window, eagerly seeking Al. She brushed the lace curtains aside, gazed up the street, and saw the darkened sky advancing.

What was she doing? It was still early, only seven-fifteen, but she wanted to be ready the second he arrived, again like a schoolgirl. One last look in the mirror, a quick brush of her hair and she headed downstairs, and looked out the front curtains. She couldn't help herself. The anticipation of his arrival was like no other feeling she had before, almost like she really had met Mr. Right, just like he had said. She paced in the front living room, not wanting to sit down in fear that it would cause an unwanted wrinkle. Again, she took a look through the window next to the front door. She wanted to open the door as soon as he got there, before he got there even, but the air-conditioner was on, and her parents wanted to keep the expensive air inside the house. She had to occupy herself, so she put some music on her smartphone. Her favorite songs held in her hand, and soon she was moving to the rhythm, dancing across the floor. Several minutes went by and she felt a tinge of sweat start on her forehead. She stopped immediately and faced the window again. Suddenly, a vehicle pulled into the driveway.

"He's here," she said. She turned off the music and smoothed out her skirt before opening the door.

<hr />

Al Campo spent the entire day dredging over innumerable volumes of text and manuscripts with Herman Seller, seeking clues to the whereabouts of the lost key. While Al got a headache from reading, Herman painstakingly tried to decipher the engravings on the gold box. After eight hours, Campo took a shower in the men's locker room and got dressed. Even after all his searching, he hadn't found so much as a mention of a key. The manuscript from the Crusades Herman had found never mentioned a key or referred to the box again. Then there was the disappointing news that Herman's translation of the engravings had been in vain as well. Campo needed a fresh start in the morning, and told Seller he would return late this evening after he had taken care of some unfinished business. Herman didn't question his friend as Al left.

Campo now found himself turning down Inglewood Road. He tossed the map aside, and watched the house numbers decrease, as he traveled to Domeni's house. He approached a traffic light and stopped. He counted down five more homes, and decided that the fifth was hers. He saw cars parked on either side of the road. There seemed to be one for every house, and one to his left was parked in the wrong direction. It was a Ford van, its windows clouded. It looked like a work truck. A man was powerwalking his dog toward him, and several bike riders passed on his right. Campo felt a bit strange, and his senses tingled, but there seemed nothing to be leery about. It was just another day in the suburbs. The light turned to green, and he cruised down the street to number 405, and pulled into the driveway. Al saw Domeni peek her head out the door. She motioned with a forefinger to say she would be one minute. He watched through the open door as Domeni pecked a kiss on each of her parents' cheeks, and before Al could make the three steps to open the passenger door for her, she was there. Campo gazed at her beauty, her long, silky legs. Her stride was natural, yet every-thing about her was sexy and alluring. Her velvety hair bounced, and she threw Al a smile, weakening his knees.

"Hello, Al. You're right on time," she said, a bit of shyness showing through.

"Hello, my dear. You look…for lack of a better word, simply gorgeous," he said, and opened the passenger door. Al couldn't take his eyes from her as she sat her bottom down, then swung her legs in. Al rounded the front of the car silently, praising Jesus for his good graces. He sat behind the wheel, and had to catch his breath—both because the stitches in his leg felt like they were tear-ing, and because her beauty took it away. "So where would you like to go?" he said. "I am game for anything"

"Um, I don't know. Until now, I never gave it much thought. Are you familiar with the area?" she asked,

"Not really, so anything you want to do will be fine with me," Campo said shrugging his shoulders. What he'd really like to do, he couldn't say out loud.

"In that case," Domeni said, looking him in the eyes, "how about Bertucci's? It's a brick-oven pizza place. It's in Wayne, about fifteen minutes down Lancaster Avenue," she said, and pointed out her window. The ride would give them a chance to talk in private before they entered a crowded restaurant.

Al looked in the direction she indicated, and saw a Ford van driving toward them. He could now see through the front windshield that the van was loaded with armed men. It sped toward them rapidly, and screeched to a stop at the base of the driveway. Al reacted instantly.

"Hold on," he said to Domeni, and jammed on the gas while throwing the Durango in reverse. As fast as the engine would allow, the Durango's rear bumper smashed broadside into the van. The four men were unable to react as their weapons were flung from their hands. Campo leaned hard on the pedal, forcing the vehicle sideways across the street, pushing it into a telephone pole, which broke in half and landed on the van. Campo saw that the two men on the side of the impact were knocked unconscious, while the others had been crunched under the collapsed roof. Campo's Durango pulled away from the wreckage undamaged with the exception of some scratched paint, and a dented back door.

"Are you all right?" Al asked the bewildered Domeni.

"I think so," she replied, her voice sterile and eyes wide. "What happened?"

"Nothing to worry about. I think they made a wrong turn. You did say that way, correct?" Al turned the wheel and raced west on Inglewood Rd.

Domeni's breathing was erratic, and she was pretty shook up. She remained silent for a moment to collect her thoughts about what had just occurred. They were racing away from an accident scene, and she felt compelled to return. "Al, what about the people in that van? Shouldn't we stop and see what happened? It's the right thing…Al, watch out!"Domeni screamed.

Al's eyes were fixed on her expression when she yelled. He turned to see that the traffic light was green, but blocking the intersection was a huge Square bread truck, the picture of a man wearing a tubular chef's hat holding a tray with fresh loaves of bread looming before them. Above the picture, in bold sweeping letters, was written: Dough Boy Express. The truck crossed the lane of traffic from the left. Al yanked the wheel to his right in an attempt to avoid the impact.The Durango's tires protested the sideways friction, and both driver's side tires exploded. The steel rims sparked and screamed on the blacktop road, Al hit the gas and tried to move but the metal rims couldn't get a purchase, and the two remaining tires spun in the air. The Durango rolled over and crashed against the box truck. Al and Domeni were rattled in their seats, and he struggled to remove the safety belts, but it was too late. The rear doors of the bread truck opened, and six men leapt out. Before Al could move to defend Domeni, two tranquilizer darts struck his chest, then one pierced Domeni's thigh. Campo's vision faded away as the men opened the door, and reached in for them.

CHAPTER TWENTY-EIGHT

My hands, I can't feel my hands…I can't move my legs. Where's the heat? I'm freezing, and what was the number of that linebacker who ran me over? Al Campo's thoughts ran wild as he stammered back into consciousness.

"Al…Al, wake up! Please, please wake up!"

He heard a woman's voice. It was Domeni's.

"He's coming to." Now he heard a male voice speaking in a flat tone.

Al blinked his eyelids several times, trying to focus, and realized his chin was on his chest, staring at his bare legs and stomach. He saw that, except for his underwear, he was naked. This made twice in a week he had woken to find himself that way. He hoped it wasn't the beginning of a trend. The back of his neck ached, and he slowly raised his head. He closed his eyes, let out a breath, then rolled his head around until the joints of his neck cracked in his ears. He opened his eyes again. He sat on a stainless-steel framed chair. He saw his ankles were taped to the base with duct tape. His wrists were restrained behind his back, and he felt tape around them as well. To his left he heard a subtle cry; the sound was not of fear or pain, but of relief. He carefully turned his aching head to see Domeni. Her eyes filled with moisture, mascara streaking her cheeks, and her hair was disheveled beyond a bad hair day. Through all of that, Al could still see her beautiful golden irises, and in them, a glorious light of hope and confidence, causing him to smile. She was taped to a similar chair, and although she was clothed, her appearance was of someone who had not dressed herself.

"You know something," he said. "I believe you're the most gorgeous woman I've ever met."

Domeni's face glowed briefly, and a laugh of happiness burst from her lips. She shyly turned away, then met his stare.

"Thank you, but not now I'm not."

Campo looked back at his unclothed body, rolled his neck around again, and then looked back at her. "Well, from the way I'm dressed, it appears I got lucky last night, or I passed out—and you got lucky."

Domeni laughed again.

Al suddenly felt his skin crawl, as if someone was watching him. He craned his head, and looked over his right shoulder. Beside him, two men watched him with fixed stares. The one closer to him had familiar features: a dark complexion and wavy hair, a bruise above the bridge of his nose, and a hard, fearless scowl. The other man had a crew cut, and ice-blue eyes emitting glimmers of panic. He appeared to be trying to hide his emotions by clenching his teeth, which made his jowls and cheekbones more pronounced. Both men were bound, and as naked as Campo. They were twisting their arms in an attempt to free themselves.

Campo scanned the room before acknowledging the two. It was sanitary white, with fluorescent lighting hanging from a solid ceiling, and the walls were white cinderblock. His feet rested on frigid, bare concrete flooring. In front of the group was a stainless steel table, a lone chair, and in the far corner stood a coat tree adorned with their missing clothing, and at its base sat their shoes.

"Don't I know you?" Al asked the familiar-looking man.

"We never had a chance to meet formally, but I know you very well," the agent said.

"What happened to your face? You cut yourself shaving or something?" Al asked, suddenly knowing full well who he was.

Faz grinned and clenched his teeth. "I had a slight run-in with a gun you took from my partner and threw at me."

"That's right," Al said, the memory appearing back in his head. Al was intrigued by his situation. This wasn't the first time he'd been a prisoner, bound to a chair, but the previous time he was also gagged. He didn't feel panic, nor was he afraid. The most important thing was to remain calm, especially with Domeni held captive along side him. "You're one of those FBI guys who followed me the other day," Al said and studied the room again, memorizing every square inch while he spoke. "Where's your friend, um... Tyson. That's it, Joe Tyson. I still have his card right here in my... rather, over there in my pants." Al nodded in the direction of the clothes. "Your partner told me your name, but it slipped my mind with everything I've been through." Campo talked as casually as though they had met by chance at the grocery store.

"I'm Special Agent Carl Fazolo, and this is..."

"Special Agent Craig Stortz," the young agent broke in as he wrenched his body back and forth, trying to rip the duct tape.

"I wouldn't bother with that," Al said and looked him in the face. "You'll pull your arms out of their sockets before you break ten layers of duct tape."

"Well, I can't just sit here and do nothing," Stortz said and continued his thrashing. The muscles on his chest were straining and veins on his neck near bursting.

Campo shrugged. "Suit yourself," he said and kept his tone upbeat and calm. He wanted Domeni to think he was incomplete control. Although their situation was grave on the surface, and Domeni was clearly terrified by her abduction, each time he spoke, he saw a light grow in her face, a glow of trusting faith, which in turn fueled his craving to escape. As he looked around him, he decided all was not grim. They were still alive, and in his varied experience, if their captors were going to kill them, they would have done so by now. At least, he hoped that that was the case.

"So gentlemen...and Domeni," Campo nodded toward her with a smile that brought a matching one to her face. "Since you all have been awake longer than I, can anyone tell me where we are?"

"I only woke several minutes before you, Al," Domeni stated.

"We've been awake about ten minutes now, and it's been just the four of us since then," Faz said. "I'm willing to bet Gull's behind this though." Faz hadn't paid any attention to what Campo said about freeing themselves, but he wasn't straining quite as hard as Stortz.

"No visitors,huh?" Al asked.

"No one," Faz said. Campo could tell he was angry—no, not angry, but frustrated. He had the familiar look of failure in his dark features.

"I wonder where anybody could get in," the young agent from Arizona said. "I don't see a door, or even a knob in the room."

The group turned their heads to all angles possible. None of them could see the entire room, but Stortz was right. There didn't seem to be a door.

"Well, I know how Domeni and I arrived here, but what about you two?" Al asked, and he saw Domeni start to wriggle in her chair. She too was attempting to break free.

"We were staking out Domeni's house," Faz said.

"My house! Whatever for?" she said defensively, and swung her head toward the agent then over to Campo. She looked as if she would freak out at any moment.

"We were waiting for Campo here to arrive," Faz continued. He now appeared mad at Al, obviously blaming him for their condition. "You see, no one's been able to find him for the past two days. It was as if he dropped off the face of the Earth. We thought Gull had terminated you, but Tyson had hope, so we bugged every phone imaginable, and had our ears on the airwaves—and bingo, the call to Domeni's house from your cell phone was picked up, hence the stakeout. We just didn't count on Gull's men being there also."

Faz lied about how they had known about Al and Domeni's date. The FBI had a mole at Baroque, and he wasn't about to tell anyone that, not here, not now.

"And you were taken by surprise," Al said, and then shook off a chill that ran through his veins. The room felt like it was getting colder.

"This Gull person you're talking about. It's not the same Mr. Gull I work for, is it?" Domeni asked.

"One and the same," Faz said.

"How could two agents of the nation's great FBI be taken so easily?" Campo asked, as he rolled his wounded shoulder. Despite the cold, that portion of his body was warm.

"Don't act so superior, Campo. You seem to be in the same predicament. Who in his right mind would risk coming out of hiding after the assault at your house?"

"This is true, but it was for a date with this beautiful woman." Al nodded at Domeni, who was on the verge of panic.

"Assault? What assault?" Domeni asked, fear building in her voice. "Why do you want Al, and who are the people who did this?" She began speaking faster as dread took hold. "Why am I here? What have I done to deserve this? My hands are hurting, my legs are going numb, my stomach is growling—I want to get out of here!"

"Domeni, Domeni, hold on one minute," Al interrupted. "I'm sure this is not the best first date you've been on, but it's not over yet. Please give me a chance, and I'll try to explain."

"Please do," Domeni said. She closed her eyes while Al spoke, praying it was all a bad dream. She was trying to control her breathing, but failing. She definitely was about to lose it completely.

"You see, several days ago, I was driving to work when I saw an old couch in the trash, and I stopped to pick it up…"

"What does an old couch have to do with my hands and legs being tied to this chair?" Domeni looked at him like he had three heads.

"I'll get to that in one second." *This is unbelievable*, Al thought. There they were, held hostage, and he had to explain himself to Domeni, like he was her child. Yet he knew she was near her breaking point, so he just played along and told her the story. "You see, someone else wanted it too. A man drove up moments after I had loaded the couch onto my truck. After a slight altercation, I took it to work, and then home. Later that same day I stripped off the fabric, and discovered a box with a label for radiation on it."

"The missing plutonium," Faz said. "Un-fucking-believable"

"Oh, you know about that," Al said looking away from Domeni's teary eyes.

"Yes, only we didn't know where it was. We intercepted several calls between Gull and Bracken Guttone, and he seemed pretty pissed off about his missing product. We knew he had expected a shipment of plutonium."

"What are you two talking about?" Domeni asked, bewildered.

"And after the shootout at your house, we knew you must have it. We just didn't know how you latched on to it," Faz said, shaking his head in disbelief.

"Now you know," Campo said and looked at the other agent. He was still struggling hard against his binds. He was leaning his body forward, attempting to tear the tape from his hands. His face was turning red as he strained. Then he let out a gasp and relaxed, and dropped his chin to his chest in failure.

"Did you have the plutonium when Tyson and I chased you down Interstate 95?"

"Yes," Al said, realizing too late the mistake he made.

"Un-fucking-believable," Faz said again, frustrated. "Why didn't you say so then? You could have prevented all of this from happening. Jesus Christ!" Faz just shook his head in disbelief. "You're a fucking asshole, you know that?"

"At that time, I thought it was better to keep it a secret. Besides I wasn't sure you two were real FBI. For all I knew, you could have been Mickey and Minnie Mouse working for Gull."

"You know, I just thought of something," Stortz said as he regained his strength and started his attempt at freedom again.

"What?" the arguing pair replied in unison.

"This is only an assumption, but it's probably safe to say everything we say is being heard by our captors." Agent Stortz said.

"No shit, you must have just finished your FBI training," Faz said, his rage toward Campo landing on Stortz.

Within seconds of Faz's growl, the group heard the noise of a lock turning, and a door creak open. From behind them, several men walked in. The first was a huge, broad-shouldered man, his long blond hair tied in a ponytail. The next two men were dressed in dark blue, and they were carrying steel trays. They set them down on the table. The last to enter was Jason Gull. He and Bracken stood before the prisoners as the others retreated behind them.

"Mr. Gull? Mr. Guttone…why are YOU here?" Domeni's face drew a blank, and fresh tears rolled down her cheeks.

Jason ignored her question, and sat in the chair behind the desk. He glanced down at the trays, looking at two 9mm Glock FBI handguns, six bullet clips, the agents' identification cards, along with Al's billfold and Domeni's small purse. Gull eyed the four victims sitting before him, waiting patiently, letting them sweat it out. Al guessed he was waiting for a barrage of questions, and noted that Gull seemed to enjoy the moment of suspense.

"Gull, I suggest you release us before your complex here is swarming with federal agents looking for Stortz and myself," Faz said in a commanding tone that provoked little reaction from his captor. It was a futile suggestion, but it had to be said.

"Do you really think I should?" Gull said sardonically. "You know, I've been simply terrified of you federal agents since your capture, and now you telling me I'm in danger is just driving me over the edge!" Gull said and grabbed his shoulders crossing his arms in mock fear. "Bracken, what do you think? Should we let them go before we are swarmed by FBI agents?"

The giant just smiled, brightening his occidental face. He stood over the captives; his beefy hands were folded in front of his belt buckle

"I didn't think so," Gull said and didn't hide his pleasure, smiling at the four prisoners. Gull enjoyed this feeling of power, of ultimate dominance over them.

"Cut the shit, Gull. What are we doing here—and what do you want from us?" Faz said. His face was turning red with irritation.

While Faz was having it out with Jason, Al bided his time. His hands and ankles were bound with duct tape. Campo continually twisted and stretched his bindings despite the warnings he gave the others. The movement was painful to his wounded shoulder, but he shoved the discomfort behind the need to escape. The twisting motion would cause friction, and then his wrists would sweat. Sweat was important, because he needed moisture to work the adhesive into his skin. His allergy to adhesives might enable him to escape. He wanted his wrists to blister. That reaction could cause moisture to build, loosening the glue from the silver tape, and he could slip his hands free. Bracken gave him a stare, so he ceased for the moment.

"Why you're here is simple," Gull continued. "You two FBI agents are here by necessity. If we didn't pick you up, you probably would have muffed our capture of Mr. Campo. We could have simply killed you, as Bracken would have preferred, but I thought it might be worth it to pump you for information, so you are here to enlighten me. Mr. Campo here was brought in to return my missing plutonium, which you already know about, and the sweet and luscious Domeni was merely in the wrong place at the wrong time. Besides, we don't know how much you've told her, Mr. Campo." Jason crossed his legs and arms and looked directly at Faz. "So now, let's get down to business. What does the FBI want with me?" Jason could care less about the FBI right now. He had the balance of the product, and the weapons were nearly completed. It was the game of dominance he liked so much. To see men at his mercy and watch them cower at his presence gave him sick joy. It was a game he had played many times on the road to success.

"Gull, right now you'd better be thinking about how you're going to save your own ass," Agent Faz said. "The Bureau is on to you. We know you've been smuggling plutonium into this country for the past two years. We would have arrested you yesterday if you hadn't had Dr. Salinger killed in his cell. But we didn't lose faith. We knew you'd screw up again, and by taking us hostage, you've done it. Soon enough there will be federal agents swarming the chemical facility."

"What makes you so sure we are at the Baroque Chemical Plant?" Gull reached a hand toward one of the agent's service weapons, and his anger grew. Faz wasn't playing by the rules. He was supposed to fear him, but he was attacking. "You don't even know how long you were unconscious; time has no meaning to you. A week might have passed, and my plans already might have been carried out. I could have put you on a jet, and taken you to Texas for all you know. You could have been kept drugged for a month before I woke you. So don't threaten me with your feeble Bureau, because they have no way of stopping me or saving you."

Jason enjoyed watching the bound group. All their faces showed their private reactions to his words. He let them sink in a moment.

Faz thought about Tyson giving up on finding him and Stortz. After they were missing for a week, they would be presumed dead.

Domeni wept quietly, not opening her lips. She was moaning, imagining the look on her parents' faces, seeing them suffer, the constant emptiness and turmoil caused by a missing daughter, the anguish they would suffer, never to know what became of their child maybe starving in some dungeon. They might never know if she would ever return.

Gull smiled until he looked into the eyes of Al Campo. It was Mr. Campo's face that angered him the most. He didn't appear to be shaken by their situation. He just stared back at Gull with vengeance and worse, an air of superiority, in his eyes. Gull wanted them to fear him, and now, most of all, he wanted Al Campo, the thorn in his foot, to know he was beaten, that Jason Gull held all the cards. Jason positioned himself in front of the agent from Arizona and half-sat on the metal desk with one foot on the floor. He loaded a clip into one of the handguns, clicked off the safety, and continued his game. "What you people at the FBI don't seem to understand is I am in complete control. It pisses me off to think you're trying to peek over my shoulder." Gull waved the gun around as he spoke. "And you say you're onto me and my operation. The government has been meddling in my affairs since I created this company." Gull paused. He stood, then started striding back and forth in front of the group, collecting his thoughts.

"First," Gull continued, "there are the stringent rules the fucking FDA places on my research. They have to compile thousands of pages of data—reaffirming what we've been testing for two years. Then they come in and decide they have to run their own set of tests. Years go by without a response. 'All ourducks are in order,' they say. 'We just need to complete some more tests.'" Gull's voice grew angrier, and he waved the weapon more erratically. "Then, after they finally approve the new medicine for fur balls in cats' asses, there's the upside. I get a chance to recoup some of the millions spent on research—and fucking lab animals—and technicians' frigging vacations.

"Then the government decides to regulate how much I get to charge for the fucking pills. Finally, after all that, when the money begins to roll in, the fucking IRS decides to do a fucking audit, claiming I misused research funds. I have been hammered by the likes of you, and the so-called ones who are onto me for years, and that's all going to end." Gull stopped in front of the young FBI agent. He raised the weapon and stiffened his arm.

"Gull!" Faz said, in panic, "What are you going to do?"

Gull ignored him and pointed the gun at the agent from Arizona.

"Gull, you bastard, he has a wife and children!" Faz screamed. "I'm warning you, you piece of shit, don't."

Al saw the young agent close his eyes, and tears rolldown his cheeks.

Stortz was thinking about his family. He muttered something that sounded like "I love you," then opened his eyes and stared bravely at Gull. Then the hammer of the Glock smacked into the 9mm shell.The bullet blasted into Stortz's forehead, blowing off the back of his skull. Stortz's head jolted forward and back, leaving his lifeless eyes staring at the ceiling. The floor and wall were sprayed with a mixture of fluids, coloring the area pale red.

Brains and blood ran down the front of Stortz's legs.

Domeni shrieked out a deafening scream of fright and horror. She shook her head violently, denying the sight, screaming and crying uncontrollably.

"You son of a bitch, I'll fucking kill you," Faz blurted out, furious. He was wrenching his arms and legs in a futile attempt to free himself, straining, desperate to get to Stortz's killer. "I swear, you motherfucker, I'll kill you. Let me out of this fucking chair!"

Gull nodded to Bracken, who was standing calmly with his meaty hands folded in front of him. The bulky man walked to the side of the manacled agent, and dropped a lumbering chop onto the back of his neck, rendering him silent. Faz's body went limp in the chair, and his eyes rolled back.

After seeing the blow to Faz, Domeni held in her cries of horror, biting her lip, moaning through her tears. She rocked back and forth like she was ready for the psych ward in a hospital.

Al Campo sat cool-headed, having seen far greater violence in his past. He stared at the murderer before him with wrath burning in the essence of his pupils. He was methodically twisting and stretching the duct tape around his wrists. The necessity of getting free consumed him now. He knew he must kill Jason Gull—no matter what the cost.

Gull looked blankly at Campo. He pointed the gun toward the corpse of Stortz and said, "Now there's one less person who's *onto* me."

CHAPTER TWENTY-NINE

Men were grumbling, waving their hands and sliding papers back and forth, trying to make something out of the intelligence reports from Turkey. CIA Director Bruce Kellogg passed out photos of a body being taken by ambulance from the temple of Hagia Sophia, Karuza's headquarters. The wraps on the wounded man were bloody and thick, so his face was not clear in the picture.

"How can we be sure it's him?" Nate Breechart of the FBI said.

"We can't," Admiral Faustian said, studying the photo.

The large doors to the conference room deep under the White House on Level Nine opened, and in walked Sam Haggart. As usual he was laden with a stack of paperwork and a briefcase.

"Good evening, gentlemen," he said, addressing the first three men to arrive. "Bruce, this came for you a minute after you left for the meeting." The president's chief of staff handed over a sealed file, then sat down, dumping the case and papers.

Bruce read the cover: EYES ONLY: MR. KELLOGG, DIRECTOR, CIA.

Before he could open the thin folder, the president came in the room, followed by General Morris Bartow, who carried his own stack of files.

"Gentlemen," Worthington nodded at them, and sat down at the head of the table. The group all nodded in response and waited for the meeting to officially commence.

"Well, gentlemen, I am ready for information" Worthington said. The photo was passed to him, and he looked at it intently. "Is this Karuza?"

"We're not sure, sir," Bruce said, as he opened the file, and read its contents. "Son of a bitch—he escaped!"

"Who escaped?" Morris said, interested, not having been privy to the assassination attempt planned by Kellogg's CIA forces.

"Sir," Bruce said, addressing the president. "These are intelligence reports on the status of our operation to terminate Karuza. It appears he was unharmed…"

"You mean your boys botched the job?" Morris said.

"It seems that his cousin Ammar was wounded," the CIA director said to the president. After the last meeting, he was tired of Bartow's comments, so he ignored him completely.

"How bad?" Worthington asked. The president took out a pair of glasses and studied the photos closely.

"The report says he is in serious, but stable, condition," Bruce Kellogg continued, "He is under intensive guard at a hospital in Istanbul."

"So you shot the wrong guy, *and* he's still alive," Morris said, shaking his head. The general leaned back in his leather chair and folded his hands on his chest. He could only imagine how much worse it was going to get before it got any better. Morris studied the men at the table. The president wore the determined look of the commander in chief. He was disappointed at the failed attempt, and it showed through his wrinkled brow and in how he pushed the photos away frustrated. Also, it looked like he was finally getting under the skin of the CIA director, because he wouldn't look Bartow in the eyes.

"Morris, I think the CIA had a difficult mission with little or no chance of success, but it had to be tried," Worthington said and took off his glasses, laying them on the desk.

"I understand, sir," Bartow said and leaned down to grab his own files. "But now Karuza will be untouchable. He knows he has been targeted by the US, and he will be watching our every move."

"They have no way of knowing we were behind the attempt," Kellogg said and pointed a finger at the general. "We used local agents, and their ties to us were through a secure network. I'm not an idiot, General."

Morris shook his head. "You can't be that naïve, Bruce. Karuza has intelligence agents of his own, and there is always a trail to follow. It's just a matter of time." Bartow opened his file and laid it in front of him.

"That's enough bickering," E. James said. "That operation is considered terminated. Let's move onto future plans, Bruce, where do we go from here?"

"Excuse me, sir," Morris broke in, and let his southern drawl be heard. "But I have some information I feel should precede Mr. Kellogg's findings."

"Fine, General, go ahead," Worthington said, eying the file Bartow had laid out.

Morris adjusted in his seat, pulled his coat-tails from under his backside, and leaned on the table. "Sir, in examining the file delivered by Mr. Haggart, I discovered there was a connection between my operations in the Middle East some twenty years ago, and current events in Turkey. Look at the man in the photo here." He held up a picture of Karuza standing with Ammar and Sabu, and he pointed to the Butcher. The other men grabbed their own pictures and scanned them. "This man's name is Sabu, aka the Butcher. He was involved with Saddam Hussein during the war in the Gulf, and he headed the assault on Kuwait before we were involved. He is notorious for his extreme and violent tactics. I'm sure you all remember the inhuman acts of violence that terrorized the people of Kuwait." The group all nodded. Bartow put down the photo, and then turned to the file. "Well, he was the instrument of their fate. His objective was to build a military force for Iraq, and exploit the weaker Middle Eastern countries. But Saddam became impatient, and released the Butcher on the people of Kuwait. His military might was inadequate and not yet trained for a major invasion, so he was forced to use brutal and shocking methods to bring down the government. It's been many years since then, and he had virtually disappeared from sight. Now he has reemerged, and is standing by the side of the fanatical Karuza. I feel we must take extreme action."

"General, are you saying Karuza intends to invade neighboring countries?" Worthington asked.

"We've been over this before," Sam Haggart said. "Whom would he invade? Every country in the Middle East has masses of followers pledging to accompany Karuza to his new regime after the return of the Prophet. Whom would he invade?"

"I'm not suggesting an invasion," Bartow continued, "but what I am saying is that Sabu was underground for so long that he has had ample time to build an incredible army of unknown proportions."

"Which may result in a major campaign in the territory," the president said. "General, how do you suggest we move on from here? It's obvious he will be wise to another attempt, and I can't order a military strike against Turkey—they're members of NATO, for Christ's sake."

"Have the Turkish government quash all of his activities and future speeches," Morris said. "Cut him off from the public eye, and disband his followers city by city. Then we install a small delta force to infiltrate, at which point we take out Sabu and arrest Karuza. With the three leaders gone, the revolution will die."

"We've already spoken to the new president of Turkey," Haggart said. "He agrees Karuza poses a threat, but his country has been invaded by literally millions of pilgrims, all believing in the return of the Prophet. His hands are bound by the faith of others. He can't very well topple the man everyone believes is heralding the return of their savior."

"He's just scared. Ever since his predecessor was assassinated, he'll say anything to save his ass—even making it appear he is on Karuza's side," Bartow said, shaking his head.

"Morris, I don't think we can count on Turkey for help," Kellogg said as he leaned back in his chair, and finally looked directly at Bartow. "I feel we have to sit back awhile. I can't see how he poses a direct threat to the United States. If Sabu is building an army, it cannot be too large—otherwise our satellite imagery would have recorded the activity. We've had our birds perched over the region for six months, and not as much as a bivouac has been spotted. And believe me, we've been looking."

"I hear exactly what you are saying, Bruce," Worthington said. "But sitting on our heels makes me uneasy. I still haven't heard from anyone in this room what exactly Karuza's plans are. Are they truly working for a holy cause, and is he simply a religious fanatic? Or does he intend to use his millions of followers as military might. This speculation is not helping. I still need to hear the evidence. Bruce, the attempt we made on Karuza?"

"Yes sir?"

"I sanctioned that because your information suggested he was to make another assassination attempt within two days, correct?" Worthington said.

"That is true, sir.' Kellogg said, and seemed to get into a defensive mode. "But the information did not specify the target."

"But the time frame you're sure of?" the president asked with wide eyes, like he had been given bad information.

"Yes sir. We have sources telling us a major figure—possibly two at the same time—will be taken out before Sunday is over." Kellogg opened his file and studied it to make sure of his information.

"Gentlemen." The president clasped his hands on the desk, and stared at the men. "Frustration does not begin to describe my feelings at this moment. The world counts on the United States to keep order around the globe. If I knowingly let another assassination take place, there will be hell to pay. General Bartow."

"Yes sir."

"You're familiar with these characters, Sabu and Karuza. Devise a plan for their removal immediately. My patience with the lack of information has come to an end. Once they are gone, we can discuss their motives."

Bartow sat up, happy to now be able to share the plan that he had formulated just moments before the meeting started. "Well, at this point, sir, a direct attempt to kill them would be an error on our part, because they will be expecting another attempt. So…" Bartow paused and appeared to read his file. "What I suggest is we do just that."

Worthington looked at him, leaning his elbows on the desk, but not comprehending what the general had just said. His brow furrowed, and he squinted his eyes in confusion. Then slowly his features softened, and a slim smile crossed his lips. Morris could see the president was onto his plan.

"General," Worthington said, "have a plan drawn up immediately, and we'll meet back here in twelve hours. Bruce, I want to know if Ammar is dead, going to die, or if he is going to survive. If we know one is out of the way, it will be that much easier."

CHAPTER THIRTY

Jason Gull was bothered by the sight of the open skull, all the blood and brains splattered around the room, so he ordered his men to clean the floor and remove the body of the late Agent Stortz. After the cleaning crew left, Faz was still lolling in dreamland, and Domeni seemed to be in mild shock. Her head was making small jerking motions, and every minute or so she would shake like she had a chill. Jason positioned himself directly in front of Campo, sitting on the desk.

"Now, Mr. Campo, you have no idea how much trouble you have caused me and my operation."

"Glad to be of assistance," Al said. He wanted Gull to know he didn't fear him. "So now that you've told me, can we go?"

"Very amusing" Gull half-smiled and crossed his arms. "At this time I feel it necessary for you to tell me who you really are."

"I'm the candy man—didn't you know?" Twist. Stretch. For the first time Al felt the tape slip slightly over the ball of his thumb. The tiny blisters which had been created burst under the friction, and he sensed his hands could be free in moments, but he was terribly overmatched. He thought of easily taking out Gull, then lunging with his feet still tied to the chair, grabbing one of the weapons on the tray. Maybe he could take out the two men who had returned from disposing the body, but Bracken was frightfully close to Domeni, too close for an attempt at this time. Al needed an edge. If Faz had been close to loosening his own wrists, together they could manage it. He looked over at the agent. The man was still groggy from the thump on the back of his neck, so any attempt at escape would have to wait.

"I don't think this is a time for sarcasm," Gull said, nodding to Bracken, The mass of muscle walked over, and slapped Al open-handed across the face. The stinging pain penetrated his cheek-bone and traveled across his eyes. His head was flung sideways, nearly breaking his neck. Campo's bonds were loose enough now that could easily throw a punch in retaliation, but he held in the urge. The proper time would come.

"Mr. Campo," Gull went on, "I've investigated your life in detail, and only one thing bothers me."

"And what's that?" Al said, wiggling his jaw—bringing the bells under control.

"That you did not exist before you filled out your application to the Glazier Union ten years ago. No one by the name of Al Campo was born thirty-five to forty-five years ago, and yet, here you sit. Your birth certificate is unavailable, and you've never been married. There's a Social Security Number on your application, but it leads nowhere. It is as though you were fashioned out of thin air. Simply put, you are a fiction. Also, I find it strange you knew where I was to pick up the plutonium when I was the only one privy to that information. Whom do you really work for?"

Domeni sat still in her chair staring at Mr. Gull. She was frightened beyond imagining, and she listened intently. She now feared Al Campo. Who was he really? They didn't even have a chance to talk before this all happened. She didn't know where he lived, if he had any family, and these things Mr. Gull was saying. Maybe it was just a trick. Maybe Mr. Gull was just trying to bleed information from them before he had them all killed. She didn't know the answers, but she had to trust someone—and Al was the only one possibly in her corner.

"First things first," Al twisted his jaw again, acting like it still hurt. "I work for the union, yes, and second, I had no idea your precious plutonium was in that damn couch. What idiot would leave such a valuable item in an open area? Then again, I've only just met you."

"I'm sorry, Mr. Campo. I don't believe you, and I'm not a patient man. Mr. Guttone here will gladly beat you until every bone is shattered—and until you need an intravenous line just to stay alive."

"I'm not lying, so you may as well start the trouncing," Al said, defiantly calling the bluff, only Gull wasn't bluffing. Bracken swung his fist, backhanding Al's other cheek, ringing his bell once more. Just then there was a knock at the door.

"Come in," Gull commanded. "Now I will show you all what you've postponed, and you can be an important part of a vital experiment."

From behind the three remaining prisoners, Al saw an older man enter. His coarse gray hair was neatlycombed, and thick glasses enlarged his curious eyes. He carried an aluminum briefcase, which rose up and down as the old man limped into the room.

"Wolfie, come over here," Jason said.

Wolfgang looked at the smeared blood on the floor, and the three bound captives. He turned away, avoiding their glances, and nervously carried the case to his boss.

"Everyone, I'd like you all to meet Wolfgang, a brilliant man," Gull spoke as though he was at a board meeting. "He was my mentor both in and out of college. He has created an incredible weapon, and you all are going to be part of history."

"Gull, you bastard, we are not interested in being part of your games," Faz blurted out as he regained his senses.

"I'm sure you realize, Mr. Faz, that you have no choice. Thank you, Wolfie. Now go and get the others ready for shipment. Oh, Wolfie, one other thing. Is Everett working with you at the moment?"

"No, he is home on a personal day," the old man said solemnly.

"Well, call him in; I want your best man with you to make sure nothing goes wrong. You aren't getting any younger, you know."

Wolfgang was only too glad to leave thatroom of death. He exited into the hallway with his mind in turmoil. "What have I done?" he thought. "I have given the single most powerful hand held weapon in the world to a murderous madman. I must stop him. This cannot happen." While he was lost in his thoughts, the two men from the prison chamber entered the hall.

"Mr. Gull thought you might have had a change of heart, Wolfie, so we are here to assist you in preparing the weapons for shipment." A tall, broad-shouldered man forcefully nudged the scientist down the hall to a door marked OPERATIONS ROOM. Wolfie nearly fell over as he grabbed the doorknob and entered the room.

Back in the prison chamber, Al watched as Gull, excited as a child on Christmas morning, spun the dial on the combination, and snapped the metal briefcase open.

"Ahhh," Gull said, his eyes wide. "It's beautiful."

Domeni, Faz, and Al sat in silence. They stretched their necks, trying to glimpse what Jason was gazing at with such pleasure. From within the case, he lifted a rectangular-shaped piece of dense plastic approximately two inches wide by six inches long. Its edges were smooth, and its color light gray. Next he removed a similar-colored piece, thinner and longer; a spring-activated trigger protruded from the narrow side. These two pieces snapped together at right angles. A third pipe-shaped piece, threaded on one end, screwed securely to the second piece, doubling its length. Then Jason held up two clear plastic tubes, welded together lengthwise, keeping the contents of each tube separated. He looked at the material inside, holding it to the light, twisting his hand. He marveled at what the others could not see, that the interior product was translucent.

"This is the result of the plutonium you so frustratingly kept from me," he said. Then he unhooked a hasp on the base of the handle, inserted the tubes, and snapped it shut.

"What the hell kind of gun is that?" Faz asked.

"A very powerful one, Mr. Fazolo." Gull massaged the weapon in his palm, feeling the grip. "This is very exciting. The feeling of euphoria I have is breathtaking. It must have been the same for Fermi and Oppenheimer just before they tested the world's first atom bomb in Los Alamos. Just as they were, I too am proud of my creation."

"Let me guess, it's a nuclear-powered toilet," Al said, gazing with pure loathing at the man before him.

"More jokes, Mr. Campo? If I didn't want you to witness this, Bracken would have crushed your skull. But that time will come. This is a sophisticated laser gun that can,via a beam of light the diameter of a small nail, deliver enough concentrated radiation to instantly, and invisibly kill the target. Of course, it will be equipped with an infrared laser sighting scope for pinpoint accuracy."

"You're an asshole, Gull. A weapon like that could never be created," Al said it, but he imagined it could be done. His real task was to draw Bracken away from Domeni, so he could attack their captors with minimal risk to her. With the two other goons off to keep an eye on the scientist, he was thinking of making his move.

"I'm surprised, Mr. Campo. I thought you were more open-minded than that," Gull said waving the plastic gun at the captives.

"I am," Al said, "very, but listening to a maniacal, self-absorbed, obtuse asshole like you makes me doubtful." Bracken stepped forward, but Gull waved him back, letting the restrained man speak. "People like you make me lose my faith in power of progress. You complain about rules and regulations in testing your silly products, and government involvement. Let me tell you something, Elroy. Those procedures were put in place to keep fat cats from losing their sense of morality. You could care less if your drugs kill or maim or disfigure innocent people. Your bottom line drives you past reality, and into the danger zone of greed and power. Life is too short for you, and time is your enemy. Our government stalls information to investigate, and you hold them liable for not meeting your projections. Gull, I hope—no, I *know* you will fry in the electric chair. And if I have anything to do with it, you won't die on the first jolt." Al's eyes were red with rage, and the veins in his neck bulged.

Domeni gazed in fascination, and a degree of lust.This man, tied to a chair, sitting in nothing more than his underwear, was undaunted by imminent torture. He was incredibly sexy at that moment, and she felt a burning desire to be with him. She knew he was a man she could trust with her life.

"Well, that was a very nice speech, though I'll have to point out you are the ones restrained at the moment—and I hold your lives in this hand," Gull said, displaying the weapon.Then menacingly, he pointed the gun at Agent Faz, depressing the plastic trigger. A faint hissing sound echoed, and then there was a long, quiet ring.

At first, the agent looked normal. Still sitting upright, he began to attempt to swallow, raking his tongue across the roof of his mouth.

"Are you all right?" Domeni asked, worry and fear in her breath.

"I'm feeling a bit nauseous," Faz replied between gurgles, fighting the bile in the back of his throat.

Jason stared at him with savage anticipation.

The bound and almost naked agent let out a deep, bellowing cry—his head wrenched backward, every muscle taut. Then he fell forward, vomiting fiercely, writhing in his restraints. Another screeching cry came through his retching lips. "Help...me..." Faz bubbled out as his face turned blue, suddenly unable to breathe. His chest heaved raggedly up and down, striving to siphon oxygen through frozen throat muscles. He shook his head intensely from side to side, eyes bulging, his hands and feet milk white from yanking on his restraints, cutting off the circulation. Faz's torso and waist lurched outward, sustaining the position for seconds that seemed as long as minutes. Then he crashed back into the metal seat. The agent lay pliant, his chest barely rising up and down, death still yielding to life by a thread.

Al held back his desire to thrash out at the abomination that was Jason Gull. He avoided looking at Faz, and focused his deathly stare on Gull.

The murderer was grinning from ear to ear.

"That worked perfectly. Mr. Guttone, check the counter," Gull said, keeping an eye on his test animal.

Bracken checked the radiation level in the room with a hand-held Geiger counter. "Radiation is slightly higher than a few moments ago, but we are still in the safe range."

"That's wonderful," Gull said enthusiastically.

"How could you be so horrible—you insane monster!" Domeni yelped out.

Al could tell Domeni had moved through fear and out the other side. She knew she was going to die, and holding back now was not an option. She would welcome her fate after witnessing the horror of this madman's actions.

"This is a day to remember! Today marks the successful testing of the world's first Jasonium handgun," Gull said, ignoring Domeni's comment. "I must call Mr. Vincent immediately. Mr. Guttone, I haven't any need to question these two any longer. You may dispose of them at your leisure." Jason was so excited his emotions took over. He wasn't interested in torture. His weapon was successful beyond his expectations.

The mammoth Bracken grinned, his smile radiating his happiness.

Jason placed the deadly weapon back in its case, and snapped it shut. "Mr. Campo, though I would enjoy finding out whom you work for, I have other matters requiring my direct attention. Mr. Guttone here will see to your confession, and your imminent departure. Goodbye, Mr. Campo, and of course," Gull stared Domeni in the eyes, "my dear Ms. Conti. You have been a most professional worker. I've enjoyed gazing at your beauty these past years. I am truly sorry for your death. Adieu, my sweet." Gull blew the pair a kiss, and exited the room.

Al knew the only departure Guttone would see to would be beating them into dead rags. It was only the three of them now, but Domeni was still restrained, and Bracken stood beside her. The giant reached into his breast pocket, and drew out a stiletto switchblade. He hulked over Domeni, who peered up at her executioner.

"Hey!" Al shouted. "You piece of runny corn-filled cat shit."

Guttone disregarded his comments and smiled at Domeni. He laid the tip of the blade to her forehead. She didn't dare move. He gently slid the weapon down her nose, over her lips, then scraped the mascara from her cheeks. He slid the blade around her neck, ending at her cleavage, and stopped before cutting the shirt open.

"I must tell you, Ms. Conti," Bracken said wryly. "I enjoyed having to undress you and check your body for hidden weapons. It took twice as long as the others."

Repulsed, Domeni nearly vomited on him in shame and disgust.

"You and I are going to have a little party before this is all over," Guttone said.

"I doubt you could get it up," Al said, still trying to draw the monster away from Domeni. "You slimy, pig-headed, ugly, bald, muscle-bound piece of shit. But then again, I haven't been to the circus in a while, and I'm not up to date with the nocturnal activities of freaks."

This finally caught Bracken's attention, who darted a look at Al. "I think I'll allow you to watch, but without the use of your tongue," he said, stepping over in front of Campo, about to reach for his mouth. "Have I told you how your friend, Mr. Barrett, gurgled his last breath before my eyes? He died crying like a baby."

Filled with rage, Campo imagined the torture Bracken must have gladly inflicted on his friend. It only intensified his will to escape. "Well, the joke's on you, dickhead, because he survived."

Bracken's eyes flared crimson. "Impossible."

"Impossible, but true," Al said and saw a shadow of fear on Bracken's face.

Angry, the giant stood over his victim and reached his hand toward Campo's mouth.

He was now close enough, and with one swift motion, Campo's cupped hands boxed the hulk's ears. Guttone dropped the knife, and slapped his hands over his ears, pressing on them in an attempt to stop the ringing. From his sitting position, Al threw an uppercut into Guttone's jaw, knocking him backwards onto the metal desk. Quickly, Campo groped for the knife, hoping to cut his legs free, but it lay just out of reach. Goliath recovered swiftly and open-handed the left side of Al's face. Guttone followed that up with a left fist to the cheek. His right fist followed, knocking into the side of Al's head. The momentum threw him sideways to the floor. He crashed onto his wounded shoulder. Al wanted to cry out in pain, but instead, he reached for the knife once more. Bracken steadied himself, and kicked his victim in his wounded thigh. Al thought his leg had snapped.

"Leave him alone. I'll do anything you want, please let him be," Domeni screamed out at her former boss.

Bracken turned to her and said, "I know you will, but you'll have to wait your turn."

The distraction was enough for Campo. He pulled back his legs, swung the steel chair up and then thrust it like a battering ram, crashing it into Guttone's shins. The giant dropped onto his chest, into the pool of Faz's vomit, bursting his nose on the cement floor, splattering blood on Domeni's bare feet.

Campo finally reached the knife, and slashed the tape loose from his legs. In an instant Guttone was up and attacking again. His face was smeared with blood. He grabbed at Al's hand and twisted his wrist backwards. Al lost his grip on the knife. The two fighters wrestled, grimacing at each other. Campo was holding his own but losing ground as the massive bulk drew down his hand.

Al was ready to collapse when he called upon all his reserves of strength, and swung his elbow into Bracken's bulky chest. The effect was small, and Bracken stood stiffly, waiting for another blow. Campo was only too happy to oblige, but he would not aim for the same mark. This time he faked the swing, and thrust his knee into Bracken's groin. Bracken didn't expect it, and gasped as his testicles rose into his stomach. Al grabbed the steel chair, and brought it thundering down over the giant's back. He fell to the ground. Again and again Al bashed him. Seething in rage, he hit his back forcing the giant back down. Then he slammed the chair into his legs and finally into the back of Guttone's head until all movement stopped.

Al was panting, his chest rising up and down, but one last time he struck, letting out his anger. "Die, you son of a bitch," he screamed, then threw down the chair. Exhausted and dehydrated, Al fell to the floor, panting for air. He lay there for a few needed seconds. He looked at Domeni's frightened eyes, then felt his adrenaline rush return, and a sense of urgency flooded over him. He cut Domeni free, who immediately leapt up, wrapping her arms around him, stressing his wounds. Al cringed and enjoyed it—because to him at that time, there was no better pain in the world.

"I'm so happy you're OK," she said.

"OK?" Al whispered to himself.

"I don't ever want to let go."

"I don't either, but we have to get moving. If they heard that ruckus, Gull's men will be back in seconds." Al grabbed the handguns from the desk, inserted full clips, and offered one to Domeni. "Do you know how to use this?"

"You've got to be kidding, I've never even seen one this close," she replied and shied away.

"Well, I think it's time you started." Al said and pushed it at her again. "This is the safety. This is on and this is off." She took it reluctantly. Al had just grabbed his clothes from the corner, when he heard a faint sound.

"Whenever you're ready, I am," Domeni said, holding the gun with one hand, sliding her feet into Agent Stortz's shoes, preferring them toher high heels.

"Shhh. Did you hear that?" Campo said, and they both stood quietly. Domeni inched herself closer to her protector.

"What?" she replied.

"Shhh."

From the lips of the internally mutilated Agent Fazolo, they heard a whisper. "Caaampooo."

CHAPTER THIRTY-ONE

Al quickly went over to Faz's near-lifeless body, and held his ear close to the agent's mouth. "What's that, Faz?" he said. "Domeni, quick. Grab the knife and cut him free. Faz, we're going to get you out of here. Hang on."

Fazolo slowly lifted his head, holding it precariously upright. His entire face was swollen, gruesomely distorting his good looks. Blood was dripping from his tear ducts and ears, and pinkish bile flowed from his nostrils. He tried to spit the blood from his mouth. When Domeni cut him loose, his arms fell dead to the side, nearly causing him to tumble from the chair. Campo grabbed his shoulders, and held him steady. Then he put his arm under Faz's knees to lift him when the agent seemed to come to life for a brief moment.

"No…leave me," he rasped out.

"Faz, we've got to get you to a hospital quickly," Domeni whispered.

It seemed to take all his remaining energy, but the FBI agent reached his hand to Campo's shoulder. Campo saw the agent's dying eyes gazing into his. "You must…" Faz stopped to cough out the fluid building in his throat. The remaining words were slow and strained. "Get…to Tyson…tell danger, stop weapons…stop Gull…save lives…"

"You can bet on it," Al assured him.

Faz gave one last push, squeezing Campo's shoulder, forced out a half-smile, then expired limply in his arms. Al laid him gently on the cold concrete floor, closed his eyelids, and let him go.

Al quickly got dressed while Domeni still knelt, staring in disbelief at the dead man. "Domeni, it's time to go." Campo held out his hand to her. "Domeni, we have to get moving. Please get up."

To her, getting out seemed a dim possibility. She had now witnessed the horrible murders of two men, and watched Al beat a man with a chair like a maniac. She looked up at the dark eyes and strong face of her protector. His was a positive, stern gaze, and it renewed her confidence. They might be able to escape alive after all. She took his hand, and they both walked to the door, Al in front with the knife tucked in his pocket and the 9mm in his right hand. Domeni gripped her gun uncomfortably with one hand while resting the other on Al's back. He cautiously pulled the metal door inward a crack. He could see one man standing in front of another doorway down the hall.

"What do you see?" Domeni whispered.

"A way out."

"A window, a door, what?" she asked, impatiently.

"The room I think that old scientist is in. We're going to take him with us, and he'll show us the way out."

"Why would he do that?" Domeni said, not wanting to delay their escape.

Al turned to her, closed the door, and said; "Two reasons: first, I'll have a gun to his head, and second, by the look on his face earlier, he is as much a prisoner as we are. I'll need him to explain this mess we're in to Tyson when we get to the Federal Building."

Al cracked the door again and readied himself.

"Get where? And who's Tyson?" Domeni said tugging on his shirt.

"I'll explain later. Stop it!" Al said harshly. He needed to stop her asking so many questions. He knew she was scared and needed answers to relax her, but she would have to deal with his abruptness for the time being. He went back to the corner where the agents' clothes were still hanging. He took a shirt and wrapped it tightly around the front of the gun. He opened the door just enough to let the muzzle of the gun through, and fired a single shot, hitting the guard in the ear, killing him instantly.

"Let's go," he commanded. "Stick close."

"You don't have to worry about that. I'll be glued to you like a stamp," Domeni said as she shadowed him.

———

Wolfgang worked slowly, yet at a steady pace, organizing the parts of the monster handgun into separate aluminum cases. Through his years of research at the plant, and under the direction of Jason Gull, he had never witnessed horror like what he saw in the prisoner room. Even his experiences with the various lab animals were nothing compared to the bloodied floor and the bound prisoners. Two armed guards stood on either side of the exit, both with automatic weapons. The scientist knew escape was impossible. He now knew for sure that Jason Gull would not let him live after what he saw. He would be left alive to organize the weapons for shipment, and then the two thugs would take him for a ride, never to return. Somehow, he must disarm them, but how? It would be too dangerous to simply destroy the plutonium sleeves. A raw radiation leak of that size could not be contained, and once it escaped outside, wind or rain could carry it anywhere. The guns themselves were made of dense polycarbonate Lexan plastic, with a crystalline core. To damage them would take an explosive. Possibly switching components, maybe using two handles instead of one and a barrel, yes, switching would be the solution. Nervously, he glanced at his guards and began the process of sabotaging the weapons.

A sudden knock at the door startled him, and he dropped a handle.

"Yeah, what is it?" Campo heard the muffled response through the door.

"Mr. Gull needs you back with Mr. Guttone," Campo said.

"Both of us?" the voice said from the room.

Both? Campo thought, surprised. Where had the third guard come from? He had to answer fast, not knowing exactly what he was going to do.

"Yes, he wants both of you to come right away." Al said trying to sound convincing.

Al stood ready for attack in front of the door while Domeni was against the wall with her gun held in the ready position. The door unlocked and as it started to open inward, Al kicked it hard, knocking the two guards against one another. He leaped into the room, and shot them quickly, without stopping to think.

"Wolfgang, Wolfie? Where are you? Damn, I thought he was in here," Al said as he quickly scanned the room with his weapon held in front of him. Domeni stood by the door at the ready, watching for unwanted visitors.

"Wolfgang, are you in here?"

"Yes, here I am." The scientist was on his knees, ducking behind the table. Slowly he put his head up and smiled when he saw a face that did not belong to one of Gull's guards. "Young man, you look familiar to me."

"The last time you saw me we weren't properly introduced."

"Yes, of course, you were among the prisoners in the holding room. You've escaped, I see."

"Not yet. We need your help," Al said, and helped the old man to his feet.

Domeni, standing in the doorway, noticed a security camera across the hall. She took careful aim and held the gun tightly with both hands. She wasn't ignorant about guns. She had seen a lot of Dirty Harry movies, and she remembered seeing his hand jolt back after firing. She leaned her shoulder against the doorjamb and fired two shots. The second blew the monitor apart, and the recoil injured her elbow. She smiled, pleased by her accomplishment, since this was the first time she had fired a gun. She was rubbing her arm when Al yelled.

"Domeni, what's wrong?" Al ran forward, dragging Wolfie with him.

"Security cameras. They're watching our every move," Domeni said grimacing.

"What's the matter with your arm?" Al asked and scanned the room. He saw another camera in the far corner. "Shit, I think it's time to blow this clam bake."

"Clam bake?" Wolfgang asked.

"Never mind. We have to get moving."

"What about the weapons?" the scientist asked, resisting Al's pull.

"Can we destroy them safely?" Al asked as he looked around at more than a dozen silver cases containing the menacing handguns.

"Impossible, we have no means to…"

"Then leave them.They would be too cumbersome, and we need to make a quick exit… no wait!" Campo thought a second. "Take one with us," he reached for the closest case, snapped it shut, and pushed it at the scientist who unconsciously took it by the handle. "You'll have to carry this. My hands are full," Al said, displaying the two automatic weapons he had taken from the dead guards. "Now, Mr. Scientist, we need a car and a way out."

"And quickly please," Domeni said, sounding nervous. She kept flexing her arm, and her face looked like she was in pain.

"Yes, well, it's this way to the elevator," Wolfie said and exited the room.

Just as the three made it down the corridor to the elevator, they heard someone, or several someone's, thundering down the steps. Domeni pushed both the up and down buttons simultaneously, and the doors opened. To Al's surprise, the car was empty. Wolfgang entered first, and then Domeni, and Al backed in. The footsteps grew louder. Wolfie pushed the appropriate button, but the doors remained open. Al jammed his hand on the door's 'Close' button just as the door to the stairwell burst open. It was Jason's security force, armed to the hilt with automatics. Campo fired, taking out the front two men as the elevator doors finally closed. They traveled down, stepping out into a parking garage. Although it was not completely filled with cars, Al felt they had enough obstacles to take cover when needed.

"Where to now?" Domeni asked, tension in her voice.

"Hurry, the black Cadillac is the chauffeur car. The keys are always inside," Wolfgang said.

Al scanned the area. "OK. Move!"

Domeni ran in front, towing the old man behind her. Without warning, the Baroque security force appeared, shooting sporadically at them. Al returned fire across the sea of cars, blasting windows and side panels. They exchanged fire brutally while Domeni and Wolfgang hid behind an SUV.

"Move now! Get to the car," Al commanded as he stood and let fly a long volley of bullets until his first gun was empty. Then the enemy returned fire.Campo ducked behind a small sports car as the windows were blasted, and the tires exploded. "Jesus Christ," he said and readied his other automatic. He looked over and saw Domeni and Wolfie ducking behind a concrete column. The Cadillac was about thirty feet away. Domeni's eyes met his and he nodded. She knew what it meant, so she waited a second, and then took the German by the arm and ran hard for the Cadillac. Campo fired over the hood of the sports car and then took off after Domeni and Wolfie. Ahead of him, Al saw the old scientist scream in agony and drop to the ground. Al ran, firing blindly behind himself, and snatched up the wounded scientist. When they got to the car, Domeni turned and fired her gun while Campo dumped the German in the back seat. He got into the driver's seat, and then Domeni entered only after emptying her clip of bullets.

Lying on his back across the rear bench seat of the black Cadillac, Wolfgang felt the warmth of blood down his side and upper thigh. The bullet had entered his lower back just above the right hip, penetrating whatever organs he had in that area. Then it had torn a hole through his stomach, exiting his ninety-year-old belly. His pain was intense, and he felt burning pain shoot through his gut over and over again. To cry out or moan would only inflict more distress on his nervous system, so he lay silent, holding to his wound a blood-soaked clump of tissues Domeni had found in the glove compartment.

"Hold on," Wolfie heard Al bark from behind the wheel, and then all of a sudden inertia pushed the old man deep against the backrest. His body slipped with every jerk of the car. Campo slammed on the brakes, and Wolfie agonizingly held his left hand against the rear of the driver's seat, barely keeping himself from falling to the car's floor.

Al constantly swerved, stopped, and accelerated, crashing into other vehicles. He drove like a combination of an Indy and Derby driver. His driving ability outmatched the security forces alerted to his whereabouts, out maneuvering their smaller cars. Men on foot, firing machine guns, were just crushed by the hood of the luxury car.

Domeni sat in the passenger seat, and kept her head down by her feet, her hands clasping the door and armrest for dear life.

"Where the hell is the exit?" Al yelled half-rhetorically and half at Wolfie, not expecting an answer from his wounded passenger.

"Look for…"

Wolfie was trying to shout, but Al knew he was slipping from consciousness. The pain must be excruciating, and Al's memory of being shot was all too fresh. He knew Wolfie must desperately want to rest.

"Look for the sign indicating…" the old man tried again.

"Indicating what?" Campo asked as he wrenched the wheel to the left, tearing off the front bumper of a blue security car. Bullets peppered the trunk of the Cadillac.

"Gate G," the scientist spat out, miraculously audibly enough for Al to hear him over the clatter of the gunfire.

"Gate G," Al repeated. "Shit. We passed Gate G when we first pulled out. Hold on everyone!" He raced the big sedan down a long run, then spun the steering wheel as many times as it would allow, pounded the brakes hard, released them, then gave equal pressure to the accelerator. The big luxury car turned like a spinning top, halting to face the barrage of attackers head-on.

"Now let's see who's got the bigger balls!" Al said, as he gunned the huge, eight-cylinder motor directly at the lead car.

The security forces fired at will. Al had no intention of swerving. He lowered his head below the dashboard as the front windshield was riddled with holes. Keeping his hand firm on the wheel, he headed straight for the security men. The security driver turned to his left, T-boning a fellow car, pushing it sideways and crashing into the glass elevator lobby. The fragile material shattered, shooting shards of razor-sharp splinters through the windows, piercing the flesh and bone of the passengers.

Campo looked up when the shooting stopped, and not a moment too soon. He was heading to the left of a tunnel marked

"Gate G." He swerved and hit the brakes. He had driven into what looked like a dead end. The area was round, and he sat in the middle surrounded by expensive cars. "Wolfie, it's a dead end."

"Have we reached gate G?" Wolfie spat, then hacked out an ugly cough.

"For Christ's sake, Wolfie, you led me to a dead end." Al said, looking around the cars.

"That's good."

"No, that is not good. They will be after us in two seconds, and we have no place to run," Campo began to think it had been a bad idea to drag the old man with them; he might even have been a set-up, purposely sent to direct them to the end of the line.

'Sir if…you would kindly…" Wolfie coughed out blood, then wiped his mouth with his left hand. "Please beep your horn three times, wait fifteen seconds, then three more times."

"What the hell for? I don't have two seconds to waste," Al looked back at the wounded man, and saw the serene face of an aging man. He felt compelled to trust him—and he did as he was told. The area around the car began to rumble and in a moment it began to rise out of the floor. Domeni held on tight, and Campo looked out the battered windshield, watching the ceiling above open like a split dome, the sun visible in the clear sky.

"Oh my God…" Domeni said.

"This is one hell of an elevator, Wolfie," Campo said and looked back to see the security force re-grouping. "Hopefully those assholes don't know the code, because if they do, it's going to be a short ride." The platform came to a stop, and Al wasted no time in gunning the motor, directing the car down a dirt road. He sensed he was near the Baroque plant, because of the ever-present fog. "We must be near the plant, Wolfie. What the hell is this fog all about?"

"The cooling of the reactor requires thousands of gallons of water," Wolfie managed to say between gurgles.

"Reactor?" Campo said. "You mean to tell me Gull has a nuclear power plant hidden inside the building?" Wolfie didn't respond. "Wolfie! Shit." Al knew he was in Delaware, and his instincts would probably get him to the main road, but that could take hours in the maze of roads surrounding the plant. "Wolfie, I need to know the way to the main road." Up ahead the dirt changed to blacktop, and he barreled onto it.

"Wolfgang!" Al tried again for a response. He couldn't see the scientist in the rearview mirror, which meant he had slumped over, or fainted. Al looked around, checking out the landscape, reassuring himself that they weren't being followed. On either side of the road were dense forests, and up ahead he saw a small clearing, or what he considered a clearing.

"That's me," Al said.

"What's you?" Domeni said, pulling herself upright.

"That road to the left."

"Road? I don't see any road," she gasped.

Al turned the auto, still going at high speed, mowing down the shrubs, and thundered a hundred yards into the thicket.

"What are you doing? Are you crazy?" Domeni asked, bouncing back and forth, clawing for something to hold onto.

"It's time we stopped to check out the old guy," Al stopped and darted out of the car, and quickly grabbed broken branches and bits of brush, hastily making a screen to cover their presence. It took a few minutes, and when Al came back he got a good look at the once-luxury car. Its fenders were badly banged up. The front glass looked like a piece of Swiss cheese. Three of the side windows were shattered, but amazingly, all four tires held their air. He saw Domeni leaning into the back seat, holding her hand to the belly of the mortally-wounded scientist.

"How is he? Can he talk?" Campo said as he opened the other door.

"I...I don't think he's going to last long," she replied, tears welling up in her eyes. She had never even dreamed in her worst nightmares of experiencing so much horror and death, first the brutal murders of the two agents, and now this old man. "What is happening?" she mumbled to herself.

Al leaned over Wolfgang's face, holding his cheeks. They were gray and pasty, his eye sockets shadowed. Looking at that face, Al knew death was inevitable. Sorrow was an emotion Al had learned to place at the back of his consciousness. To feel compassion for this man was natural, yet when he died, Al and Domeni would still be lost in this forest, not sure which way to go. They could end right back in the clutches of Jason Gull. That would mean certain death for them both—that was unacceptable. Campo must take on the unhappy task of grilling the dying man.

"Wolfgang, I need to know where we are, and how to get to the main road." He spoke straight and direct, his face only inches from the wrinkled, flaccid face of Wolfgang.

The German's eyes half-opened. Al saw in them the old man's pain, and his face looked like it was in the grip of a vise. His breath was slow, his limbs were loose and unmoving.

"Sir?" he whispered.

"Yes, Wolfie, where are we?" Al asked.

"Your name, please?" The words were quiet and polite.

"It's Al, Al Campo," he replied, feeling his opportunity slipping away.

"Pleasure to…meet you," Wolfe's face went taunt between words.

Al looked up at Domeni. She was crying uncontrollably, her hand still pressed hard to the wound. Al had learned a long time ago to suppress his sadness, but the courage of this man, holding on to his life by mere threads, and yet still attempting to greet a stranger as though they were meeting at a coffee shop, that penetrated his emotional shields, and when he responded he held back the lump in his throat.

"The pleasure is mine." Campo grabbed the scientist's hand and squeezed gently.

"I never wanted anyone to get hurt. I'm so…sorry." Wolfie coughed and turned his head, retching blood onto the floor.

"I believe you, Wolfgang. Everything's going to be OK. We're going to get you to a doctor."

"No, young man…I am going to die here in this car. You must escape…save the world from Jason Gull." A long, rattling cough caught in the scientist's throat.

"I will." Al thought of asking directions again, but Wolfie spoke first.

"This road will take you to a dead end. Turn toward the hill, and follow it to the highway."

"Are we at the Baroque plant?" Al said, assuming he was right.

"Yes..." The German's body convulsed into rigid stiffness, his face shook, and he trembled in pain. He pulled his head up, squeezing Al's hand as if that could draw the anguish out of his body. Wolfgang's eyes opened wide. Death's harsh grip was tightening, but he was able speak one last time, one slow word at a time. "Pray...for...my...soul..." His head dropped. His grip on Al's hand loosened as the great, unknown German scientist died.

Domeni's face was wet with tears. She took her bloodied hand from his stomach, jumped out of the car, and was sick into the bushes, crying and panting and retching.

Al rounded the trunk and held her in his arms. She returned the hold, and buried her forehead in his shoulder, letting her tears of sorrow flow, not just for the death of this man, but for the whole situation. She cried from fear, stress—and the possibility of danger lurking ahead. He let her sob to the point of exhaustion. Soon Domeni's mind caught up with her body; she relaxed in Al's arms, no longer able to bear the burden of consciousness.

He tenderly laid her in the front seat. His emotions too were tired. He stood gazing toward the road, looking over the roof of the car. Memories thrashed in his brain. The past was creeping up on him, and he would have to face it head-on.

CHAPTER THIRTY-TWO

The sand in his teeth crunched as he grimaced. The sand blew almost constantly across his face as he waited quietly, lying on the desert floor. He wore a headdress of khaki-colored linen, using the tail to shield his eyes. His face was a weathered copper, the skin cracked from the intense heat of the day, and the extreme cold of night. He lifted a pair of night-vision goggles, and focused on the compound three hundred meters in the distance. Few men were up and around the encampment in the pre-dawn hours. Turning his attention to the left, approximately an equal distance away, he could see his partner lying flat, also facing the compound. To the right two others lay, waiting for orders, and though he could not see them, he knew six others were spread out around the area.

Major Alfonse Candalini placed the goggles back in their pocket and rubbed his hands, generating warmth. With both hands, he gripped the handle of his M-16 semi-automatic, equipped with a grenade launcher, and tensed his fingers, heating the cold steel. He looked at the timer on his wrist. It indicated there were thirty seconds to go before all hell broke loose. He planted the butt end of the rifle onto the edge of a camel chip, bracing for the recoil. The timer on his watch began vibrating, signaling the attack. His was not the first weapon to fire; across the desert his men fired parachute flares, illuminating the compound. Immediately the assault followed. The major fired six rapid-fire grenades, pulling back the shaft of his gun between launches. They exploded with ferocity. His men were spewing grenades and gunfire everywhere, flushing out the inhabitants of the compound. The victims were blasted into the air, shrapnel tearing off their limbs. As the explosions ceased, men exited the dirt huts firing blindly, only to be picked off by one of the major's snipers. A pile of corpses grew until the light from the flares died away, and darkness took over the desert once more.

The major and his men then evacuated the area separately according to their pre-planned escape routes, leading them into the blackness of the desert to rendezvous in the morning light. Alfonse ran crouched over, keeping low to the sand. He'd become accustomed to zigzagging his way to his vehicle—nearly a quarter-mile away. Tonight was no different than any of the other missions he and his men had carried out in years of snuffing out encampments deemed to be probable dangers by his superiors in Europe, who took their orders from Washington. He never questioned them—he simply carried them out. The raids were occurring more frequently lately since the Iraqis had invaded Kuwait. He and his team of Special Forces gladly caused serious damage to the Iraqi army. Up until today, the raids had takenin a similar form. Next his superiors had ordered them to infiltrate the Iraqi underground and eliminate them from within. For now, the major concentrated on his escape, not allowing his mind to wander onto the next mission. He eventually stood straight as he ran more slowly, approaching his truck.

Something was wrong; the blackness of the sky was playing tricks on him. His vehicle was no longer there. Standing in the spot where he had left it, he spun around in circles looking along the horizon. Tire tracks were barely visible, yet they were there. As strange as it might seem, his truck had been stolen, but by whom? Alfonse was vulnerable, standing there in awide-open space, so he quickly made his way to a low rock formation, and huddled into a crevice naturally bored into the rock by blowing sand. He sat with his back to the stone, his weapon drawn, and weighed his options. Radio silence was critical at this point of the operation, and he refused to equip his men with radios, just to rule out any urge. He was no different, and now he was alone. With darkness changing over to morning, he would be exposed to the rescue party sent to the compound he had just annihilated. He could have a go at jogging into the desert toward the scheduled meeting with his men, but he would arrive hours late, if at all. Or he could count on his men seeking him out after he was discovered missing. But all in all, his chances were grim.

Without wasting anymore time, he stripped off the heavy ammo belt and bag, leaving himself enough for one assault, in case he encountered anyone he couldn't hide from, and made out on foot at a steady pace. Sweating heavily after only a half mile, he opened his garments, cooling his body. The sun was rising in front of him, and he knew his pace was too slow to get to cover before the heat of the day really hit, yet he trekked onward. In the distance, he saw a dust cloud, and he knew it was a vehicle heading his way. He slowed his run and stopped to rest. The cloud of dust grew larger, inching its way toward him, and he now could distinguish three tan-colored jeeps coming at full speed. He bent down, rested his arms on his knees,and looked into the auburn sand, panting, seeking a solution. The answer eluded him as he rose, and was surrounded by the jeeps. Perched over the windshields, men dressed in Iraqi military uniforms aimed Russian AK-47 assault rifles at his chest. The answer he sought in the sand was now clear: give up or die.

<hr>

Al Campo snapped out of his daze, and checked on Domeni lying in the front seat. She slept peacefully. Al was hoping she was dreaming of flowers and rainbows, because when she woke it might be to a world of thorns and thunder. He didn't know what getting away from the plant would be like, and he needed time to think about his next move. He saw the dead scientist in the back seat and decided to bury him. He lifted the German, and carried his limp body toward the trees. He smelled like cologne and sweat, but the strong scent of blood overpowered it all. His body was heavy and with Al's wounds and bruises, now throbbing all over his body, he set him down only ten feet from the car. He used the knife he had stolen from Bracken and scratched at the leaf-covered dirt. It loosened the surface soil until he could scoop out the dirt in handfuls. He repeated the process several times and dug a shallow grave. He rolled the body in and gently covered him with the loose soil and leaves. It wasn't much protection from the scavengers that roamed the woods, but it would have to do. He marked the location with a broken tree branch.It had grown naturally in the shape of an imperfect cross. He didn't know if Wolfie was a Christian or not, but Al was, and since *he* was burying him, a cross and a prayer would suffice. He said the Lord's Prayer silently, and then found a yellow wildflower and laid it on the mound. If he lived till tomorrow, he would make sure someone came and took the old scientist to a proper burial site.

He returned to the car and lay on the mangled hood. Al found himself at a crossroads in his life. He was facing the evil of a madman in a place he called home. He couldn't even begin to imagine how far Jason Gull's claws dug into governments here and abroad. The simple fact that he could kill without remorse, and worse, with a sort of happy excitement, meant he was out of control, especially when his victims were federal agents. Gull had no fear of ever getting caught; he must have protection at a high level.

Al needed to focus on his next move. Escape first, and get Domeni to safety. Then his next step was clear. By any means possible, stop Gull before his deadly weapon could be used on innocent people. The only way to do that would be to kill him. Campo knew he must wait until dark before he could safely drive out into the open and make it to the highway. He allowed his tired body and mind to relax and fell into a quiet calm, not sleeping—just a self-possessed state of relaxation.

Major Candalini awoke to pain. His body was suspended over a cold, dank, wet dirt floor. His arms were forced behind him, draped over a wood beam, anchored to the walls of a dungeon-like cavern. His shirt had been removed, along with his shoes. His bare feet dangled just inches from the moist ground, while his hands were tied to metal rods protruding from the bottom of the beam. He raised his head, and felt stinging throbs pound his skull. Rolling his head, he discovered blood dripping from his scalp, and to his dismay he realized the wetness on the floor below him was his own blood soaking into the sand. If he raised his head up, half-cocked to one side, he could see his captor. The face was dark, with hair covering most of it. The eyes were black as coal, and a sinister grin shone through the bushy beard. He wore a tan beret with matching desert military clothes Candalini recognized as the uniform of the Republican Guard of Iraq's elite force. Several other men dressed in similar uniforms surrounded him, but none of their faces held the same cold cruelty as the first.

"Who the fuck are you?" the major asked in his best attempt at Arabic.

The man didn't even hesitate. He immediately swung his fist into the major's jaw. The major felt his bones rattle, but they remained intact. The man then thrust his fist into his gut, causing, Candalini could feel it, internal bleeding. The beating continued as the man worked every part of his body. The major's ribs were broken as a metal rod was used like a Louisville Slugger. Then his legs were crunched, all three bones in each. The only parts not touched were his upper arms, and he could only reason that was because they were required to hold him upright. The torture lasted for hours; the man would take breaks, catching his breath between blows. He was the only one inflicting the pain. The others stood indifferent. Some leaned on their rifles, others sprawled out on mats, watching silently. No questions were asked of the major. Only torment and misery were delivered. Ultimately, his torturer tired of beating him. Then he pulled out a long dagger and cut the Achilles tendon in both ankles, then the patella tendons in both knees, then at last, he cut the major down. The major collapsed to the blood-soaked ground. The group of men dragged his limp, beaten body across the room. Blood trailed behind him like an oil spill. He was thrown into the back of a truck, and dumped onto the road in the town center. During his last conscious moment, he felt his ragged hair yanked tight, and saw himself face-to-face with his torturer. The image was etched into his brain, never to disappear, for he was looking into the eyes of a madman.

"If you survive, you can tell your American pig friends that Sabu the Butcher did this to you, and I will punish all Americans who come to my land. *If* you survive." The evil man spat at him, then shoved his head into the hard ground. The truck pulled away, and the last glimmer of light vanished from his eyes.

———

Moisture draped across his skin. The heavy clouds of humidity fell to the earth as the familiar fog rolled through the trees. Al opened his eyes and saw the dim light of dusk clouded by the haze. It was time to move into the open, under the protection of night and shadows. He sat behind the wheel, with Domeni's head at his side. She curled up in the fetal position, and stirred as he started the engine.

Slowly, she opened her eyes, wishing it were all an awful dream. Scanning the dashboard, gripping reality, she followed the panel toward the wheel. Then she met Al's gaze. His dark features and piercing brown eyes, smiling in a sturdy and sympathetic grin, were a pleasure to view.

"Did you rest well?" he asked, moving the gearshift into drive.

"Oh Al," she said, putting her arms around his waist, resting her head on his lap. She held tight, never wanting to let go. His physical existence re-energized her. Somehow, she knew he would bring her to safety, bring the nightmare to an end, and she could rest in his arms forever. Domeni pulled herself up to his face. Tears dripped down her cheeks, feeling a profound and unbounded trust in her protector. Al stopped the car and shifted back into park. She rained a flurry of kisses onto his cheeks and forehead, around his neck and ears, but avoiding his lips. Then her hands came around his head, pulling him closer to her, as finally their lips met. Al returned the passion he felt rise in her as they lost control of their inhibitions and desire took over. They rolled sideways onto the leather seat of the once luxury car and made love. For a few moments, they forgot all that had happened, and they became partners in the seduction of one another.

CHAPTER THIRTY-THREE

J ason Gull was furiously swearing at his security force. He paced back and forth across the lower level of the parking garage, cursing at them like they were dogs. For most of the men, it was their first meeting with the man who signed their paychecks, and what they saw was not anything at all like the talk in the break room had suggested. He was sweating heavily; his shirt collar was unbuttoned, and his tie hung loosely. Lastly, he smoked feverishly, lighting one cigarette after another. "If those three people are not found in the next two hours, I'll remove every one of you from those fucking comfortable homes the company has helped you all purchase! Your fucking families will be out on the street—I guarantee it!" Gull said, glaring at each of the twenty or so men in his presence.

Without another word they scrambled to their vehicles and headed out after the escapees. Gull hit the elevator button with the fleshy part of his fist. He raked his nails through his thick hair and then grabbed another cigarette. He entered the elevator and punched the button for the operations level. Minutes later, he entered the room where Wolfie had been preparing the weapons, and took a quick look around.

"Everett, we are missing a weapon!" Gull screamed at a tall man dressed in a white coverall standing by a group of tables. A long row of aluminum cases were all opened toward Everett.

"Yes, Mr. Gull," Everett said as he snapped shut one of the cases. "Apparently one was taken during the escape."

"Son of a bitch!" Jason's temper was at a dangerous level, and he knew it. Perfection had always been his trademark, and now with his life on the line, that was the furthest thing from his credentials.

"Sir, if you recall, Dr. Wolfgang prepared sixteen weapons, the first being the prototype. I do believe it is fully functional," Everett spoke with a commanding air, his voice almost bitter. He had been Wolfgang's assistant for the past three years. Only thirty-three years of age, he was a genius at nuclear fission and kinetic energy. In a way, he was as responsible for the final creation of the weapons as Wolfie. It was his insightthat creating a totally polycarbonate casing for the weapon would make it seem harmless to the naked eye, as well as undetectable by any type of metal detector. Now he was in total control, and Gull was going to rely heavily on his knowledge. Gull knew Everett was only too happy to be rid of the old German. Now he could be top dog.

"Yes, yes, I remember. Pack it in another case, and ship them out immediately," Gull said between puffs. He rolled up his sleeves.

"I'll see to it personally, sir," Everett said.

"Don't fuck this up, Everett. I'll hang your balls from the flagpole." The statement was delivered in a voice so grating it sent a chill down Everest's spine. Gull returned to his office, sat at his desk, and stabbed a code into his keypad. He spun his chair and watched the two large panels slide open. The familiar image of Mr. Vincent appeared, his pudgy hands resting on his bulky stomach.

"Yes, Jason, what now?" Vincent said. He seemed to be ready for another blunder.

"The apples have fallen from the tree. They will touch down in eight hours."

"Very good, Jason. I knew you would accomplish your task on time. In two days, you will be sitting by my side in the White House," Vincent said as he began rocking in his chair comfortably. The news was refreshing, and a pleasant smile shone on his cheeky face.

"Yes, Mr. Vincent. I am looking forward to joining you." Gull was a bit relieved at finally being able to report success to Mr.

Vincent. Seeing how happy he was, Gull even allowed himself a thin smile.

"Tomorrow, Jason, we will witness the fall of many nations, and behold the creation of a new, more powerful one. It will stand side-by-side with the United States. The new Most Holy Nation of Believers—not a nation separated by geographic boundaries—but joined by faith, all followers of the Prophet throughout the world will live securely under its strong wing. Our leader, His Holiness, Caliph Karuza, will bear witness to the return of the Prophet, and show him the path we have prepared for him. The time has come, and we have played an integral part in its success."

Mr. Vincent's ramblings made Gull very uneasy. Although Jason sought power within the government, he did not have much confidence in the New Age of Believers. After he received his payment, he would probably opt for retirement in a sunny part of the world.

"Gull, I expect you will arrive in Washington tomorrow evening, and we will meet privately on my yacht on the Chesapeake," Vincent said, raising his eyebrows like the question only had one answer.

"Yes, Mr. Vincent. Tomorrow will be fine. I just have to tie up some loose ends here before leaving for the airport." Jason knew his loose ends were extreme, and he chose not to bother Mr. Vincent with the fact that two prisoners had escaped along with Wolfgang, and that they had taken with them a weapon powerful enough to change the world.

"Jason, you've never had loose ends in the past. For your sake, you better not screw this up, not when we're so close to success." The pudgy man ended the conversation, and the picture on the screen faded to black.

For the first time in Jason's memory, he felt fear, not for his life, but a fear he might not succeed a hundred percent. What if Al Campo reached the FBI—and with him an aging German scientist who had disappeared in the Sixties? And more importantly, carrying the handgun that scientist had created for Gull? They would have to listen to his story, no matter how far-fetched. Then, the FBI would come after him like a swarm of killer bees attacking a rival nest. Gull's next moves had to be calculating and swift. An entire legion of men was seeking Campo, but he must assume the worst, and prepare for the FBI. The plant and offices needed to be cleaned. Once the weapons had shipped, the remaining data, and all items containing information on the project, would need to be completely wiped out.

Gull typed in a series of numbers on his phone.

"Yes, Mr. Gull?" the gentle voice of Mrs. Anderson asked over the monitor.

"Mrs. Anderson, have everyone working on project Jasonium 11-215 make a clean sweep, leaving no trace. Make sure they understand—CLEAN SWEEP!"

"But Mr. Gull, most of the employees have already left for the weekend," Mrs. Anderson said.

"Then call them at home, call their cell, or send security to their houses. This is Priority One. Do you understand, Priority One!" Gull was yelling. He just wanted a simple "Yes sir," not a fucking song and dance.

"Yes, Mr. Gull, I understand," Mrs. Anderson's subtle voice was somber. Jason had never spoken to her like a subordinate in all their years together. It troubled her, and panic made her hands tremble as she retrieved the phone list from the computer.

Jason pressed the cancel button, hanging up on his secretary, and contacted the operations room.

"Everett," he spat out.

"Yes, Mr. Gull?"

"What's your status?"

"The cases are packed and on their way."

"Excellent. Now sterilize the room, and double—no, triple check the Geiger counter. If anyone comes looking for radiation, I don't want so much as a radioactive atom found. Do I make myself clear?"

"Yes, Jason." Everett used Gull's name for the first time, defiantly letting his superior know he was not an idiot. "I've already begun purification of the operations room and the holding chamber. I also have six men on their hands and knees scrubbing the cracks on the floor." Everett wasn't that extreme, but it's what Gull wanted to hear.

"Good. When you've done that, go to the kennel and destroy all the experimental animals, and scrub that room as well." Things were moving in the right direction, and Jason's confidence lifted as well. The weapons on their way meant his mission was complete, and now was the time to secure everything. He punched out a call to his secretary once more. "Mrs. Anderson, have you contacted everyone?"

"Nearly, Mr. Gull, except I haven't been able to contact Ms.Conti," she said, feeling she had done a good job making all her calls and confirming them in such a short time. Her good feeling wouldn't last long.

"Ms. Conti? I never gave her security clearance on the project. I wasn't aware she was involved," Jason tried to maintain his calm.

"Ms. Conti wasn't directly involved in the project, sir," Mrs. Anderson said, her voice shaking, "but this week I was overwhelmed with work, finishing the filing of the project, and I asked her to take home two hand written files and copy them onto a computer disc. You see, she is a much faster typist, and she has the software at home to do it," Mrs. Anderson said, as dread rose in her stomach. She had given Ms. Conti those files without permission—and Mr. Gull was adamant about security.

"Mrs. Anderson, are you telling me Ms Conti has vital information concerning the project?" Jason was boiling over with rage. Here another cliff to climb, another blunder by incompetents. He held back the urge to blast her.

"Yes, Mr. Gull, that is correct. Those files were handwritten by Dr. Wolfgang. I think they were his final logs connected to the project."

Gull's face turned pale, then took on a shade of red only seen on the surface of Mars. The veins on his temples nearly split as he slammed his fist down, splitting the arm of the chair.

"Fuck!" he yelled, and Mrs. Anderson didn't need the intercom to hear him. His voice traveled through the wood door to her ears. She closed her eyes and ducked her head, imagining the force of his breath on her neck.

He dialed again, and contacted Simon Baird, his new head of security. Baird had left an hour ago in a dark blue security van.

"Yes, Mr. Gull?" Baird answered.

"Simon, what is our situation?"

"Well, sir, I have four vehicles, including my own, circling the plant area, moving progressively outward, searching for the Cadillac. Also, I have four more running to the main roads in an attempt to cut off that route, and then…"

"Listen, Simon," Gull cut him off. "I want you to leave the search, get to this address, and remove two files from the home."

"Would that be Ms. Conti's home, sir?"

"Yes, it is. She has two files, and they may or may not have been copied onto a disc. I want those files—and as a precaution, take her whole fucking computer. And I don't care about casualties. Just get those files."

"Sir," Simon said quickly. He didn't want Gull to cut him off again. "I have already dispatched two units, one to Ms. Conti's home, and one to Mr. Campo's. I understand the situation, sir, and I intend to cover all angles. Every avenue of escape will be cut off, and I will capture the three of them. The units will arrive within twenty minutes, armed and ready for any instruction."

Simon's confidence filled Jason with pleasure. For a change, he didn't have to think of everything. "Excellent, Simon. I trust you will see to the retrieval of the files personally. And Simon, I don't want this to travel into the public eye. Have your men obtain the files at all costs—yet without drawing attention to themselves."

"I'm on my way, sir." Simon hung up and Jason let a half-smile cross his face.

CHAPTER THIRTY-FOUR

Four marble columns grew like tree trunks from the floor, the tops spreading like branches of solid pure white. Stone leaves decorated the undersides as the tops flattened out, forming a smooth surface. The table was massive in girth and thickness. Its edges had been left rough and coarse. The sculptor, losing sight of his masterpiece, had decided to leave it as it was. Seated at this table was Caliph Karuza dressed in his usual white linen, his hands folded in silent prayer. Beside him was Ammar who had been in surgery two days ago, and was now under constant care by his personal physician. Karuza needed him close, and once the doctors allowed him to leave the hospital, he brought him back to the temple. Ammar sat stiffly, wearing bandages around his neck, and a sling supporting his left arm. His neck was sore and throbbed, but he did not complain, for he must of course be present while shaping the new ruling of his caliph. The large mahogany doors opened, and the caliph's general, Sabu the Butcher, entered.

"Your Holiness!" Sabu said, "the weapons have arrived from the Americans!"

Karuza opened his eyes and glared at his general. "Excellent. Allah has been gracious to them and our cause. See to the men, and brief them once more. Ensure they all are able to use the weapons, and execute their mission on time."

"Yes, your Holiness. Our time has come—and I pray the Prophet's return will be swift!"

Sabu stood erect, nodded to Ammar and Karuza, then exited the room.

"My cousin," Ammar said, unmoving. "Tomorrow begins the reign of Caliph Karuza. Hundreds of millions of followers will worship you worldwide. No one will be able to stop us from uniting all of our peoples into one nation—and you will be Allah's messenger of the New World. The United States will surrender under the pressures of the new order, and the Republic of Georgia will give us protection from the East. It shall be a momentous day indeed!"

"After tomorrow, Georgia will come under the power of our rule."

"What didyou say, my cousin?" Ammar said and cocked his head slightly."Andropov expects to remain in power after the new nation has formed."

"Tomorrow," Karuza looked over at his cousin, with whom he was raised like a brother. The sinister stare bore through the coarse beard. "With the army Sabu has been building for the past two years, we will storm the borders with a million men, and remove Premier Andropov from his powerful seat, and display his corpse from the capital. Then we will stand alone as the only superpower in the world. We will take control of their nuclear weapons and launch them against any and all who will not obey our rule. The time has come for the return of the Prophet—his path will be cleared of all infidels. Only true believers can ensure his repossession of the Earth. I can feel his strength as we come near to the day when all surrounding us is one. The Prophet will break down the Christian belief, destroy the tales of Buddha, and thwart the meaning of Judaism and their pitiful hope that someday their Messiah will come. I can take no more of the ramblings or false preaching."

Karuza bowed his head, clenching his eyes shut to purge out his hatred. "The New World shall be no different than the old, when the Arabs ruled the known world for six hundredyears before the time of the Crusades. This time,the presence of the Prophet and his Reign of Justice will allow no more heresy among the people of the world. Tomorrow will be the day of judgment."

"I did not know you had intentions of killing Andropov."

"Ammar, my brother, while you slept, and you regained your strength—Allah spoke to me, and told me of the betrayal Andropov was to commit. He will die with the other leaders, so the prophet's path is clear. I never trusted that fat bastard, and Allah in his infinite wisdom bestowed upon me the task of destroying all who stand in the way. It is to be the Most Holy Nation, and I, Caliph Karuza, shall stand next to the Prophet upon his return." The pair clasped hands and bowed their heads in silent prayer.

Meanwhile, outside the walls of Hagia Sophia, the pilgrimage of believers grew. Families crowded the streets and gardens. All hotels and inns were jammed with news media covering the story. The city of Istanbul burst with bodies. People slept in alcoves and on doorsteps, continually looking to the skies, which most believed would be the avenue of the Prophet's return. The grounds echoed with prayer and calm. No one fought or argued. It was the calm they knew the Prophet would cherish.

Sabu's men stalked the streets, corralling men, enlisting them in his army. Unruffled, they would follow his soldiers in aircraft to one of twenty sites set near the Turkish-Georgian border. The sites themselves were hidden under the shroud of True Believers. Their true intentions were unknown to the Georgian defense. Weapons were stored in underground bunkers, tanks and artillery hidden inside buildings designed to look like mosques. Sabu was organizing his greatest army of all time; he would not make the same mistakes as before. Time had been his enemy in the past. Now it allowed him to give birth to his dream. Tomorrow possibly two million men would storm the republic like ants, decimating all that stood in their way.

In the United States, religious fanatics congregated, hundreds of thousands packed into the Mall in Washington, DC. They left their jobs and careers behind, hoping to send a strong message to the government that they believed in the return of the Prophet and that Caliph Karuza would be their new leader. The sentiments of the crowd spilled over into the back rooms of the higher political powers—yet some believed that's where the sentiments were contrived.

———◆———

In a spacious apartment overlooking the Chesapeake, on the outer rim of the capital, the congressman from the fifth district of the state of South Carolina sat cross-legged, leaning his elbow on the soft armrest of a tan suede sofa. His dark skin was freckled with specks of black, making him look even older than the sixty-five years he had. He wore a brown suit and tie, and poised on his head was a Muslim cap decorated in African colors of bright yellow, red, and green. He was the current leader of the underground movement of the Nation of Believers. His name was Fattah Abdullah, and he was outspoken inhis full support of Karuza's visions and promises of a new Nation of Believers, and the return of the Prophet. With all the activity occurring in the Middle East, he had been sharing the media attention with the new movement. Each day and evening, after an update on the Turkish situation, he was all too happy to give an impromptu press conference, urging Americans to come to the capital, and to join the True Believers movement. He had secretly been funding the pilgrims all over the country, paying their way, feeding, clothing, and sheltering them on their travels. Unlike Sabu in Turkey, who was creating an army for military intentions, Fattah was building a peaceful gathering with direct orders from Karuza—a non-violent takeover was necessary in the US. Only after a sign from Allah would it occur, and his caliph assured him it would be soon.

"Are they necessary?" a man sitting across from Fattah asked, pointing a heavy hand at two men standing behind the congressman. The men were tall and broad-shouldered, standing with their hands folded in front.

"As far as I'm concerned, they are always necessary. They help me sleep at night," Fattah said.

"Fine then," the man replied, with no attempt at hiding his displeasure. He leaned down and picked up a glass of brandy, sipping it before continuing. "His Holiness assured me he will allow you a position in the government after the change over has taken place. Which position, he hasn't said."

"Secretary of state is what was promised to me at the beginning, and I intend on holding him to that promise," Fattah said, as his expression turned stern. "My influence and stature among the Believers here in the US has almost guaranteed a smooth and controlled takeover. That was the goal set forth by His Holiness, and I have come through with full public support—I have everything to lose if this operation goes awry. You have remained shrouded, your anonymity complete. If Karuza fails, you will remain in your position as vice-president of the United States. After the rise of Karuza's believers in this country, I deserve the promised position—and fully expect it."

"Like I have said, Mr. Abdullah, the position you will hold has not been decided as of yet. Besides, if Karuza fails, which he won't, you still have the hundred million dollars in raw diamonds to fall back on. I'm sure that is worth sacrificing your measly reputation for." Mr. Vincent spoke directly, knowing Fattah had no idea how much the diamonds were worth, and he saw a gleam in the black man's eye. "Mr. Abdullah, I sense doubt and a lack of faith." He swirled the cordial around in the glass before sipping again, allowing Fattah to take in his comments.

The congressman shifted in his seat, crossing his legs. The last thing he wanted was to lose his position with Vincent, knowing he was to become the next president. "No, Mr. Vincent, you misunderstand. I have not lost my faith. I am only concerned my hard work has been taken for granted. I have complete confidence in His Holiness and am at his service."

"I am happy you are with us," Vincent said and set his glass on the desk in front of him. "Now, Karuza has sent instructions that tomorrow you will give your most powerful speech immediately after the president falls ill. You will swear Allah has delivered the sign of the Prophet's return, and now is the time for our total commitment to His Holiness, Karuza." Vincent slid his glass aside and reached into his briefcase. "Here is a copy of the sermon for you to study and memorize. Remember, you must be convincing enough to sway public opinion, and garner congressional support. After

I'm sworn in as president, I'll send for you and publicly endorse your cause, and contribute whatever is necessary to prepare the way for the return of the Prophet. At the same time, around the world, similar speeches will endorse Karuza, and finally the Caliph will speak, bringing all Believers together into a single, powerful nation.

"May I ask how the president will fall ill and die?" Abdullah asked.

"Karuza and I both agreed I would not be privy that information for my own safety and deniability," the vice-president drank down the last of the brandy. Then he stood, straightening his tie. He walked to the door and turned. "Remember, just do as you're told, and everything you ask for will be granted—after the return of the Prophet."

CHAPTER THIRTY-FIVE

The sun settled into the distant west, falling deep into a deep slumber for the evening. A three-quarter moon rose as shadows stole over the Baroque chemical plant. Al Campo, with Domeni clinging to his side, cautiously drove the mutilated sedan out to the roadway. Campo scanned the road in both directions. No headlights or search beacons loomed in the darkness, and the area was quiet.

"What do you think? Should we make a runfor it?" Al asked, locking on tight to her shoulder.

"No time like the present. After last night, it can't get any worse," she said as she dug in and held her head low.

Campo turned onto the unlit road, heading in the direction Wolfgang had indicated. He kept the headlights off and trusted his night vision to slowly guide them out to the main road. Domeni was now feeling more secure, so she sat up straight with Al's permission, still holding tightly to his side.

"I think we're out of the line of fire for the moment," Campo said glancing around.

"I couldn't feel any safer sitting in a police station surrounded by men with guns than being next to you," Domeni said, snuggling her head into his shoulder.

Al felt the warmth in her words. He leaned down, and gave the top of her head a long kiss. Her hair still had the smell of sweet perfume.

"Al," she said, "now that we are not running, burying someone, or tied to a chair, could you please tell me what in God's name is going on? Why is Mr. Gull doing this—and what do you have to do with it? And what was all that about you not having a past? Like you appeared out of nowhere?" Domeni spoke without looking at his face. Despite her lust, and the sense of security he gave her, she still didn't know a whole lot about her knight in shining armor. That began to bother her, and she couldn't bring herself to stare him down, fearing to see an unwelcome truth in his eyes, but she would listen before she judged.

"Domeni, apparently you've been working for an evil man. I'm not exactly sure what he is up to, but one thing's for sure—the only purpose for those weapons we saw at the plant is to kill. Wolfie died before he could say anything, but the way he acted in the plant, it was strange. He didn't know what the weapons were to be used for until the last day, and it bothered him enough to want out. Gull knew he couldn't be trusted, so he dragged him along until he finished them, and then killed him anyway. He was preparing them for shipment, but to where? If they were to end up in one location, they would have been shipped in the same box."

"Why? They could have been sent different routes to the same place."

"Too risky. Anything could go wrong with one or more of them during shipment. No, they were sent all over." The thought floated through Al's mind for a few moments, while he tried to figure out his enemy's weaknesses.

Then Domeni broke his concentration. "And what about you? How were you involved?"

"Purely coincidental, like I said to Faz—the couch started it all."

"Oh, that's right, I forgot," Domeni masked her feelings. She was sure he was holding back, just the way he had with Gull. "What about me?"

"What do you mean?" Al asked.

"Do you think I have something to do with all of this?" Domeni asked, testing Al's faith in her—and she also wanted him say it out loud.

"Are you kidding? No way! He had to take you in with me. He couldn't just drop you off at a mall or something. But then again, his company is huge; he couldn't possibly know every move of every employee. Maybe there's something you know, but don't know that you know."

"But I don't have any knowledge of the terrible gun, or any of Mr. Gull's personal dealings," Domeni said defensively. "I've worked for the company for fifteen years, and for three different people, but never with Mr. Gull directly."

"When you say 'directly,'are you saying that maybe through the chain of command you have done work for him?" Al asked as he flicked on the headlights, turned onto the highway, and blended into the light traffic.

"Of course, everybody works for him indirectly. It's his company," Domeni stated.

"That's not what I'm saying."

"Then please tell me what you are saying," she said, beginning to get a little uncomfortable at his questioning.

"I mean, do you do any projects for Jason Gull through another coworker?"

"No, I don't. Mrs. Anderson is his personal secretary, and she is my boss. She runs the entire floor. I've never seen Mr. Gull's…" Domeni caught herself. Suddenly she remembered Friday afternoon. "Oh my God! Shit!" She said and sat bolt upright.

"What is it?" Al said.

"Quick, Al. Turn off the next exit! I have to get to my parents' house right away!" Domeni's voice was frightening Al. Desperation and anxiety filled her face.

"Domeni, tell me what's wrong!"

"I will, just turn!"

Al flung the wheel, crossing three lanes in one swift motion, looping around, and heading north on Interstate 476. He gave her a stare, prompting her to speak.

"Al, on Friday I wanted to leave an hour early to get ready for our date, so I asked Mrs. Anderson if it would be OK if I left. She said yes, but could I take home two files, and transcribe them onto the computer at home. She knows I am a fast typist. She wanted me to bring them back on Monday."

"Did you look at the files?" Al said, and actually thought this might be a turn for the better. If he had files directly linked to the weapon, it would be easier to explain to the FBI.

"Briefly," Domeni's expression turned blank; she could see the wording of the papers in her mind. They had not been in any great order, or neatly written. She remembered the name jotted on the lower left corner. The letters were scribbled, and they ran together, but she knew the name. It was Wolfgang.

"Well?" Al prodded.

"They were Wolfe's notes. Wolfgang signed the bottom of the front page. They were his personal notes concerning the new weapon. That's why I was brought in with you. Mrs. Anderson probably gave them to me without Gull's knowledge."

"No way," Campo shook his head. "Had Gull known you had them while we were prisoners, he would have asked you for them."

"Not unless he already sent his goons to get them from my parents' house."

"Here," Al tossed his cell phone to her. "Call your parents' house. Tell them to get out immediately and drive to the nearest police station."

Domeni dialed, the phone rang and rang. "There's no answer, and they don't have an answering machine," Domeni said in panic.

"Keep trying. They may have gone out for something to eat. Is that possible?" Al asked, fearing the worst, but hoping it would plant a positive thought in her mind.

"They could've gone to Atlantic City for the evening. They were talking about it before I left."

"That's good news, but keep trying anyway. They may come home."

"Al, your phone is beeping."

"Shit, the battery is going dead. The fucking thing must have been on all night. Quick. Call 911 and tell them a burglary is in progress at your home!"

Domeni dialed 91…Then the phone beeped one last time and turned off.

"Al, it's dead," she said, looking at Al in disbelief. Tears dripped down her face. The thought she might have put her parents in danger was too much to bear.

"Don't worry," Al said, patting her thigh. "We'll be there in ten minutes."

———

The battered Cadillac approached the Conti home on Inglewood Road, and proceeded slowly through the first traffic light. They could see the house in the near distance.

"There is a van parked across the street from your home. Do you recognize it?" Al asked, knowing instantly it was the same type of vehicle used by Gull's men.

"No, I don't think so," she said, straining her eyes through the darkness.

Campo turned the car down an adjacent street. "Domeni," he asked, "I'm not familiar with the area. Is there a back street or alley or parallel road behind yours?"

"Yes, the back yard butts up against Mr. Burton's house, and he is at the end of a cul-de-sac."

Al made the appropriate turns, and then cut off the lights, parking at the end of the road. They could see Domeni's house through a thicket of trees and shrubs—a perfect cover for approaching unseen. "Good. That's my way in."

"Al Campo, what do you mean, your way in?" Domeni grabbed his arm, and pulled his face toward hers. "Let's go to my aunt's house and call the police before we make any rash decisions. I don't want anything to happen to you. I didn't see my parents' car in the driveway, so there're probably not home. There's no need to rush in now."

"Sweetheart, relax," Al said, rubbing her cheek softly. He surprised himself by saying that word. It had been a long time since he'd uttered it. His feelings must be genuine. "There is a possibility no one is there. I'm just going to give a look-see."

Campo reached to the floor and grabbed the Glock handgun and the knife he had taken from Bracken. He removed the cartridge from the handle of the gun, and saw that only two bullets remained. He replaced the clip, and stuck the gun in his pants. "OK, now where did you put the files?"

"The computer is in a closet at the bottom of the steps in the basement. They are in a caddie next to the printer."

"I suppose it would be silly to ask if you have a key on you," Al said looking at her disheveled attire.

"Al," she looked at him hard and folded her arms across her chest, "You do realize I've been drugged, unconscious, undressed, dressed again, involved in a shoot-out, a car chase, made love in the front seat of a Cadillac, and then dressed again? God only knows where my house key would be." Domeni watched his eyes travel over her body, and she realized he wasn't serious. She smiled at his dark eyes.

"Sorry, I had to ask," Campo smiled. He checked the bullets again, and turned to Domeni, staring into her golden eyes, which glistened with a hint of tears once again. He was on edge and felt a wave of desire creep down his spine. He leaned forward abruptly, grabbing her from behind and pressing her to his chest. He kissed her on the lips, slid his hand down her back, and brushed against her butt. He pulled back and held his face inches from hers. "I just needed that," he said, not waiting for her to ask. "Is your aunt's house far from here?"

"No, just down the block. Why?" she said and leaned in close for another kiss.

"Because I want you to go there and…"

"No way," she stopped him, knowing he was about to brush her off. "I'm coming with you."

"Oh no, you're not," Campo blurted.

"Why, you said yourself probably no one is in there," Domeni said and opened her car door.

"I said possibly no one. Besides it doesn't mean someone can't come later. It could get dangerous." Al got out of the car as well as she rounded the front to meet him.

"I don't care; I'm coming with you. I won't stay here all alone, and going to my aunt's is impossible. If she saw me looking like this, she would panic and have a heart attack."

Campo knew this was an argument he wasn't going to win, so he instructed her to stay close and quiet. Together they moved swiftly, stealthily traveling through the brush. Domeni momentarily caught her hair on a tree branch and gasped out loud. Al turned and untangled it. He raised a finger to his lips, gesturing to her to be quiet. She mouthed the words:"I know, I know." They crept low, hunching down like two armadillos. Al held the gun drawn and stopped before stepping into the open yard.

"Listen," he said, turning back. "I'll move in for a closer look, and then signal you to follow. Remember! Stay low, and watch me."

"Wait a second," Domeni said, and before Al could speak, she planted a kiss on his lips.

"What was that for?"

"I guess I just needed to. Besides, I liked the last one." Domeni smiled and crouched low behind a shrub.

He accepted the explanation, because he would have taken a thousand more. Now he sped off toward the house. The back spotlight was beaming out over the open yard, so he skirted its light, scampering through the shadows, and ended with his back pressed against the red brick. He stood erect for a moment and held his breath.Then in one quick motion, he spun around the corner of the house, visible for a split second in the spotlight. The back wall had a solid wood door with no glass. Next to it was a large bow window about six-foot square. He scrunched his body between the two, holding the 9mm with both hands in front of him.

Al peered through the window. The house was dark, and he could make out the shadowy shapes of a sofa and an end table at the far end of the room. To either side were openings into the front of the house. Looking up at the window above his head, he saw flashes of light. He assumed they were flashlights, and looked back into the window. Now he could see flashes of light in the opening to the left of the sofa. He reasoned the stairs were there.

Campo squatted on his haunches to think. He guessed the van brought—at most—five men. One would stay in the van, most likely the driver, so that would give him four targets. His best chance would be to take them out while they were still upstairs, but without a key, his entry would probably give him away.

Al looked down, staring at the ground, racking his brains for a solution. His eyes moved from his feet, crusted with dry dirt from Wolfie's burial, then along the concrete patio, sizing up the various cracks and seams. He was aware of the flowers across from the patio, the slight scent of roses, and an orange aroma from a nearby citronella candle. He looked at the doormat. WELCOME the mat read in black letters, and it struck him. He reached down and lifted the rubber and felt doormat. To his surprise, a shiny key was wedged in a crack. He inserted it into the lock slowly, and turned it gently. The key twisted smoothly and unlocked the door without a sound. Just before entering, he stopped and put his back against the brick again.

He asked himself if he was nervous or scared. Neither, he decided, just unsure of the terror Jason Gull would unleash if Al got himself killed, and couldn't warn anyone about Gull's evil intentions. He pressed hard into the wall, closing his eyes—finding that place in him that was divorced from morality, without respect for human life. He wanted desperately to forget his past, yet each moment he found himself deeper into it.

His mind wandered back again…

The long, rotting, wood beams running parallel across the ceiling sagged, almost at the point of collapsing. Slats of hand-sawed lumber, their knots ugly and now separating with age, connected the beams and stabilized the roof. Low-wattage bulbs hung precariously on open electrical wires as water dripped past the bulbs. The room was familiar, along with the smell—an odor of mildew and damp soil, smoldering ash from makeshift stoves, and most of all, natural body odors. It seemed no matter how much they bathed, the stink of sweat still filled the air. He rolled his head. Sore, stiff muscles stretched in his neck. The pain was harsh until his vision fell on her. She removed a veil and headdress, uncovering her cherubic face. Her hair was long, and utterly black. Even in the limited light, it shimmered with a silky ripple, falling past her shoulders. Her eyes were dark as well, set in her face like oval stars floating above strong cheeks and full lips sweeping into a curve. Outwardly, she displayed a frail and passionate façade, but he knew she could become a ruthless, merciless assassin. He noticed she was holding his hand, but he couldn't feel her warm touch. Major Candalini smiled through swollen lips and bruised flesh. Her smile grew as her eyes dampened. Tears did not fall—her will was strong, and she knew he needed her strength if he were to survive.

"Sarita, my love," he whispered.

"No, no, don't speak," she said, touching his lips. "You are safe with us."

Sarita Mondeaux was part of the commando team that had blasted the encampment the day before. She had escaped, found the major's body on the street, and dragged him to safety. The two had been together for four years, working undercover in the Middle East. They met due to fate, as Candalini would put it. The major was escaping the realities of home, and Sarita sought her freedom. Sarita was French on her father's side, but had been raised by her mother in Israel. She witnessed the cruelties of hatred during her childhood, and after her two years of mandatory military service in the Israeli army, she had joined the fight against terrorism, securing a position in the commando forces of the United States. That's where she met Alfonse Candalini, her love.

The major watched her as she scanned his body. His head was propped up at such an angle that he could see the remnants of his blood-soaked tunic, torn and crusted with mud, barely covering his muscled physique. The commando medic must have cut open the cloth, bandaging gashes and slices with hurried amateur dressings. He looked like he had been caught in the middle of an explosion, flung into the air and then crashing to the ground.

"My love, soon we will take you to the hospital. Ghali and I will ensure your journey is safe," she said. He saw her squeeze his hand tighter, but he still had no feeling. Sarita looked across his body and muttered prayers.

Alfonse let his head fall to the side, and saw the friendly face of Ghali, a tall, dark man born in Libya, but raised in the US. He had come to the area with Alfonse. His face was long and narrow. He had short, grainy hair and a slender build, but his most distinguishing feature was the egg-shaped birthmark on his forehead. It partly disappeared into his hair but covered the right side of his brow.

"Where are the others?" the major asked, looking back to Sarita.

She looked away, avoiding his eyes, and said in a low voice. "Just the three of us survived. Joseph and Nicholas and the rest were captured and terminated."

Alfonse absorbed the blow with a sinking feeling through his numb chest. Ten men gone. Guilt and shame tore through his heart. He failed his country, his men, and himself. Those men were his family—and he had let them down. Tears welled up and dripped down the side of his battered face. Sarita wiped them with the back of her hand and then kissed his cheek.

"All must come to an end. You will regain your life, and go home to America, to doctors—and all will become good again," she whispered in his ear.

"And you will come with me?" he said. Now tears fell from her eyes. He knew she couldn't leave with him. They had talked about it during many nights alone. Now was not the time to tell him, though, she thought. He needed strength, most of all emotional strength, to survive his wounds.

"Yes, my love, but first you need to let the doctors save you…" her voice trailed off as voices were heard yelling outside in the dark street. Sarita whipped out an AK-47 rifle from behind her back, pointing it across the major's body, toward the door. Her angelic face in an instant became stern and hard.

"Ghali, quickly! We must move him now!"

With those words Alfonse felt the concussion of the doors blasting open and felt something hard slam into his skull. He saw Sarita's hair blown back, and her eyes squinting against the flying shrapnel. Her arm rose to fend off the debris. Ghali ducked, spinning to look into the cloud of dust and smoke. The doors were burning, and the floor littered with pieces of smoldering debris. Delirium took hold of Candalini, and he watched the next few moments unfold in slow motion. Sarita opened fire, blasting out into the street. Empty bullet casings cascaded onto his chest, the hot metal sizzling on his blood-soaked clothes. He saw her lips move, yelling something at Ghali, who was shooting as well.

He watched her determined face. She never looked away from the doors, shooting constantly, and then it came. She jolted forward, her elbows landing on him. The shot came from behind, slicing into her back and out through her chest, red stains immediately bursting onto her clothes. Without wasting a second, Sarita regained her footing, turned, and fired back, emptying her weapon. She reached under her clothes and grabbed a full clip, inserting it into the AK-47. She turned to Ghali once again, saying something. Alfonse couldn't hear her but he read her lips.

"Ghali, remove him. Take him down into the tunnel. I will protect you."

Ghali, as always, obeyed orders without question. He grabbed the major's shoulders and dragged him to the floor. The major didn't feel anything, no pain, not even the thump of his body on the floor. He was all but dead, except his eyes remained open. Ghali dragged his heavy body over burning pieces of wood and torn clothing, over bullet casings littering the ground. Alfonse looked into the havoc. Smoke and more fires erupted as another explosion rocked the house. The roof was shifting. He could see it move. The walls were about to topple. Through the haze he made out Sarita's kneeling figure—firing in all directions, she refused to yield. Al wanted to say something, to call to her to join them, but a wood beam fell from the ceiling and landed on his chest, driving the breath right out of him. It was on fire and the smoke and heat scorched his face. There was no pain, but Alfonse was losing consciousness. Ghali used his bare hands to lift the debris, and his face registered searing pain, but he didn't stop till the major was free. Alfonse looked through the haze of smoke and flame and caught a glimpse of Sarita. She turned and looked him in the eyes; her expression transformed from that of a determined killer to one of love. She was like an angel, pouring grace and love into the major's soul. Just then there was another blast. The ceiling collapsed, and he never saw Sarita again.

"Al, Al! What's wrong?" Domeni pleaded, shaking him, startling Campo back to reality.

"Nothing…nothing. I was mentally preparing myself to enter. I found a key under the mat." He blinked himself back to today. "Domeni, I want you to stay right here. Take the gun."

He handed her the weapon and pulled the knife out, extending the blade. "If anyone other than me comes through this door, don't hesitate, just fire. There are only two bullets left, so after that you'll have to make a run for it."

"But you're going to need the gun. You can't go in there with just that knife," Domeni said, grabbing him by the collar.

"OK, when you're right, you're right. Sorry."

"Sorry for what?" She barely got out the words beforeAl thrust a fist into her jaw, knocking her unconscious. He didn't hit her all that hard. Campo figured she must have fainted.

"Sweetheart, I just have to do this on my own," he whispered as he carried her limp body and hid it under a picnic table nearby. He made sure her head was supported so she would only wake up with a headache. She was going to be pissed off enough. Al stepped up to the door and slowly turned the handle. Gently he pushed into the darkroom. The house smelled like baby powder, and some kind of candle that reminded him of peppermint. He stayed low, closing the door behind him. Crouching in the shadows, he made his way to the opening on the left of the sofa. He quickly looked around the corner. There was a staircase leading upward. He could hear the intruders searching through drawers and closets, banging the doors open and closed. Silence was not their best skill, and the noise would help him remain unnoticed for the moment. He turned around and went to the other side of the couch. Another opening led into a kitchen where there was a candle burning on the counter. There were some dirty dishes in the sink, and the dishwasher door was open. Through the kitchen he could see into another room, the dining room, with a long table and china cabinet, and a glass chandelier hanging over the center. Next to it was the living room, furnished with a sofa and chair, a couple of round tables with lamps. To his left was the staircase again, from the other side. He crouched and made his way to the bottom of the stairs, backing against the wall under the railing. It was a wooden rail with metal S-shaped supports. He tucked the 9mm in the back of his pants, and pulled out the stiletto, holding it like a butcher ready to carve a roasted turkey. He couldn't risk going upstairs—the first man to spot him could take him out. He needed to draw them down where they would be bottled up on the stairs. He needed a diversion, so he grabbed a porcelain statue and heaved it across the room. It shattered, and the noises upstairs ceased.

Beams of light flashed across the stair opening and then went out. He had to wait nearly a minute before the first man came down the steps, two steps ahead of another man. Each carried a small automatic weapon, with long silencers projectingfrom the barrels, and flashlights taped to the top. They were dressed all in black, with hoods covering their faces. Cautiously, they trekked down the steps, waving their weapons from side to side, scanning the steps below. Al pressed tight to the wall, looking almost straight up. Sweat poured down his cheeks. He gripped and re-gripped the knife, made sure his muscles were loose. He waited until the ankles of the second man were at eye level. He thrust the knife between the railings and sliced the man's calf muscle. Blood spurted out in a stream over Campo's hand and onto the floor. The man let out a moan and stumbled and fell into his partner, sending them both tumbling to the base of the steps. They landed in a mangled heap, unable, for the moment, to fire. Al leaped onto them, cutting into their throats with fury and a murderous gleam. The ruckus was loud, but Al could hear a third man at the top of the steps radioing another man in the van. He cautiously came to the top of the steps and flicked on his flashlight.

"We have a problem…" was all he managed to get out before Campo shot him in the face with one of the automatic pistols he'd taken from the first two men.

Al raced to the front window. The van in the driveway started to pull out. Al took careful aim, and fired a quick burst of three bullets, shattering the driver's side window. The vehicle rolled to a stop against the curb, its engine still running.

CHAPTER THIRTY-SIX

Al Campo searched the rest of the house and was relieved to find that Domeni's parents were not home, nor did he find any other intruders. He went outside, pulled the van onto the driveway. He dragged the dead driver out and brought him inside, piling him in a heap with the other three dead men at the base of the steps. Domeni was still outside, *asleep*, so he brought her in, and laid her on the sofa. Out of breath and exhausted, he went to the fridge. There was a carton of OJ, a couple of containers of leftovers, miscellaneous condiments, and as he slid a half-gallon of skim milk aside, he saw two cans of Bud Light. "Praise be to the king of beers," he said and downed one without breathing. Then he popped open the other one and sat down next to Domeni. He remembered the card Joe Tyson had given him, and hoped it was still in his billfold. Luckily, it was, crammed between two one-dollar bills. He hammered out the numbers on a portable telephone he found in the kitchen, and took another long drink while the phone rang.

"Hello?" a female voice answered. "Federal Bureau of Investigation, Philadelphia Office. How may I direct your call, please?"

"Special Agent Joe Tyson, please?" Al said, and saw that it was eleven p.m. Tyson still had his secretary working?

"May I ask who is calling, sir?" the woman said.

"Yes, you may. Tell him it's Al Campo."

"One moment, please." Then soft orchestra music played.

Campo felt like he was ordering furniture from a computer—then a startled Joe Tyson got onthe phone.

"Campo, where the hell are you?"

"Nice to hearyour voice too, Mr. Tyson. Working late tonight, huh?" Al asked. He knew Tyson was probably a bundle of nerves, wondering about his missing agents.

"Cut the shit, Al, and tell me where you are!" Tyson was mad.

"Oh, I'd say I'm in the middle of a serious bit of espionage, mixed with some conspiracy." Al spoke jokingly, as if they were watching a game together, but he was totally serious. "I and a friend of mine were recently the guests of Jason Gull…as were, I'm sorry to tell you, two of your agents."

"Faz and Stortz, let me talk to them." Al heard the immediate relief inTyson's voice, and felt bad that he had to tell Tyson the bad news.

"I'm sorry, Tyson…they're both dead. And we barely made it out ourselves." There was a pause on the other end. Campo waited for the news to sink in. He was about to speak when Tyson beat him to it. This time his voice was slower and calmer.

"Al," the agent said, "tell me where you two are. I'll send a car."

"I think you better send a clean-up crew as well. I just had a run-in with four of Jason's goons, and it got messy. We're at Ms. Domeni Conti's home." Al proceeded to give the agent the address.

"Don't move. A clean-up crew is on its way, and we'll extract you both."

Ten minutes passed. Al finished his beer and found one more in the back of the fridge. It was a bit staler than the others but who cared. By the time he heard cars pull up outside, he was comfortably sitting on the living room sofa, an automatic nestled on his hip, and Domeni's head lying on his legs. Then a crowd of FBI men charged into the room, their guns pointed at Campo. They were ordering him to drop his weapon and put his hands behind his head.

"Wait a sec, guys," Al said as he let the weapon fall to the ground. "Didn't Tyson tell you…" He was interrupted by two agents thrusting him to the floor. Two other men seized Domeni.

She woke up startled and screamed as they put her hands behind her back and clicked handcuffs on both of them. Campo was struggling to speak, but they pinned his head to the coarse carpet. He could hear the men charge up the steps and saw their black shoes scurry past. The men called out to each other.

"I've got four corpses over here," he heard a deep voice say.

"All clear upstairs," another man said,

"Clear in the basement and on the first floor," he heard a woman's voice say.

Campo was then picked up by the scruff of his neck and his cuffed hands. "Wait a sec…" he managed to get out, but then a piece of adhesive tape was pushed over his mouth. *That's going to blister* He thought and was turned toward the door and forced to walk behind Domeni out into the street to an awaiting black car. He looked about and saw no fewer than five unmarked cars and about six local police cars, lights flashing. It was an army of activity. His head was pushed down as he was helped into the car, and he saw Domeni shoved roughly into another car, and they sped away from the madness.

She is either going to hate me, or love the fact we will have great stories to tell our grandchildren, he thought as the car raced down the road.

It was only a thirty-minute ride to the Federal Building in Philadelphia, but Al found himself lying down in the back of the FBI car and decided to close his eyes. He knew this wouldn't last. He had first hand knowledge of the murder of two agents, and they were sure to find the aluminum case with the monster handgun in it. They would need answers for both. He just hoped that Domeni was being treated fairly. He had barely dozed off when the car bounced over a speed bump and they entered the underground garage of the Federal Building. He couldn't see much of the garage through the windows. The lighting was dim, and his hazy vision wasn't strong enough to penetrate it. He was bounced out of the car and forced into an elevator, two agents by his side, both dressed in dark suits. Campo could see body armor protruding from their collars. They were lean and tall, both an inch taller than Campo. He guessed they were to ensure his cooperation. Campo had no intentions of struggling. He knew they needed him, and he was going to bide his time.

They exited the elevator, and Campo was shoved down a short hallway to a doorway bearing the universal sign for a men's room. He was led in, and the men ripped the tape off his mouth. He wriggled his nose and lips but remained silent. Next they removed his handcuffs and shoved him toward a pair of sinks with a large mirror over them. It was his first chance to look at himself in a while. He was a mess. His lips and mouth started to form small blisters from the tape. His hair was matted and curly. He had a partial beard, and dark circles rimmed his eyes. Dried blood was caked at the corner of his lips and running down his forehead. The bridge of his nose was swollen and his eyes were bloodshot. He cupped his hands under the silver faucet and washed his face. He scrubbed around the back of his neck and in his ears. He glanced in the mirror every few seconds and saw that the two agents never took their eyes from him. He didn't care. He was happy to be able to clean up; he just wished he could get a shower. He was pulling some paper towels from a dispenser mounted in the top of the counter when he saw the one agent look at his watch.

"That's enough," the agent said and reached for Campo's arm. "We have to move."

Al Campo rubbed the damp paper towel through his crop of hair. He felt ready for another twelve rounds, this time with the FBI. He was led to Tyson's office.

Joe Tyson was sitting behind his desk, flanked by two middle-aged men. When Al Campo walked in, the three stared back at him in horror. The two agents who had escorted him this far remained outside. The office was plain. A picture of the president hung on the wall. There was a neatly folded American flag in a triangular glass case on a table under the picture. On the left stood a tall black file cabinet, and Tyson's desk was straight ahead of him. Behind Tyson were two large windows, one of which was open, and the lights of the National Constitution Center shone up at them. Tyson was smoking a cigarette, and he had his elbows leaning on the desk. The smoke drifted past his face.

"Hello, Mr. Campo," Tyson said. "We've just finished reading the preliminary report from the clean-up team. Amazing. Four men all by yourself?"

"I was lucky,"Al said.

"Yes, I believe luck had a great deal to do with it," the man sitting on Joe's left said. He had black hair receding from a broad forehead.

"Al, this is Marc Coli," Joe said.

Marc didn't extend his hand, so Al kept his at his side. Al figured him to be with the National Security Agency. The man was wearing a neat, light gray suit, his hands were folded over a bent knee, and his gaze restedfirmly on Campo.

"And this is William McDonnell," Tyson introduced the other man.

"Call me Bill," he said, leaning forward to shake Al's hand. Al figured this guy must be a politician, from the way he was so eager to impress. He wore a checkered sport coat with a black polo shirt, black slacks, and very expensive Italian shoes. He sat back comfortably and smiled, in awe of Al.

"Please, sit down," Tyson said, and Al let himself drop into a leather chair across from the oak desk of the FBI agent. "We'd like you to go over the events of the last week, starting with your first meeting with Jason Gull."

"Yes, tell us what that device is that you were found with," Marc said in a tone that rubbed Campo in an odd way.

"Well," Al said, "how about you two start by telling me who the hell you work for—and why in God's name I have to tell you anything? As a matter of fact, I think I'd like to take Ms. Conti on a little vacation, so if you'll please tell her I'm here, I'll be on my way. "Al didn't like this situation one bit. These men cared little for him, and as soon as he gave up the info, they would cast him aside in some safe house…prison, rather—where he would remain silent and out of the way. *Screw them*, he thought. He had a score to settle with Gull, and he intended to ensure his participation was required.

Before they could answer, Tyson spoke. "William is with the FBI. His specialty is biological and chemical weapons, and Mr. Coli is from the Pentagon."

"Which of the five sides are you from, Mr. Coli?" Campo said, studying the man. He didn't like him. Even the way he sat annoyed

Al. He was too cocky. He had his hands clasped on his lap and kept a sneer on his face like he was smelling an old shoe.

"All of them," Marc said with a stare. "Now Mr. Campo, we feel that time is of the highest importance—so would you please humor us by recounting the events of the past few days? Mr. Tyson has said you witnessed the deaths of two agents. This in itself is of the utmost importance. We can't very well go barging into Gull's office with our guns blazing without confirmation." Marc paused a moment, brushed an invisible bit of lint from his pants, and then continued. "You know, Mr. Campo, he also told us you withheld information during your first meeting, and after your home was attacked, you failed to inform the authorities. In my eyes, these are both crimes, and one happens to be a federal crime that may have directly led to the deathof those two agents."

"You know, Mr. Colin," Al mispronounced his name intentionally, "I don't like you, or your insinuations. You must be from the National Security Agency. I never liked anyone who got their job by sucking up to political assholes." Campo looked him directly in the eye. Then he turned to Tyson, "And on top of that, I don't care for the way I was brought in here. If I had known, I would have never called you. I should have taken Domeni and left the country, and let you fuckers sort it all out without me, so don't fucking threaten me. I've killed more men in the past twenty-four hours than I care to remember, and one more won't make a difference." His stare returned to Coli.

"All right now—that will be enough," Tyson said quickly, playing referee. "Al, I know you've been through the wringer already, but if we are to have any shot at arresting Jason Gull, you are going to have to cooperate. Now, please tell us what is in the case."

"Did you study the files from Domeni's home? I'm sure you found those as well. They should explain everything."

"Unfortunately, they don't," Bill said. "The contents of the files were of no use. They were the writings of a man seeking help. He wrote about being a prisoner, and how he was being forced to work on radioactive material, and that he was not permitted to leave. He rambled on and on about no escape and such."

"That would be Wolfgang," Al spoke with a lump in his throat. The death of the old man crept back into his head. "More like a diary I guess. He had no contact with the outside world. His only way to cry for help was in his notes. He must have hoped someone on the outside would be reading them."

"Who is Wolfgang?" McDonnell asked.

"A German scientist," Campo said, turning to the chemical expert, "who was held captive by Jason Gull, and whom we helped to escape. No…he helped us escape. He developed that weapon in the case."

"A weapon!" Coli said.

"Yes, a gun powered by a derivative of plutonium, or something like that. I didn't get all the specifics. I was too concerned about staying alive," Campo explained. "But I did see first hand what it can do. Gull was going on about it being effective from a distance. Its range could be a thousand yards, I don't know, but its effectiveness may not be the same. And then again, it could be what they were looking for."

"What do you mean by that? Why would they not want it to kill from a safe distance?" Bill asked.

"Well, because Faz was its first victim. Jason pointed it at his chest. We saw nothing for a few moments, and then he seemed to suffer the effects of extreme radiation sickness. Vomiting, burning eyes, reddened skin, blood seeping from everywhere." Campo saw Tyson's jaw tighten, and he looked down at the ashtray as he put out his cigarette. He had to hear this, but of course he didn't like it. "Doesn't that sound like the effects of extreme radiation, Mr. McDonnell?"

"Yes, they are, but how long did it take for him to be sick?"

"It was only about thirty seconds after Gull fired the weapon. Then he vomited immediately. I only put the two together because after Faz had a fit, Gull asked what the radiation levels were in the room. Then I remembered reading all about the victims in Japan after the atomic bombs were dropped. They had the same ill effects, only those victims were miles from the impact site. If this weapon was fired from a greater distance, the illness wouldn't begin until the assassin was long gone and out of harm's way."

"When you say you saw nothing, you mean you weren't present when Gull shot the weapon?" McDonnell asked.

"No, we were there in the room, all together," Al said. "What I mean is the gun made very little noise, and we saw nothing exit the barrel. If there were any background noise, an assassin could fire the weapon, and no one would know the difference."

"It doesn't make any sense. How did the radiation only affect Agent Fazolo, and not you all?"

"Gull didn't seem to be worried about the radiation until after he fired it," Al said. "I think it was some sort of laser beam. I kind of remember Gull saying something like that."

"My God!" Coli said. "An assassin could eliminate at will, without detection."

"We have lasers that can pinpoint a grain of sand from a thousand feet," McDonnell said. He was shaking his head, lost in thought. "The power of the atom concentrated into a laser beam. Genius."

"That's the idea behind the invention, I suppose," Campo said, concerned.

"Fired from a distance, the effects could be mistaken for anything. A concentrated blast of radiation could lead to many illnesses hidden within the body," McDonnell spoke as a teacher mighton the first day of school. "For example, someone with a weak heart could very well suffer a heart attack, and die suddenly. Once his body expired, the radiation sickness would not spread. Or flu symptoms could lead to pneumonia, or even a stroke. Any number of deaths would be caused by such a weapon, and the true cause would go unnoticed, unless of course the victim was aware of the contact."

"How many weapons does Gull have?" Tyson asked.

"None," Campo said.

"You took the only weapon?" Coli asked, surprised.

"Not at all," Campo continued. He figured he had to educate them. "When Wolfgang brought one into the room where we were being held, Gull instructed him to pack away the other fourteen for shipment. So I would have to assume there are a minimum of fifteen, including the one we brought in. I couldn't risk taking all of them because we were under constant attack, and it was either the cases, or a machine gun. I chose the latter. The others were shipped to any number of locations."

"There could be hundreds of them out there by now," Coli scowled.

"Not likely. I remember Gull being excited as hell after the first weapon was brought into his room. He needed the plutonium I had in my car, and the box wasn't that big, maybe one foot square and three inches deep."

"That size box could hold approximately twice what we extracted from the dog," Tyson said, and Al looked at him, puzzled. "The destination of the weapons—any ideas?"

"Not a clue," Al replied, shrugging his shoulders.

"How much time since you escaped?" McDonnell asked Campo.

"Well, I haven'treally had a good sense of time since we woke up as prisoners, but I'd have to say between twelve and twenty-four hours."

"My God, they could be halfway around the world by now," Coli said. "What about Ms. Conti? Do you think she knows where the weapons were to be sent?"

"Why don't you ask her?" Al directed a cold stare atColi.

"We did. She said she didn't know either," Coli said. He didn't seem intimidated, but he avoided Al's eyes.

"Then she doesn't," Al said sternly. It irritated him, thinking about how they had probably grilled her the moment they arrived. "Listen, why don't you send a team into Gull's plant, confiscate everything, and grill him for information. He can tell you everything you want to know."

"We have to find out as much information as possible before force is used," Tyson said.

"Yes, Mr. Campo. We here in the FBI know when to arrest someone. We certainly do not need the advice of a civilian," Coli said.

Al guessed he wanted him to feel inferior, but it didn't work. As always, Campo was holding the trump card. "So you're not going down there at all?" Al said and cocked his eyebrow.

"When and how we go is classified information," Tyson said, leaning back in his chair. "Mr. Campo, any information you can provide will help. I want nothing more than to see Jason Gull behind bars, but I have to do my job. I'm responsible for the lives of the men and women who undertake these missions. I don't want to take unnecessary risks."

"Well then, I guess I'll have to go it alone," Al said, and waited for the reaction. The men looked puzzled and glanced at one another.

"What do you mean, go it alone?" Tyson said.

"I mean, if you pack of idiots are going to sit on your asses while Jason Gull sends those weapons to who knows where to do who knows how much damage, I, me, Al Campo, is going to connect Gull's testicles to a car battery, and get some answers before it's too late."

"I'm confused," Marc said. "Why would you want to go back down there, and risk your life again? This matter no longer concerns you. You are free to leave here and return to a normal life. We won't interfere, and you can do as you please. We'll call you for the trial."

"First of all, Marc," Campo had a bitter taste on his lips, and he spat out the words. "I don't want to risk my life, and second, that freedom you said I have to go back to my everyday life comes at a price. Thousands, perhaps millions of men and women died creating and preserving it, so I guess I feel I need to do my part to hold onto the freedoms this country gives me. I need to remove Jason Gull, and to do so, I will use all means available to me, and if that means risking my life, then I guess that means risking my life."

"Why would you think your freedom here is being threatened?" McDonnell asked. He was more curious than irritated, unlike Marc.

Al leaned back in his seat, asking himself how these three men could have been entrusted with such responsibility. When he spoke, he tried not to show his contempt. "Gentlemen, it seems I need to spell thingsout." The men looked at him silently, just waiting. "I witnessed Jason Gull personally kill your two agents, Stortz and Faz. He did this with pleasure. Agent Stortz was bound and practically naked, completely defenseless. Gull blew his brains into next week, and then casually smiled at us all. Then he was almost overcome with joy when he used Agent Faz as a human guinea pig, experimenting with his new toy. The man is ruthless, to say the least. Those weapons he created are not for some carnival side-show, or for a bank robbery. Their development must have taken years, and millions of dollars of funding, I'm sure you would agree with that." Campo motioned to McDonnell, who nodded. "Gull is interested in something on a global scale," Campo continued, "and if he's not, the people who bought the weapons from him are. In the wrong hands—world power is at stake. The guns must be found before they reach the hands of a madman or terrorist group. This is basic deduction, right? Especially if you're in the FBI, wouldn't you think?"

Tyson was annoyed, and Campo could see the agent clenching his teeth. Al enjoyed the moment of power he held as Tyson fidgeted with a pencil. Then Tyson spoke up. "Marc, William, would you please give me a moment alone with Mr. Campo?"

"Certainly," McDonnell said, but Coli grimaced, mumbling something before he rose abruptly. Campo kept a firm eye on Tyson while they left.

"Mr. Campo," Tyson said and dropped the pencil. "I sense you feel we are taking this situation lightly. No one is unhappier than I am about the deaths of those agents. But I can't let my emotions decide our next move. Every precaution must be taken. We've been watching Jason Gull for two years, and this is the first time we can connect a crime to him. Sure, we could haul him in for murder, with you and Ms. Conti as material witnesses, but with his power and influence he could have thirty people confirm an alibi, and he would just walk. We can't waste time with uncertainty."

"That's bullshit. Screw arresting him," Campo said and threw up his hands "Are you kidding? There should be no thought of putting him in a penitentiary, and getting a feather in your cap for doing so. Grab him now, this minute, beat him until he cries 'uncle,' and maybe you can find out where those weapons were shipped, and what their intended use is. If you wait, who knows how many will suffer?"

"Mr. Campo, that won't be necessary. Our moles will find out their destination. I appreciate your help. Thank you for all you've done. We will take over from here," Tyson motioned toward the door.

Al knew Tyson didn't wish to babble on any longer. Getting him and Domeni to a safe house and out of his hair was the best solution for him right now. Al wasn't looking forward to being cuffed again. "You can't just brush me off and make me forget everything I've been through," Al said casually. He still had an ace up his sleeve, and he intended to use it. He knew his life would again be changed if he left quietly. The threat of Jason Gull would hang over Domeni and him like a storm cloud. To ensure his life was his own again, being able to go back to his antique collecting, working an honest job, and going to the taproom with friends without looking over his shoulder, he would have to take matters into his own hands.

"Why don't you pick up the phone and call Morris Bartow," Al said, his voice confidant and crisp.

"General Morris Bartow?" Tyson paused.

"The same."

"You mean Major General Bartow of the joint chiefs?" Tyson said with a smirk, and looked like he had just won the lottery. Campo had given him a name Tyson would be all too happy to call. That would put this wiseass in his place.

"Joint chiefs, huh," Campo pondered. "Ten years ago he wasn't even in Washington. Never thought old man Bourbon Street wanted so much. Hell, he never wanted to leave Italy, or his position as Special Project Director of the Middle East."

"And how would you know that?" Joe sat down slowly, surprise showing in his furrowed brow.

"Why don't you just give him a call, and tell him Alfonse Candalini is in your office."

Time to call his bluff, Tyson thought, and rid himself of this thorn. He spoke into the intercom. "Millie, direct a call to General Morris Bartow in Washington, use Code Seven." Code Seven was not an emergency line, just an alert signal so Bartow would take the call.

"Thank you," Al sneered. "Code Seven. That way he'll take the call, but not be alarmed. Very smart Tyson."

Tyson was growing tired of Al's remarks. He wanted nothing more than to kick his ass out into the street. The pair waited, Al sitting cross-legged, arms softly resting on the arm rests. Tyson sat, nervously tapping his fingers on the desk. He pulled out another cigarette and lit it, while he stared at the phone. *Ring, dammit,* he thought, wanting to end this bullshit and move on. There's no way this guy could know the general. How could he? He was just a civilian caught up in a crisis—a civilian with extraordinary insight, but still a civilian. *Once I speak to the general,* Tyson thought, *this will all be over.* Then he recalled the file on Campo—incomplete, his past unavailable, and Tyson wondered who this man really was. Was he a mole of the opposition? This could all be a set-up. Suddenly, his phone sprang into life and a jittery Tyson lifted the receiver. "Joe Tyson."

"I have the general, one moment," Millie said.

"Hello, this is Bartow," the general said in his southern drawl.

"Hello, General, thank you for calling, I'm Special Agent Joe Tyson, Director of the Philadelphia office…"

"Yes, your secretary briefed me as to who you are. What is this about please?"

"Yes, of course. I have here in my office a man who claims he is Alfonse Candalini." There was a long pause on the phone. At first Tyson thought the line was disconnected, but he listened hard and faintly heard the general breathing on the other end. Tyson spoke again. "General, are you still there?"

"Yes, I'm on the line. I don't think what you said is possible, Mr. Tyson. Major Alfonse Candalini died some time ago."

"I knew it!" Joe blurted out.

"If you knew it, Mr. Director, then why the call?"

"I don't mean I knew he was dead, just that the man sitting in front of me couldn't have known you." Tyson smiled and took a long draw of his cigarette, filling his lungs completely.

"Just because Candalini is dead does not mean the man in your office doesn't know me." Bartow said. "Describe him to me, if you would."

Tyson took another puff and studied Campo. "He's approximately six feet something, dark hair, dark complexion, brown eyes…"

"Does he have an odd, star-shaped scar on his chin?" Morris asked, having heard enough.

Tyson looked over at Campo, sitting with a crooked smile, looking at his squared jaw, and a thin growth of hair. He saw a clear spot on the front of his chin, an irregular-shaped star where no hair grew. Tyson's mouth dropped open and the cigarette fell to the desk. He quickly recovered and picked it up before his papers caught fire. "Ah…yes he does."

"Hell, Mr. Director, the man who sits before you is someone from my past. Him just being there, and you making this call tells me there is one hell of a nasty predicament going on—and I'm sure he's smack dab in the middle of it."

"As a matter of fact, sir, he's the one who feels a sense of urgency, but we have the situation under control."

"Put the man on the phone, would you, Mr. Director," Bartow said, the command delivered as kindly as he could. Although he had no direct authority over the FBI field director, certain courtesies were to be granted to the joint chiefs. Tyson was about to hand it over, when Bartow stopped him.

"One second, Mr. Director."

"Yes sir," Tyson said and puffed on his smoke again.

"Is this a secure line coming out of your office?" Bartow said.

"Always, sir."

"Thank you. Now I'd like to speak to him in private, and I'm in a little bit of a hurry, so if you'll excuse yourself from your office for a few moments, I'd appreciate it greatly."

Tyson felt his face turn red, mostly from embarrassment but also from anger. He placed the phone down in front of Campo. "The general wants to talk to you," he said. Then he got up and stalked outof the room, joining Coli and McDonnell in the outer office. They looked at him in surprise.

"Where's Campo?" Marc Coli said.

"He's in there, on the phone with Major General Morris Bartow," Tyson said.

"What in God's name for?"

Tyson took a last draw from his cigarette, shrugging his shoulders.

Al waited until the door was completely closed before picking up the receiver. "Morris," he said jovially, "how have you been these past years? Up to no good I see, getting yourself promoted to the joint chiefs."

"Never mind all that," Bartow said."What in the Sam Hell are you up to? You're supposed to be dead, remember?"

"Well, at this point in my life, I've never felt more alive."

"Enough of the bullshit, son. What is going on that you invited the FBI in Philly to call me?"

"I'm glad you asked," Al kept his attitude light. "I'm in the middle of some serious domestic espionage, and I fear it's going to become global if they don't respond to it immediately. They are playing with fire and won't listen to what I have to say."

"OK, son, give me the lowdown, leaving out the particulars."

The general listened quietly while Campo took five minutes to explain the whole situation, implying he had a plan to stop the terror before it started, and that he wanted to be part of the FBI raid he was sure was about to happen.

"You mean to say two agents have been murdered, and this Tyson fellow is just sitting on his hands?"

"Morris, I think he's forcing me out of the picture because he thinks I'm a civilian."

"You are, you know," Morris said.

"Not any more, General." Campo's tone changed, calling him "General" for the first time. "I'm back in the war, whether anyone likes it or not."

The general sat silent for a moment, reflecting on the past. Al had been a sublime operative in the Middle East; his covert actions and military planning were renowned in their time. If the situation was at the level of seriousness he suggested, the FBI couldn't have a better man working with them. "Is that the way you want it, son?" Bartow said.

"It is, General."

"Fine then, but your status as a dead man will not change. These people cannot know who you were, otherwise your life may be compromised. I will instruct Mr. Tyson to allow you onto the team as an advisor. After this situation is over, your life will be yours to deal with. As far as Washington is concerned, Major Candalini is dead, and Al Campo is a private citizen with first-hand knowledge, who is assisting the FBI in an investigation. Do we understand each other?" Morris said.

"That's all I wanted to hear, General." Al smiled and felt a tinge of satisfaction roll down his spine.

"Good, now put that Mr. Tyson back on the phone, so I can give him the low-down."

"Thank you, General," Al said, then held the phone to his chest. "Yo, Joe!"

Tyson heard Campo yell through the door. In an instant, the Philadelphia director popped back into the room and quickly sat at his desk.

"The general would like a word."Campo held the receiver out.

"Yes, General?" Tyson said, staring at Campo.

"Mr. Director, I believe it would be in your best interests to have Mr. Campo on your team for the Baroque Chemical operation. He will be invaluable in delivering information concerning the security of the facility." Morris tried to use his best sales pitch on Tyson

Tyson listened intently as his eyes grew bloodshot and his face red with anger. How dare he attempt to control Tyson's position as director and issue what amounted to a soft-soaped order?

"General, with all due respect, I appreciate your advice, but I feel I have enough personnel working with me as it is. And without orders from my superior, I could not involve a civilian in this, or any other operation we are conducting. Again, I appreciate your advice, but your authority does not oversee this office."

"Mr. Director," Morris continued, "I believe you are correct in what you say, so if you'll remain in your office I will be speaking with Mr. Kellogg, the FBI director here in the Pentagon in a few moments, and he will call and give you your orders. Does that sound like something you would pay attention to? Because I feel you've taken my kindness a little lightly."

"No sir, I…" Morris hung up the phone, and Joe listened until he heard a dial tone, and then slowly replaced the receiver on its cradle. His reddened face paled to white as he clenched his teeth.

Campo sat amused, and didn't waste the opportunity to joust with Tyson. "Is there a… problem, Mr. Director?"

The two heard a knock at the door. "Come in!" Joe said louder than he probably should have, but he was lost in thought. The door opened, and McDonnell poked his head inside.

"Is everything OK? May we return?" McDonnell said with a furrowed brow.

"Yes, yes, of course, come in, Bill," Tyson said, waving his arm. The two men returned to their respective chairs.

"What's the situation?" Marc asked.

"Well…" was all he got out before the phone rang, and Tyson nearly jumped out of his chair. "Tyson," he answered, and peered at Campo. Joe felt like he looked, like a frightened chicken watching a prowling wolf.

"Yes, sir…of course, sir…yes, but…no, no problem, sir…I will…yes, follow orders, yes…thank you, sir…good day, sir."

Joe hung up, fingers clasping the desk, rage pouring from every vein. Then he got hold of his feelings, managing to remain professional. He reached into his breast pocket, pulled out another cigarette, and quickly lit it.

"What is it?" Coli said.

"It seems Mr. Campo here has friends in high places. That was Kellogg. He ordered me to put him on the team for the Baroque Chemical operation."

Coli and McDonnell were stupefied, and looked over at Campo—who stared right back, wearing a Cheshire-cat grin from ear to ear.

CHAPTER THIRTY-SEVEN

Upon opening the door, Al noticed an orangey glow against the ceiling. It was the dim lighting reflecting through the lampshade. His eyes panned the room, looking for her— and there she was, lying peacefully on the white linen. A chill was present, but warm air flowed in from a window she must have opened; only a sheet covered her shapely figure. He approached her, careful not to disturb this beautiful creature God had bestowed upon him. He sat smoothly on the side of the bed, looking at her peaceful countenance. Through the sheets he could tell she was naked. Her bare breasts shone through, the nipples protruded, and the tan skin shadowed transparent sheets. She laid on her side, with one arm down her hip, her other hand resting under her chin. She looked like an angel from a painting by Rafael. The linen clung to her shape, her body still moist from the bath. Al stared in fascination, following her arm over her hip to bare legs.

"My God, she is beautiful," he thought. Her image would be etched in his mind forever.

Al did not want to wake her, even though he was about to leave and might never see her again. But desire led him onward. He removed his shirt, and the dim light shrouded his battered, torn torso. Next he took off his pants and lay down next to her. His hand followed the contour of her arm, sweeping around between her legs with the back of his hand. Her eyelids flickered, and a quiet moan of desire escaped her lips. Domeni's eyes opened into slim, dreamy slits. She smiled and drew her hand to his face, rounding his cheek. Her arm left her side and rode down his hairy chest to his groin. He was fully aroused, and she laced her bare leg over his hip reaching behind to his buttocks and pulled him tight. She kissed him warmly, and the two fell into tugging and pulling each other closer and closer. She pushed him over onto his back, positioning herself onto him. They moved rhythmically, like a chorus, and they caressed each other's chests as their passion mounted, fervently moving without words. They gazed at one another—she saw in his face pleasure and love, yet he was away in some far-off land. She knew then that he was leaving, and she saw in his eyes the harsh truth that he might not return. Their passion mounted, and they climaxed together.

Dropping to his chest, she laid her head down, listening to his beating heart. The rhythm was intense. She kissed his neck and all around his face, then pressed her face again to his heart. Its beat was still fast. Then she hugged him tightly around the waist.

Al drew his fingertips down to the small of her back, sensing the threads of life pumping into her heart. Love was silent, and she was satisfied with no words. Raising herself, resting her hands on his chest, her golden eyes dripped tears onto his chest. He had to leave, and she knew it, but before he left, she wanted more, and she saw he did as well. Her hips moved in a circular motion arousing him once again, and time was erased as their love moved into ecstasy.

Single file they rode, five black Chevy Suburbans, windows tinted, and all markings blacked out. Even the normally shiny aluminum tire rims were darkened. The engines hummed in unison, quietly rolling on the blacktop. The cloudy sky dulled the moon's glow, which aided their stealth as they converged on the Baroque Chemical plant. Al Campo sat in the passenger seat of the lead vehicle as Special Agent in Charge Joe Tyson drove. Four other agents crowded into the back seats, armed with M4 carbine rifles, and wearing body armor. The letters "FBI" were printed in fluorescent yellow on their backs. Each of the trailing vehicles also contained six men; each dressed the same, and all heavily armed. Al was the exception. He wore his street clothes, the same ones he had had on for the past twenty-four hours, and a borrowed bullet-resistant vest. He carried an FBI-issued Glock 9mm with five extra clips.

Following Al's directions, they drove in on the main road, and then the lead car turned off onto the dirt road, while the others headed toward the main gate. Tyson navigated the rough path with the assistance of parking lights only, and as soon as they could see the fence, he extinguished those as well. He stopped in front of the barrier, reading its sign, and turned to Campo.

"Is this the right place?" Tyson asked.

"Looks like it," Campo said, peering around the area. "I remember seeing that sign in the rearview mirror as we rose up."

"We better hope so because Team B is counting on our infiltration," Tyson said. He still had some doubts about the entry point. "OK, here goes."

Tyson tapped the horn in the sequence Al had told him. For a few moments, nothing happened. He glared at Campo, and then rapidly the car shook and trembled. It sank below the surface. Everyone other than Al jolted in their seats. The car reached the bottom, and the automatic lights switched on. The area looked different to Campo.

"The cars…where the hell are all of the cars?" Al whispered to himself.

"Which way?" Tyson asked, looking down the brightly-lit long path to open space.

"The elevator we came out of is at the far end of the garage," Al said, pointing beyond the concrete columns.

"Everyone, keep your eyes open, and your weapons ready— they may already be aware of our entry," Tyson said.

"Not to worry, Joe. It's a good bet they're watching us right now." Campo glanced up at the camera globes hanging from the ceiling.

"Let's hope Dunn is the one viewing the monitors," Tyson referred to his mole working in the security central location. Tyson stopped in front of the elevator, and then the men in the rear jumped out, and scanned the area with rifles drawn.

"Clear…clear…clear…clear," the four sang off.

Al inserted the key card he had obtained from Wolfgang's corpse, and the elevator slid open.

"Jake, Steve, you two wait here," Tyson ordered, "and we'll send it back to you. If it doesn't return in two minutes, break radio silence and call Armstrong. Switch to level five intrusions. And secure the entrance to the garage. Turn on your headsets."

Jake nodded as he and Steve took up positions with their backs to the corners of the elevator bay. Inside the elevator, Campo pushed the third button from the bottom, and the four rode up silently. It was at that moment of silence that Al felt his first butterfly in his stomach. Until then his intense anger had driven him on—pushing aside fear and the pain of his many wounds—but within the enclosed doors, and not knowing what to expect, his belly rebelled. The plan was thin and hastily contrived. Only after Campo told them of the existence of a reactor inside Gull's plant did Tyson sit up and take notice of Al's sense of urgency. McDonnell explained the danger of the possibility that Gull, if sufficiently determined to cover up his actions, could very well set off a chain reaction ending with a nuclear meltdown, destroying all evidence—and forcing radiation into the sky, making the plant inaccessible for thirty years.

Their plan had Tyson's team entering the garage and heading right to the reactor operations room, hopefully taking control of the area. Meanwhile the main assault at the front doors would cause a diversion. The two teams would meet in the middle, securing the plant. Dunn had last been contacted an hour before they left Philly, and he reported that Gull was still in the plant. Tyson said the best-case scenario would be to capture Gull, and take over the facility without incident.

Yeah, right, that will happen, Al thought as the elevator came to a stop.

The stainless steel doors slid open, and all four pointed their weapons into the brightly lit hall. Agents Simon and Paulson entered first, and darted their M4s side-to-side. The area was empty, so they stepped into the hall. Tyson reached around into the car and pushed the button, sending it back to Jake, then followed Al, who led them to the room of his incarceration.

It was empty as well, no bodies of Faz or Stortz. No blood-stains on the floor or wall. Not even the smell of Faz's regurgitation remained. The room had been sterilized.

"Shit," Al whispered. "They must have cleaned this room with a fucking power washer."

"Al, we need to get to the operations room," Tyson said, tapping his shoulder.

"Right, OK, this way," Al said and walked down the hallway. He held his 9mm with both hands.

They crossed the hall to the door of the reactor operations room where Al had found Wolfgang. The door had no markings. Al rubbed his hand across the blank panel, and could feel irregularities on the surface where the paint had been removed. This was the room, he thought. They opened the unlocked door, and again, found it devoid of everything: fixtures, desks, tables, and computers were all gone.

"What the hell?" Campo said. "How is it possible to remove an entire operations room that fast?"

"Al, we're running out of time," Tyson said, burdened by the thought they had been set up.

"Give me two more minutes. Follow me." He guided them to the other end of the hall to one last door. Just as Al turned the handle, they heard a thundering sound, and the floor beneath them rumbled. The trembling grew more intense as the noise reverberated from the elevator.

"Move now!" Al screamed as he pushed Joe into the last doorway. Agents Simon and Paulson reacted a second too late as the elevator doors shook, then exploded outward in a fireball of metal shards and pieces of molten concrete, their bodies were incinerated instantly. Al thrust the metal door closed and held his feet against it as the intense heat penetrated the steel, and the soles of his shoes. He rolled over in a reverse somersault grabbing the fallen Tyson as he ran down the passageway.

"Level five! Level five! Jake, do you read me? This is Tyson! Level five!" he yelled into the headset but received no response. "Al, I think we have a problem!"

Campo looked back at him as they raced toward another door twenty feet away. "No shit, Joe, really? I thought we were experiencing technical difficulties!" He stopped at the door and turned the handle. All of a sudden the door was yanked inward, taking with it his body, and his momentum carried him to the floor. He landed hard, bumping his nose on two large Italian leather shoes. He turned his head upward, and saw the enormous figure of Bracken Guttone staring down at him. *What the hell, this guy must be made of concrete, why aren't you dead?* Al thought. The giant grabbed Al by the scruff of the neck, and tossed him into the wall. Campo fell to the concrete, howling in pain, his weapon lost as he stared back at his foe. Bracken's face was bruised and swollen. He wore only a white T-shirt, and through it Al could see the dark shadows of his many bruises. A bloodstained bandage was taped across his neck. His customary perfect ponytail was gone, and his stringy hair fell below his shoulders.

Tyson stood with his hands clasped behind his neck as one man frisked him for weapons and another held the agent's own weapon to his head. Jason Gull stood across from them and bent down to pick up Al's 9mm.

"Mr. Campo," Gull said. "Again, you grace us with your presence, only this time you arrive without an invitation." He aimed the gun at Campo.

"Well, shit head, I figured the best was yet to come." Al paused to catch his breath. "And I never miss out on a party," he said finally, grunting through pain.

Gull smiled, amused at Campo kneeling on the floor in discomfort. Then he turned to stare at the FBI agent. "Mr. Tyson, we haven't met, though I'm sure we know much about one another. I'm Jason Gull."

"I know who you are. You're the murderous psychopath who killed Faz and Stortz."

"Ah, I see Mr. Campo has been keeping you up to date," Gull said and folded his arms in front of him. He smiled like he was a proud parent. "Yes, I killed your men—but I am not a psychopath. I'm a businessman, engaged in something far beyond crazy. You see, I'm going to be rich and powerful beyond your wildest dreams.

I'm going to be the richest of the one percent, and your men died to ensure that happens, just as you two are about to do. Don't worry. Your nobility will be remembered by my many followers, and I will tell them about your sacrifice."

"Gull, its over," Tyson ordered, his voice full of feigned confidence. To hear Gull admit to two murders meant that he underestimated him, he wasn't a Psycho, he was a murderous lunatic. Jason Gull would stop at nothing to carry out his plans. Murder was simply a stepping-stone. Now Tyson second-guessed his decision not to bring a second unit from Philly, and not to call in local law enforcement. They were alone, and Tyson only hoped his surface team would be more successful than his. He stood now, his only defense to possibly making Gull uneasy, maybe unbalancing him enough that he made a mistake. "It's time to surrender," Tyson said. "Waves of state troopers are on their way, and once I don't respond that our infiltration was a success, they'll put this place under siege. A larger assault team will be arriving soon enough, and there will be nowhere to hide."

"You fool!" Gull barked, his anger growing," I know everything your pitiful FBI schoolboys do. You must consider me an idiot. I have ten men from your office on my payroll. There is no second unit coming, and the men you have attacking from the surface have been met by a hundred armed men. They're plenty busy. They will be battling for hours before they realize it's time to call for help. Then, way before the cavalry can arrive, there will be a little accident, and no one will come within a fifty-mile radius of the plant, not now, not for years."

Campo was quiet, listening to the two square off. His thoughts were whirling, working out a plan of attack. He knew he had to stop Jason now, before anyone else died. He needed something to throw the balance of power back into his hands.

"We're prepared for your radiation leak, if you've got the balls to do it," Tyson said.

Gull's rage grew more intense. He had spent his life earning respect throughout the world as a genius and inventor. This prick talking to him with such disrespect was maddening. He stepped up to Tyson and thrust a fist into his stomach.

The senior agent bent over, gasping for air. Although he was in good physical condition, the punch hurt. Then, before anyone could react, Tyson stood up and spit into Gull's face. Quickly, the guard holding his gun struck Tyson in his head, hitting his clasped hands. Tyson winced, yet stood his ground and held back the urge to retaliate.

"Again, you insult me with your stupidity," Gull said as he paced back over to his original position, making sure his back was toward the wall, flexing his hand around Campo's 9mm. "A simple reactor leak might scare a few people away, but a complete meltdown, followed by a nuclear explosion, will rock the entire northeastern United States. A crater a mile and a half wide, devastation ten times that of Hiroshima. Now that will cause a sensation."

Tyson and Campo cringed. Even though they had thought about the remote possibility of a nuclear explosion, they never imagined Gull would kill millions of innocent people.

"New York, Philadelphia, Baltimore, and Washington D.C., will experience such major fallout they will become ghost towns, full of men, women, and children dead or dying of radiation sickness. Mass hysteria will ensue, and a new government will take over, leaving your inane FBI in ruins. It has already been set in motion."

"Now you insult me with your idiocy," Campo spoke up incredulously. "First off, you fool, no matter where you hide you'll be found, and even if we two don't survive there is another eyewitness to two murders. Plus, a certain German scientist has been having conversations with the feds about his imprisonment, and forced him to create weapons of mass destruction. So you could leave a crater the size of the Grand Canyon, and it wouldn't make a difference because you're still going to spend the rest of your sorry-ass life in Leavenworth."

Al's contempt incensed Bracken, who reached out and swung his arm. Al ducked and the fist grazed the top of his head. Campo moved in, welcoming the chance to make a diversion. He swung his fist hard into Guttone's stomach, but it had almost no effect. Bracken stood straight, fire burning in his eyes.

Payback time, the giant thought. He was about to pounce on his prey when Jason ordered him to stop. Bracken paused and gave his boss a look of fury, but he wanted his revenge on Campo and would not be denied. Guttone grabbed Al by the biceps, squeezing the muscles like grapefruits, and then flung him like a cardboard box. Campo crashed against the wall on his wounded shoulder. He grunted and slid to the floor. The massive man took two steps towards Al and then kicked his midsection, the force tossing his body across the entire width of the room. Al spun in the air and landed on his rump. Guttone was toying with him like a killer whale hurling seals in the frigid Arctic waters before devouring them for dinner—and Bracken was looking hungry. From one end of the room to the other, his body was being flogged by the cinder block walls and concrete floor. Guttone picked up Al by his throat, holding him at arm's length, high in the air. Tyson looked in amazement at both Bracken's strength and Campo's endurance.

"I said, that's enough! Bracken, cease!" Gull ordered again.

The giant stared at Gull, panting, holding firmly to his prey. Al's thoughts were blurry, and he was confused about his whereabouts. He could feel the blood pounding in his skull as his oxygen supply diminished, and his arms fell, dangling at his sides. He was about to let go, visions from his past rose up unbidden…Stortz's demise, Faz's plea for vengeance, Wolfgang's last rites, and then Domeni, her beauty and the satin feel of her skin…the warmth of their bodies together. He couldn't let go, not now, not ever. His vision cleared enough to see his one opportunity. With his remaining strength, he stiffened his fore and middle fingers and stabbed them into Bracken's eye sockets. Campo heard the brute howl in pain, felt the chokehold loosen, and he dropped like a stone.

Goliath bent over, blinded and overwhelmed by shock. Al lay on the floor between Guttone's legs, Gull still pointing his weapon right at him. He glanced to his left, making eye contact with Tyson, who was still standing with his hands held behind his head and his two guards close by. Campo winked to him, and Tyson prepared for anything. Al called up his rage and anger, and with all of his strength, he swung a fist upward, crashing it into Bracken's nose. Blood splattered out as his upper body bent back. Quickly rushing forward, using the large man's own weight and momentum, Al pushed the massive body into Jason Gull.

As Gull fell, he fired his weapon, shooting the giant in the back, killing him instantly. The huge body of his former security chief pinned Gull to the floor, and his gun spun away, toward Campo. Simultaneously, Joe Tyson plunged double chops into the throats of his guards; they grabbed at their necks and went down, shot by Campo using the gun Gull had dropped. Joe Tyson secured two automatic weapons and met Al standing over Jason Gull, who was struggling to get free, clawing at the concrete floor, his legs immobilized by the dead weight of Guttone. Al stepped on his hand.

"Now, Mr. Gull, what core meltdown are we talking about?" Al said, panting and enjoying his vantage point.

"You idiot, we have to get out of here. In thirty minutes, the radiation will reach a dangerous level," Gull responded, half in pain from the shoe pressing on the back of his hand, and partially in panic at the thought of becoming a victim of his own terrorist plot.

"What do you think, Joe? Do we believe this idiot? Or do we kill him now, and figure the rest out for ourselves?" Campo dug his heel harder into Gull's hand, enjoying watching the agony on his face.

Tyson was busy replacing his headset, his injured fingers clumsy. "Al, let him be for the moment…Jake, do you read? Reply. This is Tyson, respond."

"You're wasting your time with Jake. He died in the fireball from the elevator shaft," Al said.

Tyson looked him in the eye, knowing it was true. He tried another channel. "Armstrong, reply. This is Tyson."

"Yes sir. Armstrong here."

Tyson heard through the crackle of static the tell-tale sounds of a firefight. "What's your status?"

"We were surprised by a barrage of gunfire from the main entrance, but we've managed to enter the building, and have secured the main area." Tyson could hear men yelling and shots fired intermittently. "It seems we have driven them back into the center of the facility. Resistance is weakening, and we've begun taking prisoners."

"Good. When you've completely secured the plant call me and…" Tyson was cut off by Armstrong yelling through the noise.

"There's one other point of information, sir."

"What's that?"

"Agent McDonnell and our nuclear tech, Ted Billings, have warned me radiation levels have been rising, and the deeper we penetrate into the building, the more rapidly they rise."

"Shit!" Tyson said, looking up at Campo, then down at Gull. "What have you started? Armstrong, how long before levels become dangerous?"

"Sir, this is Ted Billings, and at the current rate of expansion, in an hour we will be beyond saving ourselves. We have to locate the control room and contain the leak if at all possible."

"Understood," Tyson said. He stood over Gull and aimed the automatic at his head. His years of training and hard-won composure went out the door, and he was ready to do anything to force Gull to reverse what he had done. He knelt down, gazing into Gull's face. "You're going to take us to the operations room and help us shut down the core meltdown, or I'll let Mr. Campo here take you to a place where no man has gone before."

"All right, all right, I'll do it! Please get off, and get me out from under this corpse." Gull said. He was at the brink of tears.

Al was enraged by his cowardice. He leaned his full body weight onto the foot crushing Gull's hand and jabbed the end of his weapon into the sobbing man'scheek. "You'll help us from where you are."

Gull yelled in anguish and looked up at Al. He was frightened—and that only made Campo's temper worse. He reflected on how just twenty-four hours ago this man had been bold and sarcastic, buoyed up by his own ambitions and self-indulgence, tossing away lives into oblivion without misgivings or regret. Al wanted nothing more than to blast his head into the floor.

Gull looked up at Al through his distorted face and mumbled something.

"What's that, Mr. Gull? Oh, I'm sorry! Does the gun jammed in your face make you to slur your speech?" Al said and pulled his pressure back a bit.

"I have the only access to the control room. Hurry! We're wasting time," Jason said.

"I don't believe him. Do you, Joe?"

"I'm serious! The elevator that just exploded was the main entrance. There is another elevator only Wolfgang and I knew about, but you need me to enter. It's the only way..." Gull was pleading for them to listen. Campo felt it was a trick, but what other option did they have? Al looked up at Tyson, who shrugged his shoulders.

"He may be telling the truth, and if Ted Billings is right, we don't have much time," Joe said. They dragged the corpse of Bracken off Jason Gull, pulled him roughly to his feet, and handcuffed him.

Gull explained to Tyson how his men could meet them at the secret elevator, and Tyson passed the information on to Armstrong. The three made a series of turns and went up a flight of steps. Their ears were suddenly blistered by alarms, and red and yellow lights flashed in their faces. Al held onto Gull's arm, twisting it behind his back, making sure the pain was constant.

At the top of the steps, they met up with Billings, McDonnell, and Armstrong. Armstrong was a big man; he had broad shoulders enlarged by his flak jacket. His face was light, and his blue-gray eyes fixed on Tyson's bleeding hand.

"Sir, are you all right?" he yelled over the noise. "Do you need a medic?"

"What's that?" Tyson asked, not realizing his wound was open. He lifted his hand and said, "No, I'm fine. We have to keep moving. What is the status outside?"

"The plant is ours," Armstrong said. "We are loading prisoners now and questioning the security guards."

"Ted, what about the radiation?"

Ted lifted a handheld Geiger counter and spoke into Tyson's ear. "We are being exposed to tolerable levels but radiation levels are still rising."

Tyson nodded and looked at the big man. "Armstrong, get topside and tell everyone to get as far away from the plant as possible, as soon as they secure all prisoners. Then radio for the clean-up crew to stand ready. And see if you can turn off this goddamn alarm."

Armstrong nodded and quickly left.

"Gull, make it happen," Tyson ordered.

"My key card is in my front pocket," Jason said, his voice barely audible.

Al took Gull's card and through the flashing lights he saw a slot under a keypad. He inserted the card, and a small panel slid open, allowing a padded chin rest to project outward. With Campo's help, Jason placed his face into it, and a light flashed into his eyes, scanning his retina. The elevator doors slid open, and the men entered.

"Wait a minute; you don't need me any longer. You guys can enter and disarm the reactor. Let me go with Armstrong!" Gull spoke fast, but Campo knew it was just another trick, so he shoved him into the elevator.

No markings or buttons were visible within the shiny metal car, and the doors closed automatically, which thankfully cut off the flashing lights and dulled the blaring alarm. Their stomachs rose in their torsos as they descended rapidly. Campo looked through the crease between the doors. There were none of the typical flashes of light that signaled the passing of floors. There was only darkness. It seemed as if they had been falling forever when their momentum ceased.

The doors opened, and a wave of intense heat blasted into their faces. The area was bathed in amber radiance. The group bounded out into a stadium-sized room containing the reactor and operations facility. A wall of gray-painted steel rose up ten feet on the left. It was covered with knobs, buttons, and dials, some bright yellow and green, and others blinking an intense red. From the top of the giant panel ran dozens of thick black cables and silver metal tubing, all twisted together. These were strung across the ceiling, hanging from chains and wires, connecting a jumble of round mechanical piers located throughout the perimeter. In the center of the vast space was an imposing tower of concrete, reaching a ten stories into the air. Above the mass, the moon shone through steel grates. Campo reasoned the tall structure was the cooling tower, which emitting the billowing fog always present during his trips here.

He suddenly realized that today, as they had approached the plant, there had been no mist. He saw Billings make the connection at the same time.

"Mr. Gull," Billings paused as he stared at a console between the wall and the concrete tower. Its surface was angled at forty-five degrees; a keypad and a monitor were recessed in the center, and a phone and headset lay next to it. The balance of the table was covered with diagrams and documents, along with a pattern of system checkpoints labeled for each component of the single reactor. "I assume this is the main control panel, and the place where you directed the reactor coolant flow to be stopped. Am I correct in assuming you had the coolant flow decreased to cause the reactor to overheat?"

Gull stood, sweating, frozen in his shoes, staring at the wildly swinging needle of the Geiger counter in McDonnell's hand. "Yes, I had the coolant flow stopped, and a single boron tube raised above safety level," Gull said with wide eyes. He was perspiring uncontrollably.

Campo's knowledge of nuclear reactor technology was sparse, but he did remember that boron was the key to absorbing radiation. If the tubes were removed the reactor would overheat and explode.

"Can you start the cooling process again?" Tyson asked Billings. The tech's gaze was fixed on the computer monitor as he frantically typed out commands on the keypad.

"It's still not that simple. If we allow the water current to flow into the core too quickly, it might explode from the shock, like pouring hot coffee into a cold cup. It would shatter. We need heated coolant to start the flow, and then we can slowly let the water back in, gradually decreasing the temperature."

"Um, guys," Campo said, as he too saw the Geiger needle. "This thing Bill is holding is swinging off the chart."

"If we stay down here much longer, there won't be enough time to scour off the radiation. We'll have absorbed too much," Bill interjected.

"Son of a bitch, it's there," Billings said, startling the others.

"What's there?" Tyson asked.

"A reserve of heated coolant. I'm surprised your men didn't think to drain the tank to ensure the meltdown, Mr. Gull. Now it will only take a series of commands, but we have to find the raised tube and re-insert it first. Mr. Gull, which zone was opened? I see an alert, but the dial is unmarked. I have to know which command to give the computer, or else we risk other malfunctions delaying the cooling process."

"I…I don't remember," Gull said, looking like he was about to pass out.

Campo grabbed him by the throat and squeezed. "You do remember, and you're going to tell us which one," Al said, shaking Jason, but it was no use. Gull was in shock, and he only made guttural noises through his closed esophagus.

"We'll have to check them by foot and close it manually," Billings said. He turned to Tyson and looked at him like it was the only option.

"Is that safe?" Tyson asked, surprised to hear Ted's candid tone.

"Not entirely, but it will be a hell of a lot worse if radiation continues to contaminate the air. We'll all die before the reactor is secure." Billings was getting antsy as he wiped the sweat from his face

"Fine then," Tyson said. What he was about to do made him fear for his life, but he couldn't ask anyone else to do it for him. "Bill, you, Ted, and Al take Gull out of here. Tell Armstrong to wait for my signal, and then bring the decontamination unit in full tilt."

"Sir, that would be difficult," Bill said, his eyes wide. He rubbed his forearm across his face. "Our radios are dead. The signal won't penetrate the radiation clouding the air."

"Shit…" Tyson paused. He too was sweating, and Al thought it was more than just the heat. "Then give me ten minutes to find this damn thing and five minutes to reach the surface. If I don't come out, evacuate the state of Delaware, and call the president. Then call the country club. I won't be over to play the back nine tonight."

McDonnell nodded. He was all too happy to leave the oven. He shoved Gull's apathetic body toward the elevator while Campo stood beside Tyson.

"I said to get moving topside with Bill," Tyson said to Campo and started to shed his flack jacket and weapons.

"I'm going to make sure we both make it to the back nine," Al said, standing his ground. He removed his jacket as well and looked over at Billings. "Where do we begin looking?"

"Well, Ted?" Joe said to Billings, who was typing commands into the computer.

"All right...I am instructing the computer to begin the coolant flow once the boron tube has been secured. You should notice a temperature change immediately and thousands of gallons of water will stream under the concrete tower. And believe me, you'll hear it coming! The thing you have to remember—if you don't see the steam rise out of the tower or hear the flow of fluid, it means the computer needs a physical command."

"What do I have to do—rub its back and buy it a drink, for Christ's sake?" Al asked.

"In a manner of speaking, yes." Billings said as he rose from his chair. "You have to return to the control console and punch in 'system secured,' then press enter. Beside the tower, there are steps leading down to the core area. On our way in, I saw safety suits. Put them on—and head down. It shouldn't be difficult to spot. If I'm correct, there will be a series of glass panels encased insteel, and one will be elevated. There may be a control panel or a lever to close the portal, and that will lower the boron tube—that's it. But judging from the heat and radiation levels, you'll have five maybe six minutes tops before you pass out from exposure."

Al took note of the time on the computer screen: 2:47 am.

"All right," Tyson said, looking back at the elevator, to where the safety suits were hanging. "Ted, you get out of here and wait for us. Tell Armstrong to just wait for the fog to begin, then come in running. If not, tell him after fifteen minutes he has to consider us dead, and he should begin the evacuation."

Ted entered the lift. Campo and Tyson quickly put on the protective suits. They were made of a flexible, thick, clear plastic. The suits were designed to close at the back, and the two men had to close each other's suits by zipping, then folding over a plastic flap, sealing them inside. Tubes ran into the suit from asmall, handheld compressor with a dial to regulate the air current. They turned the knobs, and the plastic inflated. The suits were bulky-looking, making the men appear as if they were trapped inside balloons, forcing them to move with stiff, awkward steps.

They clumsily made it to the bottom. There, the heat was nearly too much to bear, but they pushed themselves forward. The area was lit with deep, red emergency lights, and the extreme temperature made the images hazy and distorted. Campo squinted. He could make out a gray wall to the left; it was smooth and flat. Every few feet he saw a glass view screen, each with two large circular knobs under the pane. He stepped in front of one and looked inside. There was a blinding flash of light, and he turned away, his eyes burning.

Tyson grabbed him from behind. "Let's keep moving, not much time," he said, his breathing labored.

Al saw fear on his face; Tyson was becoming ill, and his strength was fading fast. Campo sluggishly walked on to more portals. Time had no meaning as he felt the burning effects of the radiation penetrating his chest and bloodstream. One after another he found the glass doors closed. Maybe it was a trick by Gull, one last effort to kill innocent people, knowing his time was up. Or possibly Billings didn't know everything about this reactor. His assumptions could be wrong. The will to survive drove him on; murky, doughy light billowed in front of him, until, several feet ahead, the haze exploded violently outward from one of the glass openings. Relieved at finding the open gate, Al smiled and tasted salty sweat pour into his mouth as he now realized how wet he was.

He turned to tell Tyson and saw no one behind him.

"Tyson…Tyson!" he yelled and looked down, the FBI agent was laying face down on the concrete floor. He fought the impulse to go to his aid. Six minutes must have passed hours ago. He had to close the door. Al got down on his hands and knees and crawled toward the flush of heat emptying into the chamber. Then he saw the glass door wasn't open. It was broken. He panicked. Pulling himself up next to the opening, he was nearly knocked over by the billowing heat. Remembering what Billings said, he looked for a control panel or lever. There was no control panel, but there was a lever. It was flat and long, extending from a fulcrum bending at right angles. The other end was hinged to a wide, flat, steel door several inches bigger than the glass opening. It was positioned above between two guides running parallel to both sides of the broken portal. Campo grabbed the lever and pulled downward. It didn't budge. Again he tried, lifting his legs off the floor screaming, but it wouldn't move. He stopped and punched it in frustration.

"Move, you son of a bitch!" he latched on a third time and grunting, pulled at it with his full strength, when suddenly he felt someone at his back. It was Tyson. Both men pulled with all their might until suddenly, the lever gave way, and the safety door slammed down. Immediately, the heat decreased, but not enough to make them comfortable. Together the two men walked back towards the exit, arms around each other's shoulders, assisting each other. They had just reached the top of the steps when Tyson fell to his knees.

"Hurry, type in the command to begin the flow," he said, pushing Al forward.

Campo stood in front of the keypad, but he couldn't see. The moisture in his suit was clouding the plastic. If he typed in the wrong command, God only knew what would happen. He made out the image of a pen sitting on the desk. He took it and jabbed it into the suit, tearing open the plastic. He poked his dampened head out.

Without hesitation, he typed in the command and pressed enter. All of a sudden, the room began to roar, lights flashed on and off, and the thunderous sound of a tidal wave echoed in the chamber. Al looked at the clock: 3:02 a.m. Only fifteen minutes had passed in what seemed an eternity. He lifted Tyson's body over his shoulder, carried him to the elevator, and tumbled him to the floor. The agent was now unconscious. Al felt nauseated and light-headed, but forced himself to stay awake long enough to drag Tyson out of the building. Immediately personnel wearing similar protective clothing swarmed them, taking the agent away, and leading Campo to a mini-decontamination camp that had sprung up in the parking lot.

Campo was brought into a shower area, stripped of his clothing, and scoured down by three men using coarse brushes and smelly soap. Al leaned on a plastic wall, enduring this necessary punishment to cleanse him of the radiation.

The men viewed Campo's body in wonder. There were bruises up and down his back and sides. Two bullet wounds were only partially healed, the flesh swollen and purple. His skin was marked with a hundred scrapes and cuts, and yet this man spoke not one word of complaint.

How much longer? Campo thought, fighting the desire to collapse. He held onto whatever reserves he had left, his hand clinging tightly to the plastic wall. Finally the torture stopped, and he opened his eyes.

"Sir, are you all right?" one man said from behind his plastic shield.

Campo's vision was fuzzy, and his head now whirled around. He stopped trying to remain conscious and fell to the wet floor.

BOOK TWO

CHAPTER THIRTY-EIGHT

ampo's eyes flickered. Dim light pierced his retina, like he was staring through a telescope at the sun, and he closed them. He could smell soap, and rubbing alcohol, and a trace of urine. There was a television playing in the background. He attempted to roll onto his side, but his arm was strapped down. Again, he opened his eyes, blinking feverishly, clearing the haze. To his left, a shadow slowly resolved itself into a welcome form. Domeni was sitting by his bedside. His arm wasn't restrained; it washer hand squeezing his tightly. The sight sent comfort throughout his beat-up body. He turned his head and looked directly into her eyes.

"Al, I'm so glad to see you again," she said with a warm smile. She was perfect, her face bright, maybe a couple of bruises hidden by light make up, but her dark hair was full and her cheeks rosy.

Campo tried to lift his other arm but intravenous lines dangled from it, so he raised the hand Domeni held, and brushed her cheek. "I dreamt of you while I slept. You were covered in white, and I held you close. How about you joining me in this bed, and we'll cover ourselves with this white sheet."

Domeni giggled, but she knew he was serious. "There is nothing more I want to do right now, but…" she said, and glanced towards the foot of the bed.

Joe Tyson sat cross-legged, his hands folded on his lap. Light shone through the window behind him. "How are you feeling Al?" he asked, grinning happily to see his partner alert.

"Like I went ten rounds with a concrete truck, and lost miserably. Aside from that, and the twenty or so throbbing muscles and bones I have, I've never felt better." Al adjusted the backrest of the bed. Humming, it brought him upright. Then he leaned forward to stretch his back muscles. Domeni stood and massaged his shoulders and rubbed his back. "How about you? You seem pretty well off." Campo bent his head down, as Domeni's hands pressed on his neck and squeezed his shoulders. She was giving it her all, digging her thumbs and fingers deep into his muscles. She's done this before, he thought.

"Yes, I am," Tyson said and rubbed the back of his knuckles. His finger was broken, cased in a metal and foam splint, and two fingers were taped together. "The doctors gave me some pills to relieve the nausea, which I can't say are completely working, but they gave me a clean bill of health after the scrub down." Tyson looked down at his pants and brushed them off. Then he took out a cigarette from inside his suit jacket pocket. He knew he couldn't smoke in the hospital, but the feeling of it between his fingers and the taste on his lips was soothing. "I'm glad to hear you're doing well," he said. He took an imaginary drag and then blew out imaginary smoke. "Because it's not over yet."

Al's head jerked upward. "What do you mean not over yet? You've got Gull, his operating power is finished, and I'm sure your guys persuaded him to divulge the destination of the weapons. Oh that feels good, sweetheart," he said to Domeni as she worked her way down to his lower back.

Tyson stood and leaned forward. His splint clinked on the white metal frame at the foot of the bed. His knuckles were black and blue. "It's a little more involved than that. Ms. Conti, would you mind leaving us for a moment?"

"No way," Al said. "She's already involved. Besides, this back massage is wonderful."

"It's OK, Al," Domeni said and gave a last rub across his back. "I don't want to hear any more than I have already—I'm petrified enough." She stood and leaned towards his face, looking into his eyes. "And don't worry, I'll finish this massage later—you can count on it." She gave him a long kiss on the lips, then turned and gave Tyson an affirmative stare, and left the room.

Al leaned back and asked, "All right, what the hell is going on? Did the FBI botch up another one?" Al saw a tray table where Domeni had been sitting and rolled it over. There was a metal lid and he lifted it. The plate held cold turkey and stiff mashed potatoes, and beside it was a tiny plastic cup with jellied cranberry, and a half-pint of apple juice. He ripped off the foil and sipped. "Well, did you or what?"

"No, actually, we've completed our interrogation of Gull, and his plant has a new owner, the Federal Government. And we know the destination of the weapons, so to speak."

"So you don't know?" Al's eyebrows rose. He ripped open the plastic fork and knife and dug into the cold food.

"We do know they were sent on a private jet to the Middle East, and then sent on as many as twelve trucks to different locations." Tyson put his briefcase on the table, pushing Al's plate to one side, and removed a manila folder. "We've traced the trucks and the drivers to Karuza."

"What's a Karuza?" Al asked, wrinkling his brow, shoveling the food in his mouth. The turkey was a little rubbery and the potatoes tasted like cornstarch, but he was so hungry he was determined to eat it all.

"You've obviously not been watching the six o'clock news lately."

"Forgive me. I've been busy," Campo said incredulously, as he adjusted his body in the now-uncomfortable bed and wiped his mouth with the napkin.

"He's a powerful religious zealot in the Middle East, and a self-proclaimed prophet who has been speaking loudly of Allah," Tyson said as he passed the file over to Al.

"Sounds familiar," Al said, opening the document. "Isn't there one of these guys popping up every couple of decades?" He read through the document, his eyes nearly popping out of his head when he saw the name Sabu…the Butcher. Flashbacks twisted in and out of his head, the beating, the torture, the endless pain he had suffered at the hands of the Butcher. A lump in his throat grew to almost choking size; his blood vessels expanded, turning his face red. He held the napkin to his lips, fearing he was going to vomit.

"Yes," Tyson said. "Sabu is involved with Karuza. General Bartow said you might be interested in helping us further our investigation and stopping whatever plan of destruction Karuza has."

"You can be damn sure of that," Al said as he flipped through the file, turning to a page of messages written in a foreign language, the translation written beside it. Campo looked at it quizzically. "This writing here, what language is it?"

"It's Arabic; we found a dozen messages translated in Gull's office. Those first few are self-explanatory. Karuza was obviously demanding shipment because Gull was late—thanks to your stealing his plutonium. But we haven't been able to decipher the meaning of the last one."

Campo read the decoded message: "'Operation Slaughter to commence on the next Sabbath. The Americans will suffer all the more upon his return. Complete your task, and all will be well." Campo reflected on the message for a moment, but its meaning eluded him. He stared long and hard at the Arabic version. The writing held something familiar in its odd print. "Where have I seen this before?" he mumbled.

"What's that?"

"This writing seems familiar to me."

"You understand the message?" Tyson asked eagerly.

"No, not yet, it's the Arabic writing. I've seen this before."

"Were you ever in the Middle East?" Tyson asked, recalling how Campo's file was incomplete, and then his close ties with General Bartow, whom Tyson now knew had been in control of Special Operations in that area before, during, and after the Gulf War.

"Yes, I can speak some Arabic, Farsi, but I can't read any of them." Then it hit him. It was the message he found inside the room of the patient in the state hospital. Al reached out and pointed to his clothes draped over a hanger. "Joe, grab my pants over there. There may be a clue in there."

Tyson tossed them over to Campo, who dug through his pockets, pulled out his billfold, then riffled through it, tossing money and receipts aside. "Bingo!" Al said.

Tyson looked at him intently, hoping for a breakthrough.

Al compared the notes, holding his paper under the file, and searching through each line. He found an exact match. *But now what does it mean*, he wondered. He was lost in thought. He leaned his head back and closed his eyes, eliminating all interference, charging his memory to recreate the past; strangely the sounds of the television became apparent. FOX news was delivering footage of the president, and the commentator spoke: "You see here the president's caravan arriving at the front gates of the Delaware State Hospital; he is arriving at his regularly scheduled time to visit his sister, who has been a patient here for almost twelve months now. He looks in on her frequently since she checked herself into the hospital just under a year ago, battling depression and anxiety…"

"Tyson shit! That's it, quick! Grab the rest of my clothes!" Al said and tore off the open-back hospital smock. He stood there naked, yanking the tape and the IVs from the back of his hand.

Tyson was baffled at Al's actions but threw the rest of his clothes to him. "What the hell are you doing? Have you lost your mind? You're in no condition to be jumping up and down like that—sit and we'll go over the message…"

"No time! We have to get to that hospital! The president is in danger! I'll explain on the way!"

Campo gave Tyson a detailed explanation of what he had stumbled across at the hospital, and the strange behavior of the patient. Tyson listened intently as he drove his dark Chevy sedan like a madman; he propped a red flashing light on the roof, and beeped the horn furiously. The FBI agent handed Campo his cell phone and a series of numbers to dial to get them through to the president's secretary. Campo jacked it into the car phone speaker. The two heard the ring on the other end, and then a woman's voice answered.

"Hello, this is the White House. How may I direct your call?"

"Yes, Connie, this is Special Agent Joe Tyson from the Philadelphia office. I need you to patch me through to the president's Secret Service detail. I think Jim Richards is the one in charge." Connie wasn't flustered a bit but responded immediately.

"Mr. Tyson, the president is visiting his sister in Delaware, and it will be difficult to reach him, but I will try to link you with Mr. Richards."

"Connie, this is an emergency, and the president's life may be in jeopardy, so please don't try—just do it."

Campo watched Joe talk to Connie, honk the horn, drive through a maze of traffic, dodging pedestrians, and screaming obscenities out the window at the other drivers on the road—all at the same time. It was a magnificent show of skill and concentration. "I commend you on your driving abilities, Mario; the academy has a good training course, I take it."

"Academy, shit. I used to race stock cars in high school. This here is training from backyard round-ups."

"Hello, sir," the woman on the phone said. "I have the president's Secret Service Agent in Charge on the line. I'm putting you through."

"Yes, Special Agent Phillips here," the man said dolefully.

"Phillips, this is Special Agent Joe Tyson, FBI Philadelphia." Tyson spoke quickly as he could, as he raced onto the median, swerving around a group of cars. "I have information that an attempt to assassinate the president is planned at the Delaware Hospital. It is imperative that he be removed immediately from the premises."

"Nonsense," Phillips said, "the Secret Service has combed the building, and nearly twenty agents surround him…"

"Phillips! Listen to me! Where is Jim Richards? Let me talk to him," Tyson yelled and barreled back onto the roadway. He swerved all the way into the right lane.

Campo bounced and banged against the door and seat. Never one for wearing a seatbelt, he decided now it would be a good idea and managed to strap himself in. It didn't help much because now the straps constantly tugged on his wounds.

"I'm sorry, sir, but he is with the president right now and can't be disturbed…"

"Phillips! You warn the president right now, and tell Richards this is Joe Tyson, or when I get there, I'll personally tear your throat out and shove it up your ass—do it now!"

"Mr. Tyson—if that's who you are—I think our conversation is over!" Phillips hung up.

Tyson was enraged, and he put his fist into the dashboard, cracking the plastic panel. "Son of a bitch! We'll have to do it on our own! When we get there, you lead the way. I'll tote my badge and try to find Richards."

Twenty minutes later the big sedan rumbled to the front gate and was approached by two Secret Service agents.

"Can we help you?" a short man asked. He wore dark glasses and a dark brown suit. The other agent, similarly dressed, was even shorter than the first. He leaned in to stare at Campo in the passenger seat.

"Yes, I'm Special Agent Joe Tyson, of the Philadelphia FBI," Joe showed his ID. "This man here has information critical to the safety of the president; he is the only one able to make out a physical conformation of a possible assassin. We need to enter immediately and stop the attempt."

"Sir, if you'll pass along the information to me, I'll radio in to the president's aide and..."

"Are you deaf?" Campo asked, agitated. "He just said I have to see the fucking guy! I don't have a name or description good enough to be sure, so just let us the fuck in, and warn the president."

The agent looked at Campo indifferently, and motioned with his arm to the left of the gate. "Sir, if you'll pull over there, we'll see to your assassin, and secure the president's safety."

"You asshole, the president will be dead by the time you act. We're coming in. Tyson, head over there!" Al said.

"Right! Screw this!" Tyson said, as he stabbed the pedal and raced toward the building Al had pointed out. The Secret Service agents were thrust away and shrouded in a cloud of smoke of burning rubber and blacktop.

Inside the hospital, the president and his entourage walked down the long hallway leading to the nurse's station atthe apex of K pod. E. James Worthington walked briskly and smiled at the nurse who was standing in front of her station.

"Hello Nurse, how are you today?" President Worthington said as he passed.

The halls were filled with patients, unaware this man was the leader of the Free World. They took to their own simple lives, ignoring the men in black. As always, E. James agreed to the security following him into the building, but he insisted on not disturbing the residents. They had carried awful burdens on their backs, and he wished not to disturb them any further. Mr. Wilson, who was the first one to take care of his sister, stood poised, his hands folded behind his back. This was the fourth time he had met the president, and each time was as exciting as the last. Worthington saw him, and went right over and shook his hand.

"Jim Wilson, how have you been? Still keeping the lid on this place, I see?"

"Yes, sir, Mr. President. It appears they won't let me go until I can afford to retire," the big man said, glowing at the fact Worthington remembered his name. "You'll see your sister is waiting in her room at the end of the hall as always, and the rest of the residents are milling around like it's just another day."

"Thank you," the president said smiling. "Jim, maybe afterward you could see me to my car, and we can have a chat about your retirement."

Mr. Wilson smiled from ear to ear. "Yes sir, thank you, Mr. President."

Worthington motioned to the Secret Service men to wait at the nurse's station while he proceeded down the hall so he could be alone with his sister. He marched down the discolored white tile floor, passing a woman resident wearing a grimy fur coat, curling her hair into twisting dreadlocks, mumbling to herself. Then he saw a short man, his head pointing down, and a crop of black, curly hair gonewild. His hands were tucked into the pockets of a soiled, white terrycloth robe. One end of the belt dangled freely, dragging on the floor. He dragged his slippered feet at a slow, methodical pace, and the president heard the swooshing sound of each step. Worthington would never stare at anyone askance; he would thrust a hand out and look the person in his face, giving him his full attention. But this man oddly seemed to avoid—yet seek—Worthington's attention.

———◆———

Yavuz was nervous, but for the first time in nearly a year, he felt his heart burn with martial fervor. After so much time away from his home and people, he was beginning to forget his commitment to the cause. Fragments of fighting the war, and verses of the Quran sprang into his brain like mushrooms in a lightless birth. His blood, which until now had been stagnated by medications and lethargy, thrummed through his veins, and there came upon him a merciless desire to kill. He listened to the footfalls clack against the hard floor, as the commander of all that is evil— America—approached. His head hanging low, he raised his eyes enough to see the shoes of his victim. Within the pocket of his robe, he gripped the weapon, loosely massaging its strange material. When he first opened the package, he had been disappointed at its appearance; small and square, it looked like a child's toy. But after he read the instructions and put the pieces together, it took on a now-familiar shape. Once he realized the weapon's power, he was certain he could achieve his goal. He hid the packaging in the concealed door in his closet, and then placed a small cyanide capsule under his tongue; he was ready to fulfill his promise to clear the path for the return of the Prophet.

———◆———

Campo jogged as best as he could, hurrying down the hallway with Tyson by his side.

"Which room number is it?" Joe asked, pulling the struggling man along.

"He's in K pod, in the middle of the hall. We turn this corner and enter past the nurses' station." Campo was breathing heavily, his wounds draining his stamina, and he pushed on as hard as he could, past the pain, past the throbbing in his muscles. The two men turned the corner, and were met by three Secret Service agents.

"Out of the way, the president is in danger," Tyson protested, flashing his credentials and shoving aside the first agent.

Campo now used the cinderblock wall as a crutch, looking down past the men. He saw the president walking freely down the hall past the rooms. Then he saw Yavuz just ten feet away. Worthington's back was to the assassin. Campo wanted to lunge forward to save the president but knew he would never reach him in time. He examined Tyson arguing and made his decision. He pushed himself off the wall and thrust a fist into the jaw of the closest agent, knocking him out, then threw his body against the other two, freeing Tyson.

"Tyson!" he screamed, "The dark-haired man in the middle of the hall. Go now!" he said, resting his full body weight on the downed men.

Joe saw the assassin's gaze and understood. He drew his service 9mm, and ran down the hall yelling, "Move, move!"

The residents ignored him, staring blankly. He pushed through one last guard and came upon Mr. Wilson. His huge frame stood between Joe and Worthington. Tyson wasted no time and pistol-whipped the pod bouncer across the neck, dropping him.

———◆———

Yavuz poked the end of the weapon through a hole in his smock. The minuscule red dot danced across the president's shoulder as he passed, arcing around to his back. Yavuz had read in the brief directions that the closer a target was, the quicker death would come. He stared down the target, centering the red dot. It was time to become a hero to his people.

———◆———

Special Agent Joe Tyson came down the hall like a maniac, but he worried that if he fired his weapon on the run he would hit one of the unmoving residents, or worse, the president, so he threw himself at the assassin, flying fifteen feet to collide with Yavuz just as he fired the Jasonium gun. Tyson's tackle diverted the deathly ray, which harmlessly penetrated the acoustical ceiling. He collided with his target, knocking him onto the ground. The agent quickly recovered and crushed his knee into the man's back. He grabbed a clump of Yavuz's hair, yanked his head up, and jammed his pistol into his cheekbone.

Even from behind, Tyson could see the assassin smile. "We will win. He shall return and bring justice," Yavuz said in perfect English. Then he wiggled his jaw and crunched down on something in his mouth.

By that time Campo had been restrained by the Secret Service and handcuffed. Down the hall the president was on the floor with two agents on top of him. Tyson looked up and saw the president's stern face through the arms of his guards.

"You're safe now, Mr. President," Tyson said as he felt for a pulse in Yavuz's neck, confirming his demise. "Now where the hell is Special Agent Phillips?" Tyson said and glared around at the crowd.

CHAPTER THIRTY-NINE

The air was thick with dust and the smell of diesel fuel. Engines billowed out black smoke. The workers, some wearing bandanas over their mouths, wore dismal expressions, drawing in slow breaths as the clammy dust was continually kicked up by the scuffing of boots. An army of workers and machinery had constructed a cavernous room underground. Sabu the Butcher walked along a path towards the entrance tunnel, which was a hundred feet wide, and as high as it was broad. He jumped from his jeep before it came to a complete stop and gazed out at his military might. Hundreds of soldiers lined the cavern walls, dressed in tan and gray camouflage military attire, some sitting cleaning AK-47 assault rifles, some leaning on oil-soaked barrels chewing on tobacco. Others were sitting in groups, listening to orders from superiors. As the general passed, they jumped to attention and saluted their leader. Sabu returned the gesture smiling and left the shallow tunnel hall, proceeding into the main subterranean area.

He felt the noise in his chest, and high above him dangled giant halogen lights that slowly rocked back and forth, illuminating a room the size of an Olympic stadium. The floor was of ground-up rock, and other than the heavily traveled roadways, the surface was jagged and awkward. Sheer walls rose upward, possibly twenty stories, hacked out of the mountain by thousands of slave laborers. This room was built as a holding area. A battalion of tanks, artillery, and rocket launchers, countless numbers of soldiers lined the cavern with his most vicious fighting regiment nearest the front, all readied for the first assault. Furthest away were tubular-shaped tunneling machines spaced a hundred yards apart. These massive mechanisms looked like monsters from a Godzilla movie, towering fifty feet high and twice as long. Huge steel tank tracks—taller than any man—were hinged on an array of gears and pulleys lining the lower sides. At its front, thousands of drill bits came together, forming a cone shape. Mounted on every drill-bit head were tiny diamonds embedded into the points, all allowing fast and smooth cutting through earth and rock. These diesel-burning machines laid in wait, engines idling. Any moment the order would be given to break the surface just ten feet away. The tunneling had taken months of continuous labor. Sabu's engineers had started outside the Georgia border city of Akhaltsikhe within Turkey and dug deep under the valley, covering nearly a hundred miles to the capital city of Tbilisi in the Republic of Georgia. The plan called for the machines to all break ground simultaneously, and drive onto the land surrounding the Georgian capitol building. Cannons would swing out on all sides of the tunneling machines and fire a barrage of shells, destroying everything in sight, clearing the way for the armored division and ground troops to complete the invasion.

Sabu stood akimbo, marveling at his powerful, invincible military. He reveled in thinking how Premier Andropov would look, staring at those machines garnered with the diamonds he had supplied, bashing down the perimeter walls of his state house, plowing through his treasured gardens and onto the capitol building itself. This was his euphoria: soldiers, tanks, and guns. Death and destruction were his prescription for power, and moments before the storm, his shadow cast over the army waiting to create his thunder. A soldier marched up to him and saluted. At attention, Sabu returned the gesture, and the man handed him a radio handset. The receiver clicked and a voice from Istanbul crackled through.

"Allah's will has been achieved," the voice announced. "Now my soldiers must go and prepare the way for the Prophet's return."

Sabu smiled and said, "It will be done." Then he changed the frequency on the radio, and now he could be heard on a loudspeaker, broadcasting throughout the cavern and deep into the various tunnels. "Believers of the new order!" His voice echoed loudly, so he spoke slowly. "We have been blessed with the task of destroying our enemies…His Holiness Caliph Karuza announced to me that the leaders of all nations surrounding ours have fallen, as His Holiness has foretold. Beyond this crust of earth and rock the last infidel waits. Karuza has foreseen our triumphant victory…and brought within our grasp the military might that will catapult one nation, our nation, into the world as leaders, no longer the persecuted. Then Allah will send back the Prophet and he will garner the power of the New Age. It will be a New Dawn, with the Prophet and His Holiness Karuza side by side. Now we fight… one last fight…to prepare the Way!" Sabu shouted and pumped his fist into the air. A bellow of cheers and screams of joy shook the cavern, as the soldiers cheered their leader. The roar of the tunneling machines grew, and black smoke and debris flew into the air. The cavern sky looked like a thunder storm was approaching, and many men covered their faces with rags and colored cloth, the air chokingly full of dust. The machines ground boulders to pebbles, the front diamond drills spun, breaking the ground and jets of light burst into the room. Waves of smoke billowed outward as the surface was broken. The debris was funneled safely away, and the tanks and artillery began following the enormous tunneling machines, spearheading the massive number of troops.

＊

Inside the capitol building in Tbilisi, Premier Andropov sat with his cabinet. All his generals, the prime minister, and various political leaders crowded around the lone table. The men were bickering across the furniture, waving their hands, and shaking their heads in confusion. All the while Andropov sat calmly, watching the spectacle.

"How can we be sure the United States will remain neutral? There are no guarantees or treaties in place for such things!" General Olaff spat out.

Andropov watched Olaff's round belly shudder as he yelled, and his crop of gray hair puffed upward. His khaki suit was plastered with medals that reflected the lights in the room Andropov noted a colored ribbon draped around the general'sneck. He remembered giving him that very medal, but the reason escaped him.

"Yes, how can we be sure?" the prime minister asked. "And what about Russia? Surely they too will not stand for our position in protecting the Arabs?" He was a young man of forty-five and new to the government. Andropov despised him. He, of course, had been elected in the first free elections held inthe republic.

"Russia is nothing! They will cower to any government holding their oil resources," another man said.

"Gentlemen! Gentlemen!" Andropov yelled, quieting the room. Then he continued in a strong, deep voice. "The leaders of all the Arab nations across the Middle East, North Africa, and Israel have perished, and soon we will receive word that President Worthington of the United States has also died. We are once again a superpower in Asia."

"How is that possible without the support of the old Soviet Union?" Olaff asked.

"The Soviets kindly left behind three hundred nuclear warheads. Fifty of them are in missiles, and our scientists have unlocked the codes. They stand ready to thwart all opposition." Andropov's words caused mixed feelings, and he saw it in their faces. "Caliph Karuza shall join the Arab nations together, and thus will control ninety percent of the world's oil supply. With his power, we will choke the United States and Europe, causing them to drain their reserves. This way, we will, without any violence, conquer the West. They will be but territories of our United Republic."

The rumblings began again. Some present showed fear, while others enjoyed this declaration of power and progress. Valissi Pandanko stood against the wall to Andropov's left; a defiant pride gleamed in his pale features.

"The people of the USA will never tolerate a fascist government," the young prime minister said.

Valissi stepped to the table and said, "They will if their only other option is no gasoline in their cars, buses, or trucks, and watching all transportation come to a stand still. Heating oil will be unavailable, and they will freeze, like we have for decades. We can hold the world hostage, supplying oil only to those countries willing to negotiate with us. Slowly our vice grip on them will take its toll, and they will succumb to our rule."

"The new president of the United States," Andropov said, "will sympathize with Karuza, and he will sway the majority of the liberals to do the same. And once Karuza has them, we will take over."

"Why would the new president do that?" The minister asked.

"Because he was placed there by the republic of Georgia." Andropov said and held a thin smile. The men looked astounded. They could not imagine how Andropov's influence reached the vice-president. Silence captured them for a moment; Andropov thought he had them in his pocket when the prime minister spoke again.

"What about this Karuza?" the prime minister asked. He was pouring a glass of water. "Can we expect him to sit back while we exert all of the power through his ownership of the oil? I refuse to believe he will take a back seat to our government."

"You may be right, Prime Minister, but I feel Karuza's goal is to have total control of the new United Nation of his True Believers, whatever that may be; he has no concerns with America or Europe. Once he is proclaimed Caliph over all, he will cooperate with our rule, and we will share the wealth generated by the oil prices we intend to set, starting at one hundred and fifty American dollars per barrel."

Finally the men sat up and took notice. At $150 a barrel, hundreds of billions of dollars would flow into Georgia—eradicating poverty in their country. They would become a true superpower, with a nuclear arsenal, and the entire country living the life of the sheikhs. As they sat—each lost in his own world of thought— they started to feel strange vibrations. The prime minister looked under his seat, seeking the cause, then to his glass of water that was sliding toward him. The rest of the room's inhabitants started to panic as the vibrations grew. The table skated across the floor and pictures fell from the wall. The men rose and headed for the door, pushing each other aside, when the rear wall came crashing inward exploding fragments all around. Premier Andropov was knocked to the floor and stepped on by his cabinet. Only Valissi returned to help.

When Valissi bent over, something struck his shoulder. The premier looked at the red stain on Valissi's suit, realizing the man had been shot. His face went blue, as agony caused his body to wobble. He fell back, banging his head—and died on the floor next to Andropov. The premier looked up. A giant machine twice the size of any tank barreled into the room. Screaming and panicked, men ran—only to be met by the same fate. Bullets exploded from every direction, peppering every wall, shredding bodies and furniture alike. Andropov inched away, still lying on his back, using his elbows to pull himself along. The sun broke through behind the gargantuan tank as the ceiling collapsed and debris rained down everywhere. The sunlight lit a million tiny reflections, making a grotesquely huge revolving cone sparkle, as gunfire continued to thrash the room.

Then it suddenly stopped. The machine's cone stopped spinning and retreated several feet. Yet, the assault wasn't at an end. The pause was to allow foreign soldiers to come running in around the machine, their weapons firing sporadically. Their uniforms were unfamiliar to the premier. Several of them grabbed the premier harshly, lifting him to his feet. The soldiers half-dragged, half-carried him outside. He then saw what had happened; standing amid the chaos was Sabu the Butcher—a sinister smile on his face. Andropov was on his hands and knees. From the steps of the capitol he looked into the distant countryside; all around were thousands of soldiers laying siege to his city. Tanks fired rockets, destroying structures everywhere he looked, as those massive machines devastated the landscape, flattening all in theirpath. Flames and smoke billowed into the sky, blocking out the sight of his beautiful mountains. Men and women were crushed beneath tank tracks. The soldiers killed all, indiscriminately shooting men, woman, and even children who were running, falling, dying in pools of blood. A man in the distance stopped and raised his hands in surrender. A running soldier fired a burst from his machine gun and his head exploded in a red cloud. A woman was cowering with three children grabbing at her skirt. They were crushed by a tank.

Andropov watched helplessly as his land was decimated. He only had one thought: Satan had a new name, and it was Sabu.

"Sabu, I beg you! Stop this madness!" Andropov pleaded from his knees.

"Surrender is not an option!" Sabu shouted. "Death is the only way to complete victory, Andropov! You, yourself, should know this—you were a murderer yourself in your youth. Many Arabs died, and their blood is on your hands. The KGB never showed mercy to my fellow countrymen—why should I show mercy to yours?" Sabu stepped forward and nodded to his men. They grabbed Andropov and lifted him so he was standing on his knees. For a brief moment, Andropov stared Sabu in the eye, so the Butcher slapped him across the cheek.

Andropov took the blow and looked back with a bloodied lip; he held back tears as he saw the destruction behind Sabu. "What does His Holiness Karuza want from me? I am his servant," he said and dropped his chin to his chest.

Sabu grinned. "You now speak, and I have heard you." Sabu knew he couldn't kill the premier yet. He needed the codes to the warheads, and he had to use Georgia's people as leverage.

"Stop the madness, and I will do all you ask." Andropov finally let himself shed tears as his dream of a New World died, and Karuza's nightmare began.

CHAPTER FORTY

Al Campo had been deprived the luxury of complete relaxation for nearly forty-eight hours, and finally he reached the point where nothing mattered, physically or mentally—his body was able to shut down. He slept, deep, dreamless sleep that was like being plugged into a power charger. Once he awoke, he was allowed to shower, dress in a pair of blue jeans, a black V-neck shirt, and some new track shoes. He felt great until he was told they were going on a long drive. He must have still been tired, because he immediately fell asleep again, until he found himself jarred and bouncing on the rear bench seat of a Chevy Suburban. He looked at his watch: four hours straight.

When the car arrived at the front steps of the White House, Al was still supine, staring across his body through the window at the strong, white columns and marble steps. A White House security guard checked the driver's ID and allowed him to exit the car. The man looked in and grinned, seeing Al's amusing face. His hair was a mess. The imprint of the leather seat cushion was pressed into his cheek, and a line of drool ran out the corner of his mouth. Campo squinted, focusing on the bemused look of the driver, and realized his appearance must be grungy at best. His driver was Campo's only escort as they entered the presidential residence. His name was Tom or Jim or something like that. The man was tall and lean. When they left Philly he was going on and on, boasting about a triathlon or some shit when Campo dozed off. Now Campo wanted to use the restroom and couldn't remember the guy's name.

"Ah…buddy, where's a bathroom? Long ride, you know. Gotta release the dragon," Al said and raised his eyebrows. Five minutes later he left the bathroom with a fresh appearance and a certain bounce in his step. He was as ready as he could be to formally meet the president.

The elevator opened into an anteroom outside the Oval Office. Jim or Tom, whoever, suggested he sit down while he informed the president they had arrived. The room was white and had two doors, one to the elevator and one his escort knocked on. He heard a voice from the other side, and the guy stepped through, closing the door behind him, leaving Campo all alone. He scanned the room, simply passing the time. Its walls were painted perfectly, not a mark on them. The ceiling was ten feet high, and there was a huge crown molding that graced the perimeter of the sparkling white ceiling. Positioned around the room were portraits of famous Americans of the past: several former presidents, and paintings of what Al assumed were the president's dog and cat. All were framed in heavy-looking wood and painted, guess what, white. Jim-Tom reappeared and motioned to him.

"The president will see you now," he said.

Al entered the naturally lit office. Huge windows looked out to a beautiful lawn, several secret service men were standing at different angles looking out into the gardens. The room was crowded, a coffee table in the middle with several mugs and a carafe, a wood-framed sofa on one side and several chairs on the other. Starting to his right sat Joe Tyson, then General Morris Bartow, a man Campo recognized as the president's chief of staff, Sam Haggart, the CIA director, whose name escaped him for the moment, and finally, E. James Worthington at the center.

Immediately, Worthington rose from his chair and met the slow-moving Campo in the middle of the room, standing over the presidential seal printed on the deep-blue carpet. He gave Al a hearty handshake.

"Mr. Campo, a pleasure to meet you at last," the president said, looking him dead in the eye.

"The pleasure is mine, sir." Al said as he returned the president's firm grip.

"Special Agent Tyson over there was just finishing his summation about your heroic escapades," Worthington said nodding toward Tyson who had his legs crossed and a tired look on his face. "First, I want to thank you for saving my life." The president dropped his smile and looked serious. "I'm indebted to you for that, and I thank you on behalf of the people of this country for saving it from possible devastation," he said as he placed his hand on Al's shoulder, squeezing his wound without knowing it. "I believe you know General Bartow." E. James waved out his arm, beginning the introductions.

"Know me, hell. We were practically father and son during the Reagan/Bush administration," Morris said, giving him a bear hug and a kiss on the cheek. Campo was too surprised by the general's affection; he forgot to moan from the general's tight grip.

"This is our CIA Director, Bruce Kellogg," the president continued and pointed to Kellogg who was dressed in a deep green suit and lime green tie. Campo wasn't a style guru—hell, he never wore anything but jeans and a T-shirt, which is what he had on—but Kellogg's tie was blinding.

"Pleasure to meet you," Kellogg said, reaching out a hand from his sitting position. "These stories Mr. Tyson has been telling are quite fascinating...if you ever need a job, just give me a call."

"I'll remember that, sir," Al said with a half-hearted smile.

"And this is Sam Haggart, my chief of staff."

Sam set down a pile of papers and shook his hand. "Pleasure, Mr. Campo." Sam looked as tired as Tyson. In fact, all the men in the room were a bit peaked.

"And you already know Joe Tyson," Worthington said, finishing the introductions. He pulled out a leather chair for Al and then sat in his.

Tyson's gaze had changed. Three days ago he would have liked nothing more than to have Campo thrown in jail. Now a look of respect showed every time his eyes met Campo's.

Al sat directly across from the commander-in-chief. He had never been in the Oval Office and was enjoying the view. Around the elliptical room, the walls were covered with more pieces of art, many of which Campo remembered seeing in reference and history books. Washington, Lincoln, and many other presidents' portraits hung on the walls. A moment of uncomfortable silence fell over him as these powerful men stared in fascination at this new model of American virtue. Campo knew he had to break the tension, and they were waiting for him to speak.

"So what were we talking about?" he asked, panning his head around.

"Just the recent events that have occupied your life these past few days, and the remarkable path you traveled to be sitting in this office," Sam Haggart said. Apparently he had been leading the meeting before Al's entry.

"Sounds good, but I had first-hand knowledge of that. Now, let's get to the real reason I'm here, because we all know it's not because you're going to give me a medal." Campo paused and watched their faces. The CIA director held a rigid glare. He saw Tyson allow himself a thin smile, and the general an even bigger one. Campo looked back at the president and continued. "Sabu the Butcher, let's get to him." Al leaned over and grabbed the carafe. "Coffee? Is there an extra cup?" he said. Campo was to the point of not giving a shit and showed no feelings of inferiority among the men in the room. Tyson slid a cup across to him. Al poured himself some coffee and drank it black.

Worthington grinned and glanced over at Bartow. "You did say, General, he had a "no bullshit" way. I like that. Now, Mr. Campo," Worthington continued, his inflection more serious. He leaned his forearms on his knees and looked Campo in the eye. "General Bartow here has briefed me on your dedication, and the valiant sacrifices you made for this country for fifteen years. It is my understanding you didn't receive the respect and rewards which should have been yours." Worthington was watching Al, searching for something in his face.

Campo sipped again and said, "So, what are you going to do? Give me a bunch of money and the retirement I deserve? Undo keeping me unconscious for six months, changing my name, and reconstructing my face without my consent? I don't think so." Al spoke with contempt, not toward Worthington, but toward the whole political arena that had taken control of his life all those years ago. So many years, so many memories of death, murder, and suffering, lost love…and now he wanted to vent the way he should have done all those years ago. He had forgotten those moments, stored them away in the rear of his mind, but they were waiting to surface like teeth under babies' gums, erupting when reality shocks and disturbs them. He wanted to lose himself again, and disappear into obscurity, but Sabu was within his reach. Vengeance and a thirst to be back in the game again drove him here. He tried to compose his bitterness.

"Mr. Campo," the President said, "your country needs you again."

Al remained silent, waiting, and not jumping.

"Mr. President, may I?" General Bartow asked, and E. James nodded. "Alfonse, Joe here said he had a brief conversation with you in the hospital about Sabu's involvement. And son, you've always known me to be a straight shooter. Sabu is in the middle of a military uprising that makes Hitler's Nazis look like a boys' choir. We need to head them off before there is a nuclear holocaust."

"How can I stop a nuclear war?" Al said and put the empty mug on the table.

"That's why we're all here," Kellogg interjected. "We need to know what you know. You figured out the president was going to be assassinated, and no one, and I mean no one else did." Kellogg gave Campo a nod of approval.

"He is involved with this man here," Sam Haggart added and passed over a photo of Karuza.

"Do you recognize him?" Bartow asked.

Al studied the face of Karuza in the picture, the rugged lines crossing his dark skin, and solemn eyes wrinkles feathering outward. His headdress was bright white with spiraled gold trim. He had a beard, trimmed tightly along his cheekbones. Campo scanned his memory. He knew the man, but only a younger version, and Karuza wasn't his name. "Mr. Haggart, do you have any more photos of this man? I don't want any current ones. Any from older files?"

The group of men in the room became excited. The president was clearly surprised. Kellogg leaned forward, and Morris smiled.

They knew he was onto something, and they liked it. It was what they had expected, no, what they had hoped. The chief of staff fumbled through a selection of pictures and produced a handful. Campo leafed through them, playing with different angles, holding some up in the air. He tossed a couple on the table then stopped at one that showed Karuza without his headdress. Karuza was younger, with fewer wrinkles and a thinner beard. Suddenly the name hit him like a brick.

"His real name is Adhar Atahollah," Al said. He looked at the picture but watched the men in the room at the same time. "The name means 'waiting gift of God.' He was dredging in Northern Africa twenty odd years ago. He used to preach in the middle of the street, claiming he had been sent from Allah and was on a mission. We briefly had our eyes on him because he seemed to be gathering followers, and the government thought he was a cover for a weapons-smuggling operation. But after a year or so, our efforts came up dry, and soon afterwards, he vanished from the public eye." Al tossed the photo and it stuck at the base of the carafe. Then he clasped his hands on his lap.

"Do you remember if he had any ties to the Russians back then?" Kellogg asked.

Campo screwed up his face. "Russians? Maybe something about being tolerant of communism, and 'down with the Americans,' some shit like that, but it was typical for that time. Not too long after the fall of the Soviet Union, he dropped out of sight."

"Are you sure of that time frame?" Worthington asked, and Campo sensed his appetite for information.

"Yeah, pretty sure. It was about the middle of my tour in the Mid-East. But I have to say, gentlemen, aside from all of that, if Karuza is shacked up with Sabu, it can only spell disaster. Sabu is a malignant disease. I suggest you send in an elimination force and take them both out. Once they are removed, his flock of followers will run for cover. It was my experience, only the elite commanders knew of the details of the operations, and once we eliminated them, the rest dispersed."

"Those were the same comments the general made a few moments before you entered," Worthington said.

"And yesterday, and the day before, I might add," Morris said looking at Kellogg.

Worthington ignored him and continued. "Now for the difficult part. Karuza is now untouchable. After the deaths of all fourteen leaders of the Middle Eastern countries, he has gained superior power over all of the True Believers in Europe and Asia. They believe his prophecy has come true, and now they regard him as a true prophet."

"You'll have to brief me, because I don't understand any of that," Campo said.

"You've been out of touch a while," Tyson said.

"Son," Morris spoke, "in the past forty-eight hours the leaders of the fourteen primary Middle Eastern countries have perished at the hands of Karuza's assassins."

"If they were assassinated by Karuza, I find it hard to believe people would follow him," Campo said and changed his position in the leather chair. The room was getting warm.

"That's the catch," Morris continued. "Those weapons you discovered were sent to his killers. The leaders all died, it seemed, in strange but apparently natural ways. The King of Jordan died of a sudden heart attack. Ahmadinejad became mysteriously ill with vomiting and diarrhea.He died of dehydration. All the rest perished in similar fashion. Our experts say all of the deaths can be explained by the power of the weapons created by Baroque Chemical."

"Well, that really sucks for the Middle East," Al said with a slight sense of satisfaction. "Half of those leaders were criminals anyway. And if I may say so, Ahmadinejad deserved to shit himself to death. Mr. President, you were on the hit list and survived. We as a country are still on the safe side. Where does this nuclear holocaust bit come in?"

"Sabu, under Karuza's orders, launched a massive invasion into the republic of Georgia, a former member state of the Soviet Union. He has succeeded in the largest military takeover since World War Two, killed Premier Andropov, and now controls…"

"The nuclear arsenal the Soviets left behind," Al finished his sentence, having a revelation about the seriousness of the meeting.

The room suddenly grew hot, and Campo felt like he was going to get burned any minute.

"Exactly," Worthington said. "We estimate he has at his disposal fifty warheads."

"Now what? He demands the world on a string?" Campo asked.

"Almost," Kellogg replied. He sat forward and his tie hung straight down like an emerald pendulum. "He also gained control of ninety percent of the world's oil supply with his dominance in the Middle East. Therefore he is going to squeeze the world for all he can. Already barrel prices have doubled in a day, with no end insight. He wants the US to evacuate all military bases, embassies, and government offices immediately—leaving behind all weapons, computers, and every bit of data stored in those facilities. It's absurd."

"If we don't comply, he'll start World War Three by wantonly launching missiles in every direction," E. James said.

The president seemed uncharacteristically worried. Campo saw the president's tight jaw, and he flexed his fists in anxiousness.

"How much time do we have?" Al asked.

"Seventy-two hours," Morris said. "And he's holed up tighter than a bayou gator egg nest in that temple in Turkey."

"Turkey?" Campo said shocked. "What the hell is he doing in Turkey? That son of a bitch is from Egypt."

"He claims Istanbul, Turkey is at the center of the world, bordering the European and Asian continents," Kellogg said.

"And where else would the so-called Prophet decide to make his reappearance?" Joe Tyson entered the conversation, speaking sardonically.

"And it doesn't hurt that Turkey borders the Republic of Georgia," the president added.

"OK, how are you planning to take him out?" Al asked, looking at his former boss.

"We had planned a combined Delta/Seal team, but the likelihood of success without a tremendous loss of life is nil," Kellogg said, answering for the general, and it looked to Al like he had a plan that had been shot down.

"Then again, we feel a smaller team entering from within the ranks could penetrate his defenses and remove him," Morris threw back.

Campo knew where the general was headed, and it's what he wanted to hear, a chance to settle the score with Sabu. But the chance of success was thin at best; he'd been away from the area so long he might be rusty, and getting up to speed would waste precious time. He would need help, and that help would have to already be inside the temple. "I would need local assistance."

"Of course, we have a team on site, awaiting orders," Morris said bluntly.

"Are the men loyal? Not some ragtag group you just recruited a week ago?" Campo said tersely.

"The leader of the team is named Ghali," Morris said, and watched Campo's reaction.

Al stared back and grinned slightly, sharing a private moment with Bartow as the others debated.

"We have to send in a larger assault team," Kellogg demanded. "We can't depend on one man making the difference."

"I have no intention of sending in a suicide team, large or small," Worthington said. "I want a foolproof plan, or I'll have no choice but to order a complete and total evacuation of our men and women."

Campo listened to the conversation while planting a seed in his brain. It had to grow into a way to eliminate Karuza—and return alive. Alive? Well, maybe. He could see in his mind's eye the Turkish countryside, its mountainous landscape, and the hills hemming in the great basilica of Hagia Sophia. He could work out an escape into the mountains, but how could he take out Karuza and Sabu? Campo's eyes drifted beyond the talking group. He felt a chill run down his spine, remembering Sabu beating him nearly to death, the Butcher sweating and panting as he swung fists and batons. And the sound of his own bones made when they broke still rang in his ears. He tried to focus on the now, the time for revenge would come. He just had to work out how. His eyes drifted, focusing on the hanging portraits. This time he viewed Washington fixedly. The father of the country looked back at him with that confident, commanding chin, and broad forehead. Then he gazed at Lincoln's portrait, past his farmer's appearance and heavy eyes, onto Grant, and the others. None smiled until he saw the painting of Benjamin Franklin, whose lips curled, almost like he was hiding something. The painting was similar to the one Al had seen at the philosopher's home in Philly. This was the original painting; the copy hung in Philly. As he studied it, he realized it was nearly identical but not quite. This painting was longer, and included the scientist's chest and torso. Al looked at Franklin's puffy collar and the gold chain hanging around his neck. Campo's eyes widened. At its end dangled a key, a gold key! Simple in design, it had a round handle, a slim shaft, and flag-shaped teeth. Campo smiled inwardly then suddenly heard the men speaking again.

"I'm going to say it again," Worthington continued, getting aggravated. "I will not place any one man up against insurmountable odds!"

"That won't be necessary, sir," Campo chimed in. All heads turned toward him. "I may have thought of a way to remove this Karuza joker without placing anyone in harm's way."

"Would you care to enlighten us, son?" Morris looked over at Al.

Campo knew he had Morris on his side, and whatever scheme he concocted Bartow would be with him to the finish. They all looked at him and knew he was the one to *volunteer*, but no one said anything. They waited for him in silence.

"First," Al said scanning the group. He was fixating on Kellogg's tie again. The CIA man must have noticed and he smoothed his tie down his chest. "I need to ask a few questions. Karuza, is he the oldest in his family?"

"What the hell does it matter?" Kellogg spat out.

"Bruce, let's see where he's going first before we shoot him down," E. James said. He raised his hand to Kellogg. "Let him speak."

"Fine sir…he's an only child." Kellogg spat out.

"That's even better," Al said, confusing the group. "Next, Mr. President, are you familiar with the painting on the wall there?"

He pointed behind Morris. He remembered the president was an American history teacher before he became a lawyer. It was one of the reasons Al had voted for him. He appreciated anyone who was dedicated to history.

E. James looked peculiarly at Campo, but took his question as serious. "Yes, that portrait of Benjamin Franklin was done by an unknown artist toward the end of his life. It is rumored he was also buried in those same clothes."

"And the key hanging around his neck." Campo rubbed his hand down his chest, describing the area in the painting. "Any idea what it was?"

Worthington looked at the portrait, then back at Campo. "Many scholars have suggested that was the famous key he used in his kite experiment that discovered electricity. It was said he was never seen without that key hanging around his neck."

"So it would be a good guess he was also buried with that key as well?" Al was now excited, and could feel the bewildered eyes on him. He could feel the blood rising in his face.He must be red with glee.

"What's this all about?" Worthington asked squinting his eyes, trying to see inside Campo's mind.

"You all wouldn't believe me if I told you," Campo said and looked at Morris. "Now, one last question. In Persian or Middle Eastern history, new rulers were traditionally…paid homage…or sent personal messages of loyalty by the lands or kingdoms they conquered. Have the surrounding nations, especially the ones who just lost their leaders, been sending gifts of devotion, asking to be welcomed into Karuza's new empire?"

"Yes, as a matter of fact they have been," Kellogg said. "So far our intelligence reports have seen at least six major acting leaders from the surrounding nations traveling to Hagia Sophia with an entourage. The meetings are private, but our moles have seen them enter with gifts and leave empty-handed. Apparently Karuza accepted the gifts and sent them back home with new instructions. We are attempting to bug those meetings, but it's too risky at the moment. We have reports the other major nations in the region are planning similar trips to Turkey."

The CIA director looked at the president; his face was filled with uncertainty. Most of the other men in the room looked the same, with the exception of General Bartow. His typically rigid features were softened, and a peculiar smile played over his mouth.

"All right then," Campo said, he clasped his hands in front of his face, closed his eyes, and thought hard. When he broke his silence, all the men looked at him like he was crazy. "This is what we have to do. I need twenty-four hours to get ready, and in that time, the White House must let the public know the president here has become ill, then died, and suffered the same fate as the other leaders. Then set up a meeting for me to meet Karuza and Sabu, pledging our loyalty and devotion to His Holiness, telling him the US will be behind him and his New World. Once I'm there, I'll do the rest."

"What the hell will that accomplish?" Kellogg asked.

"First of all it will flush out any accomplices here in the US," Morris said. "You, yourself, said Ammar had contacts here, and I'm sure if they find out the president is dead, they will want their reward. Secondly, our window of opportunity will open, and Karuza might let his guard down long enough for us to get close to him."

"It's insane. You can't expect to just walk up to him and shoot him—they'll be expecting that—and they will kill you before you get within fifty feet of him," the CIA director said.

"But I'll be bearing a gift he can't refuse," Campo said smiling.

They all saw the gleam in Al's eyes. He knew they wanted more answers, but time was running out. It was what they brought him here in the first place for, he figured. They wanted him to volunteer, not be ordered to do it. And that's exactly what was happening. He was on a mission of his own making. The scenario was perfect.

Worthington looked long and hard at Campo. He knew many men: world leaders, famous people, tycoons with extreme power. He always stared them straight in the eyes and felt he could read their minds, knowing their choices long before they themselves knew what they were doing. But Campo was different. His face was wild and determined. He knew the man's history, how Sabu had tortured him, nearly killed him, but there was more than vengeance in his eyes. Somehow he felt he could trust him. Worthington contemplated his options. On the one hand, Campo was falling right into their scheme; his willingness to go it alone was humbling. Worthington had never been in the military—his closest stint would have been in Vietnam, but his application to Dartmouth had already been accepted. He remembered he had the opportunity to postpone college and go to war, but his fear of the unknown and the possibility he might not return caused him to leap on a plane and head to Dartmouth. He never regretted his decision. His ego made him think that he could do more in this office than on any battlefield. As president, he now held the power to send men and women off to risk their lives, something he himself was unwilling to sacrifice. He was just beginning to feel shame and regret, as he stared at the fearless face of Al Campo. It would only take a moment for him to refuse Campo's request and save the man's life in so doing. But the country needed a scapegoat, and Morris had explained how the operation would be ten times as likely to succeed, and that many lives could be saved if the man before them could be maneuvered into volunteering. Worthington pondered his own past and then the needs of the country. He found himself feeling guilt and embarrassment at what he must do, but his dedication to the government meant he must risk the life of one to save the lives of many. After a drawn out moment of silence, E. James Worthington spoke. He cleared a lump in his throat, put his fist to his mouth, and coughed.

"All right, Mr. Campo." Worthington kept his eyes on the desk for a moment, then looked at Campo, whose face showed effortless courage. Worthington felt the lump return and coughed again before continuing. "Because of the general's high regard of you, your past service to this country, and my own intuition, I am going to grant you your twenty-four hours. Sam, Bruce, set in motion the fictionof my death and find a safe house for me. Sam, you'll have to brief Congress and the vice-president. Let's flush out the traitors. In the meantime, start evacuating all non-essential personnel from the region. If nothing else, it will show good faith. Mr. Campo, the fate of the nation lies with you. I feel a strong confidence in you. I pray you are successful, and that you can put an end to this fiasco."

CHAPTER FORTY-ONE

Herman was slumped over the desk; piles of papers were strewn around his resting body and by his feet. His back rose and fell slowly as air flowed in and out of his lungs. He wore a white, button-front short-sleeved shirt, the same one he had on all that day. It was soiled under each arm and yellowed by his deodorant. Herman Seller slept quietly. He needed sleep as much as anyone, though he rarely made time for it. Unlike the rest of the world, who expected to go to bed at one time or another, Seller just worked until his body gave up and he collapsed wherever he was at the time. It was a practice he had started back in the days of digging in the earth and uncovering relics; he was known as the tireless machine. Students envied him for his stamina—while rival professors placed him on a pedestal, thinking him a cross between a dedicated scientist and an obsessed adversary. On this day at midnight, he took off his glasses to rub his eyes for the hundredth time, and simply fell asleep.

He was awakened by the quiet hum of the telephone ringing in his ear. He lifted his head from the pillow of papers and peered around. He couldn't see clearly, and he squinted at the desktop. He groped around for his wire rim glasses and wrapped them over his ears. Now he just had to find the phone. He could hear it, yet it seemed so far away. He slid the books and folders around. The noise increased, and he knew he was close. He lifted one last stack of papers and discovered the black base and handle. He lifted the cool plastic and blinked his eyes a few times.

"Hello," he coughed and cleared his throat. "Hello, this is Herman Seller,"

"Herman, old buddy, how are you this morning?" the familiar voice of Al Campo bellowed in his ear.

Seller stole a glance at his wall clock and saw the hands at two-thirty a.m.

"Have I caught you at a bad time?"

"My, my, Mr. Campo, you seem very spirited this early in the morning, very spirited indeed," Seller said and scratched his head.

"Well, Herman, I feel like I just got a blood transfusion. How's the research coming along? Any progress in finding the key to the box?" Al asked with a bit of hope his friend might have some conclusive evidence proving his theory.

Herman looked at the mountain of information piled in front of him, reminding him of the project at hand. "No, I am afraid I haven't any leads to its whereabouts. This is a difficult task, a difficult task indeed. Mr. Franklin was a very public figure and thousands of documents have been published on his life. I've scoured nearly all of them, including hundreds of personal letters and writings, and other than the two you produced, I can find no mention of this mysterious gold box, none indeed!"

"Well, old friend" Mr. Campo said, his voice almost too cheerful for this time of the day. "I think I may have stumbled onto a major clue, and I need your help."

"Yes, of course, of course. How may I help?" Herman said. He rubbed his eyes and scratched the top of his head again

"I need you to meet me at the corner of Fifth and Arch Streets and bring the gold box with you. Do you have a car, or do you need to take a cab?"

"Mr. Campo, are you aware it is two-thirty-seven in the morning? This is a very strange request, strange indeed!" Herman could feel his clothes clinging to his frail skin, and knew he was a mess. He wouldn't feel proper unless he showered first.

"Old buddy," Campo said, still a bit too jovial for Herman at this hour. "You're going to have to trust me on this one. It'll be worth it, I promise. I need you here in fifteen minutes."

So much for a shower, Seller thought. "OK, Mr. Campo. I'm coming. I'll go to the motor pool, and get my car."

———◆———

The streets were empty. The overhead lights shone down onto the blacktop. All alone on the corner was parked a large, dark-colored van. Al's shadowed figure exited the back, leaving the rear doors open. Campo grabbed a yellow construction barrier and a couple of traffic cones and placed them behind and in front of the van. He walked over to the tall decorative brick wall. The base was sloped like the leg of a chair, and then the middle rose up flat and straight, and the top crested like a wave on both sides. The wall ran continuously for the entire block in both directions—except at the corner—where there was an opening. Mounted between the two piers was a wrought iron fence: spiraled steel shafts with an arrow head top connected by a horizontal bar, each rod was about hand space apart. Through the fence was a marble slab flush with the ground. On the other side of the wall was the Christ Church burial ground, dating from 1719. Mounted on the brick was a bronze plaque:

The last resting-place of
Benjamin Franklin
1706-1790

———◆———

Venerated for benevolence, admired for talents,
esteemed for Patriotism, beloved for Philanthropy. Washington.

———◆———

The sage whom two worlds claimed their own. Mirabeau.

———◆———

He tore from the skies lightning and from Tyrants the scepter. Turgot.

Al Campo read the plaque in the dim light. "That about says it all," he said, then went to the other side of the opening, and read through the chronology of his accomplishments. How could one man achieve so much in one lifetime? Although Franklin did live far beyond the average life span of the time period, it was still extraordinary. Al thought he heard a police siren in the distance, then screeching tires. It was too far away to concern him. He felt confident the police wouldn't harass him because his last phone call before he called Herman was to Joe Tyson asking for a favor to ensure his task would be trouble free. The only possible problem could come from the Park Service. Tyson said they might be difficult to fend off but that he would make the call anyway.

Al grabbed a stepladder from the van, set it next to the fence, then grabbed another one, and set it on the other side to get down on. He climbed down into the graveyard and heard the faint sound of someone whistling. It became louder with each moment. He climbed back out, jumped the last two steps, and was met by a tall figure.

"Dr. Jonathan, glad to see you again. Thanks for coming," Al said to his old friend's nephew. Campo threw his arm around his shoulder and squeezed in friendship and in thanks. He'd never forget he was alive because of Jonathan.

"Not a problem. Like I said, anyone my uncle calls son is my brother." Jonathan adjusted his red Phillies cap that had been knocked askew by Al's hug. Then they both turned up the street to look at an approaching car.

"You expecting someone else?" Jonathon asked, looking back at Al.

"Yes I am, and by the speed this car is going, I feel pretty confident it's him." Campo shook his head and smiled at what he saw. The headlights traveled slowly up Arch Street, stopping at the Fourth Street intersection while the light was green, then proceeded up and pulled in behind Al's van, bumping into one of the orange cones. The car wasn't as inconspicuous as Al had hoped.

Herman opened the door to his cherry-red 1963 Ford Falcon sport car. It had an original ragtop, a plastic rear window, and low-profile whitewall tires. It looked like he just drove it off the lot.

"Mr. Campo, Mr. Campo! Is that you?" Herman asked, poking his head out.

"Yeah Herman, it's me. Come on over. I want you to meet someone." Campo waved to him. "Professor Herman Seller, I'd like you to meet Dr. Jonathan Thomson, the man who saved my life."

"Professor, it's a pleasure," Jonathan said and studied the vintage car. "And may I say, that is anawesome car you're driving." Jonathan rubbed his hand over the warm hood and then shook Herman's hand.

"No, no, the pleasure is mine, mine indeed, my pleasure to meet you." Herman looked at Jonathan, unsure how to respond to the comment about his car. Al saw the tension in his face and broke the silence.

"Herman, did you bring the box?"

"Yes, yes, of course. I have it on the floor by the front passenger seat. Would you like me to retrieve it now?"

"Later. First we need the key," Al said and moved back toward the van.

"The key!" Herman said. He took several steps back toward the car and the box.

"Yes, the key…let me show you something, Herman," Al said, bringing him to the front of the van. Herman walked cautiously, Al prodding him along. He shone a flashlight on a picture of Benjamin Franklin that he had laid on the hood. "Does this look familiar to you?"

"Yes, yes, that's the famous portrait hanging in the scientist's home." The old archivist was leaning close to the picture, having dificultly seeing inthe limited light.

"Right," Al said. "I got this postcard from the park ranger this afternoon. Now do you see that chain hanging around his neck? It doesn't show it in the picture, but at the end of that chain hangs a key. Our key." Campo patted Seller on the back, nearly knocking Seller's glasses off.

"Are you sure, Mr. Campo, that the key is the key to the box? Mr. Franklin never mentioned it in any of his memoirs. I have checked every paper ever written by Franklin himself. There was no mention at all." Herman was speaking nervously; he was aware of his surroundings and knew Campo was up to something strange, something very strange indeed.

"Herman, I also found out that he kept this chain and key with him at all times and died with it around his neck. It was rumored to be the key he used in his experiments with electricity, you know, with the kite?" Al said and walked over to the ladder and pointed through the grate at Franklin's tomb. "I also have a strong suspicion he was buried with it."

"Mr. Campo! You don't mean to disturb his grave...do you?" Herman's face darkened with trepidation.

"Wait a minute," Jonathan asked in his quiet manner. "What grave and what key to what box? Are we talking about *the* Benjamin Franklin?"

"OK." Al had left him in the dark long enough. "Jonathan, we have to retrieve a key from a grave, yes, Benjamin Franklin's grave." Al again pointed a finger through the metal bars at the cemetery. "The key is to a priceless gold box. I need it for a reason I can't explain right now. So I called you two here to help me dig it up, because I knew I could trust you and Herman. I promise, in a week I'll tell you the rest of the story. But right now, time is against me." Al looked at Jonathan and saw some doubt on his face. Al felt like he was a little apprehensive about disturbing one of the founding fathers graves. Who wouldn't be? "Jonathan, if you have an issue with this I understand. I brought you here, I admit without any info as too why and I thought I could trust you no matter what. But if you want to bail now you know my real reason. No hard feelings. OK?"

"I have to admit," Jonathan said and rubbed his face and took in the scene of Franklin's grave. "When you said on the phone you needed my help. I wasn't expecting to dig up big man Ben. But when I told uncle you needed my help. He said I should not ask questions and just go. You know Al; I did graduate school and go to college and med school. No one and I mean no one else in my school did that. I owe it all to uncle. But, I did grow up in Camden after all, and I wasn't a saint. So if you need my help I am willing to go the extra mile. Let's get started."

Campo placed his hand on Jonathan's shoulder. He smiled and gave an approving nod. Al went to the back doors of the van, grabbed some tools, and passed them to Jonathan. First came shovels. "I don't know if we'll need those, but just in case," he said. Then he pulled out two crowbars and a long digging tool called a pinch bar. It was a heavy, solid round steel bar, with one end flattened like a spade, and the other end rounded into a ball to be used for leverage. Then he pulled out a couple of ditch-digging picks, and finally, two long, black Maglite flashlights. Jonathan slid the tools between the bars of the iron fence, then climbed the ladders and jumped to the ground.

"I don't believe I can make it over the gate as capably as Mr. Thomson did. No, I don't think so," Herman said, shaking his head.

"Sure you can, Herman—it's easy," Al said as he picked his friend up. He felt heavier than Al had expected. The frail little man only weighed a hundred and thirty pounds, but all Campo's injuries made lifting even that much a little painful. Aware of Herman's body odor, he hoisted the old man up the ladder and passed him to Jonathan, who set him down as gently as a feather.

Before Seller knew what happened, he was standing on top of a marble slab in which were carved the names *Benjamin* and *Deborah*. The men glanced around the cemetery. The graveyard was littered with stones; the street lamp bounced light and shadows off of their worn surfaces. The engravings for the most part were unreadable—and some of the gravestones had fallen over, or had broken edges. The cemetery was from colonial times, and all those buried there, other than Franklin, had been long since forgotten by their heirs.

Campo jumped down next to Jonathan and passed him a flashlight. They both turned them on and shone them at Seller's feet.

"Herman, I believe you are standing on top of our landmark," Al said.

"Yes, yes, of course," Seller said, stepping sideways onto an adjacent slab, engraved with the names of Franklin's daughter and son-in-law, *Richard* and *Sara*, and the date, *1811*. There were pennies and coins littering the Franklins' slab, maybe in homage to his famous phrase "A penny saved is a penny earned."

Al and Jonathan bent down, sweeping the pennies aside, and they inspected the edge of the slab. It was approximately twice as wide and longer than a typical casket and about as thick as a clinched fist. The marble lid lay over a granite curb they deduced was the top of the vault itself. A continuous mortar joint bonded the two together.

"Yo, man, this is like cemented down. We're goin' to have to make some noise," Jonathan said rubbing the mortar with his finger.

"I was afraid of that," Al said, looking at the joint. "Wait a minute—here on the short side the mortar is deteriorated. I think we can fit the pinch bar inside." With that said, Al slid the heavy iron crowbar quietly into the crease. Jonathan grabbed another crowbar and put it between the ground and Al's bar, to serve as a fulcrum. Jonathan stabbed the point of a pick into the long side, and the two men pried simultaneously. To their surprise it squeaked and slid slightly. They swung around to the opposite end and did the same, and then the entire slab was freed from the mortar. Slowly and steadily, they inched the marble gravestone over to one side, uncovering half the opening. Jonathan squeezed his legs into the opening, and used his arm strength to shift it completely off to one side. A dank odor seeped into the air around them.

"I'll tell you something," Jonathan said as he took off his hat and rubbed sweat off his forehead with his arm. "It's going to be a lot harder to replace this than it was to get it off."

"Let's worry about that later. Hand me that flashlight, Herman," Campo said. He poked the beam into the open grave. Seller inched his way closer to the edge, his glasses hanging loosely on the bridge of his nose. "Well, Herman, does this bring back memories?"

"Yes, yes, indeed, it's exhilarating. The same feeling overcame me each and every time we excavated a new site. May I be the first to see?" Herman said eagerly. He put his hand out and Campo gave him the flashlight.

"Of course," Campo said. He realized that Herman's interest was in the discovery. He had made it clear that he didn't want a key found. But he never said he didn't like looking for one. Campo moved aside for his friend, and he and Jonathan lowered Seller into the opening.

The former Director of Archeology found himself standing on something like a bed or a sofa cushion. He had to steady himself with one hand on the wall and hold the light with the other. The light beam illuminated the shadowy compartment. Herman immediately thought it odd that there was no coffin; the bodies were just laid in the marble tomb. The one on the left was apparently Deborah. Herman studied her briefly. Her white silk dress had grayed from age and lay crumpled over the skeletal remains. Her frail hands were at her side, her skull was empty, and long coarse gray hair streamed from the top. His mouth opened wide as he moved the beam to her husband.

"Holy shit," Al said.

"Damn!" Jonathan said.

Benjamin Franklin's appearance was entirely different than Deborah's deteriorated remains. The first thing Seller noticed was his clothing appeared new. Franklin's bright, navy-blue velvet shimmered, his fur collar was puffy and soft-looking, and his body was rounded out, showing off his proud belly. His skin… "He still has skin!" Herman Seller said aloud. He saw the face of the man himself, the smooth, bald forehead, the pinkish cheeks and nose, and he showed signs of needing a shave. Franklin's eyelids were closed, and Herman felt like the corpse might awaken any moment.

"Well, Herman, what about the key?" Al asked.

"Ah, Mr. Campo," Herman said glancing back at Al. "I'm afraid I don't know what to make of this. It's very strange, very strange indeed."

"That man was just buried yesterday!" Jonathan said, looking in disbelief.

"Herman, look at the center of his chest! The chain, pull it out," Al said, kneeling down on the edge and pointing.

Seller hesitantly reached down and tugged on the gold chain. Slowly it came, and then stopped; he had to pull harder until the key popped out. It was so brightly polished the reflection of the flashlight briefly blinded them.

"Can you remove it from around his neck, Herman?" Al said, ready to come in with him.

Herman nodded slowly. "Please take this," he said, handing the flashlight to Jonathon. He supported himself with his left hand, resting it on Franklin's chest. The lifeless mass felt soft and solid like a stiff pillow. Herman was able to tug the chain from behind the head and free it from the corpse. His fingers tingled as they had, he remembered, when handling the gold box.

"Oh! My heavens," Seller said, watching in disbelief. Franklin's body, so strangely preserved just moments before, began to rot before his eyes: the hands shriveled, the chest sunk under his weight, and the face deteriorated. Flesh melted from the bone; the bump of the eyes diminished and vanished, becoming empty orifices staring back at Herman. The sight was grisly and amazing.

Seller gasped as he found himself pitching forward, his hand falling through the suddenly brittle ribs. He was leaning too far forward to save himself. He was sinking into the corpse.

Campo grabbed him by the belt, Jonathan by his arm, and together they lifted him out of the grave. Seller accidentally kicked one of the flashlights, and it fell into the hole, landing on Franklin's chest, shining into a gruesome face. As the distance between the key and the body increased, they saw the fresh blue velvet fade to a charcoal gray.

"Am I glad you two guys saw that!" Jonathan said, straightening out Herman. "Because I don't believe it just happened."

"Well, one thing's for sure, I'm certain that's the key," Al said.

"How so?" Herman asked, as he felt the electrical vibrations flow into his palm.

"Because I remember the velvet sack around the box. It looked brand new when I found it," Al said excitedly. "The rest of the things in the couch were as old as dirt. The only thing that touched the box was the sack. And that key was lying between his clothing and his skin, somewhere on his chest. Once it was removed, its power went with it. Herman, let's get the box."

Seller was standing back from the grave, the key dangling from his hand. "Mr. Campo, I...I don't think we quite understand the power of the box, no...no, not at all. We have to do more research before we can risk opening this relic. We have already stepped too far into the unknown."

"Herman..." Campo said in a controlled tone. "Herman, old friend, I understand your concerns, but I have to use the power of this discovery for a reason of unbelievable complexity. For me to explain it now would take usinto the afternoon hours, and I have to get this box and the key on an airplane within two hours."

"Mr. Campo," Herman said. He could feel the energy creeping up his arm to his shoulder. "I don't believe you have a full understanding of what we have just uncovered. We have to research its power. It holds life within. You saw the corpse. It looked alive until we removed the key. What is in this box may not be the Angel of Death. It could be the Fountain of Youth. It has to be studied and fully understood. It cannot be used selfishly."

"Herman, I don't want it for selfish reasons. Its power will be used to benefit everyone in the world, I promise you that," Campo spoke to his friend compassionately. "Please, I need to see if that key works in the box. Let's just try it out."

Jonathan was moving stealthily toward Seller and was about to snag the key from his hand when Al stopped him. "Jonathan don't...Herman understands I'm a man of my word, don't you, Herman?"

Seller nodded nervously, gripping the key and its golden chain tightly. He could feel energy charging through his veins: the tighter he squeezed, the more intense the feeling. It was as if he were being injected with euphoria, a sense of energy and well-being reaching into his chest, spreading into his extremities. The professor's hunched frame unfolded, straightening. His body began to vibrate, and Seller watched the skin on his hand smooth, the gray spots evaporate, and the protruding veins diminish. The sight frightened him, and he yelped, dropping the gold key onto the ground. He immediately lost the sensation, and the skin on his hand reverted to old age. He rubbed his hand and arm briskly, as he slumped back into his customary posture.

"Now that was some wild shit," Jonathan said. Grabbing a handkerchief from his pocket, he used it to pick up the relic and handed it over to Campo. "Al, I hope you've got a good reason for needing this, because I agree with the old guy. We shouldn't mess with the man upstairs."

"Herman, are you all right?" Al asked. Seller nodded and kept rubbing his arm. Campo led the three to Herman's Ford. He reached in for the velvet sack, placed it on the hood, and removed the box from its wrappings.

They stood in silence, Jonathan's mouth wide open, and Seller's gaze fixed.

Al held the velvet on top of the box, careful not to touch the metal surface with his skin. Even through the cloth, he could feel the energy within. He stood unmoving, contemplating his decision to open it.

What if Herman was right? How could he be so presumptuous to think he had the right to disturb something that hadn't been opened in two hundred years? But he had to know what was inside. Images of Agent Faz's distorted face blinded him, Wolfgang's shallow grave, his friend Stanley lying in critical condition—how many more would die if Sabu were allowed free reign? He thought of Domeni, and of leaving his past behind and starting over with her. But Sabu, someone had to stop him. And there was no one better to do it than Alfonse Candalini.

Al pushed down on the lid. When he turned the key, he didn't want it to open any more than was necessary. "All right, here goes!" He inserted the key slowly; it fit snugly and without any resistance. Then Campo twisted it clockwise. It didn't move. He paused and looked at his friends with trepidation. He was perspiring now from pure tension. He removed his hand shook his fingers, and re-gripped the handkerchief around the key carefully. Then he turned it counterclockwise. It spun easily, and Al felt the tumblers shift. The box opened a crack, despite his hand on the lid.

"It works!" Al whispered, looking over at his companions. He expected to see them smiling with glee, but their faces were blank and their eyes wide.

Campo looked down and saw a strange mist begin to seep from the box. It curled around his wrist, and traveled up his arm.

"Oh shit!" he said, and leaned his body weight down. Then he quickly twisted the key clockwise. He pulled the key out in a jerking motion. The mist vanished back into its tomb. He stood back and became aware of his breathing. It was erratic and heavy.

Jonathan stepped over by his side and put his hand on his shoulders. "Now that is some scary shit...I don't think there is any doubt that is the key, and if you ask me, we should put it back into the old man's grave along with that box. It's just a thought," Jonathan said, seeing Al's chest rise up and down.

CHAPTER FORTY-TWO

THE PRESIDENT IS DEAD! The president was found dead in his bedroom in the White House this morning, found by Chief of Staff Sam Haggart. Apparently he suffered a heart attack in his sleep. Vice-President Carel Vincent will be sworn in at ten-thirty this morning, as soon as he returns from a fishing trip on the Chesapeake…

"Perfect! Simply perfect," the president said joyfully. "This should draw them out—don't you think, Bruce?"

He was reading the headlines of the *Washington Post*, sitting casually on a suede recliner. A fireplace was to his left, unlit of course, on this hot summer's day, and his dog lay at his feet on a circular area rug. Worthington was dressed comfortably in a black jogging suit and sneakers.

"To be honest, Mr. President…I don't," the director of the CIA said. "But it will cause the attempted assassins to believe they have succeeded." Bruce Kellogg sat on a floral sofa across from the president. His legs crossed, he swirled the liquid left at the bottom of his glass of scotch and ice. He had been nervous about their plan from the beginning, and the scotch eased his tension. He loosened his orange tie and unbuttoned his collar.

"That will be enough for Mr. Campo to get into the middle of the fire, while you send in a Delta force to annihilate this Sabu the Butcher and that crazy Karuza. Do you have them ready to leave?"

"They left this morning and should be meeting up with British intelligence…" Kellogg looked at his wristwatch. "…inside of three hours, in the mountains outside Tbilisi—ready to invade the capitol building, securing Sabu and his men."

"I hope we're not underestimating this character—and putting our men into a fire of their own." Worthington leaned over to pet his dog, which had nestled his head on his foot.

"Sir, I think Mr. Campo entering Turkey will cause enough of a diversion. Our Delta force should have no problem in securing the capitol."

"What is the status of our men and women leaving the area?"

"All non-military personnel have already begun leaving. The balance are awaiting further orders." Kellogg sipped the dregs of his drink and rested the glass on the arm of the chair.

"Don't have them wait any longer. Get the order out." Worthington leaned back and folded his hands on his lap. "I want everyone to leave immediately. If the Delta team is successful, I will call for their return. I'm not going to risk Karuza thinking we're stalling and have him decide to launch a missile to let us know he means business."

Bruce nodded, but silently the president could tell he disagreed with his commander-in-chief.

"What time does Mr. Campo arrive in Turkey?" Worthington asked, looking above the fireplace to a burnished wood mantle clocksitting on a dark stone ledge.

"He already has, sir. He's expected to meet up with General Bartow's team within the hour."

"I thought he was to arrive as our emissary, and not secretly," the president queried.

"Well, sir," Bruce said with a bit of loathing, "I guess he has plans of his own. All the better, once he starts the ball rolling, it will make it easier for the Delta team."

<hr />

Vice-President Vincent got the call while sitting in a deck chair on the back of his boat, a thirty-six foot Sea Ray. His rod was cast into the blue-green depths of the Chesapeake. His rounded belly stretched hispolo shirt to new limits of expansion as he sat with his hands clasped over the mass. He wore a pair of Bermuda shorts and weathered Docker shoes. The fishing rod was perched in a cradle, and as he watched, the line began to jump and thrash in the bay. He immediately thrust his pudgy hand out and stole the rod back, locking the reel. He spun the knob slowly, finding some resistance. The fight didn't last long, as he pulled a ten-inch flounder up the back of the boat. Its flattened body curled upwards as he looked into the two eyes so strangely perched on the same side of its head.

Just then a short man of Latino descent called to him from within the cabin, waving a cell phone in his hand.

The vice-president called for the man to remove the hook from the fish and release it back into the bay. He entered the cabin. It was ornately decorated in dark oak paneling. The side windows had deep red curtains, and the floor was polished oak planking. Several paintings were secured to the walls, mostly of the large fish he had caught over the years. He took the cell phone from the short man's hand.

"Hello, this is Vincent."

"Mr. Vice-President, I'm afraid I have some terrible news." Carel recognized the voice as belonging to Sam Haggart. "President Worthington is dead."

"Dead! Oh my God!" he said in mock surprise. "When? How?"

"Last night, apparently. The doctors say it was a heart attack; they are going to perform the autopsy tomorrow. You are required at the White House immediately."

"Without a doubt. I'll be there in two hours," Carel said, then hung up the phone. He pressed a button next to the door and spoke into an intercom. "Mr. Cruz, take me back to Washington."

"Yeah, sir," the man said in a heavy Spanish accent.

He then stood and stared out the window for a moment to reflect. He wasn't surprised—no, he was just now relaxed for the first time in nearly two years, and he wished to savor the moment because he knew it wouldn't last very long. He sat down on a comfortable leather chair. It was oversized, comfortable for a man of his girth, but it seemed too large in the small room. Next to the chair was an oak end table with a single drawer with a keyhole. He struggled to reach into his shorts pocket and withdrew a key ring. He located a minute, simple key and unlocked the drawer. Inside was an address book overloaded with loose papers, names and numbers hastily written on the covers outside and in. Miraculously, the book fell open to the page he needed. There was the name Fattah Abdullah with his home address, phone number, and private cell phone number.

"Mr. Abdullah," he said with a tint of superiority in his tone.

"Yes, Mr. Vincent, you have my ear."

"It is time to make your speech." Vincent's voice was broad and deep, pride clear in his tone. "Allah has sent the message, and the return of the Prophet is imminent. All who stand in our way will perish, and those who join us shall rejoice in the New Kingdom."

"I am ready to leave my office now," Abdullah said enthusiastically. "We are setting up a podium in the mall area and contacting the networks. I want this speech to be heard across the country."

"We need it to be heard across the world," Vincent said stoutly. "What time do you expect everything to be in order?"

"I should be able to make it onto the six o'clock news."

"That's perfect." Vincent pressed the end button, and placed the phone into his shorts' pocket. He felt the vibration of the engines spinning the screws. He was about to become the next president of the United States.

◆

The man sat staring at the stack of equipment, hovering above the single monitor that was a blank gray. Perspiration beading on his forehead, the cumbersome headphones were clamped to his ears, and he had to wave off the continual smoke that always seemed to drift in his direction. Why was it that the smoker was never surrounded by smoke? It always drifted, and punished the innocent.

"Jesus, Jack!" he said, turning around to his partner, who was in the middle of lighting up a new cigarette with the hot ember of the last. "Do you ever stop smoking? Christ, give yourself some fresh air once in a while."

Jack raised an eyebrow. His face was light-colored with smooth, billowy cheeks. He had blond hair combed straight down, cut around the ears with a slight part on his forehead. His green eyes were bright, and they squinted as he put uphis hands.

The two were back to back on swivel chairs. Jack monitored the airwaves, filtering out the static and black noise, while his partner, Tom, listened for the designated cell number to be called by the chief of staff. That was to happen at any moment. Tom sat tall in his seat; he was thin and athletic, with sharp shoulders, and a dark crewcut. His face was round and shiny under black eyebrows and blue eyes. Their van sat poised in front of a partially constructed beach house in North Beach, Maryland. The van was white, and labeled "Jack's Painting."

The vice-president came under suspicion after the president had a meeting with Sam Haggart and Bruce Kellogg. The CIA director had been informed that Carel Vincent had several unscheduled meetings with the congressman from South Carolina, Fattah Abdullah. While the meetings had not been bugged, and their intentions unknown—the FBI was suspicious. After the events that had just taken place in the Middle East, the group sat down and discussed who in this country would most gain from the president's death. All agreed it was Vincent, and that's when Kellogg made the connection. They had been watching him closely and were waiting for him to make the mistake they all knew he would.

Tom heard a click and sat up, and then the voice of Haggart came through, garbled:

"What's that, sir?" he said holding his hand to the headphones, looking at his partner. "Jack, I can't hear a fucking thing except frigging rock and roll music, Jesus. Mr. Haggart, please repeat that."

"Tom," the chief of staff yelled into the phone. "I said I'm going to make the call now, are you ready?"

This time he heard Haggart loud and clear. "Yes sir, we're ready." Tom turned to Jack. "Keep the fucking line clear. He's going to make the call." Jack crooked his mouth and blew a long puff of smoke into his partner's direction. Tom was listening intently, and he switched on the recorder. He could hear as plain as day the conversation between Abdullah and Vincent. After they hung up, Tom replayed it, making sure he got every word. Simultaneously, the discussion was played back for the president to hear in his private residence.

"Thank you, Tom. It came through perfectly," Haggart said.

Jack smiled and blew out another plume of smoke.

"Sir?" Tom asked. "Should we follow him to the White House and keep our ears on?"

"Hold for a moment, Tom." There was a long pause before Haggart's voice returned. "That won't be necessary, Tom. You can pack up and bring the tape to the office with you. Give it to Mr. Kellogg's secretary. Then go home. You two need a break."

"Thank you, sir," Tom said, and then Haggart hung up. Tom removed the headphones and looked back at Jack. His partner sat relaxed. He deliberately took out another cigarette before the one in his mouth was finished, lit it, and put it in his mouth alongside the first, puffing on two butts at the same time.

With lightning quickness, Tom snatched them both and crushed them on the metal floor. "You're an asshole!" he said, as he jumped into the driver seat.

CHAPTER FORTY-THREE

Al had forgotten how dry and hot the air was. It took him some time to learn how to breathe again, drawing in slow, steady breaths. He walked along the tarmac of a small airstrip outside of Istanbul, Turkey. Campo's arms were full. He carried a small brown suitcase in one arm, and the other shouldered a large travel bag of the same color. He was all but dragging the suitcase along the ground, using his wounded arm to carry it toward a green Mercedes pickup truck, circa 1950. The driver wore a dusty tan tunic and weathered beige sandals. He had a turban on top of his head with the tail half-covering his face. Campo slowed his pace, not recognizing the tall figure staring at him with dark eyes. His trip was not secretive, so he did not practice stealth, and he walked on cordially, prepared to pass the man indifferently. The tall man waited, leaning on the front of the musty pickup. His gaze left Campo momentarily, then shot back, eyes wide. The gap between them closed, and the man darted toward him. Campo dropped the case and prepared to defend himself. It was too late. The tall man threw his arms around Campo's chest in a bear hug.

"My brother, you have returned—and by God's will—alive and well," the man said. Then he pulled away. Now that he was standing next to Campo, Al could see he was a full three inches taller. He had to look up into the eyes pooling with tears. Campo was still at a loss for words as the stranger unwrapped his face, revealing the smooth, brown features of his old friend Ghali.

"Ghali, is that you?" Campo said.

Ghali removed his headdress, displaying a pronounced birth-mark on his forehead. The pair embraced again, Al was overwhelmed—and felt his insides turning. When General Bartow told him Ghali would be his contact, his emotions were hard, and he acted like it was just another mission from his past. Now in the presence of his old friend, he was suddenly aware that he had never thanked him for saving his life, or ever said goodbye. Ghali had rushed him out of the country, and Al had spent the next year learning to forget his life and start new. They separated and held one another's forearms.

"It is so good to see you again, my brother," Ghali said, holding onto Campo's shoulder in warm friendship.

"You have no idea!" Campo said, his heart pounding. "I didn't understand how much I missed you—missed everything—until now."

Ghali grinned, displaying a set of yellowing teeth. The wide smile brought more memories back. Ghali's warm face always made Campo smile.

"Come, I will take you to my home." Ghali said and grabbed Al's bags. There was a quick buzz of activity. Al thought Ghali wanted to take him away before they were spotted in public.

"Home…isn't there a safe house or command post?" Campo asked.

"Major, I am the only one; my home is the command post," Ghali moved the bags into the truck and opened the passenger door.

"Where is your team?" Al said. "I was expecting at least six men to assist in my operation. Weren't you briefed by the general?"

"I was told of your arrival. The general called me an hour ago, but he made no mention of an operation or the need for six men," Ghali said.

Al looked down at the dirt, once more lost in time again; the government had duped him again. He was here to be out of the way, or maybe he was a decoy. Nonetheless, Morris was now playing the political game. Al decided instantly his mission would still go ahead, with or without the US government. His risk had doubled, yes, and he knew he might not return home this time. His only asset was Ghali—whom he hadn't seen in more than a decade.

"My friend, let's go to your home, where we can sit and talk," Campo said and slid into the seat.

"Yes, of course." Ghali's face beamed with sympathy.

They rode silently, though the noises around them were deafening. Thousands, if not hundreds of thousands, of people crammed the streets. They were everywhere: on the streets, in the alleys, milling in doorways. Campo even noticed children gathering on rooftops. The outlying area of Istanbul was being pushed to the limit. He could only imagine how terrible the city proper was. Adding to the din was Ghali's truck. It lacked a muffler, and despite their slow rate of travel, the sudden bursts of a choking engine were attracting attention. The windows were down, and the back window was completely missing. Dirt seemed to swirl around the cab, making for a very uncomfortable ride.

"This truck of yours isn't very conspicuous," Al said with a smile as they bounced up and down while dust blew into the cab.

"No, not at all," Ghali said and showed his amber teeth. "I maintain a low profile in the city. I bring the obvious, and curious onlookers take me for a local."

"Whatever works." Campo said. He was still at a loss about what the government was up to.

"These people do not worry over the common peasant," Ghali said, keeping one eye on the road and the other on Campo. "They have come to bear witness to the return of the Prophet. They wait for the clouds to open and Allah to send him back to his people. A loud and disturbing truck carrying two passengers will hardly be noticed amongst the millions."

"Millions?" Al said.

Yes, it is believed there are fifteen million pilgrims thronging in and around the city, along with the pre-existing ten million inhabitants who make this the largest sardine can in the world," Ghali said and turned the rusted truck down another crowded street. "The people will not take the slaying of their caliph lightly."

Al looked at him. He just said the general had not briefed him on his plans, but then again, Ghali was always one step ahead of him. "Who said anything about an assassination?"

"It has been many years since you left, my friend." Ghali looked at him without moving his head, then stopped his truck in front of a one-story building. Its façade was sand-colored stucco. Chips of cement were flaking to the ground and cracks could be seen everywhere, the obvious result of the many earthquakes in the region. The front door was hardwood, painted but the color was a faded gray. "My brother, this is my command…my house. You must exit now so I may park. Once I do, there will be no room for you to exit the truck."

Al exited and watched Ghali park. His friend wasn't kidding; he pulled into a space between his home and the building beside it. The truck's side view mirrors were missing, and the vehicle wouldn't have fit with them attached. The reason for the missing back glass became apparent as Ghali climbed out into the bed of the truck. He jumped to the ground, grabbed the suitcase, and then lifted Al's larger shoulder bag.

"In the name of God, my brother, what do you carry in this sack?" Ghali asked, as he had to put down the smaller suitcase in order to hoist the shoulder bag.

"Let's go inside and I'll show you," Campo took the smaller bag, following Ghali. He was let into a one-room apartment; the walls were similar to the exterior stucco, but smoother in texture. The same chipping and cracking were apparent under makeshift repair work. To the right, a green cot, lacking blankets but with a yellowish pillow, was nestled against the wall, under a window. It was open to Ghali's truck. On the left, there was a square table with three chairs. There was simple kitchen with a small refrigerator resting on a counter next to a sink along the back wall. Further to the right, Al could see a toilet half-hidden by a curtain. The floor was made up of worn wood planks, and a lone lamp dangled from the ceiling. It must have a 300-watt bulb, Campo thought, because the lone window was blocked by the truck, and the door was closed, yet it illuminated the entire room like the sun.

"How did you manage such a fine home in such a short time?" Campo was joking. The home was depressing.

"My brother, this has been my home since Karuza began his assault on the minds of the good people of the world two years ago." Ghali gestured toward the table and set his luggage on the floor next to it.

Al looked at him. "If we've had undercover agents here this long, how could it have come to this, with Karuza holding the world on a string?"

"I am one of Karuza's devout followers." Ghali let this sink in before an explanation. "I have managed to gain the confidence of his cousin, Ammar. Two years ago, I was working in the market outside of Ankara. Long forgotten was the fight for peace by the Americans, too busy with inspections and sanctions. After you left, the general left also. Bartow made no further contact. He left us… out in the cold without a paddle, as you say in America."

Campo didn't bother to correct him; he wanted to hear this.

"So there I was," Ghali continued and sat at the table. Campo joined him and they looked each other in the eyes. "I was working for a living, haha, selling garment bags to tourists, and then came a day when Karuza paraded in the street. His entourage strode past my wares, Karuza at the head, with Ammar and the Butcher beside him. Yes, the Butcher. My weakness forced me to seek knowledge as we once did in the desert together. The face of Karuza was familiar, so I sought out files, not official papers, only the ones you, yourself, had encouraged us to create. 'Store knowledge in places that may be forgotten, yet remain in the open,' you once told me. When your body was taken away, I felt a terrible disgust in men, and I began to remember and log the events of our time together. It was a way to workout the demons. So I first made notes in the margins of books, then the notes became journals, then the journals became books. I have every memory of every mission on record."

"But where would you keep it so it was not discovered?" Al said and licked his lips. The dry air was getting to his throat.

"Again, as you said, forget, but keep in the open, where it could be seen. The Public Library of Istanbul. The volumes of text have never been loaned out contain my diary. Those books led me to the discovery of Karuza's real name."

"Adhar Ataollah." Campo said.

"Yes…and I knew while the Butcher was by his side, he was a danger to good people. Only death follows in his wake. Through what was left of my network of trusted friends, I was able to contact the CIA working in Europe, and from then on I was a spy again. Although I feel my efforts have gone to lesser concerns, because here we sit and the Butcher commands millions." Ghali said.

"Exactly why I've come to Turkey," Al said, and the tingle of revenge raised the hair on the back of his neck. He could almost feel the presence of Sabu. "Can you get me close to Karuza?"

"Yes," he said. "But why?"

"I have a gift to bestow upon His Holiness. I come as an emissary from the United States." At least, that's what the original plan was. After hearing that Ghali was all alone, Campo didn't know what to think. Ghali went to the little refrigerator and pulled out a jug of wine and two cups. He filled them, returned the jug, and sat at the table. A moment passed as they sipped the wine. It tasted sweet, like blueberries or boysenberries, and it wasn't particularly potent.

"Sabu has become very powerful. It is much different than before," Ghali said and drank his wine, tilting his cup to empty it. "When you were here last, no one supported the assault. I mean all of the Middle East condemned the acts of terror and violence. Now, Karuza has gained the support of the people." Ghali got up and went to the small refrigerator and poured some more wine into his cup. This time he brought the jug back to the table. "Look out into Istanbul; he has brought hope and inspiration to the many who have nothing—and had hope for nothing. Even the American believers in the region sympathize. Karuza's prophecy has come true! And all who come are peaceful, only Karuza keeps them strong, Allah did send a sign. All leaders fell sick and died, including your President Worthington."

Al grinned.

"What, you have not heard of this?" Ghali said.

"Ghali, my friend, President Worthington's death will cause the traitors in Washington to reveal themselves, and even more important, it will bring comfort to Karuza. He will let his guard down, knowing America is no longer a threat. I am here to exploit that subtle feeling of omnipotence he has. First, I am going to bring this gift to Karuza, and eliminate him—then we will travel to Tbilisi and deal with Sabu."

"My brother, there will be no need to travel to Tbilisi," Ghali said, again looking puzzled.

"Ghali," Al shot back, he leaned closer to his old friend, his face a mask of seriousness. "If you believe I only want Sabu for vengeance, you're wrong. Karuza is the leader—and once he is gone, his civilian followers will follow. But Sabu is the key. Destroy his military leadership, and we will destroy the revolution. Once the figurehead is dead, all who look up to him will fall."

Ghali smiled and patted Al's shoulder. "You misunderstand, brother. After word came that Worthington was dead, Karuza sent for Sabu to return to Hagia Sophia. Now the three of them stand together, as they have for the past two years. He arrived an hour before you did—just when I received the general's call, a messenger arrived to tell me so."

Al was elated. Two pigeons in one place. Although he only had one bullet, he would have to make use of the situation. "I thought I could smell his stench when I arrived. How soon can you bring me to Karuza?"

"Brother, to bring you before them now would be suicide. There will be a hundred guests arriving at once; a private meeting is not possible. He will have armed guards, and, I might add, Sabu has cunning instincts. He will not allow any harm to come to His Holiness."

"I understand that." Al finished his wine and grabbed the jug.

"Then why do you wish to give your life for theirs?"

"I have no intention of giving my life willfully." Campo shook his head and sipped the wine again; apparently he was wrong about the alcohol content, because he felt warmth rush into his face and a tingling on top of his head. "I know the risks, and in my attempt, I may be killed. Every day I have nightmares of the torture, the pain, the hours of agony." Campo closed his eyes, fighting off the memories of torture. He opened them again. He was growing angry. He didn't know if it was the wine or just how close he was to vengeance with Sabu. "It didn't end in Iraq. The suffering continued for months through rehabilitation. Sabu stole from me one life, one I was very fond of. And not only my life—but he killed others close to me, and the anguish of knowing I was safe while she lay dead was too much to bear." Campo squeezed his eyes tight, he saw Sarita's image over and over again. A pain in his chest grew; he was suffering from heartache. He looked Ghali in the face and calmed himself down. "I then set out on a journey to establish a new identity and forget all of my past. And now the Butcher threatens my new existence, and I will not tolerate any threats."

Ghali looked at him. Campo was earnest in his feelings. "Karuza has hundreds of guards surrounding him at all times; any attempt to kill him would result in death."

"His guards will scatter from his side as I unleash a monster sent from God or Allah, whichever they prefer. His strength will kill Karuza, and then it will be only me and Sabu."

Ghali's expression turned blank, wondering if his friend had gone mad in the years since they had last seen each other. Monsters! How unlike his friend to use phantoms to convince him. He had one more thing to tell Campo, one more piece of information to convince him not to throw his life away for revenge. "Brother, there is something else I must tell you. Something the general had asked me not to tell."

Campo was curious now but not surprised. Bartow had a thousand secrets up his sleeve; another revelation would not shock him in the least. Ghali took a long drink of his wine, as did Al, who had been neglecting his. He stared at his friend as he tilted the cup.

Ghali clapped the cup onto the table and spoke quickly. "She is alive!"

"Who is alive, my friend?" Campo asked, with a furrowed brow.

Just then a subtle rapping was heard at the door. Campo went into a defensive mode, setting down his cup, and sliding his chair out slightly. "Are you expecting someone?"

Ghali's face was still and plain, like a stone. He couldn't read his thoughts.

"Yes," he replied, rising to answer. Before he opened the door, he looked at Campo, closed his eyes briefly, and prayed silently.

Al watched in wonder. *What is wrong?* he thought. The door opened toward him, so he couldn't see the visitor immediately. Ghali bowed his head and said, "Welcome back." Then in walked a woman with dark features, carrying a basket of fresh fruits and vegetables.

She looked at Campo, and her eyes burst open, displaying dark irises, and an expression of mixed alarm and excitement. She pulled back the linen covering her head, letting jet-black hair fall down.

It was Sarita.

Al's heart sank into his stomach as a throbbing lump grew in his throat, nearly choking him. He couldn't even speak her name.

Sarita slowly handed her basket to Ghali. "Alfonse?" she asked in a raspy, whispering voice. "Is that you?"

Campo rose to meet her, and the two embraced. Sarita dug her head into his chest and wrapped strong arms around his waist. Al squeezed tight, putting his lips to the top of her head. She began to sob, grabbing the front of his shirt with her fists, angry and blissful simultaneously.

She looked up at her old lover. "You have finally returned!"

Then they kissed; she brought her hands to the side of his face, caressing his cheeks, around his thick hair. The lump in his throat was drowned by affection. He felt he was in the midst of dream, ten years of separation erased in one embrace. They lost themselves within one another until they heard Ghali clear his throat loudly enough to wake the dead.

They parted lips, and finally Campo was able to look at her. Time had aged her, but her beauty shone through. He noticed a scar running from her left ear down her jaw to her chin. Another was almost hidden at her hairline, and where her neck met her shoulder, there was one more jagged line.

"You survived?" Al asked.

"I have, Alfonse, but until now, I've only recovered physically—seeing you…" she paused while tears ran over her cheeks. She shook her head slowly, unable to comprehend his face being so close to hers after so many years. "Now my heart shall heal… now you are in my arms again, safe and well. Sit and we can talk together as we once did so long ago."

At that moment he wanted nothing more, but time was his enemy, and he did not know how long it would take Ghali to get him near Karuza. "Sarita…my sweet, dear Sarita…I did not know you were here, or even thought you were alive. I am so happy, and my insides turn with love—and our past. I want more with you."

He looked down at their clasped hands, rubbing her weathered palms, smoothing away the tear drops that fell onto them. Then he looked at her angelic features, seeing the scars. How could he have let it happen? How could he have left without knowing the truth? He burned with regret, and here she was—ready to take him back—all forgiven, all forgotten. In spite of the pain she endured, she seemed simply contented with his presence.

"Sarita," he said, "I have come here with a mission to complete."

"Of course," she said looking at him. She saw a different face. The surgeons in America had changed his nose and his chin, and his crushed cheekbone was reconstructed, making it slightly more pronounced than she remembered. But in his eyes, in his eyes she saw the same man, determined, methodical, professional—and most of all loving. She was also still determined, although when America withdrew, her support team and funding went with it. Now all that was left was Ghali, her rock, and her partner in strengthening the information junket they created. Her faith in America had dwindled, and so had her determination to assist them. Her glance dropped to the floor. Releasing her hands from his, she sat down, putting her palms flat on the table. She took several deep breaths, bringing back her professionalism, and her unyielding desire to be with him—no matter what the situation.

"Major Candalini, how may Ghali and I be of service?" she said with a steely calm.

Campo sat in the chair across from her, shoved the cups aside, and grabbed her hands. "Sarita, so many years have passed. I thought you were dead—I was dead for all that mattered. Once I returned to the States, it was nearly a year before General Bartow contacted me. I immediately asked about you. He said you were gone." Al closed his eyes, reliving the moment in his mind. He pressed his lids together, but the tears squeezed out. "Bartow ended my existence as Major Alfonse Candalini. I had to start a new life, one without you—a life I rejected at first, but I grew into the world around me, slowly making contact with people again. I started over, but I never forgot our past, more than a decade gone—and now I find myself back here with you…

Sarita's stare was polar. She listened and understood she was about to lose him all over again.

"I have a mission," Al continued. "And there are others waiting for my safe return."

She held back the tears this time. How could she expect it to be the same as it had been so long ago—a lifetime ago. He had been remade, and her life had been altered as well—only in different ways. She too, had been abandoned, spent time in a hospital recovering, but her struggle remained. She had been fighting for what she knew was right, and she took on that task gladly. But to see him alive again—she missed him so, and she wanted more. However, she couldn't ask for it. Just seeing him would have to be enough.

"Sarita, I must complete this mission," Al said, attempting to reassure her. "You and Ghali will be part of it —only this time we will not fail and separate again—after this we will be together."

"Do not speak of us any longer," Sarita said, tears still welling in her eyes. "I loved you—and that was enough for me. You must have many friends who depend on you, and I'm sure you cannot disappoint them. I don't want you to make promises to me." She stopped and took a deep breath, "Because then you'll be breaking promises you made in America. I don't want you to break the heart of the one you love. It would be too much for her to bear. I know what a broken heart feels like…" She again lowered her head, avoiding his gaze, looking at their clasped hands, regaining her strength.

Al was taken aback, but then she always was strong and self-less—and most of all—in tune with his thoughts. After Karuza was gone, he would make it right again. She would know how much she was adored.

After a prolonged silence, Ghali spoke. "Major, His Holiness has been receiving guests daily, usually in the morning hours. I will speak with my contact within Hagia Sophia, and arrange a meeting with Ammar and the caliph."

"And Sabu!" Campo spat.

"Of course. The Butcher will be by the caliph's side. You mentioned a gift. May I see it?"

"Certainly." Al picked up the travel bag, placing it on the table in front of Sarita. Unzipping it, he first took out an old *thobe* and *ghotra* made of gray linen. He would have to don them before he met with Karuza. He wished not to stand out like an American on vacation. Next, he removed the bright purple velvet sack; he held it in his hand as he swept his suitcase to the floor. Then placed the velvet down carefully, one end at a time.

Sarita and Ghali waited intently as he untied the cord. When the shimmering gold was displayed the two gasped. Ghali reached a hand toward the relic.

"My friend, I'm sorry, but its surface cannot safely be touched by human hands." Campo gently took hold of his wrist and eased it aside.

"What is this artifact so beautiful that only Allah himself could have created it?" Ghali asked.

"It is magnificent," Sarita said.

"Ghali, my friend, you have no idea how close you are to deducing its origins. It is of holy creation, and within its luster and its alluring promise of wealth and power, something unholy and terrible lies hidden. This is my gift to Karuza," Campo said as he stared at the engravings, each ridge flashed diamonds of light. Campo slowly became lost in thought before he snapped out of the trance. "It will destroy them, and then I will deal with the Butcher."

"It will be difficult for His Holiness to refuse such a beautiful gift," Sarita said.

"That's the plan."

"How does it open?" Ghali asked. "I see no seam or hinge on its sides, only a slot shaped like the full moon resting on a pedestal."

"With this," Al said as he pulled the chain from around his neck, he had it coated in a flexible plastic that kept his skin from touching the metal. He tugged until the key itself popped out. The gold seemed drab and tarnished through the film. "This will unlock the end to Karuza's reign, and return power to the people of Georgia. Once we destroy Karuza…"

"We destroy his revolution," Sarita finished his sentence.

"Yes," Campo said, giving her a tender glance. He then gathered the velvet around the box, and pulled the chord tight.

"Major, I must go now and meet with Ammar's agents." Ghali adjusted his turban, throwing the tail under his chin. "I will arrange for you to meet with His Holiness tomorrow morning."

Al thought it odd his friend suddenly had to go, right after viewing the box. Nonetheless, he had to meet with Karuza soon. He looked at his wristwatch and saw it was still on Philly time. His timetable was based on its hands. He had twelve hours left before Karuza's deadline for the United States expired and he unleashed the missiles. "What time is it now?"

"Nine o'clock," Ghali said looking at his own watch.

"Ghali, my friend, time is a commodity I have little of. Would it be possible to meet with Karuza privately tonight?"

"My friend, I will do my best, as I always have for you," Ghali said reassuringly and left.

Al and Sarita looked at one another with desperate eyes, their elation of moments ago turned to somber, withdrawn smiles.

"You must be hungry. I will prepare some food," she said, breaking away and going to the exposed kitchen.

"That sounds wonderful," he said, attempting to squeeze comfort between the tensions. The two sat and ate together, talking only of the past, avoiding the future and events that might separate them forever. An hour of reminiscing had passed when Ghali reentered the house.

"My friend," Ghali said from the open doorway. A slight wind blew dust across the floor. It ceased as he shut the door, but a cloud was now overhead. Ghali stomped his feet and dusted his pants off and said. "I have not all bad news. We may see His Holiness, but only at his calling, tomorrow at eight a.m."

CHAPTER FORTY-FOUR

A mmar rapped his knuckles on the teak paneled door. The intricate pattern of its grain shot out from the center where it met in an apex of jagged ridges and smooth lines. The color was rich amber; its thickness muffled the gentle knock, so the visitor struck the hardwood with more power. There was still no answer. Ammar reached to the center of the door, turning the knob, pushing the door inward. The room was dark, with the exception of a sliver of light from the open door.

"Holiness?" he said into the obscurity. He reached around to the adjacent wall, flicked a light switch, igniting a huge brass and crystal chandelier. The chamber was vast. To the left a tall spindle bed, made of the same rich colored wood as the door, stood like a majestic throne. The mattress was high off the floor, and its covers were turned down, but empty. He scanned the room, past lace draperies hanging in front of divided glass panels. Karuza now considered the windows a threat, so Ammar had pulled an opaque screen over them. He turned to the center of the room, looking for his cousin among several beige, billowy sofas separated by a rectangular bronze table. Moving further into a darkened area, a Persian carpet was laidout. He saw Karuza kneeling, sandals removed, hands folded in prayer, his eyes closed.

Ammar looked past him, the Caliph's shadow tattooed the far wall. It was as though there were two of them: one of this world, and the other a Holy Ghost. Ammar removed his sandals and moved to kneel next to his cousin. The pair appeared as two unmoving statues, Karuza's bright white robes contrasted with Ammar's pale tan. He lost himself in meditation just when the caliph opened his eyes.

"My cousin, I have awakened." Karuza looked at his cousin wide eyed.

Ammar looked over and smiled. "Holiness, Sabu has returned from his victory in Tbilisi. He has brought a gift for you," Ammar said, not wanting to divulge the contents of the present, hoping his cousin would not ask.

"Ammar, how are you feeling today? Your recovery by the grace of Allah has been swift?" Karuza was looking at the bandage taped to Ammar's shoulder and neck. His face was taut, and his tired eyes were like two holes in the black sky.

"I am well, my Caliph; the doctors say I will make a full recovery."

"As Allah has told me in my sleep, you shall." Karuza flapped his folded hands in approval. "Sabu has arrived, and he brings with him the power of the new age. Where is he?"

"When you are ready to receive him, he will meet us in the Great Hall of the Sun." Ammar bowed.

Karuza nodded. "Ammar, Allah has spoken to me of a messenger bearing a gift of power and beauty. It holds the secrets of the Prophet and will bring about his return. Has he arrived?"

Ammar looked astonished at Karuza's clairvoyant thoughts. "A man has arrived. We have not brought him in. He brings a gift—a box—of such beauty it could not be described by the agent. What it holds is unknown."

"It contains the future for us and the future of the world. First we will meet with Sabu. He carries the power the Prophet shall wield. Then deliver the messenger before me as the sun crests the hills. His gift carries the power for the return of the Prophet. The new era of our people will begin upon his use of the weapons to continue his reign of justice." Karuza stood and started for the window. "Ammar, follow me to the glass." Quickly Ammar rose and came to stand beside the caliph. Karuza slid his hand between the drapes, separating them in the middle. "You see how the people cascade across the gardens into the hillside.

They come here because the future is here—and the New World begins here."

They looked out into the landscape of Hagia Sophia; a plethora of pilgrims prayed, gathered in family groups, milled about, helping others, or simply gazing skyward, looking for the Prophet to descend. They were millions of peaceful followers wanting only the promise of a new beginning.

"They also come to see you, my cousin," Ammar added. "You are the vessel, the only way to the future. They pray for you and your safety. Without your holiness, none of this would be possible. Sabu has brought the power of the West into our grasp. They sleep peacefully now, without the threat of the Americans, without the threat of the Jews. You have brought peace to their world, and now when the Prophet returns, they can return to their homes and kiss the soil beneath their feet and call it their own. Not since the Middle Ages, when the caliphs ruled the Middle East for eight hundred years, has that been possible."

Karuza gazed out at the multitude as Ammar spoke. His dreams were becoming reality. Only the final step need be taken, and the world would be his.

Sarita and Ghali offered Campo the lone bed to sleep on, but he refused, insisting he would feel more comfortable on the floor while Sarita was in the bed. It wasn't much of a discussion because they knew Campo rarely—if ever—changed his mind.

Al expected this to possibly be the longest night of his life, with the fate of the world lying on his shoulders and the woman who once was his only love lying just a few feet away. He was flat on his back, hands clasped on his chest, with Ghali to his left already sleeping, curled in the fetal position, facing away from Campo. To his right lay Sarita. She too was supine, her profile glowing in the light of the single candle Ghali had lit. Its smell of ginger filled Campo's nostrils. He turned sideways, crooking his elbow, resting his head on his hand. Sarita opened her eyes and turned to look at him. She saw his look of desire and smiled.

"Alfonse," she whispered. "Tomorrow all may change; you must sleep, and prepare for your mission."

"All may change…everything but the fact I still, and always will, love you."

Her smile turned to a frown. She knew he was telling the truth, but also knew he belonged to someone else. She could not have him. His words—unknown to him—were cutting her deep.

"Alfonse, think of your mission tomorrow," she said and tenderly rubbed his forehead. He reached to grab her hand, but she pulled away quickly. "Prepare your mind for that, and we will talk of us after tomorrow."

Al would have to be content with that, because she closed her eyes, and turned to face the wall. He went back to looking at the ceiling, breathing deeply the fragrance of the candle. Its odor seemed to permeate deep into his lungs, and slowly he realized he felt unexpectedly sleepy. He looked over at Ghali with weary eyes. He blinked. Was his friend missing? He went to rub his eyes, but his hand would not move. He was paralyzed! He struggled with the thought, and suddenly Ghali was standing over him. Al could see his friend's eyes, but his mouth and nose were obscured by a breathing apparatus. The candle was tainted. The airborne drug was taking over. His immediate thought was for Sarita, but he was unable to look over at her.

Next came blackness.

◆

Campo awoke in pain; his head throbbed as he opened his eyes. His arms were pulled taunt over his head, chained to a concrete wall behind him. His shoulder muscles were stiff from the unyielding stress. From a misshapen concrete ceiling, a light dangled, casting a ghastly light. Campo judged the room to be ten by ten, the walls of the same texture as the ceiling. Across from him stood a flat, riveted steel door with no knob or keyhole of any kind. A gruesome pile of deteriorated bone and flesh fragments lay scattered among ragged, bloodstained linen.

The floor was slimy and cold under his bare feet; he could only assume the wetness was the remains of the deceased. He could see the pile of remains moving in small jerking motions, and in the dim light he watched rats scurry down the corners carrying a meal into an enlarged crack, disappearing into the wall. The pain raging through his skull subsided as a sense of failure trickled down his spine. Perspiration burst from every pore, though the air was damp and cool. The beading sweat from his shoulders matted his bare chest. Yesterday he worried how it was all going to end; the thought of a miscarriage of trust on his part never crossed his mind. How could it be? Ghali? He remembered the words his friend—no, not friend, but foe—spoke of the good Karuza brought to the people—his sudden departure once he viewed the box. Twenty years ago it never would have got this far. Removed from his element for so many years, his once-calculating instincts were stale.

Ghali! How could you? he thought, shaking his head. But Sarita too, was she an accomplice, or was she also a victim? She wasn't wearing a gas mask the last Campo remembered, but she had rolled to her side, facing away from him. Did she feel the effects of the candle, and slip a mask on seconds before the poison took hold? But Sarita was not here with him…

How could I have failed so miserably?

Now the question remained, would they keep him there, leaving him to die, his corpse devoured by the rats, or would they bring him to some sort of trial, and promote it in the media as a captured spy, and have him publicly executed? He had to concentrate, had to push this despairing contemplation to the back cavity of his brain. He knew no matter how grim the situation, escape would always be an option.

He took stock of his position. The chains seemed to reflect the light, sparkling dots on the opposite wall… they must be newly made…breaking them would be nearly impossible without proper tools. The wall anchor holding them tight was another matter: it was an eyebolt embedded into the concrete. Al saw rust flaking from the pin where it entered the damp wall. Certainly it was not as secure as the chain itself. But it was mounted high, maybe three feet above Al's hands. He would need strength that eluded him then. He shut his eyes and dreamt. Sarita's image passed through his mind's eye, and then Ghali's smiling face. He went back further, drifting past the meeting in the White House, seeing Domeni lying in the room, her figure under the transparent sheet. He remembered their clasped bodies, her golden eyes moist with tears, her request, and his promise.

"Al, I know you must leave, and I won't ask you to stay." She was lying on top of him, her chin wresting on her overlapped hands on his chest. A pillow was propped under his neck. He listened and brushed her hair with his fingers. "But all my life I've dreamt of someone like you, waiting for you to walk into my life. And now that you are here, all I want is for us to be together…" *Forever.*

That word she kept within her mind; she didn't want to push him. Not that he wouldn't go because of her. They had only just met a week ago—but what a week it was. It had been lifetime of events jumbled together: excitement, fear, love she couldn't have imagined possible, her life on the line more than once, and Al Campo as her hero, there to save her.

Not quite a fairy tale—but her knight in shining armor, he was.

She wanted the happy ending more than anything else in the world. When he left that night, he might never return and her fears, her once-upon-a-time story, would end not so happily ever after.

"I want you to promise me…" She turned on her cheek, not letting him see the tears, not wanting to influence the decisions he would have to make. She wanted him to say it. That would mean everything.

"Hey," he said. "Look at me." With the back of his fingers, he smoothed the tears from her face. "I've been waiting just as long as you have for that special someone, and believe me, you are she. Fate brought us together, and I have no intention of messing up our fairy tale. I don't want to go, but I need to do it. And I promise you, when I return, we will be together."

She climbed up to his lips, and made sure he felt the fervor of love she had deep within the core of her being, elated to think of the happy ending that was soon to come.

Campo opened his eyes and once again was entombed in his dungeon, but now with the emotional strength he needed. He spun around, facing the wall, and grabbed the manacles with both hands, reaching one over the other in short distances, only a palm at a time. His shoulders burned with pain as his partially healing wounds tore open again. His exposed feet pushed on the oily surface, slipping hard to the ground each time—but he didn't stop the movement of his hands. His back started throbbing and his bicep muscles were vibrating with stress. He pulled his body off the ground, and now used his knees as additional hands, digging into any crevice, scraping the cloth free, and gouging into his skin, where the grimy surface oil burned into his blood and felt like stabbing knives. Finally, he was able to bend his arms down to his chest. If he thought it would help him to climb more quickly, he would have used his teeth. He managed to become like a spider scaling upward, inch by agonizing inch. He made it to the eyebolt and hung there, dropping his knees. He bounced up and down, dangling his lower body outward, but the corroded steel was unforgiving. The burning in his shoulders was overwhelming, and he was about to give up. He attempted to rest, hanging there, with his hands clasping the eyebolt, and his chin set on his fists.

He looked at where the bolt entered the cement. Dust surrounded the pin—and he realized the downward pressure was causing it to bind in the hole. He would have to exert outward force to free it. More climbing was required. He took several short breaths and threw his legs out, lunging his body off the wall, then bent his knees. They came crashing onto the hard surface, blood spouting in a web around his knee. His left gave way, but the right managed to find a purchase in a slight depression, and held while he brought back his left. He was able to hold himself by leaning his entire upper body outward at a forty-five degree angle. He released the chain through his hands, slowly bringing him almost parallel to the floor. With enormous effort he swung his body to the right, releasing his left knee, and brought his foot up, landing it flat on the wall, and then he did the same with the other.

His shoulders and back were suffering torrents of stinging pain as he hung suspended like an amateur rock climber scaling a building. He heaved, though he thought the pure weight of his body would be enough to dislodge the anchor. The bolt did not move, and he was losing his grip on the chain. He yanked again, harder, and the chain slipped two links through his fingers. He regrouped and tried again. Now three links slid throughhis grip—but he also saw concrete dust escape from the hole.

"It moved!" he gasped in a strained, hoarse voice, as though someone could share his triumph. He took hold of the chain, wrapping it around his hand, and gave one final tug, keeping up the pressure, clawing at every ounce of energy left in his body. If it didn't give way then, he would have to drop to the ground still bound to the wall.

"Drop to the ground!" he said aloud. He didn't foresee the after effect. He was nearly ten feet in the air, and once he freed the anchor, his momentum would carry him backward to a hard, slimy concrete floor. His eyes popped open, turning his head to see his landing, and he began to reconsider his situation. Just then the bolt moved a fraction of an inch, with frightened speed he thrust his knees back onto the wall—but it was too late. The bolt popped out like a bullet shooting overhead. He thought the only way to save himself was to go with the momentum already established, so he arched his back, kicking his feet onto the wall, and pushed his body into a clumsy back flip. He surprised himself. His feet were the first bit of him to come down, but his perfect landing was foiled by the moist floor. His legs slid outward, and he struck the floor in a wide split. The chain bounced against the steel door, clanging loudly, then landing behind him. He rolled to his side and winced, massaging his groin muscles.

Surely the loud noise of the chain would be heard for some distance, and someone would be coming to see what had happened. He had to prepare himself for a fight. Rising first on all fours, then to his feet, he gathered the chain, twisting it around the knuckles of both hands, leaving a length between them. Then he backed against the wall with the steel door to his left and remained stone still. With the lack of a knob or even the presence of a hinge he did not know in which direction it would open. To the right would be his best guess, and he wanted to surprise his keepers. It wasn't long before he heard footsteps—more than one set—traipsing toward his cell. He heard a lock disengage, and the door swung outward. Al didn't even see the person coming through the door, but he thundered his chained fist into the man's nose, splattering blood—it seemed everywhere. He wasted no time running into the hall, pushing the man backward onto another guard. Al jumped on top of them like a maniacal psychopath escaping from elec- troshock treatment. He bludgeoned the two with steel-wrapped fists, showing no mercy, savagely pounding their skulls until their bodies lay still and breathless. His heart was pounding, and he was breathing heavily as he leaned on the dead men. His knees were on their stomachs, and he looked at their destroyed faces. He could not remember the last time he had to kill a man with his hands, but he knew he would get used to the idea again before today was all over. Thinking of murder, one image entered his mind: looking into the bloodied eyes of Sabu the Butcher.

CHAPTER FORTY-FIVE

Colonel Michael Barzanian didn't like it one bit. He was reading a decoded message sent just five minutes previously, and he was shaking his head. The message said in so many words that his mission had been canceled, and new orders were to be carried out immediately. The colonel was of medium build, with a well-defined upper body. He was fifty-five years old, the oldest active Delta Force member still willing to leap out of airplanes from 15,000 feet. The skin on his face was taut, showing few wrinkles aside from small crow's feet splaying from the sides of his eyes, giving him a look of experience, while still preserving a youthful glare. His nose was narrow, with wide-set eyes set below dark eyebrows. His hair was thick and straight. He let it grow a little longer than most men did in the service, or most men his age even, letting it come to his shoulders. Tied into a tight ponytail, it appeared shorter than it was. He was known as a rebel from his younger days, and never much liked following the well-traveled path. Instead he chose his own methods in combat and missions such as this. That is to say, he had a plan—until these new orders arrived. He sat in a swivel chair mounted onto the upper deck of a monstrous Lockheed C-130E Hercules cargo plane. They were flying at 30,000 feet above the Black Sea, skirting the Turkish border about a hundred miles west of the Republic of Georgia. His team consisted of twenty-nine Delta Special forces—he was the thirtieth. Twenty-seven of the men were in the lower cargo hold, preparing to jump out of a perfectly good airplane, to descend on the unsuspecting forces of Karuza's military, who had taken control of the republic.

Captain Stram was just walking down the main aisle, a lump of papers under one arm, and managing three cups of hot coffee wedged between his two hands. The third cup of coffee was for Sergeant Thomas Donato, who was sitting in his own swivel chair to Barzanian's left. He sat listening to the coded message being repeated over the radio, awaiting any changes. There were none.

Before they left the base in Sicily the colonel had been offered more men. There was ateam of 130 Rangers stationed on the carrier USS Harry Truman floating in the Mediterranean Sea with nothing better to do. But that would mean him having to board the carrier, and then take off from there in separate planes because the C-130 Hercules' girth prohibited it from landing on a floating airstrip. The other option would be to rendezvous somewhere outside of Turkey, and time did not allow for that. Besides, his mission objective was to seize control of the capitol building and capture a man called Sabu. He had been assured once Sabu was apprehended, the fight would be over. He thought it best to enter with a smaller team, able to infiltrate under the cover of darkness, and accomplish the objective quickly and with minimal losses. Now this changed everything. He had spent the last five hours going over satellite photos of Tbilisi, along with intelligence reports, and he was moments away from briefing his men on his plan of attack. Now the C-130 had been ordered to turn around and head for Istanbul. Amazingly enough, they had been ordered to land at Istanbul International Airport after ajump from a mere two thousand feet into the heart of the city.

Sergeant Donato signaled Barzanian that a new message was coming through.

"Yes, Donato, what is it? Another message changing these orders here in my hands we received not ten minutes ago?" Barzanian said jokingly, but he knew it could be true.

"No sir, it is actually not a message, but a photograph being faxed to us. It should come up in a few seconds."

The colonel watched as the fax machine came to life, and an image began to appear. It was a floor plan of some kind. Donato waited for the transmission to stop, then plucked the paper from the machine and handed it to Barzanian. The colonel studied the floor plan silently.

"Sir, another message coming through," Donato said.

Barzanian simply nodded and trained his eyes on the photo. Something about it intrigued him. It was in part a vital piece of information, but there were notations on the plan, marking varying entrance and exit locations, also the possible location of Sabu, and one other target—Karuza. The photo also had an arrow jutting off to one side, pointing to a set of stairs, apparently leading to a dungeon of some sort. In fact, the word cell was underlined.

"Sir?" Donato asked, offering the new message.

Barzanian took it and read it silently. It began with the typical garbling of codes and nonsense to be picked up by the enemy, misinformation that would send them on a wild goose chase if they intercepted the message. Then he came to the message at hand.

New targets located in temple, eliminate as previously ordered. Diversionary incursion set in motion. Complete objective, then locate American prisoner and extract. First priority targets, then extraction, repeat first priority targets, then extraction.

From General Morris Bartow,

USMC, Joint Chiefs

"An American prisoner, that's fucking great," he whispered under his breath.

"What's that, sir?" Donato said taking his eyes off the monitor and taking a drink of coffee.

"Huh…oh nothing," Barzanian said, looking up from the message. "Are there any more messages, Sergeant?"

"Not at this moment, sir," Donato said, checking his instruments.

"I'm going down to brief the men. Let me know immediately if anything else comes through." The colonel turned and walked briskly toward the center of the plane. Then he descended the steel stairs to the lower deck. The colonel entered the vast chamber he called the basement. His men all waited patiently, each seated against opposite walls of the cargo hold. They all wore black uniforms and body armor, and black Kevlar helmets. Every man was carrying a standard M4 Commando assault rifle. Barzanian appraised his men with a fatherly grin. He was proud of his soldiers and expected only the best from each one of them. As always, he took a no-nonsense approach to his briefing.

"Men," the colonel said, folding his arms on his chest, "it looks like the United States government decided our last mission was some sort of cakewalk, so they've decided to give us the impossible task at removing the military leader of a rogue army in the middle of his fucking city. Then if that wasn't challenging enough, we have to liberate a fucking American citizen held prisoner somewhere inside a mosque."

Just then the C-130 began to bank sharply to the left, and the walls of the cargo plane tilted. Barzanian leaned one arm against the stair rail, and continued. "In thirty minutes, we will jump into the lion's den. I want everyone sharp and locked, cocked, and ready to rock. Captain Stram will be down in ten minutes to give you an idea of how each of you will be deployed. Remember, no one gets left behind. Good luck." The colonel retreated up the stairs and saw Donato holding out another message. He read the paper with a disgruntled stare.

Priority. Mission must be completed by 0900 Istanbul time, timeframe of utmost importance; Karuza has planned launch of ICBMs. You must intercept…

Barzanian looked at his watch—which he had already tuned to Georgian time—and he knew Istanbul was an hour behind. The dial was positioned firmly at nine o'clock. There was only one hour left, and it would take more than half that time just to get his men on the ground. Barzanian looked over at Donato and said, "We're fucked!"

CHAPTER FORTY-SIX

Campo searched the dead bodies for a key to unlock his chains; he found it in the shirt pocket of the first man. Now free from his bindings, Al picked up the two Uzi machine guns previously carried by the guards. Both men also had holstered Beretta 9mm handguns that he also commandeered. He sized up the two uniforms, and since he was scantily clad in a pair of torn pants, he undressed the taller man and put on the desert-tan military uniform. The fit was snug, and he knew it would be noticed, but that was insignificant compared to the bloodstains covering the entire upper portion of the shirt. Al knew he would have to remain out of sight regardless.

There was a set of concrete stairs down the dark corridor on his left, and he decided to head up them with an UZI in his right hand. He slung the other over his shoulder and stuffed the two handguns in his pants. He crept up the steps, holding his weapon in front, looking upward. The two guards had arrived so quickly, they would have had to have been stationed close by. Campo approached the top, crouching on the uppermost step. He peered over it, and saw another hallway with an open door at the far end. Inside the room another guard was sitting on a metal chair leaning on the back two legs. Al also noticed another staircase to his left leading up to another floor, but once he stepped into the hall, the guard would definitely see him. He knew there wasn't much time; this guard would be expecting his partner's return any moment. Campo reached back and pulled out the 9mm. He took careful aim and fired a single shot that tore off one of the legs of the chair. The guard fell backwards and slammed his head onto the floor. Al darted from his position and was instantly kneeling on top of his prey with the muzzle of the 9mm crammed into the guard's mouth.

"Shh…" Al put his index finger to his lips. "Sabu?" he said, looking his victim in the eye. The guard was defiant at first, shaking his head from side to side. Campo pulled back the hammer of the gun and shoved the weapon deep into his throat, cutting off his air supply.

"Sabu?" Al said again, ready to blow the back of the guard's head off if he were obstinate. The guard wisely nodded, and Campo got him to rise slowly. He had the guard put his hands in his pockets, and Al grabbed a clump of hair on the back of his head, jabbing the 9mm into his neck.

"Let's go," Al said. They moved into the hallway and up the stairs.

CHAPTER FORTY-SEVEN

Sabu stood in front of an ornate metal and stone table. He set down a thick aluminum briefcase, spun the three dials to the appropriate combination, and popped open the case. Inside was a two-piece computer. The base had a Cyrillic keyboard. He taped over several of them with symbols, indicating the codes he had tortured from Andropov. The top was a flat computer screen, and to the right of the screen were two slots shaped like octagons. After tapping several keys the screen came to life. At the top it read "Targets" and listed below it were two symbols: USA and ISA. Beside them were the codes to enable two nuclear warheads that could be launched from where he stood. All he needed to do was to insert the two keys, highlight one, and press Enter. Sabu clicked on the USA, and then put his hand in his pocket, pulling out two keys in the shape of long octagons. Their surface was pockmarked with microcomputer chips. Their ends were flattened like a wing nut about two inches long. Once the keys were inserted, they would send out signals to a satellite floating high over Asia. The two separate signals would be reconciled in the satellite's internal computer. Only the codes would have to be entered, and the satellite would relay the remote signal to the silos in Georgia—and the missiles would be launched.

Sabu couldn't wait.

He toyed with the thought of just ending it all right then by inserting the two keys and erasing Washington, DC, from the face of the planet. He grinned a sinister smile under his bushy black mustache and inserted one of the octagons. The second one he let roll back and forth in his palm, the wings of the key humming as he did. "Why not force the hand that feeds," he said in a low voice, speaking to himself. "Karuza and his dreams of the return of the Prophet, bah, I say. It has been because of my strong arm and military genius that we now hold the weapons of mass destruction. It is I who brought Georgia to its knees, and it is I who will reign supreme once America surrenders."

He gripped the key hard and spun it in his hand—pointing it toward the slot under the first one.

"Sabu!" Karuza said from the doorway. "You have returned in triumph and glory!"

Sabu looked at his caliph, squeezing the key in his fist. Sabu, with all his military might and prowess still cowered before Karuza, because deep inside, he somehow believed in Karuza's divinity.

"Your Holiness!" Sabu cried and bowed his head as his caliph approached him.

"Sabu, my general, you have returned a hero, and your name shall be revered throughout the new Nation."

"You are generous and benevolent in your faith in me, your Holiness," Sabu said, rising from his bow. "My caliph, I have brought back the power of Andropov's former Soviet Union. Within the computer lies the power to launch revenge against the United States." Sabu waved his hand over the keys, then pointed to the USA icon.

"What is the hour?" Karuza asked.

"It is thirty minutes after eight, on the first morning of the new reign of His Holiness, Caliph Karuza," Ammar said.

"Sabu," Karuza said in an unexpected tone of excitement. "Prepare your instrument for launch at precisely nine o'clock. Now, my cousin, bring to me the deliverer of the Prophet's return."

Ammar walked to the huge bronze doors and opened the one to the left. In walked several of Sabu's elite military guards, all carrying AK-47s slung over their shoulders. Five guards filed in, taking positions around the room. One of them was Major Satchan.

"Major!" Sabu said. "Your reward as promised—I will have you sit here by the case; at the exact hour of nine you will release the missiles onto the Americans. Here, I will show you."

The major beamed with pride as his general explained the process.

Next in through the door came two people: a very tall man known as Ghali, Ammar's agent, and the other, a woman carrying a heavy sack. She was all in black, her head covered by a dark veil; only her glowing eyes showed. Behind her walked another pair of guards. The entourage all bowed before Karuza. Ammar went over to Ghali and took him by the hand.

"You have done well, Ghali. We are proud and satisfied with your return to the faith. Show us the prize."

"Blessings of Allah upon you. You are gracious in your words." Ghali motioned toward Sarita, and she set the heavy object on the table a few feet away from where Major Satchan was sitting. Ghali was about to open the bag, but Karuza stepped forward.

"Wait!" Karuza said. "Where is the deliverer? He must be present; I have seen it in my dreams. The Prophet shall only return as he witnesses."

Ammar looked at the last two guards to enter. "Where is the prisoner?"

"Your excellence," the guard to the left answered as he snapped to attention. Fear flooded his dark face. "We called the guards in the prison but received no response. We assume the radio has failed. I immediately called for the corporal to go down to the cell."

CHAPTER FORTY-EIGHT

Campo led his prisoner up the concrete stairs; he moved his head from side to side, looking beyond the black crop of hair in his hands. Just as they rose to the top, they were surprised by another guard—and without hesitation the guard fired his AK-47, tearing off the arm of Campo's prisoner. He screamed in agony and fell to the ground. Al looked at the new guard now without his human shield and raised his weapon, as did his opposite.

Campo's bullets blasted into the guard's AK-47, shattering it, but his foe was unharmed. The guard alertly jumped toward Campo, his hands reaching for Al's neck. Just as his hand met Al's throat, Campo fired again into the man's stomach, but his attacker kept coming wildly. They both fell down the stairs, but Campo was able to turn his body to land with his foe under him as they struck the concrete. Al's weight came down onto the guard, breaking his back. Then the two rolled violently down the flight of hard stairs, crashing into the wall. By the time they reached the bottom, Campo had no control of his movements, and he struck his head on the unforgiving concrete.

Al woke bleary-eyed and out of sorts. He found himself restrained by chains once again only this time he stood upright. A wooden staff was behind his back, tucked under his armpits, and his hands were chained to the outer ends. *How many times in one week have my hands been tied or chained or cuffed It's getting to be a nuisance*, he thought as two men held him up by these ends with his feet just touching the floor. As his vision cleared, he saw a menacing stare that could only belong to one man. It was Sabu the Butcher, breathing a foul stench onto his face.

Sabu was looking at him in a strange way. He wasn't gloating, but rather he looked curious. Al saw his prying regard and smiled morosely. It was all he could do to keep the nagging thought of failure deep in the recesses of his brain. Escape was always an option, he thought, as the hair on the back of his neck stood on end.

"Your name?" Sabu said.

Al remained quiet.

Sabu slapped him across the face. Blood was already dripping down Campo's cheeks from his fall, and his head throbbed. The slap had little effect. Sabu squinted and inspected his prisoner at close range. Campo spit in his face.

The Butcher jumped back in a natural reaction, but then came forward, ready to backhand Campo again. He saw Campo's eyes shine back at him. Usually men cowered in his presence, but Al was defiant. Hate and rage, yes, those he was used to, but it was the look of pure fearlessness that caught him. Only once before had he seen such doggedness. Then Sabu remembered and stopped before his hand reached Campo's face. Sabu stood straight and grinned. Then he turned to face Karuza.

"Your Eminence, this man is a fraud," Sabu snapped. "He cannot be the vessel of the Prophet's return. He is a spy sent here undoubtedly to assassinate Your Holiness. Ammar, who is this man?"

Ammar approached Ghali. "Ghali, is this the man who brought the gift?"

"He is, your Grace," Ghali replied, standing calmly with his hands folded in front of him.

Al looked straight ahead and appraised the room without moving his eyes. Karuza stood silently and his eyes were fixed on Campo. He seemed to enter a trance as the rest spoke. Al also saw Sarita over by a large table, ten feet to his left. On the table was his travel bag containing the gold box. Beside it was an aluminum briefcase with a man sitting behind it playing his fingers over a keypad. Ghali was also to his left but closer. He could see his folded hands and his wristwatch. The arms were poised at eight-fifty. Only ten minutes before Karuza was to launch a strike at the United States. But with Karuza here, along with Sabu and Ammar, Campo felt a bit relieved. The US might have persuaded them to delay their plans. He needed more time, and it seemed it was in front of him. Then the guard behind the metal case spoke up.

"General Sabu," the man said, looking over the screen, "I have keyed in the launch codes, and set the default timer for nine precisely."

Campo heard the word "launch" and nearly vomited. The case was apparently a remote launching computer from the captured republic of Georgia. Campo tensed as the challenge before him clarified. He had only ten minutes to get out of his chains, kill seven armed guards and Sabu, make it over to the keypad—and somehow disarm a Russian remote satellite-launching computer, without the slightest knowledge of how the computer worked, or the codes. Plus he might have to fend off one or both of Ghali and Sarita, not knowing how far they would go in a fight.

No problem.

"Your skills have no bounds, it seems, Major," Sabu said, smiling at the man behind the launching computer.

Al saw Sabu turn his head and figured now was as good a time as any to die.

Fuck it.

He swung his shoulders like a helicopter's rotor, surprising the two men holding him up, blasting them away and the staff hit Sabu's head, knocking him down to the floor unconscious. Then he spun wildly, thrashing into the other four guards who were standing in a circle around him. Men went flying everywhere. Campo ran past a shocked Ammar, knocking him against a marble column, then lunged past an entranced Karuza and dived at the soldier now standing behind the launching computer. Campo saw a flash of gunfire from the guard and heard a bullet whiz past his ear, and then another flash. This time the projectile slammed into Campo's armpit tearing skin and splitting the staff holding his chains.

His arms were now free and he collided with the guard as he let off another shot. Al barely felt the burning sensation in his side. He only knew he must pounce and destroy. The major was crushed under 220 pounds of raving maniac.

Al heard Ammar barking out orders to his men. Campo finished choking the life out of his victim, turned, and saw six men getting up, ready to fire all at once.

He knew it was time to die.

Then all of a sudden, the six men were met with an unexpected barrage from an Uzi sub-machine gun. Ammar quickly got to his feet and tackled Karuza a split second before being shredded by the hail of bullets.

Campo ducked behind the table and looked for the source of fire. He saw Sarita standing with the Uzi in her arms, emptying sixty rounds in an instant. She tore out the empty magazine, and drew out another from under her clothes. Cramming it in, she waved her weapon from side to side.

"Ghali," Sarita said. "Quickly, seal the door."

Ghali ran and braced the door with a large flush bolt mounted on the inside. He turned and ran back to meet Campo at the remote launching computer.

Sarita walked over toward the table while leveling her weapon at Ammar and Karuza who were crouching on the floor.

Campo was trying to figure out how to signal the satellite and stand down the missiles. The keys were in Cyrillic, and he spoke Russian, but he didn't write it. The screen was flashing red letters, counting down from thirty.

"Holy shit, ten minutes gone already," he said out loud.

Just then Ghali gave him a slight shove and said, "May I have a try, Alfonse?"

Campo looked at his old friend and realized he had had to turn him in. It was the only way to get so close to Karuza. "It's all yours, old friend," Campo said.

Al received a smile from Ghali. He watched as he rapidly tapped the keys in a series of combinations. The red lights counting down...0:09...0:08...0:07. Ghali smacked the Enter key and Al saw the look on his face as the numbers continued down. Ghali feverishly typed in another series of codes, Al watched and was about to smash the case with his fist in frustration. 0:04…0:03… Ghali jammed all four fingers at the Enter key, and with two seconds left, the numbers stopped. Ghali twisted the wings of the two octagon keys and removed them from the panel. Campo and Ghali smiled at each other.

"Piece of pie," Ghali said and laughed.

Al did the same, and then looked over at Sarita, her gun still trained on Karuza and Ammar. She stole a glance at Campo. Her smile was warm and filled with love as their eyes met. Campo was about to move toward her, but in the moment that she had taken her eyes off Karuza, Sabu had pulled out one of his Lugar pistols and fired at Sarita. The bullets entered into her midsection, and she dropped to the ground in a pool of blood.

Sabu kept firing, taking aim at Al and Ghali. Campo tumbled the table over for cover and ducked behind just in time. Ghali wasn't as swift. He was shot in the forehead and fell like a stone beside him. Campo heard Sabu telling Ammar and Karuza to remain where they were. Then he ordered for Campo to stand and throw out his weapon.

If only he had one.

Sabu held his side arm pointed at Campo's sternum. "Your Holiness, it is now safe for you to rise," he said. "You will come out from behind the table," Sabu said to Campo.

Al rounded the overturned table, and noticed the gold box had tumbled out of the bag, and more importantly, the remote computer had been smashed under the table's edge.

"Your Holiness, he has destroyed the launching device!" Sabu said in a fit of rage.He walked towardsCampo and pressed the Lugar into his face. "I should kill you right now!" he said. His face was beet-red from anger, and he pulled back the hammer of the gun.

Campo wasn't ready to die yet; he still had one more roll of the dice. "If you kill me, your caliph will never know how to open the gift I brought."

Ammar and Karuza were standing close by when he spoke, and Ammar had been looking at the gold box lying on the ground half out of its velvet casing.

"Nothing can save you now, Major Candalini," Sabu said his name; somehow it just sprang to his lips. He gripped the handgun and prepared to fire.

"General Sabu, put down your weapon!" Karuza yelled as he blinked several times, moistening his eyes. "Allah has commanded me to allow him to live, to bear witness to the Prophet's return."

God bless that Allah, Al thought to himself.

Sabu was visibly frustrated. However, he lowered his weapon slightly, bringing it to his side but it was still aimed at Campo.

"Ammar, my cousin, set the gift here next to me." Karuza said and waved his hand. Ammar lifted the gold box and removed it completely from the cloth. Campo could tell by Ammar's eyes that he felt that same electrical tingling.

"Your Holiness, it is true. I can feel the power of Allah emanating from within." Ammar placed the box on the floor at Karuza's feet. "Holiness, I see a hole made for a key to fit inside. It looks like the sun rising from a stone."

Sabu raised his weapon again, nestling it squarely between Campo's eyes. "Where is the key?" he said, with a murderous grin.

Campo looked down at his chest; he no longer had the key. Ghali must have taken it—unless Sarita had it. Al wondered if one of them had had it with them. He hoped they did.

"General," Karuza spoke up, "he no longer possesses the key. You will find it around the neck of the traitor on the floor," he pointed toward Ghali's unmoving corpse.

Ammar promptly found the plastic-encased chain, and brought it to his cousin.

Campo stood there perplexed. How in the world could Karuza have known where the key was? He could have easily guessed that one of the two had it, but to know it was hanging around Ghali's neck seemed like a fluke. All this talk of the Prophet was making Campo start to rethink his decision in bringing the box here. Had he unknowingly brought the actual vessel of the Prophet's return? Was Herman's research wrong? Was it perhaps not the Angel of Death, but the Angel of Mohammed? What if Karuza was actually doing Allah's work, and Campo was just a pawn in that game? Campo was about to tell them not to open it, but Karuza was already working the plastic, exposing the metal.

Karuza touched the bare metal of the key. His fingers felt electricity channeling into his pores. He feverishly rubbed harder and faster, finally exposing the entire chain. His hands trembled, and he fought to steady them as he raised his arms high above his head spreading the gold chain, letting the flag-shape of the key dangle toward his face.

"Allah! It is time! Send us the Prophet!" Karuza spoke. "Bow before the son of Allah," he commanded.

Ammar knelt and laid his head to the floor. Sabu motioned for Campo to bow using the gun as a pointer. He hesitantly got to his knees but held his head from the ground. Sabu bent to his knees and sat on his heels watching the caliph revel in glory.

"Once the Prophet returns, he will have no need for a remote launching device," Karuza continued. "He will wave his arms and destroy the Americans as he begins his reign of justice against all infidels. His glory shall bring the masses together as one, and the world will bow down before his goodness." Karuza slowly bent down and rested his knees on the floor. He kissed the key and smiled at its brilliant sparkle. "Allah, return to us your most blessed son," he whispered as he inserted the key and twisted it in the chamber.

Immediately, a seam appeared around all sides and smoke seeped from the crack. Karuza held his place while Ammar rose up on his haunches. Sabu watched Campo, waiting for an attack that was sure to come once he took his eyes off him. The mist spilled onto the floor and rolled out around the men. Karuza lifted the lid and fully opened the box. Now the smoke gathered from the floor and rose into the air above them. They arched their necks watching the smoke spin into a funnel cloud. At ten feet it gathered, and they watched it take shape. Their mouths were agape. Even Campo was amazed at how the mist seemed to have a mind of its own, as it took on the form of a massive man-like creature.

A huge chest rose as muscular arms shot out from the sides. Last to form was the head, a hooded skull. The being was facing Campo, and he watched as black eyes glowed at him. He now felt true fear about his choice in bringing the gold box. He pictured the leathered face of Herman Seller pleading him not to seek a key, warning him that evil lurked within the beautiful box.

The beast seemed to complete its form and the smoke ceased to move upward. The smoke was dense and opaque, and Al noticed that it remained connected to the box at all times. It turned from Campo and rested its deathly gaze on Karuza. The caliph raised his arms, opening them to receive alms.

"Mohammed," Karuza said. His eyes were wide open and his face pale, "Divine one and most celebrated of all the prophets. We are your children and we have made the path clear for your return to glory and righteousness. I am your servant. Command me and I will obey."

Ammar had his hands clasped and was continually bowing up and down, murmuring prayers. Sabu was now totally engrossed in the event, and he too clasped hands and started praying. Al couldn't help but stare at the colossal figure hovering above their heads. The creature moved slowly, studying Karuza, its black pearl eyes examining the caliph. Karuza opened his mouth, ready to speak again when the ghost transformed into a stream of luminous mist and disappeared into Karuza's open mouth. The others watched in awe.

Ammar smiled. He could have only believed the form was truly Mohammed's spirit and had entered Karuza to use his body for his earthly deeds. But soon his smile vanished as all emotion fell from Karuza's face. He stood unmoving, like a statue. Then the life in his eyes went dark, his skin turned ashen white, and, with his arms still raised in praise, the caliph fell forward. His body exploded in an eruption of dust, a cloud of ash rose into the air around them. The men knelt in shock. Sabu and Ammar shook their heads in doubt, hoping this was some sort of ritual for the Prophet's return to the mortal world.

But their optimism was dashed as the frightening hooded skull materialized from the remnants of Karuza's clothing. It rose within the cloud of dust, hovering once more, a ghost within a ghost. The face of the monster next set its mortal stare on Ammar. The black eyes glowed brilliantly, freezing Ammar where he knelt.

The beast thrust itself at Ammar's chest. Its murky hands turned to sharp claws and sliced open his robes and tore into the flesh. Al thought he was going to be disemboweled, but no blood spilled, though the internal organs could clearly be seen. The ghost penetrated through the open wound, and turned to face Sabu and Al, its black eyes flashing at them as the seam of skin closed. The intense, luminous eyes blazed as Ammar suffered the same fate as his cousin. He fell, face first and a cloud of dust and debris plumed into the air.

Sabu snapped back into consciousness. Fear should have been his first instinct, but his hardened emotions turned him to an attacker. He trained his pistols at the monster as it rose from the vestiges of Ammar's clothes, and Sabu fired several quick bursts. The creature was unaffected and charged at the general's body. Sabu's face lit up like a star, and he lost his breath for a moment. He reached for his throat and opened his mouth as his face distorted into an ugly, disfigured grimace. Then slowly the mist began to leak out of his open mouth. It gathered above his head back into its horrid form. Campo expected Sabu to fall forward like the others, and then remembered Sabu wasn't Egyptian. He was Syrian. Sabu stood straight and watched as the ghost dashed into Campo's stomach and quickly appeared out his back. The creature floated, circling above them for nearly half a minute, then dived back into its tomb, and the gold lid slammed shut.

Al and Sabu stood as equals for a brief moment, both witnesses to the Angel of Death. Then voices echoed from the outer room as the locked door was pounded on from the other side. Campo became aware of his surroundings, but only a split second before Sabu started raising his weapon. Al dove straight for him, and tackled Sabu at the waist. The general's weapons fell to the floor, and they rolled together, thrashing at one another. Campo wouldn't release his grip around Sabu's waist, and squeezed with all his might. Sabu was fighting for air. He put his hands together and brought them down hard onto Campo's back, but Al held on. They stopped rolling, Campo on top. Sabu beat his fists over and over on Campo's back as his lungs desperately sought air.

Campo lasted longer than he thought he could, but eventually, his grip loosened. Sabu attempted to box Campo's ears, but his hands hit the side of his head, causing thundering pain in his skull. Campo held on, but his hold was weakening. If he could only hold on until Sabu passed out.

Then Sabu grabbed the hair on the sides of Al's head, wrenching his head back. Campo saw him gasping and growling wrathfully. Campo fought past the pain of the tearing hair and flesh. He still held tight, squeezing until his hands went numb. The menacing face of the Butcher was turning red and his eyes bulged. Campo knew he was close. Then Sabu violently thrust his forehead into Campo's nose, crushing the cartilage and spraying blood into both their eyes.

Campo finally released his grip, and Sabu pushed himself free. The pair rose quickly, Campo's vision was distorted from the blood that covered his eyes, and searing pain penetrated his sinuses. He didn't have time to wipe his face because Sabu hauled off and punched Campo on the cheek knocking him sideways, then dealt him another blow to the other side. Al staggered back, barely able to see his foe— he threw a forward kick at what he thought was Sabu's stomach. Sabu blocked it with his hand. Sabu kept coming and was able to clasp his hands around Campo's throat. Al grabbed the Butcher's wrists, trying to pry them off, but Sabu's strength was too much for Campo.

Al was getting dizzy from the loss of oxygen. He stumbled with Sabu still holding on. The Butcher then kicked Campo's legs. They buckled but he remained upright. He struggled to free himself, but he was drifting away to a far-off place. Sabu started talking, and Campo barely distinguished the words.

"I should have made sure you were dead all those years ago," Sabu said through clenched teeth, spittle flying from his lips. "But my superiors thought it was more important to use you as bait and find your hiding place." Sabu grinned and panted, holding tight to Campo's throat, "It worked perfectly. Your men had an unusual loyalty toward you and it became their ultimate fate. And now you've returned and spoiled everything I have worked for."

Sabu squeezed harder, and Campo was fading fast, Campo dug his fingernails into Sabu's hands, digging deep, drawing blood, but the pressure only increased.

"I see the loyal Ghali lying dead on the floor," Sabu continued. "And over there lies your true love, Sarita. Both have died because of their unyielding devotion to you, and your pitiful American faith."

Campo's eyes flared into burning red suns as he listened to Sabu's words roll into his foggy ears. A rage burned in the depths of Campo's soul.

"Yes," Campo gurgled out. "My faith…my men…my love!" Then, without warning, he swung his fist in a windmill and sadistically punched Sabu in the testicles. The Butcher released his grip and grabbed his groin. Campo was a man of fury. He struck Sabu with hardened fists, faster and faster, left, right, left, right, his knuckles met their mark, snapping bones. Sabu staggered back, raising his hands in an attempt at defense, but he was bludgeoned in the face, the chest, the stomach, and finally forced against the wall. Campo didn't let up the blows until Sabu ceased defending himself.

The Butcher's arms dropped to his sides, and his head fell to his chest. Campo held his hand against the Butcher's chest, steadying him against the wall and measured him up for one final blow. Then he grabbed a fistful of blood-soaked hair and pinned the back of his skull against the marble wall.

"This is from Sarita, the woman I LOVE!" Campo announced. He reached back his bloodied fist, screamed in hatred and anger and revenge, and blasted his fist into Sabu's nose crushing his face, killing him without remorse. He let the body drop to the ground. His heart felt like it was going to erupt from his chest, and he panted and tried to control his breathing. Suddenly, it felt like his hand was on fire. He looked at it. Two broken bones protruded through the back of his hand. He grabbed it with his other hand and pushed them back under the skin with his thumb, moaning. He tried to wriggle his fingers and couldn't. He was unable to twist or bend his wrist without severe pain, so he just tore a piece of cloth from his shirt and wrapped his hand tightly.

Campo leaned on the wall, then turned around and looked at the macabre scene. Over his heavy breathing, he heard soldiers pounding on the door. The bolt was straining as the door was being forced inward. He needed weapons, and he pushed himself off the wall with renewed effort. He reached down to pick up Sabu's Lugar, inspected the clip, and found only one bullet remaining. He remembered Sarita had emptied her gun, and then reloaded another magazine before she…he couldn't think the words.

Al hobbled over to her. He found her lying on her stomach. He had to see her face one last time, so he rolled her over gently.

"Oh my God!" he gasped. "Sarita, my love, you are alive!"

"Yes, my love, I still have not surrendered to my living God!" she said, and held her hands over her bullet-pierced stomach.

Campo saw blood oozing over her fingers and replaced her hands with his, pressing to stop the flow. He felt the torn flesh and knew she was badly wounded. He heard the soldiers at the door, but they were louder this time and something else struck him.

He heard gunfire. There was a fierce battle going behind the door, but who could it be? Then he heard American voices screaming, and then there was a blast as the entire door was blown to pieces and suddenly fire erupted everywhere. He picked up Sarita. She moaned as he positioned her behind the overturned table, and he pressed his hand onto her wound once again. He looked into her eyes; the once beautiful light that shone from within her soul was dimming.

"Place your hand upon my chest, my love," she said.

Al held his one arm around her back, supporting her upper body and took his bandaged hand and placed his palm on the center of her chest.

"Do you feel the music my heart plays?" Her voice was weak and strained. She coughed blood onto her chest and stared into his eyes. They were dark, almost no white visible.

Al felt her heart rumbling like a storm; the rhythm was erratic but powerful. "Yes, it plays like it always has, strong and persistent," he said as tears welled up.

"No, Alfonse. The music has just returned…returned since you reappeared." She paused to catch her breath; a bloody mist sprang out of her mouth as she coughed again. "I had no life while you were gone. I walked in a daze, never resting, never seeking anything, always…always alone, no one but you in my heart, and you were not there. I had never been loved by anyone but you. And I could never love anyone but you. Then you came back…back into my world, and the music became more powerful than ever."

Sarita stopped and grinned through the fierce pain in her battered stomach. Al saw it, and held her close. He looked around, searching in vain for help but there was bedlam all around. Flames licked the walls and smoke billowed toward the high ceiling. He saw soldiers run past the fiery doors letting off quick bursts of bullets. One soldier was shot running past, and his head evaporated in a mist of blood and brains. He crashed to the floor as others ran stumbling over him. The noise was deafening as more explosions rocked the temple, and the floor shuddered under them.

"Hold me close, Alfonse, my love," Sarita said and began to shiver in his grasp. She ducked her head into his chest and grasped at his shirt. The pain was stabbing her, and yet she did not moan or cry out in anguish. "You are the reason I am alive again," she said, looking back at him, her eyes nothing but slits. "Cradle me in your arms…so I may die as I have lived…with you in my heart."

"No, you won't die! I can't bear to lose you again." Campo was pleading, crying, squeezing her tight; he rocked back and forth groaning. "Not this time, I am stronger now. I will save you." He said it as he looked carefully over the table's edge. The fighting was intense, and from his position he saw Sabu's men through the smoky haze firing wantonly and several bullets flew above his head, shattering the capital of a stone pillar. Debris pouring down on top of them, he shielded Sarita's body with his own. When the rain of rock ceased, he looked at her once more, her eyes fluttering as she spoke.

"Alfonse, my love, return your hand to my heart." With her last bit of energy she grabbed his wrist and put his hand to her chest.

Campo felt the organ throbbing through her bosom; only it no longer had the intensity it had before. It was slowing rapidly, her grip on his wrist loosened, and he felt her heart giving up. Through pale lips and closed eyes, she spoke her last words. "I love you, Alfonse." Then he felt the last thump of her heart, and she passed on.

Al squeezed her tight, moaning and crying uncontrollably, bobbing up and down, holding her in his arms. "No, not again, not again, no, no, no." He was like a mental patient unaware of anything else, when suddenly a massive explosion rocked the chamber propelling the table and Campo backward, pinning him and Sarita to the wall. The room was suddenly crowded with soldiers locked in a brutal gun battle. They were Sabu's men retreating; a dozen men ran into the room. Something clanked and tumbled on the floor around them. Campo stole a glance over the table's edge—four concussion grenades.

Shit.

In a split second, he ducked behind the table, covered his hears and prayed he would survive the blasts. In succession the four grenades went off: BOOM! BOOM! BOOM! BOOM! The floor and walls shook violently, parts of the stone ceiling came raining down, and the windows shattered, blasting glass, metal and wood into the streets below. Sabu's soldiers went flying in all directions. Their eyes exploded in their sockets, eardrums burst, men screamed, cried, and then died as their ribs were crushed into their lungs and heart. Soldiers lay crippled everywhere, blood was everywhere, the flames were everywhere, black smoke choking the oxygen out of the room. Campo was partially protected by the table and the distance, but he was still rocked into delirium. He removed his hands from his ears and saw they were soaked in blood. His eardrums had burst. His eyes failed to focus and he was straining for air.

Campo was on his hands and knees. He tried to get up and looked over the edge of the table at the carnage. Flames and bodies were shadowy, distorted images. Then his eyes honed in on red laser beams darting across the floor and walls. Men dressed in black barreled into the room through the still blazing doors, assault rifles with laser sights pointing in all directions. Campo stood and tumbled over the table, crawling toward the soldiers he hoped were friendly. He was approached by three men in black. A tall one lifted Campo's face, grabbing him by the hair, studying his features. Al saw through bleary eyes a middle-aged man with a ponytail looking him in the eye and saw his mouth moving, but heard no sound.

Colonel Barzanian could see the man on the floor was not an Arab. "Are you an American?" he asked, but got no response. "Captain Stram?" he yelled across the room. "Are we secure?"

"Yes sir, all units report the resistance has stopped, and we are now in control of the temple."

"Good," Barzanian said and leaned down to the wounded man. "Bring me the description of the American prisoner. I think I've found him."

EPILOGUE

Deep in the recesses of the archives department, Herman Seller fidgeted with an ink pen between his thumb and forefinger. He read the story from the *Philadelphia Inquirer*.

Vice-President Carel Vincent was sworn in yesterday as President of the United States. Within anhour of being sworn in, he was taken into custody and placed under arrest, charged with treason. President Worthington and his cabinet have been suspicious of his dealings with Fattah Abdullah. It was learned that Vincent and Abdullah had been in secret talks with the self-proclaimed caliph, Karuza. President Worthington faked his death, and when he did, Vice-President Vincent was discovered talking with Abdullah, and mentioned he had first-hand knowledge that the president would be assassinated, only he didn't know the CIA was listening. Federal authorities attempted to arrest Fattah Abdullah at his congressional headquarters but Abdullah could not be found. The FBI is conducting a nationwide manhunt.

The self-proclaimed caliph, Karuza, was assassinated by his own men late last night in Turkey. The reason for his demise is not known at this time. President Worthington will be back in Washington today, a press conference is scheduled for nine p.m., when the president will answer questions related to the vice-president and the recent happenings in Turkey.

Herman was startled from his reading. Someone was banging on the door to the archives department. He took his eyes from the news and stood. He arched his back, stretched, and then opened the door. A man wearing a brown shirt, hat, and brown shorts was standing at the door. He was holding a package with both hands.

"I have a delivery for a Mr…" The man braced the package with his knee and cocked his head to read the name on his computer clipboard. "…Seller. Herman Seller."

"That would be me, young man," Seller said, and stepped out of the way, motioning his hand towards the desk and giving the man a clear pathinto the room. "Would you mind setting it on the desk over there?" The deliveryman walked the package over the crowded desk, and with a loud thump, dropped the package onto the newspaper.

"I need you to sign here," the deliveryman said.

Herman pushed up his glasses and looked at the funny cursor pen and the plastic face of the screen, "What do I do, young man?"

"You sign your name in the screen. The cursor will see it."

Herman did what he was told and scribbled his name onto the plastic screen. "Amazing, amazing indeed," he said and handed back the pen.

"Sure is," the deliveryman agreed and shut the door as he left.

Seller inspected the package. It was wrapped in thick, crinkled, gray paper. A string was tied around it like a Christmas gift. Herman withdrew a pair of scissors from the drawer and cut it open. Inside the paper was a bunch of bubble wrap around a velvet bag. He immediately recognized it. There was also an envelope with his name on it. Without opening the velvet he satand read the letter.

Dear Herman,

I am dictating this letter to one of the nurses because my hand is broken, and I am currently unable to move due to my many injuries, too numerous to mention. As I promised you, I return the box. I hope it has arrived intact and unopened. I wrapped it myself, even though I had only one functioning hand at the time. It had been bounced around in a duffle bag in the back of a transport truck for over thirteen hours. Herman, I want you to know. You were right. The box should never be opened again. What sleeps inside should remain hidden forever. I have firsthand knowledge of its inhabitant and trust me: the Egyptians never stood a chance. Herman, I trust you will know how to proceed from here. Open display is not the right course. Not the right course indeed.

"Indeed." Herman said aloud. Then he read on.

There's one other thing I need you to do for me. I need you to contact Joseph Tyson. He works for the FBI in Philadelphia. I am unable to call myself because the doctors say if I'm not operated on immediately, I'm not going to last the night. I had to fight them off just to dictate this letter and send the package. Call the Federal Building in Center City and tell them you have an urgent message from Al Campo. They will put you through. Then tell Tyson he has to keep Domeni safe until I return. He has to tell her I'll return as soon as the doctors let me go. He has to tell her I will be back. Make sure he tells her that.

Well, old friend, the nurses are jabbing me with needles, I have to go. Don't forget to tell Tyson. I'm coming back.

Your friend,

Al Campo.

Herman set the letter down and wrote the words *Tyson*, *Federal Building*, and *Domeni—coming home* on a scratch pad. Then he inspected the velvet cloth. It was flawless. The rough ride had had no effect on the ancient cloth.

Herman put his hand to his chin and tapped his forefinger on his lips, contemplating.

"Where do I hide the Angel of Death?" he wondered aloud.

He spun in a circle, staring at the bookcases and piles and piles of papers strewn about. This building was two hundred years old, and on the national historic registry. He had been the sole caretaker of the archives for thirty years. Wherever he decided to put it, it would surely be safe. He looked down between a wall of shelves and a freestanding bookcase. The base of the wall had a sixteen-inch high raised panel that hid the air duct. He grabbed the velvet bag and took it over to the wall. He rapped his knuckles on the panel, and discovered it sounded hollow. He went back over to his desk and took out a letter opener. Returning to the case, he slid the point of the letter opener into the edge of the wood panel. To his surprise, the whole panel popped open. It contained nothing. There was an old metal pipe, some brown powdery insulation, and more dust than he cared to think was in the building, and—except for a few cobwebs—it was empty. He carried the heavy box in the velvet bag over to the open panel. He struggled to bend down and nearly fell from the weight of the gold. His knees were shaking as he lowered his back and pushed the Angel of Death into the open compartment.

"Oh my, I almost forgot," he said and went back to his desk. He opened a file folder and took out Dixon Hancock's original letter and the letter Campo had found in Franklin's desk. He carefully untied the cord of the velvet and slid the letters inside, making sure he didn't touch the metal. Back at his desk, he grabbed the newspaper he was reading, and crumpled the pages, packing them all around the bag. Then he pushed some of the dank insulation over the top and when he had finished, he thought he had done a pretty good job. No trace of the velvet could be seen. He replaced the wood panel. Then he stacked a waist-high pile of folders and books (which hadn't been read in God knows how long) in front of the opening, concealing the panel completely.

"That should do it. No one will discover that for hundreds of years, hundreds of years, indeed." Herman stood and clapped and rubbed his hands together. "Now, what else was there…"

Then his phone rang.

"Yes, this is Herman Seller. Who is calling, please?"

"Herman, it's me, Margaret. I just wanted to call and thank you for the beautiful flowers you sent me."

"Margaret? Flowers? Oh yes, yes, indeed, Margaret from the library. I'm so happy you like them."

"They're beautiful," she said. Her voice was soft and friendly. "Herman, I was wondering…would you like to have a cup of coffee with me? I'm just ready to leave, and I thought I could buy you a cup."

"Yes, yes, of course. I enjoy drinking coffee," Herman said. Her voice was so sweet and sincere, he couldn't resist.

"So I'll meet you outside of Starbucks on the corner of Thirty-Forth and Walnut in five minutes?"

"I would be delighted, delighted indeed. See you soon." Herman hung up the phone and prepared to leave. All the while there was something tugging at his mind, something else he had to do, but he just couldn't remember what it was.

"Oh well, it will come to me while having coffee," he said, and then left for his meeting with Margaret.

What Herman didn't realize was that Al's letter was crumpled in with the newspaper stuffing in the wall panel along withthe scratch pad he had written the note on.

THE END

19389552R00240

Made in the USA
Middletown, DE
17 April 2015